Meadow House

by

David Fabio

Avid Readers Publishing Group
Lakewood, California

The opinions expressed in this manuscript are those of the author and do not represent the thoughts or opinions of the publisher. The author warrants and represents that he has the legal right to publish or owns all material in this book. If you find a discrepancy, contact the publisher at www.avidreaderspg.com.

Meadow House

Avid Readers Publishing Group

http://www.avidreaderspg.com

Photographs by David Fabio

ISBN-13: 978-1-61286-298-9

Printed in the United States

Contents

List of Characters

Edward Gray –
- wife Kathleen LaPoint Gray

Marge – waitress
Bonnie – innkeeper
Jean – innkeeper
Jason Willard – accountant
Frank Crawley – Realtor
Carl Johnson – employment counselor
Maria Wagner - innkeeper
- husband Ethan
- daughter Ashlee

Leslie – Ashlee's friend
Dawn Swenson – classmate
Oscar Davis III – Red – classmate
- Red's father – Benson

Bob –
John and Helen Schmidt – grandparents
William C Edgar
- wife Marjorine

President Herbert Hoover
President Calvin Coolidge

Introduction

Every once in a while, you run into an interesting story that you keep telling yourself, someone ought to write this down. Well, this is one of those stories.

It is a book about several people with whom I found myself working with and observing in my town, and the special relationships that developed.

As it is in many locations, it is about the emotions people establish from within their environment. Often, we forget how the feelings we develop from where we live, can affect the type of person we become.

I'm sure, most of you have heard the old line – I'm going to move to start a new life. Does this really happen? Do we really need to move to start to modify our outlook? On the other hand, does our historical existence simply stay with us no matter where we end up?

In working as an accountant and financial advisor for many years, I had come into contact with many people. Most of them, you could figure out in about ten minutes. They usually fell into one of several characteristics.

There were the aggressive people – those that looked for any and all opportunities to get the best of someone else.

At the opposite end, was the placid individuals – those that went with the flow no matter what the decisions in life presented.

In general, I enjoyed working with people that were willing to stick their neck out a little bit, making their own paths to the future. Those were the interesting people to watch. Yes, they were not perfect. Failure happened every once in a while. However, they were the ones that usually learned from one attempt and tried hard not to repeat the same experience. Most of all, they were the interesting people that made observations a fun activity.

For my part, I was always too conservative to follow that path. I preferred to be part of the team that attempted to fulfill the objectives. It was a path of less risk with ample rewards to keep me happy.

Perhaps you can see yourself or someone you know in the story about my friends.

However, before we get started with my story, I felt you needed to get a feel for what makes our little corner of heaven something special to all of us that live here.

Jason Willard - Financial Advisor

Background

The Valley

Nestled in the calm backwaters, which were showing nary a ripple on this sunny summer day, a bald eagle, perched high in a majestic pine that was leaning slightly over the river, was watching the activity in the river. Below, two young beavers swam in and out of their lodge.

The lodge had been fashioned over the past years from willow branches and mud, knit together into a mound that extended from the bottom of the shallows of the river to almost four feet above the water. The soft willows had provided the building material needed for their mound as well as a source of food during the long winters. In anticipation of the extremely cold winter days, which might prevent the beavers from wandering off to cut live trees, many of the smaller branches of a tree had been lodged into the bottom of the river providing them a reserve source of food. The beavers knew they could swim underwater and retrieve their food whenever the severe winter storms came through.

On this day, the two young beavers were learning the skills of cutting and retrieving branches from the willows by the adult beavers. The willows grew close to the shoreline of the many islands in the river. With their sharp teeth, it did not take long to cut through a three-inch diameter willow tree and drop it into the riverbank.

There were several lessons to learn this day. The adult beaver was teaching its youngsters how to cut the trees so that they would fall towards the river. Also, another important lesson to be learned by the young beavers was to cut the trees upstream of the area of their lodge. Pulling large branches upstream was not as easy as heading downstream with their prized food source. Even so, the beavers showed enormous strength by easily moving large branches through the backwaters.

The beaver lodge was intentionally located in an area where the shallow backwaters narrowed, and the current started to pick up as the water funneled back towards the main channel. Keeping busy, the beavers were placing new branches in areas where the river's current had been diverted. By strategically weaving the branches in the area, they could create a dam that would raise the level of the backwater. Yes, they were an example of nature's dam builders at their best. The dam they completed blocked off an area over a hundred feet wide.

During the daytime, only the bald eagles, and an occasional osprey, paid any attention to the beavers activity in the water. Along with a great blue heron, they found the dam as a place to watch for fish. By damming off the area, it made fishing in the shallow waters easier for the eagles and osprey. The eagles would either sit high above in the majestic white pines that lined the hills along the St. Croix River, or soar just below the light whispering clouds. With a vision that resembled a good pair of binoculars, they could spot fish near the surface from several hundred feet in the air, and swoop down to catch it with its long talons.

On this day, the parent was teaching its two immature bald eagles their new territory. For the past month, they sat in the huge nest that hung high in a white pine near the river. From a nest made from tree limbs that weighed over two thousand pounds, the immature eaglets had watched their parents snatch fish from the river. Then, they would fly up to the nest and feed their young. Now that the eaglets were older, it was time for them to learn their territory and eventually start to hunt for themselves.

The adult eagle sat patiently in a white pine just down the river from the nest. Beckoning the young eagle, it cried out for ten minutes before the first eaglet finally flew down the shoreline to the white pine where the adult was sitting. Slowly, the second eagle was coerced into leaving the trusty tree and took flight to join the others. It was an event that happened the same way every year.

While the eagles were flying, they spotted a family of river otters playing along the shoreline. They too would be searching the waters for their next meal of fish or clams.

As far as the eye could see up and down river, two hundred foot tall white pine trees lined the river with a protective green ribbon that provided the shelter for the birds and animals that inhabited the area. It had been this way for thousands of years.

***

Over ten thousand years earlier, glaciers had covered the area, along with much of North America, to a maximum depth of up to a mile thick. Then, something changed. The earth started to heat up and the ice sheets slowly started to melt. As the melt advanced and the giant sheets of ice retreated north, formed glaciers again and retreated once more, great chunks of the glaciers broke off and were left to melt by themselves. They looked like small white islands left sitting in water, or on the gravel carried by the glaciers. These heavy pieces of ice, often several hundred feet thick, formed the depressions in the soft soil that became many of the area lakes.

However, it was the rivers that were formed out of the huge volumes of meltwater that made the deep cuts through the hills and valleys. One must remember, it didn't happen just once, these rivers of melt water came and disappeared at multiple times over thousands of years.

One of the many areas that collected the tremendous volume of runoff from the ice was Lake Superior, or as it was called then, Glacial Lake Duluth. As the enormous volume of water collected in Lake Superior, it put pressure on the surrounding shorelines. Eventually, a river formed that helped drain the excess volume of water, which had been naturally constricted by the high hills and ice blockages that had surrounded the lake.

***

Before that, over a thousand, million years ago, the huge plates of the earth's crust that had moved the continents, as we know them, were still moving. Their previous movement formed the continents, as we know them. Now, as the glaciers covered the area, the earth trembled as the land once again tried to divide.

The North American Continent tried to split in two from north to south. The split went from the area of Lake Superior south. However, the forces that moved continents in the past, which were beyond anything we can describe, were not strong enough. As the continent rift healed itself, molten rock from reservoirs deep in the earth were shifted into the deep crack. The period of the attempted rift lasted approximately 20 million years.

The western half of Lake Superior was surrounded by igneous rocks, which were formed from molten material close to the earth's mantle. It rose up thousands of years ago, when a rift in the continent formed across the area. Dynamic pressures pushed the molten rock up in layers, forming the hills and mountains. There was even evidence of volcanic activity in the area.

The igneous rocks that formed were extremely hard. Even the glaciers had problems reducing the rock's size. However, eventually, the force exerted by a sheet of ice, a mile thick and hundreds of miles long, was indeed able to move mountains.

Evidence shows that the high hills and mountains on the shores of Lake Superior were much higher prior to the glacial period.

The center of the lake formed when the molten rock dome that had supplied the material that was pushed up into the hills, collapsed downward, back towards the earth's mantle. It was this action that created the deepest of the great lakes. When the glaciers started melting, the water found the depression, which was left by the molten rock dome. The rivers formed one of the largest freshwater lakes in the world – Lake Superior.

***

There was one problem with glacial Lake Duluth; there was no place for the water to go. To the east, what would eventually become the natural outlet to the lake was still covered by hundreds of feet of ice.

The big lake rose to the height of the surrounding hills above the current city of Duluth. At its maximum height, it was over 300 feet above the current lake. It sounds huge, but we have to remember, the glacier's ice was up to a mile thick, and a mile equals 5,280 ft. To the ice sheet, the hills and lake were but a ridge and a puddle.

Unfortunately, there were no cameras or people recording history back then. Therefore, the exact details will be left to speculation. However, nature has left us many hints.

The result of the continental rift, millions of years earlier, left numerous fault lines due to the folding of the rocks. As the glaciers melted, the enormous forces caused by the weight of the water, renewed the old, built up pressures in the rocks. Things were approaching the breaking point. Something had to happen.

It probably started with an earthquake. Stresses contained deep in the rocks were allowed to build until something finally had to move. The ground shifted violently.

The resulting earthquakes along an old fault line simply created the necessary leak in the lake's dam. It started slowly. However, as the water found its way south along the fault line through the rocky hills covered with sediment, a massive river quickly formed.

The rapidly flowing stream that eventually formed down the fault line was the start of the St. Croix River, which carried a massive torrent of fresh water from Lake Superior all the way south to the Mississippi River and eventually the Gulf of Mexico. The volume of water it contained was so great that the flow cut massive river valleys along its length. Some of the valleys had been started years earlier by the melting of Glacial Lakes Grantsburg and Glacial Lake Norwood. Eventually, almost three hundred feet of Lake Superior's almost seventeen hundred foot maximum depth was released through the combination of the St. Croix River and a newly formed river leading through the other great lakes to the east. However, it was not over yet.

The water that formed Lake Superior came from the melting of the glaciers and was assisted by the fact that the northern area of the huge Glacial Lake Agassiz was still blocked by the glaciers. None of its meltwater could flow north through Canada into the ocean. The water from Glacial Lake Agassiz flowed into Lake Superior on the east, the Mississippi River on the south and the Minnesota River on the west. As a result, massive amounts of water were still being melted and supplied to the rivers.

Eventually, the other cork was pulled. The ice melted from the eastern end of Lake Superior allowing a massive river to exit the lake. In fact, it was such a massive outflow of water when it burst, that when it hit the ocean after flowing out the St. Lawrence River, the huge volume of fresh water temporarily stopped the Gulf Stream, which flows up the coast from Florida. The differences in water temperature and densities of fresh versus salt water stopped this natural current that is presently propelled by the glaciers of Greenland and the arctic ice pack.

The big lake was slowly coming down.

About the same time as the water started flowing to the east, the glaciers in southern Canada were melting, which allowed the Red and English Rivers to begin draining to the north. The volume of water heading south was slowing down.

As the weight of the huge glacier and water in the gigantic Lake Superior was reduced, the land around the lake shifted once again, slowly rebounding upward from the forces caused by the changes in weight. The land to the south was uplifted. Along with the lowered lake level of Lake Superior, it blocked the flow. Now, the St. Croix River was no longer able to drain Lake Superior to the south. Lake Superior's massive waters would only be drained to the east.

Well, almost!

Because of the hydraulic pressures caused by the huge volume of water in Lake Superior, and the moving of the lands surrounding it, springs were formed. To this date, the land around the lake is still rebounding from the loss of the weight of the huge glaciers.

The headwater of the St. Croix River shifted to the south approximately 20 miles, to an area near Solon Springs, Wisconsin. There, a river was once again formed by springs, which allowed water to be forced up through the ground, and fed what remained of the once mighty river. It was this spring along with the other tributaries also formed from springs – the Namekagon, Kettle, and Apple Rivers, that kept the St. Croix River flowing.

Once again, the St. Croix River had been reborn.

Over the next ten thousand years, the pristine water would flow uninhibited, except for the efforts of the beavers to slow down its route to the ocean. Instead of a river over a hundred feet deep, a gentle river of three to four feet flowed through the remains of the river valley.

As the river proceeded from the basalt rock formations that lined the westerly Lake Superior boundaries, to the sand and limestone regions that formed miles below the Taylor's Falls region, the river, and its tributaries, occasionally dropped through a set of rapids, until finally finding its gentle grade through the remains of the sandy sedimented region.

West of the river, the receding glaciers left many lakes and flat prairie lands. Most of the huge hills and mountains had been leveled into scattered gravel deposits, which had been carried by the advancing glaciers hundreds of miles to the south. As the glaciers receded, the glacial lakes, which formed from the meltwater, slowly drained via the Mississippi and Minnesota Rivers, leaving large areas of sandy soil that had once lined the enormous lakes.

Further, to the west lie vast prairie lands that looked like a great sea of grass that waved in the wind. The grasslands seemed to go on forever and ever. Occasionally, these grasslands caught fire from mighty bolts of lightning that accompanied the numerous thunderstorms, which traveled the plains like mighty sailing ships in the sky. However, it was the sheltered hills of the upper St. Croix River basin that formed the nursery area for a newly developed mighty forest of white pines.

Eventually, the white pine forest stood so tall that many of the other varieties of trees were slowly starved out of the valley by their need for sunshine. The long green needles of the white pine trees blocked the sunlight, and when some of the of needles fell to the forest floor, they prevented seeds from other trees to gather enough sunlight to grow. Hints of mighty oaks and maples that dominate other stretches of the river, struggled for glimpses of light while over-shadowed against the taller pines. In the upper tributaries to the St. Croix River, oaks and maples grew only in areas where storms or fires had temporarily cleared a section of the mighty pine forest.

For the majority of the forest, the pine trees stood so tall that even minor fires would slowly burn through the moist forest floor, leaving the majority of the tall trees green and untouched except for scars on the bases of their trunks.

Other than the tall pines, it was only the willows and cottonwoods that survived in the river valley. They had the ability to grow along the shorelines and steal some of the sunlight from the bright rays reflecting down the river. In addition, they had the ability to stand in high water for weeks at a time, allowing them to survive the massive runoffs of the spring melt, as well as being tilted by the massive sheets of ice that flowed down the river each spring.

***

The beavers went about their normal routine in the calm backwaters. The playful creatures climbed in and out of the water. Nothing seemed to disturb them from their regular routine except for the occasional flood. When high water washed out their dams, they would simply rebuild them.

For the wildlife, life was predictable. That is, until humans invaded their territories.

Little is known about the area until about 1679. Sometime, long before that date, the Native American tribes of the Ojibwe and Dakota were known to inhabit the area. The bands of the Ojibwe in the area included the Chippewa and bands of the Dakota included the Sioux. They were semi-nomadic tribes and they only left us hints of their previous existence.

The backwaters, where the beavers helped control the water depth, made excellent areas for harvesting wild rice. Along with harvesting rice during the summer, the shallows made excellent areas for catching fish during the spawn. Abundant with walleye/

sauger, smallmouth bass, and the occasional seven-foot long sturgeon, the area made an excellent territory for the tribes in the summer. The hills were populated with whitetail deer along with the occasional black bear. From here, the tribes could travel the river system back to camps along Lake Superior or south to the Mississippi or Minnesota River areas.

For the tribes, one of the most important things about the valley was that the area was home to numerous bald eagles, whose feathers played an important part in tribal ceremonies. Many a young brave was required to climb one of the huge white pines to snare an adult eagle. Only the adult eagles had the required white tail feathers. It was a ritual that was followed for years. To the Native American tribes, the area was sacred. As such, they protected the area so that it would continue to provide for their needs.

The only exception was the occasional tribal warfare. They fought to the death for territory and occasionally for lost lovers between the tribes. The Chippewa and Sioux were enemies of each other. Both felt the other was invading their land. Even with that rivalry, it did little to change the environment. The tribes only took what they needed. However, the tribes did leave us clues that they were there. The Native American tribes left markings in caves along the limestone bluffs of the St. Croix River, and on the rocks near the rapids of what was later name Taylor's Falls.

However, for the beavers, it was the exploration by French fur traders that started their problems. As early as 1679, fur traders that explored the St. Croix River and its tributaries started trading with the natives for pelts. Beaver pelts were worth a lot of money in England and France at the time. The felt made from the inner fur of their skins, was used in expensive men's hats. The gentle backwaters of the rivers were prime areas for beavers. For the first time, significant numbers of an animal in the area were in danger.

There were reports by trappers of catching over a hundred beaver in a single season in a tributary to the St. Croix. As they hunted the beaver, other fur-bearing animals became prey.

The looming threat would affect the environment as the animals knew it.

It was in 1683, that Father Louis Hennepin wrote in his diary about exploring the river along with the great falls upstream. He named the river the Mausoleum "The River of the Grave." Father Hennepin named it because of the death of a Native American guide that was bitten by a rattlesnake and died. However, it wasn't until 1688 that Jean-Baptiste-Louis Franquelin recorded a location for a fort on a map. Labeled Fort St. Croix, the name carried over as the new name of the river, and it stuck.

It appeared that "civilization" had moved into the area. From that point on in the history of the river, which had survived basically untouched for thousands of years, it would never be the same.

For the next eighty years, the French fur traders were in control of the area. The Ojibwe bands traded with the French fur traders based out of Lake Superior. They ranged from the top of Lake St. Croix north. The Dakota bands traded with the merchants from St. Louis. The Dakota's range overlapped the Ojibwe near the lower areas of the St. Croix and ranged south.

It remained that way until the 1760's when the British Northwest Company entered the region and began trading with the Native American tribes that had become unhappy with the way the French companies had treated them.

As late as the 1850's, the numerous Native American tribes were still inhabiting the area. Although it had become obvious over the past twenty years, they were quickly becoming outnumbered by the fortune seekers from the east. Pressured by these intruders, their territorial fights became stronger.

Over the past 30 years, there was one thing that stood out in the minds of both groups of fur traders. There were enormous forests of timber in the area, just waiting to be harvested.

News of these forests were quickly spreading back east.

Background

Change is Coming

It didn't take long for word of the mighty forests to get out of the territory. Probably the most convincing initiative was the new development of the city of St. Louis at the junction of the Mississippi and Missouri Rivers. Because of its location as the gateway to the west, it quickly became one of the fastest growing cities in the nation. As such, lumber was king and the need for building materials was great.

Lumbermen, who knew where the next fortunes were to be found, were already moving into the area, mapping out the vast forests of timber that could easily be harvested.

It wasn't until 1837, with the Treaty of St. Peters in Mendota, when the Ojibwe tribe signed over the vast tracts of land to the US government that covers what is today north central Wisconsin and eastern Minnesota along the St. Croix and Mississippi Rivers, that the lumber industry started in earnest.

Logging was the game and the rivers provided the transportation of the massive logs to the mills. During the 1840's and 1850's, sawmills were created in locations from St. Croix Falls to Marine on the St. Croix, to Stillwater, and downstream, as far south as Hudson. The lumbermen had scouted out the area ahead of time. They knew that they needed a fast flowing stream to power the great saws. Stream by stream they evaluated the sites down river where they could cut the mighty logs.

To get the logs to the mills, lumberjacks would spend all winter cutting pine trees along the upper St. Croix River and tributaries. Men would sign up for the lumber camps, where a bunkhouse and meals were guaranteed all winter. These were not weaklings. Double-bladed axes pruned the logs after men with enormous two-man saws cut them down. They worked long days in the cold weather wearing layers of wool clothing to earn a living. In the lower St. Croix areas, oak and maples were cut for quality interior woods.

All winter, it took massive ice sleds, pulled by teams of horses, to bring the logs over the frozen trails to the river. Then, when the ice went out along the river, a sea of wood would travel downstream to the mills. It was so massive that the lumberjacks could walk across the river, going from log to log. In order to get the logs to the right sawmill, the logs were branded – similar to the way cattle were branded. However, it was still hard to get the right logs to the right mill.

By spring, after the big melt, the loggers would travel to the towns down river to spend the small fortunes they had made running the logs. In Stillwater, several new mills opened up to keep up with the increasing demand that was developing for the lumber. A large number of lumberjacks flooded into the area looking for work.

Then, in 1856, in an effort to sort the mill's logs, several long chains were erected across the river just above Stillwater to pen in the huge logs. It was called the "boom site." Additional chains were used in similar operations at Osceola and above St. Croix Falls. At these locations, rafters would sort the logs and make sure the logging companies got the logs they harvested. The harvest was on. Fortunes were being made. Everyone wanted to make sure they got into the action before it was too late.

For the next fifty years, it was the timber from the great white pine forest that supplied the lumber for building many towns, including St. Paul and Minneapolis. In addition, the excess logs that the mills could not handle were shipped in mile long rafts of logs all the way down to St. Louis. To control the rafts, a paddle wheeler turned sideways would be placed at the beginning and another paddle wheeler pushed at the back of the raft. They controlled the direction and propelled the massive raft as it headed down the river. Many of the towns located south on the Mississippi River were built with lumber from the mills located on the St. Croix River.

In Stillwater and other mill towns, mansions were built within view of the river. The towns flourished and money was flowing as fast as the logs. The lumber barons that moved in from the east knew how to make the quick money by purchasing the land, cutting the trees, and then heading off to the next promising territory. These were not your common settlers that were clearing the land and farming it for a future living.

Slowly, the lumber harvest moved upstream. Vast forests were still needed to supply the mills and the needs of the cities. As a result, the harvest moved farther and farther up river where the huge trees grew. Soon, they were harvesting white pine from regions far above the basalt cliffs of the rapids at Taylor's Falls. The great forests were still standing north and east of the Falls. It didn't take long before a major problem was getting noticed.

As the logs were swept down river in the spring, occasionally the extreme number of logs flowing in the current would jam up in the many narrow areas of the river. Rivermen would attempt to break loose the logjams, occasionally using dynamite to get the flow started. Besides damaging some of the logs, the delay in the flow of logs would concern the mills. Since downtime was money, it caused several of the experienced log runners, called river pigs, to get injured or killed slipping into the freezing cold river, while attempting to move the massive log jams. It was definitely a dangerous job, and as a result, it was paid some of the best wages.

Usually, teams of the most experienced river pigs would work together in an attempt to free up the logjam. They would hunt for the key log. This was the single, or multiple logs, that when removed would allow the logjam to start flowing once again down river. It was a lot like the game of Pick-Up-Sticks. As you remove the sticks one by one, eventually you hit the key piece that makes the pile move. In this case, it was a dangerous move.

Once the key log was discovered, the entire log pile could start moving. What was once solid footing on the logs stuck in the river might instantly become a massive sea of moving logs. Many river pigs were injured or drowned when the logs became untangled. The trick was to discover ahead of time, which of the logs were the key logs, and then develop a plan to dislodge it without ending up in the river. For that highly dangerous work, the men could be paid up to a dollar a day.

In 1883, 1885 and 1886, great logjams formed at the narrows called the Dalles at Taylor's Falls. The 1886 logjam was two miles long. It was so severe that it took two months to get the flow of logs moving again. The jam took 200 men and 24 pounds of dynamite to break it loose. For a transportation season that lasted only a few months, while the river was flowing at a high river stage, losing two months was a huge problem. However, that was the least of the problems.

One has to remember the size of the logs that were sent down river. Many of the old growth trees were over two hundred feet tall. They were up to five-foot in diameter at the base. Even if the logs had been cut in half, it was still a massive log to travel down river. The bigger logs took a deep river depth just to float. The industry could not tolerate the constant logjams that tied up the river for months. Now, even the government was concerned that river traffic was in jeopardy.

Another side effect of the logjam was the creation of a dam by the logs, which could drastically change the flow of the river for the paddle wheelers. These paddle wheelers traveled the length of the river. Until the jam was cleared, the river level was unpredictably low. Also, a log or two wedged into the bottom of the river could split the bottom of a boat, and sink the wooden hulled paddle wheeler. Upstream of the logjams, the water level could suddenly raise above flood stage.

During the late summer, it was common for the river to be only a couple feet deep at best. The flow of logs to the mills needed to be completed before nature ran the river out of water depth. Something had to be done.

To keep the river moving and to get a better handle on the huge volume of logs, dams with chutes were designed to hold back some of the spring runoff and allow the flow of logs for a longer season down the river.

Also, in an effort to maintain an unshifting channel for the riverboats, log and rock dams were erected from the shorelines outward towards the main current. The hope was that the higher flow of the main current would help dig the center channel deeper.

The river was showing signs of changing.

In those early days of logging, up to fifty riverboats operated in the area of the St. Croix River above Stillwater. As the logging continued to grow, the risks to the owners running the boats became greater and greater. The result of those risks was that most of the riverboats were restricted to the area at Stillwater and below, where the river slowed and was much deeper.

1890, marked the peak of the logging in the St. Croix valley and its tributaries. By 1912, it was all over. That was the year of the last big log drive down river. The entire old growth forest of white pines was gone. Gone from the St. Croix valley, that sea of green that extended as far as one could see. The white pine was no longer king of the forest and the tall oaks and maples were being harvested as well.

Sadly, the great pine forest was gone forever. Today, as we look at the river, it is marked by scattered second or third growth white pines, growing along the banks and hills of the river. They are mixed in with the dominant maple and oak trees. Some of the taller pines still stand out above the rest of the trees. They become the viewing areas for the eagles that survived the massive cutting. However, today, the tallest of the great pines is only about one hundred feet.

During a very short period of history, enough logs were harvested through the mills that would fill a train full of logging cars six times the width of the US.

The result of all that progress was that the river valley and its tributaries were permanently changed. What nature had kept the same for thousands of years, man had permanently changed in less than one hundred years.

Now, over one hundred years after the last big log harvest, the valley is once again green and healthy looking. However, the white pine is no longer king of the forest. The hills are still slowly recovering. Whether it will ever return to the way nature had originally developed it, is uncertain.

Even the flow of the river has been regulated. Dams upstream, which had originally been considered for assisting the flow of water carrying the logs, were created for hydroelectric generation to provide electric to the cities.

A separate series of dams downstream on the Mississippi River were developed to regulate the flow of water, enabling a 9-foot channel for navigation all the way from St. Louis to Minneapolis on the Mississippi, and up to Stillwater on the St. Croix River.

Above Stillwater, a three-foot channel was attempted for operating shallow running riverboats all the way to Taylor's Falls.

The government attempted to control the rivers. The Army Corps of Engineers had been commissioned to keep the nation's water highways open for commerce and recreational travel.

Once again, it was the rivers that changed. New shorelines with newly created backwaters were established.

Eventually, as part of the National Wild and Scenic Rivers Act of 1968, the river valley was recommissioned once again to be under the National Park Service, in an effort to control the development of some of the nation's more scenic recreational waterways. It was one of eight rivers designated under the act.

For the St. Croix River, it amounted to a serious effort to restrict development and river travel aimed at attempting to bring back some of the original wild river attributes.

The first problem that the Park Service encountered – how do you reset the public's usage and priorities for the river? As they say, "the horse was already out of the barn." And, in this case, it had been out of the barn for a long time.

The neighboring states of Minnesota and Wisconsin had already agreed to several management plans over the years. The public had attended the meetings and understood the limitations given to them in building cabins and using the river. Everyone thought they had reached an understanding. The river valley had once again become a beautiful place to live and visit. The events of the past were long forgotten in most of their minds.

It appeared that things were about to change, once again.

***

Chapter 1

Reflections

"Ashlee, please talk to me, Maria asked. At least, mumble something."

"Mmmm."

Oh, what have I done? My daughter is slumped in the far back seat of the van, not talking, sullen, and is hardly even willing to look at me. All because I am moving the two of us for the second time in less than three months.

And now, even though we are stuck together in our car as we take a couple hour trip to Little Falls to visit my aunt, whose health is failing rapidly, once again there is no discussion. She just sits back there listening to her music as if she is ignoring the world as it passes by the window.

Having to pass through St. Cloud, Minnesota, where we used to live, and where her father Ethan was living, is obviously almost too much for Ashlee. She hasn't even looked out the window to see any parts of the place where we used to live.

I thought she seemed to have adjusted really well to the move to my parents. With the way she is today, how is she going to adjust to our move to our new home at the Bed & Breakfast that I will be managing? I honestly don't know which girl will show up at the end of the day.

I feel like the worst mother of the year. The only reason we took this trip today was that I was not sure if we would have the chance to see my aunt again before she died, especially after I start working at the Bed and Breakfast. What's it going to be like, later this evening, when we finally get to move into the B&B? Will Ashlee make the adjustments?

Nevertheless, I had to do it. I just had too. Things were falling apart faster than I could keep track of them. Ashlee's life was falling apart. Getting mixed up with really questionable kids; boyfriends that looked like they came out of some dark, Gothic movie. And then, there were her grades! Her grades were heading for the bottom of the scale after being a B+ student. Through it all, her father, Ethan, was at best mentally, if not sometimes physically, absent. It was a risk I had to take. We had to move.

After talking to my mother and dad about all that was going on, I asked them if I could move in with them for a while, until I could get Ashlee straightened out, I could find a job, and possibly go back to school to get my degree. Who knows, perhaps the results of our fifteen-year marriage could be restarted with some distance between us for a while also.

I guess what really clinched the decision to make the huge change in our family, was the last conference I had with Ashlee's counselor. She said a big part of Ashlee's school & personal performance was a reflection of her home life, Ethan, and my relationship, or lack of it to each other, and Ethan's relationship with Ashlee. He had totally distanced himself from Ashlee after claiming it never did any good to talk to her.

* * *

After we spent a few hours at the nursing home with my aunt, I was glad we came. Her health had deteriorated to the point she hardly knew who we were. Then again, it had been a few years since we last saw her. Ashlee was, at least, a foot shorter then. I used to see her every holiday with my parents before I got married. I miss those days.

We stayed for a while until the staff told us she needed her rest. Then, we headed out and got back in the van. "That wasn't too bad, huh Ashlee? I think she appreciated our visit."

"I guess," Ashlee mumbled. However, I noted that she was still slouched down in the seat in the back of the van, listening to her music.

What happened? During the past couple of months, Ashlee was definitely a different person while living with her grandparents. She had come out of the gloom she was in while living in St. Cloud. Was life up here that bad? Now, she looked like the old Ashlee.

As we drove, I wished I could find another major highway that wouldn't take us back through St. Cloud. While we were heading back to the highway that led through the St. Cloud area, before the couple hour drive to Marine on the St. Croix, my mind wandered through the events that had happened since Ashlee and I had moved in with my parents in North St. Paul. Things had improved greatly for both of us. It was as if both of us had a second chance in life.

Later, this evening, when we get back, we will be spending our first night at the Bed and Breakfast in Marine on the St. Croix. To me, it is definitely an intriguing place located in a the scenic small town along the St. Croix River. If it wasn't for our past history hanging on to us, it would be the perfect move. Time will tell.

* * *

Ashlee was definitely trying to tune-out the neighborhood they were driving through. It brought back memories that she was trying hard to forget. St. Cloud was not her source of happy memories; including the long anticipated separation of her parents. Ashlee could feel the event coming on for several years.

As she sat in the back seat listening to her music, she recalled the full set of events that happened the night before her mother announced they would be moving to North St. Paul to live with her grandparents.

It all started with a date she had with a senior at the school. Her friend had talked her into going on the date.

"Come-on, it's okay. Haven't you ever been in a boxcar before?" Lyle asked Ashlee. "They're just parked over there. It's okay, there's no one else around. Let's just go and explore. They usually leave the doors open when they are empty."

It was a dark fall night with only a sliver of the waxing moon providing light in the sky. The train cars were just sitting on a siding waiting for the railroad to need them. Ashlee wasn't too sure she wanted to be caught in a train car. She knew her mother would blow a gasket if she found out.

There wasn't anyone near the sidings where at least ten or twelve train cars were parked just outside of town. Ashlee figured Lyle just wanted to make out. His small compact car left very little room for comfort.

Reluctantly, she agreed to go with him and explore the box cars. She always wondered what they were really like inside. She had seen them parked along the tracks many times. However, that was the outside of the cars. All she had seen of the insides were short glimpses from how the movies depicted people and hobos riding the rails.

As they got out of the car, Lyle grabbed a paper bag from the trunk. "Just in case it's cool in there," he told her.

Ashlee wasn't sure, but figured he had a bottle of cheap wine in the bag. It wouldn't be the expensive stuff. Neither of them had the money for that.

She was still 50/50 about this whole thing. She wasn't into drinking, and then there was the train. What if the police or someone else spotted them on railroad property? She knew the tracks were marked "No Trespassing." Fortunately, they were both dressed in dark clothing. It would make it harder for someone to spot them as they approached the parked train.

Their car was parked on a dirt road that crossed the tracks about two blocks further down the road. It was just about 300-feet from the train cars where they had pulled off the road.

It was cool that evening. Last weekend was Halloween. In another week or two, it would probably start snowing. They could feel it in the cool crisp air as they walked through a field heading towards the train cars.

Before the tracks, there was a small drainage ditch. From there, it was two main tracks and then a set of two siding tracks where the extra cars were stored. So far, so good. No trains were coming and the cars looked deserted. Ashlee could see a light way down the tracks. There was a green light showing.

Carefully, they walked down the siding, making sure they did not trip over the railroad ties. They passed several smelly tank cars before they found a few boxcars with their doors open.

Peering inside the first car, it must have been used for hauling junk. It was a mess inside. Obviously, no one had cleaned it before parking it out of town. Perhaps that was why it was stored there. No one wanted to clean it out.

As they looked into the second car, it was clean. Only the wood interior of the car and perhaps a week's worth of dust from the door being open was visible.

"Let's climb inside," Lyle told her.

It was a big step. Ashlee wasn't very tall for her age. For a 5-foot 1-inch high school sophomore, the door height was well over her waste. Lyle was a senior and much taller. "Here, let me help you up." He laid his paper bag inside and offered to hold her foot as she climbed up carefully into the empty car. Then, he grabbed the steel handle next to the door and swung his legs inside.

"See, I told you it was no trick. Let's go sit in the corner and we can talk."

Hesitantly, Ashlee told him, "It's kind of cool in here. And what if a train comes by?"

"Look, I'll close the door near the main tracks and we can leave the other one open just a crack. That will cut down the wind blowing through. You'll see, we'll warm up in no time."

The big steel door shut with a thud. Ashlee knew that her mother would have kittens if she knew where she was. Her father would probably just shrug it off.

"Lyle, let's go slow. I'm not used to this," she told him.

He agreed to sit and talk for a while. While they were talking, he opened up the bag and took out the bottle of wine.

"What are you going to do when you graduate at the end of the year?" Ashlee asked him.

"Oh, I don't know. I know I'm not going to college. When I'm done with this year, I don't want to see another test the rest of my life. I'll probably travel for a while. Maybe I can ride the rails. This boxcar isn't too bad."

"Really, what are you going to do?" Ashlee pushed him.

"My step-dad wants me to join the Army. Maybe after I do some traveling I'll do just that. I don't know. It's too far away to worry about it. What about you?" he asked.

"I've got a couple years to think about it. I would like to leave St. Cloud. There is nothing here for me to stay. I doubt my parents would care if I stayed or left."

While they were talking, they heard a train's whistle blowing in the distance as a train crossed the dirt road. The sound was two short blasts followed by one long blast and one short blast. It slowly approached, and passed by on the tracks. "Good thing you closed the door," Ashlee told Lyle.

"Not really. I'd rather count the cars as they go by. Here take a sip of the wine. It will warm you up in this cool car."

It must have been a freight train. It seemed like it took ten minutes for the sound to pass by. Ashlee was surprised at how quiet the train was until it was almost next to them. Then, it rumbled as the train cars rolled by. Soon, it was quiet again.

Lyle put his arm around Ashlee as she took a sip of the wine. It was a fruity wine that hardly even tasted like alcohol. They sat there talking and sipping on the wine.

Suddenly, they heard a loud metallic bang as the car they were sitting in jerked violently.

"What the..." Ashlee jumped up to look out the crack in the one slightly open door. As she looked out, she felt another jolt, then, the train started to move. "Lyle, I think they are moving the train cars," she shouted excitedly.

This put a sudden damper into Lyle's plans for the evening. The train must have hooked up to the cars, and they were being pulled to the yard. He slid the door open the rest of the way and looked out.

"Don't panic, we'll just jump off. Wait till we clear the siding, so there are no rails next to us. Then, we can jump into the weeds."

The train was moving very slow. However, it felt as though it was picking up speed.

"There, see, just ahead. Just jump into the weeds on the hill and roll down. The weeds will soften the jump," Lyle told her.

Ashlee could see the spot. It was coming quickly. Fear was catching up to her. She was afraid of the steel wheels of the train. As she was nervously preparing to jump, Lyle put his hand on her back and gave her a hard shove. "Roll on the hill," he shouted to her, as she flew out of the car.

Ashlee felt the hard push Lyle had given her. Without it, she might not have jumped. As she hit the ground, the slope of the hill softened her landing. She came to an abrupt stop at the bottom of the ditch. So far, she survived the fall. All she had to do was remove the thistles from her clothes.

Ashlee looked back. Where was Lyle?

Lyle had gone back, into the corner of the boxcar, to get the wine. Now, the train was going twice as fast as before. He looked for a good spot and jumped.

Ashlee saw him hit the ground over 200 feet down the track. He rolled as he hit the flat ground near the tracks. As she saw him get up, she breathed a sigh of relief. He was okay and was walking back towards her. All she could think of was, what if???

The train passed, leaving the two of them beside the tracks. Now, they needed to brush off the thistles and other weeds from their clothes, as they hiked back to the car.

As Lyle put his arm around Ashlee, he told her with a twinkle in his eye, "I guess we'll need to warm up in the car. I saved the wine."

Just as he was saying it, his foot hit one of the switch tracks that led to the siding they were on. As it did, he tripped and fell to the tracks. The bag went flying, and there was an unmistakable sound of breaking glass.

"Damn!" He shouted.

"It's only wine," Ashlee told him.

"No, it's my ankle. I survived the jump from a moving train with a bottle of wine, only to trip on that dumb track and sprain my ankle."

He tried to get up but realized quickly that his ankle was sending signals to his brain that it was not in favor of him putting a lot of pressure on it. He could just barely move it.

"Are you sure it's not broken?" Ashlee asked.

"No! Help me to the car."

Ashlee helped him up. The ankle was hurting, but he could stand on it – just barely. It was over a block to where the car was parked. Lyle would have problems crossing the plowed field, so they decided to head to where the tracks crossed the road.

Ashlee would have to help him walk down the tracks to the road. She tried to be a crutch that would reduce the weight on the sore ankle. When they reached the road, she could probably get the car for him, so he didn't have to walk the final block down the road.

There was one unplanned problem, Ashlee didn't have a driver's license. However, it couldn't be that hard to drive a couple blocks. She had watched her mother do it for years. All she needed to do was keep it on the dirt road and bring it to a stop close to where Lyle was standing.

Walking on those railroad ties was tough enough for someone with two good ankles. By the time they got to the road, Ashlee was relieved. Not that they had gotten that far, but that the evening might have a quick ending. She was getting cold feet about making out with Lyle. Especially, since she had seen that he brought the wine.

She got the car keys from Lyle and hiked back down the dirt road to where they left the car. It was a good thing Lyle stayed at the tracks, the road was full of potholes. After unlocking the car, she looked to see where everything was located. It was definitely different from her mother's car.

She put the key in the ignition and the car started right away. One problem – Ashlee had forgotten to ask Lyle to tell her how to turn on the car's lights. After trying to figure it out in the dark, she decided to just drive to the tracks in the dark.

Putting it in drive, she drove the car very slowly down the road. Five miles per hour was fast enough under the conditions. In the dark, she could not see the holes in the road. One by one, they caught her by surprise. Now, she was straining to see where the next one was hidden. She was so nervous that she might hit something that she was totally relieved when she finally got to the tracks. Her one big break, she was relieved to find that no one else had been on the road.

Lyle watched as Ashlee drove the car with the lights off. He quickly realized that she probably did not know the light switch was on the turn lever. Watching her drive the car, it seemed like it was taking forever for Ashlee to drive the one block.

Fortunately, for Lyle, it was his left ankle. He would still be able to drive. The ankle was still sore, but the pain was slowly getting less. He figured he was right – just a sprain. Slowly, he got into the car and had Ashlee help him move his left foot past the doorframe.

Once they got back in the car, Lyle took Ashlee home before heading home himself to put ice on the ankle. It wasn't at all what he had planned for the evening. Now, his ankle hurt bad enough that everything else didn't matter. Or, did it?

Perhaps he could salvage something. Maybe he could have Ashlee put ice on his ankle at her place.

As they got to Ashlee's, he suggested to Ashlee that it would be nice if she could put a bag of ice on his ankle. Then, when the soreness went away, it would be easier for him to drive home.

Opening the door at Ashlee's place, Lyle found her mother waiting for her. Ashlee was supposed to have been home hours earlier and looking at her mother's expression, she wasn't very pleased.

Quickly assessing the situation, Lyle decided it was not a good time to stay. He quickly excused himself and limped back to the car. "*What an evening. Just my luck. What else could go wrong*," he thought.

Ashlee never told her mother what happened that evening.

* * *

Ashlee was sound asleep when I saw the road sign saying Marine on the St. Croix - 8 miles. I was still deep in thought thinking about Ashlee and me. I had been mulling over all that had gone on, in the less than three months since we moved, along with the significant changes in our lives. It really made the drive to Marine seem short. We were there before I knew it.

Still, in the back of my mind, I was puzzled as to how I got this job when other people must have been more qualified than I am.

I guess I will find out in time, and up until then, I will just have to do the best I can. At least, for now, Ashlee and I have a place of our own – kind of, and we will make a go of it.

"Ashlee, wake up, we are here at the Meadows B&B. I know the move is tough. However, it is really nice. Actually, it is really charming."

The sun was setting behind the B&B as we drove into the driveway. Fortunately, I had planned ahead while moving our clothes into the B&B, and left a frozen pizza in the freezer for us to heat up when we arrived.

Chapter 2

The View

Marine on the St. Croix

The quiet little town of Marine on the St. Croix sits along the Minnesota side of the St. Croix River between Stillwater, Minnesota and St. Croix Falls, Wisconsin. Once a hotbed of activity during the lumbering days, now the lumber mill is but a memory. Today, the river gently flows past houses and cabins that line parts of the river.

The town has changed as well. Once a community of relatives of the town founders, the town has become a favorite home to artists, scholars and those individuals that prefer a small town existence to the large city. If it wasn't for the change in speed limit signs, while driving down the highway, you might miss it.

Marine on the St. Croix has one main street. It contains the Marine General Store, bank, gas station, bar/restaurant, and a few smaller stores including a Post Office. The town was built along the river. Unless you slow down and look as you travel nearby on the highway, you might miss the other streets of the town, which were built high up on the hill above the town. Some say it is just a dip in the highway. For others that live there, it is a magical place where they proudly tell everyone it is where they are from.

It was here, that my friend Edward Gray moved many years earlier, and fell in love with the river valley.

Jason Willard – Financial Advisor

***

Edward Gray

Sitting next to the bedroom window at my reading table, I found myself lost in my daydreams as the sunlight peeked through the trees, warming the side of my face. The book I was reading lay silent on my lap. Momentarily, I sat there, lost in many memories. The only thing attempting to bring me back to reality was a reddish-orange maple leaf that gently fluttered outside my window.

The light southerly breeze had lifted the tumbling leaf high up to my second story window and was holding it there in my view. Looking at the discarded leaf, it was as if some artful magician had intentionally suspended it outside, just in my view. I could even see the veins in the leaf, which provided the chemicals responsible for changing the leaf from its summer green to its autumn red and yellow colors. Now, as the change had been completed, it had turned to its final fall color and been wisped by the breeze from its location on the tree. Oh, the magnificent wonders of nature.

I turned as I heard the sound of the door opening behind me. My wife had just entered the room to be with me.

"There you are my darling. I was wondering where you might have gone. Please come over and sit with me. Your favorite chair is calling. The sunlight feels so good today. I wish we had time to just sit here and spend the whole day talking.

"I was reading my favorite book until a maple leaf stole my attention. Come watch how the leaves magically blow around in the wind.

"You must have been fixing your hair. It looks good. Who are you preparing to go see today?

"Remember how you used to spend hours teasing your hair just to get things right to catch my attention before we were married? I do.

"I remember your sister telling me that I would just have to wait for you until you were ready. You were such a perfectionist.

"You know, I remember the first time we met. After growing up out east and working for three years as a supplier to the Rhode Island shipyards, the first time I spotted you was at a local deli. As I recall, you were on a spring break with your roommate, touring the Northeast. Remember?

"When I stopped in to meet a friend, the two of you were talking at a lunch table. Our eyes met as you looked over your friend's shoulder and watched me heading for my table. The moment I spotted you, I knew you were the one. What was it? Was it the look in your eyes, or was it your smile? Whatever it was, I told my friend, right then and there, that I was hooked.

"While the two of you were finishing your meal, I remember trying to get up the courage to walk over and ask if the two of you might be interested in joining us for a movie that evening. To my great amazement, you said yes. I still remember the look on your roommate's face. I'm not sure she knew what to say. For me, that moment was the start of a year of magic.

"You know, I still don't remember what you were wearing or whether or not your hair was combed. From then on, none of that made a difference to me.

"How come most women spend so much time making sure they look just right? Even today, you don't have to worry how you look. A quick comb to lay down the stray hairs would be good enough for me. I'd rather have you here with me than working on perfecting your looks."

"Edward, who would you look at when you go out if women didn't try to catch your attention?"

"Well, you definitely got mine," I told her.

"I think fall has always been my favorite. Maybe it's because I proposed to you in the fall. It was only three years later that we had this grand old house built. That was truly a labor of love. Everything about the design had been gone over twice, and when the house was finally finished, it was spectacular. Remember how you called it your fairytale castle. Oh how you loved to sit up here in the bedroom window looking out at the view. As I recall, you had me turn the house just slightly on the site, so that you could catch the sunlight in this window almost all day in the wintertime.

"Look, there's another bright colored leaf drifting near the window. These leaves grab my attention every time I see one of them stick to the glass. Then, I watch to see how long it will take until the next breath of wind blows it away, on its journey to the ground.

"You're not getting up to leave me already are you? Do you need to go downstairs this early? If you don't mind, I think I might just sit here a little longer enjoying the sunlight."

"Don't worry, I'll be back."

My mind wandered back to daydreams once again while I sat there by myself with the warmth of the sunlight peeking through the window.

I was thinking back again to the time after I met my wife at the deli. It was about a year later, when the love of my life, Katherine LaPoint, graduated from the University of Minnesota in Minneapolis. We had been communicating back and forth ever since we met. During the past winter, I had traveled from Rhode Island to Minneapolis twice to spend time with her. We were in love back then, and nothing was going to come between us, even my work.

My uncle had worked as a journalist in Minneapolis years earlier. I used to read some of his stories about life in Minnesota that had been carried in some of the east coast journals. He made stories about the area seem so real. I decided to give Minnesota a try.

With my shipping background, I had found a local business that needed my expertise. When I sold my bustling business to my partners and finally moved to Minnesota, we had the time to make sure we wanted to spend the rest of our lives together. Soon, the business expanded and we were shipping merchandise all over the world.

It was later that summer that we were married. With my salary and the money I saved from my partners buying me out, we purchased the 40 acres of prime land with a view of the St. Croix River. Then, we started designing this house. Oh, we had such wonderful plans back then.

The property was draped in woods. It was primarily maples and oaks, but there was a small ridge with a direct view of the river. You could even see the islands that dotted the river. As a result, we designed our house to take advantage of the view. It would sit high on the ridge. That location would make a spectacular place to invite our friends, and raise a family.

When the house was finished, it was nestled into the woods so well that if you did not know it was there, most people would have missed it. Only from the river did the house become visible. Deer, owls, eagles, foxes; it had them all. Just as I told my friends, it was my wife's fairytale house.

"Edward, I can only stay for a short while. It is almost time for me to leave."

I didn't even hear her come back upstairs. "That would be nice. I'll take all the moments I can get. Will you be off to another meeting with your friends?"

When I think back on things, I truly am amazed at how much effort women actually spend just trying to keep that special look. Their hair has to be just so, and then there's the eyes and lips. If they only realized that all that special attention wasn't needed. With Katherine, once I looked into her eyes, nothing else mattered. My mind must have fixated on her at that very special point in time. Every minor change she made to her appearance, after that time, was just a momentary change that my mind, readjusted back to envisioning that beautiful girl sitting in the restaurant that stole my love. It didn't matter that our hair had started to gray or that we lost some of our teenage figures, inside we were still the same two people, lost in love. All that wasted effort was to keep up our image with other people.

We were the only ones that counted. A comb through her hair in the morning and an embracing smile was all that we needed to start our day off right.

On the other hand, I remember when Katherine was working. She would get up early to spruce up her looks. From our bedroom, I would watch as Katherine would take ten minutes to comb and tease her hair until it was absolutely perfect. When I think back about it, I guess it was a magical moment for me. I loved to watch her, and it definitely put me in a good mood for the rest of the day.

"Katherine, are you going to see the girls later this week? If you do, could you give them my love for me? I miss seeing them. When I was looking out the window, earlier, I was recalling how I used to watch you and the girls when they were younger.

You used to push them on the old rope swing I had tied to the huge red oak in the yard. The girls used to giggle with glee every time you gave them a huge push.

"I wish we could reset the clock. I spent too much of my time at the office, or working at my desk here in the house.

"Are you sure you need to leave? We still might have some time to snuggle for a few minutes."

Even after all these years, I still loved to hold her hand and sense her presence next to me. Some things just never grew old. Somehow, I guess the only things that grew old were our bodies. We needed to be more like the trees, shed those old leaves and then start anew the next spring. Too bad people can't just hibernate for a few months to rejuvenate our lives.

I watched as she rose to leave. "Ed, you've been sitting in your chair too long. Time for me to go, and for you to move on to some activity. It will be dark soon. The shadows are showing their longer arcs across the yard. Soon, the sun will be starting to set and all its radiant warmth will be gone. I'll talk to you later. Don't worry, I'll be back soon."

I was really wishing she could have stayed just a little longer. I felt a light chill run down my spine as the sun started to set into the hills to the west. Soon, only the tallest trees would be lit by its light. My view from my window was quickly starting to grow dark.

It was time for me to move out of my chair and breathe in some of the cool fall air.

Chapter 3

Changes

My hike took me for a brisk walk around several blocks. It felt cool outside now that the sun had set. However, I needed to stretch my legs and the walk felt good. Fortunately, I had my favorite wool red-plaid jacket with me.

I crisscrossed down the hill, stopping at the local watering hole for some soup and a sandwich along with something to drink. As I did, I heard the bell at the church on the hill ring, letting the whole town know it was 6 pm.

"Ed, you're back. I haven't seen you in a while," the waitress greeted me. Marge had worked at the combined bar/café for as long as I could remember. It was good to hear her warm greeting.

"You know I can't pass up the smell of your soups. It's good to see you also. How's your family?"

"Just like always – everyone's living everywhere but here. I wish I could convince my girls to move back to town. It would be nice to see them more often."

"Well, at least you can call them once and a while and make sure they are okay. The next time you talk to your two girls, tell them I said to say hi. You know, I still remember them singing in the Christmas play a few years ago."

"Ed, I'm sure they will be happy to hear that you still remember them. Now then, what's your fancy for dinner?"

“I’ll take your walleye sandwich along with your soup of the day – chicken wild rice.”

“Have it out in a few minutes,” Marge told me, as she headed off to the kitchen.

The customers at the Brookside Bar and Grill were mostly local people that frequented the shop on a regular basis at this time of the evening. Some stopped in simply for a drink, others for karaoke night or bingo. Most of the local residents found some excuse to stop by one or two nights a week, especially in the winter.

During the prime summer months, the clientele were mainly tourists. They would stop in for a drink and listen to the babbling brook that ran through the property, or the live music they played in the evening out on the patio, during the summer months. On weekends, there would be long lines of motorcycles parked outside. It was known as a stopping point. Locals would slip in and out just to check out who was there.

By the time I had glanced around to see if there was anyone at the café I knew, Marge had my soup in front of me. If it tasted as good as it smelled, I was set for the evening.

“The sandwich will be out in a few minutes?” she informed me. “The cook had to throw a line out in the river.”

“You didn’t let him substitute the walleye for carp, did you?” I jested.

“No, but you might have to settle for something the size of bait. I’m not sure if he has caught any fish this week.”

Marge knew how to take a joke and give one back. I guess that was another reason I always stopped in for a hot meal. Having grown up out east, I enjoyed fish. It wasn’t quite the same as freshly caught cod or Maine lobsters, but it was a good substitute. I took my time eating the food, hoping that some old friends just might stop by the café. Unfortunately, tonight it was not to be.

As I was about to ask for my check, Marge came over and sat down at the table across from me. "You heading out of town again?" she asked.

"Yes, but I'll be back," I told her.

"I know you will. If you ever need to talk, you know you can always give me a call."

I thanked her for the offer. With winter coming on, she knew how the long season would feel like to me.

I drifted back home taking a slightly different route that took me up over the red bridge that crossed the brisk stream that cut through the center of town, just below the holding pond. I was hoping that since it was dark, I might see some familiar faces in some of the windows of the houses I passed. It took almost twenty minutes to walk back to the house using my irregular route. As I came through the door, the ladies at the counter looked up and greeted me.

Bonnie paused her conversation just long enough to ask me, "Edward, did you have a good dinner?"

"Yes, thanks. Once again, the Brookside filled my stomach with their soup and sandwich. This town would probably fall off the map if they ever closed it down. If I had run into any old friends tonight, I might have ordered up one of their pizzas."

They gave me a smile as I headed up to my room.

"Is Edward checking out tomorrow?" Bonnie asked her sister, Jean, watching her expressions.

"Yes! Are you going to tell him?"

"I suppose unless you want to pull the morning shift. I'm just not sure how he is going to take it. You know, he is probably our most regular customer. I'm not sure how long he has been coming to the bed-n-breakfast. He was here when I started six years ago."

Jean suggested, "I'll stop in a little early, just after breakfast, to see if you need some support. I think his room is the only one I need to clean. What are you serving tomorrow?"

Bonnie told her, "I better make something special for him. Perhaps a ham and cheese omelet with blueberry muffins would be good for the morning. It should put him in a good mood before I tell him the news."

They sat and talked for a short time before Bonnie headed back home.

***

Jason Willard Investment Services

I was relaxing at my desk in my office. It had been a beautiful morning and the traffic on my way into the office was almost non-existent. As I sat there, I was thinking: "*Things couldn't be better.*"

My computer was starting to pick up the morning's stock market ticker, while I glanced around attempting to find my schedule for the day. Then, my cell phone went off, breaking the tranquility of the morning. When I looked at the caller ID, it was Edward. It was 9:17 am, and I hadn't even finished drinking my first cup of coffee.

Edward and I had a long history that went back many years. I was working for one of the companies Edward purchased thirty years ago. When he sold the business, I started my own business auditing and consulting small businesses. To that end, for the past 20 years, I found myself being Edward's financial advisor. Owning my own business did provide me with one benefit. I had found my way into the perfect retirement job; taking care of just a few of my very best customers. As a result of my planning, I enjoyed showing up and leaving my office at my leisure. Well, that was with one exception.

"Jason, Edward here. I need a favor."

I wasn't surprised. Ed rarely called me when he didn't need something, or some information, right away.

"Well, Ed, you almost gave me a chance to warm up my chair and drink my coffee. What can I do for you today?"

"They're going to sell the Bed and Breakfast. The girl at the front desk informed me, as I was getting ready to check out after breakfast this morning. I need you to get me an estimate of its worth, and find out who holds the mortgage on the place."

"How soon do you need it?" I asked, knowing full well what his answer would be.

"I told you, they are going to sell it. I need it right now."

"Okay! Give me a little time to call a couple people. I'll get back to you as soon as I have some of the information you need."

I didn't even have to ask Ed what the address was for the Bed and Breakfast. Ed had been staying there off and on for years. The way he talked about the place; you would have thought that he had purchased it years ago. In fact, it might have been easier if he had.

Two years ago, the owners tried to sell the property. When Edward got wind of the sale, he asked me to find a straw bidder for the property. Just as it looked as though the property might sell, he had them come in with a last-minute bid – just high enough over the previous bid to get the offer. Then, as the formalities of the sale progressed, he had an inspector go over the entire house, finding a number of concealed problems. By the time the owner was able to fix all the problems, Edward had the buyer back out of the sale claiming the delay had caused finance problems with the property.

Oh yes, Edward was clever. He knew that the original bidder would be long gone and the prime selling season would be over by the time his purchaser backed out of the deal. The seller of the house would probably have to wait for another season before they could list it and be able to sell it for a profit. And, that's exactly what happened.

I wondered what Ed had planned out in his mind this time. He only had a short time to come up with an idea before he called me. However, for Edward, that was all the time he needed.

It took me a couple hours before I could call Edward back.

"Ed, this is Jason Willard. I got the information you wanted."

"That was quick. What did you find out?"

I explained to Ed that the paper for the property was still held by the same bank as it was two years ago. One advantage of a small town is that people tend to go through the local bank. "I was able to talk to the loan officer and found out that the owner was hoping to sell the place for about $100,000 over the mortgage value. He figured it was worth about $550,000. The owner told him a few weeks ago, that he had another investment in the works and wanted to unload it quickly. Apparently, he has a chance to buy into a franchise in another city that looks very promising."

"Well, Jason, that confirms what the gal at the front desk told me this morning. She informed me that I might have to find another B&B to stay at next time I was in town. They were going to put it up for sale.

"I could see in her eyes that she really didn't want to tell me. She knew how I liked staying there.

"Apparently, the girls were already talking about looking for another job, just in case the new owner did not want to run it as an investment property.

"Here's what I want you to do…"

Once again, I had anticipated the situation correctly. Edward had a plan completely worked out in his mind, even before he called me this morning. I just shook my head, while sipping on my coffee, listening to what he had planned. When it came to wheeling and dealing, I knew from experience, I was working with the master.

Edward and I had worked together several times in the past ten years. Whenever he wanted to purchase a small company, he would rely on me for making sure he had the winning bid and checking the accounting system to make sure he knew what was making most of their profits.

Now that Edward had formally retired, most of my financial work for him had been simply been in purchasing investment properties. He would buy them at a discount and sell when the market was right. In all my years of dealing with Edward, I was impressed with his ability to purchase a property or business at just the right time. His age had not slowed down his keen ability to sniff out a deal.

However, with this deal, there was something obviously special. Edward did not leave me the normal option of walking away from the purchase if he could not get his price.

As I sat back into my chair, I wondered what he had planned.

***

Chapter 4

For Sale

It was towards the end of that week that a white "For Sale" sign went up in the yard of The Meadows Bed and Breakfast. Unfortunately, for the owner, large houses in the small towns typically do not draw a high flow of traffic when they are listed for sale, especially if they are expensive.

For this specific piece of property, it would require someone that wanted it for a Bed and Breakfast, or, perhaps, someone with a large family that had made a fair amount of money and could afford the maintenance of a large home.

The seller had met with the two sisters that managed the property, hoping that he could convince his staff to stay at their jobs until a new buyer could be found. They all knew the most difficult task would be to attract new customers with a "For Sale" sign located on the lawn. Their business would either go down or temporarily go up, from customers that wanted one last stay at the Inn.

The owner was also well aware of the fact that with the house's history of low occupancy of customers, there was a chance that if the number of new customers dropped in the coming month, it might chase away many of the perspective buyers. As a matter of fact, they were quickly approaching the Bed and Breakfast's slowest season – winter. Usually, during this time, the staff spent more time cleaning snow off the steps and sidewalk than cleaning rooms in the winter. All this had led to the decision by the owner that he needed to unload it as quickly as he could.

The predictions seemed to be correct. Between the weekend and the entire next week, they had a grand total of only four room nights rented. Even though it was still mid-fall, the tourist trade had already dropped from the normal summer rate. It was looking as though it was becoming a weekend business with only a random guest requesting reservations during the week. Customers that might have come for a three-day stay in the summer were limiting themselves to day trips to the area.

It was heading into the second week since the “For Sale” sign went up that Bonnie received a call from the owner. He informed her that a realtor wanted to show the house to someone the next day. Since they did not have any guests scheduled, Bonnie told him it would be a good time for a showing; she would let Jean know as well.

The following day, at 2:30 pm, the rather short and portly realtor, Frank Crawley, came to the door with two of his customers, who were looking for a house.

Frank was well known in the small town and Bonnie greeted him by name as he came through the door.

“Mr. Crawley, welcome! I’ll get out of your way while you show your customers the house. If you have any questions, I’ll be in the office,” Bonnie told him.

Like many good realtors, Frank had gotten to know almost everyone in the community during his 40 years of selling houses. If anyone was looking for a new house, odds were they at least called Frank. Even though there were large, well known, realty firms in the general area, Crawley’s smaller firm had done quite well. He made sure that between him and his partner, they knew everyone at the local churches, both in town and in the neighboring towns, knew the servers by name at the restaurants, and even their wives had connections at the hair salon. If anyone even whispered that they were thinking of a new home or selling, the Crawley Realty knew about it.

Frank Crawley's customers were a couple in their late thirties, which were looking for an older style farmhouse, just out of town. After looking at several handpicked houses, Crawley had convinced them to take a look at the Bed and Breakfast. As a large, older house, it was a close fit to the vision given to him by his customers. He was hoping that the large lot, near the far edge of town, with mature oak and maple trees, would give them the roomy feel they hoped for out in the country. The immaculate physical shape of this house was one of the main selling points. Besides, being up on the hill with trees close by, it had that country feeling.

As the realtor took his clients for a tour of the house, he started by pointing out the fantastic kitchen, which had been improved in order to be certified for serving guests. The massive industrial gas stove was an impressive key selling point. Since the house was offered for sale as a B&B, all the furnishing were included with the house – including the large oak dining room table. Walking through the dining room, they saw it was decorated with a plate rail lined with old china plates that were on display. Crawley told his customers that they could negotiate all the furnishing into or out of the selling price, as they liked.

Throughout the rest of the house, all of the real wood floors looked as though they had been refinished in the past couple of years. With throw rugs strategically placed in the high wear areas, the wood was in excellent shape. It was another real plus.

As they climbed the curved wooden stairs that led to the second floor, they looked in at the master bedroom, which included the reading nook. It was another prime selling feature of the house along with the picturesque porch in front of the building. The reading nook was warmly lit by the sunlight coming through the window.

Crawly pointed out the fact that the four plus bedrooms would be perfect for the couple's family. They had three children and each could have a bedroom of their own. Plus, there was a two bedroom apartment attached to the back of the house that could serve as a grandparents apartment.

The couple found the interior wall coverings interesting. In keeping with the theme of an older house for the Bed and Breakfast, the bedrooms had distinctive wallpaper on some walls, while using darker blues or dark green paint on the opposing walls of the rooms. As a Bed and Breakfast, it was a very stylish building. For a personal home, however, some of the wallpapers probably needed changing.

There was one other surprising factor, which the couple discovered. It was that the house did not have air-conditioning. The house had hot water heat, and as a result, they would need to install air-conditioners in several rooms for cooling.

"Well, what do you think?" Crawley asked them. "I know your preference was to be out of town, but this house is almost exactly what you have been looking for, for the past month."

It was indeed a tradeoff. The house was perfect. The only obvious problem was they had their mind set on a rural setting. The price was less because it did not have the ten to eighty acres of land attached to it that a rural house would have. The half-acre lot gave them plenty of room, and being on the edge of town, it gave the feel of a larger lot.

"Do you know the history of the house?" the woman asked Frank.

"Funny you should ask. Actually, I do. I'll explain it to you in the car." They proceeded out of the B&B so that they could talk freely and not feel as though they were interfering with Bonnie's work at the Bed and Breakfast.

In the car, Frank explained that the house was originally built deep in the woods, in a spot overlooking the St. Croix River Valley. "The large track of land eventually became extremely valuable for developers, and about 45 years ago, they became worried that the National Park Service was going take control of the entire river valley – from the river to the top of the high ridge visible from the river. Unless homes were built quickly, they would not be grandfathered in on the land they stood. In an effort to beat the deadlines, the decision was made to sub-divide the land.

"The house was moved from its original location to this location on the hill, just above the town. At the same time, the house was converted into the Meadows Bed and Breakfast. The property on which it had been located, was divided into twenty lots, all with a view of the river. The developer, after leveling off the land, made a fortune by selling finished houses on the lots he created that had a great view of the river along with a shared river access.

"I'm not sure if the Bed and Breakfast has ever made money. There already was a historic Bed and Breakfast in town for years up on the hill, and right on Highway 95. It was built by one of the town's original founders. They gave up trying to keep it as a Bed and Breakfast a few years ago.

"This place is definitely a beautiful house, but the location doesn't draw the tourist traffic as it would if it had a view of the river or was down on the main street of town near the river. However, my feeling is that it would make a great house for you to convert back to a single family home.

"There is one other item I should inform you of. There is a rumor that the house could be haunted. I'm not sure where that rumor came from, but I figured I better mention it to you. I'd rather you heard it from me than from someone else.

"Now, I have never heard anyone say that they actually saw a ghost. However, I have heard stories of items moving at night from one shelf to another. On the positive side; if you want someone helping you with your decorating, there might be an advantage in having someone assist you for free.

"My personal feeling is that a guest that had never heard the radiation pipes of hot-water heat expand as it heats up, woke up and thought it was a ghost walking the halls. Oh, I forgot to mention, there is a large power vent in the attic that really helps keep the house cool in the summer. That's why they do not have air-conditioners."

The couple looked at each other and smiled. Haunted house?

After looking at the Bed and Breakfast, Frank Crawley took his clients to another house about five miles out of town that was located on a small creek. The house was not in the same condition, but the setting was beautiful. The house was set on ten acres of land.

From the house, you could hear a babbling creek as it meandered through the property. It was only about three feet wide and perhaps eight to ten inches deep, but it drew the birds to the many trees that dotted its shoreline. Crawley told them there was a possibility that the creek might contain a few brown trout. Since he had not caught any out of the creek, he could not guarantee it. However, many of the area creeks near here contain trout.

The other feature that appealed to the clients was along with the two-car garage, there was a pole barn that could house a workshop or several vehicles. That would be great for storing their snowmobiles and boat.

The couple estimated that it might take another ten thousand dollars to bring the house up to what they wanted. However, with the ideal setting, they felt it would be worth the investment. They had found their dream home.

In the next week, Frank Crawly showed the Bed and Breakfast to two other customers. In both cases, they decided it would be way too much house for them to keep up.

Finally, near the end of that week, Frank Crawly called the owner of the Bed and Breakfast. "I have some good news for you; I have someone who wants to put in an offer on the B&B. How's your schedule? Can we meet this afternoon?"

Crawly had not told him the amount of the offer. Knowing that the owner wanted to sell it as quickly as possible, he was hoping that he might be able to convince him to accept the offer he had in his hands.

Later that afternoon the two men met for a short meeting at the Meadows Bed and Breakfast. The offer was from a corporation that wanted to maintain it as a Bed and Breakfast. They were looking for a turn-key purchase that they did not have to refurbish. The intention was that everything would stay the same, and the current employees could continue to operate the B&B.

It was exactly what the current owner was hoping to hear. The only fly in the ointment; their offer was only $500,000 for the place.

Crawley looked deeply into the eyes of the owner. "That's about as close to what you wanted as we might see for a while," he told him. "You get to walk away, and the place continues as if it was yesterday. I checked them out and they have a good line of credit." Crawley could tell from experience that the owner was thinking it over.

The owner sat and thought about it. There were no contingencies and no transition worries with his staff. It was a clear-cut deal. He could take the money and be off to his next deal in just a matter of weeks. Even though the amount was under his asking price, the $50,000 could be made back by the end of the year with his new operation, and he could eliminate his monthly losses.

The deal was cut. The paperwork would take three weeks or less to complete.

***

Jason Willard Investment Services

My cell phone rang about thirty minutes later. It was Frank Crawley. I had been expecting the call.

"Jason, he took the deal. Tell your friend he is now the proud owner of a Bed and Breakfast."

"Good work! Thanks Jim for all the help. You didn't tell them who the purchaser is, did you?"

"No, I just did it like we agreed. I simply told him the name of the limited partnership you gave me. When you talk to Edward, tell him he owes me a fancy dinner next time he is in town. I haven't seen him in years. It will be good to sit down and talk.

"You think he is going to let the staff know he is the owner, or is he just going to stay hidden in the background like he originally planned?"

"Well Jim, knowing Edward, between you and me, we will probably be the only people that actually know who owns the property, for a long time. When he makes up his mind, I have rarely seen him change his plans."

As soon as we finished our call, I called Edward with the news he was hoping to hear.

“Ed, this is Jason. They took the offer just like you thought. What’s your plan now? How are you planning on setting up the operation for keeping the books and running the business? Did you want to run it through me, or have you come up with another way?”

“Jason, you know, I have been thinking it over. I’m sure they probably lost money for more than just the past couple years. I don’t see any easy way to turn that part around. So, if I am purchasing a business that is currently running at a loss, I might as well attempt to do something positive with it.”

I was sitting there waiting to see if Edward would finally show his cards. Why did he invest money in a business that was losing money? It definitely did not fit his previous patterns for buying and selling business properties.

“Jason, I have another idea floating around in my mind,” Edward told him. “I think I’ll run it “as is” for a few months, so I can figure out what I would like to do. Meanwhile, can I leave it to you to speak to the two women that work there? Maybe you can coordinate it with Crawley. He can let you know when the present owner is ready to inform his staff.

“As soon as the current owner informs them that the business has been sold, I would like to have you talk with both of them about whether or not they would like to stay on with the B&B. It would be for the same wages they were receiving before since they are not turning a profit. But, hopefully, they work there because they like the work.”

“I’ll get it done,” I told him.

***

Chapter 5

Plans

One month earlier in St. Cloud

Maria Wagner's daughter, Ashlee's, high school mid-semester grades had just been released. In the past year and a half, Maria had seen her daughter's grades slip from a B average to a C- average. It wasn't a huge surprise, she had seen the start of a change in her daughter's attitude ever since she entered high school.

In eighth grade, her grades were still good. However, during her freshman and now her sophomore year her grades had become a constant struggle. Even her friends seemed to have deserted her and she was constantly looking for attention.

Maria met with the school counselors. They were very good at analyzing problems and offering support. In this school district, high school started with the 9th grade class. When Maria was her daughter's age, her high school didn't start until 10th grade. As she reflected on the differences, Maria wished that the local school started with 10th grade also. Deep down, she wondered if her daughter, Ashlee, had been emotionally ready for high school in 9th grade. Ashlee's expectations and her social contacts changed radically between schools.

Unfortunately, the message she was hearing this day from her counselors was clear; it was their home life that was reflecting in her daughter's attitude and lack of desire to get better grades.

As she listened to the counselor, who was gently trying to break the news to her, Maria accepted the assessment. She realized that something had to change if she had any hope of Ashlee's education turning around.

No matter how the counselor tried to say it, this was definitely a hard message for a mother to accept. In this case, the counselor had done her homework by talking at length several times with Ashlee, and her summary appeared to be right on.

As tough as the message sounded, Maria accepted it. Things were not going very well at home. She had watched as the economic and emotional foundation that her daughter needed so badly, slipped away in the past few years. Now, Ashlee was simply reacting to it.

Maria's own self-esteem had started to slip away as well while her husband had gone from one temporary job to another in the past few years. What little extra money he was bringing in, was slowly slipping through the cracks at the local bar. To meet the rent payments, Maria had to rely on two part-time jobs and still needed a loan from her parents to make up the difference. It was Maria's late afternoon job, from 3:00 to 7:30 pm at a restaurant, that was stealing the valuable time she needed for communications with her daughter, and making sure she was completing her homework.

Maria had wondered how long the situation could continue. Her parents were generous, but they did not have the money to support her family for the rest of their life. Now, with her daughter's grades in her hands, she realized it was time to modify her life, or they would be stuck in the same situation forever.

Life hadn't always been that way for her. When she first met her husband - Ethan, it was love at first sight. Perhaps that was the problem. They quickly got married even though her parents tried to convince her to wait until she finished college. As a result of their decision, any thoughts she had of finishing college went down the tube, as she found that she needed to work to support the two of them, paying his tuition costs and their other bills. So, after fall semester her freshman year, she quit school.

The slippery slope had only started. It was only a year later, she found herself pregnant, only to lose the child in the last month of pregnancy. The emotional glitter seemed to slip from their marriage. Perhaps it was the depression from the loss of the child. Recognizing that things were floundering, Maria found herself getting pregnant once again, hoping that a child could put the love back in the marriage.

Now, as Maria looked back at the situation, she realized that their marriage never did get the opportunity to click. Most of the problems her daughter was experiencing were simply a result of the broken love in her marriage.

When her husband graduated from college in St. Cloud, the economy faltered. He never did find a job that lasted more than three years. His lack of success in life was definitely reflecting in his attitude as well. All of the events combined put a set of events in place that spiraled down, and never seemed to find a point at which it could reverse itself.

It was not very long after that point that Maria found that her husband preferred the conversations with other men at the bar, to coming home and listening to his wife and daughter. Babysitting had not been on his list of desired jobs.

The whole loss of relationship between her parents had been exceptionally hard on Ashlee. As she grew older, she watched as her friends had parents that pampered to their every wish. She wanted, so badly, to see the same kind of affection from her father that she saw in her friend's families. Unfortunately, as she grew older and did not require constant watching, their time together had become less and less.

Often, she would come home from school only to find a note on the table listing what was in the refrigerator for supper and to do her homework before anything else.

Maria rushed from the meeting at school to her job at the local restaurant. The restaurant knew that she might be a little late due to the appointment with the school counselor, however, on this day, Maria felt embarrassed coming in thirty minutes late. Each time she waited on a family at a table, she would think back to the conversations she had with the counselor. Then, she would look at the relationships one of the families at the table would have with each other. By the time she was off work at 7:30 pm, her spirit was at an all-time low. What could she do? Her thoughts weighed heavily on her all the way home.

It was Friday. She was definitely in agreement with "TGIF." This was one Friday that qualified for "Thank God it's Friday." It had been an extremely long day. Now, to finish it off, she had to figure out a way to start the discussion with her daughter about her grades.

Arriving at home, Maria discovered that her husband was still at the bar with his buddies. No surprise! It was Friday. Their gathering of the Friday "get-together" at the bar started when he was an in undergraduate in school.

When graduation time came, a few ex-students that had established local jobs and stayed in the St. Cloud area, simply converted the Friday kegger party to a regular event at the local bar. The numbers changed as people's lives changed, but the inflow of a few new graduates each year, along with a few of their friends that dropped out of school early, kept the tradition going.

As she was putting her dirty clothes from the restaurant in the laundry, Ashlee came down the steps. Maria glanced up just as Ashlee informed her, "I'm going out."

Maria looked at her; short shorts and a low-cut tee shirt. Even her makeup was a little over the top.

"Where are you going?" she asked.

"Out! A few friends and I are just going to hang out."

It was definitely not what Maria wanted to hear at the end of the day. Her daughter's friends did not have the look of the steady friends that she felt she could trust her with, especially without knowing where they were going.

"Be in by 11:00."

"Why? It's a weekend. No one else has to be home."

"I just spent an hour discussing your grades with your counselor at school today. Until they change, 11:00 pm is late enough. Understand?"

With that, Ashlee turned and stomped up the stairs in a huff. She never did give Maria an answer. A few minutes later, Maria heard the front door slamming as Ashlee went out to meet her friends.

It was the icing on the cake. Or, perhaps a more appropriate metaphor; the cake that fell as you removed it from the oven to cool. Maria broke down in tears. What was she to do? After a little while, when she got her composure back, she went upstairs and called her mother, hoping to hear some positive support.

Maria's mother had heard the story before. It was a discussion that had surfaced on and off for the past couple of years. Her mother always wished that Maria had lived closer to Minneapolis/St. Paul than St. Cloud. It would have been much easier to offer support to her daughter and granddaughter. However, Maria's husband insisted over the years that he wanted to live at least three hours away from her parents. He didn't want them "meddling" in their lives.

Actually, he would have preferred to live in a different state if he could. As it turned out, after going to college in St. Cloud, they simply stayed in the community they had come to know. Maria had grown up with her parents in a suburb of St. Paul, Minnesota before she got married.

As Maria and her mother were discussing the problems of the day, Maria's husband wandered in the door. Ethan took one look at Maria and figured that she was talking to her mother again. With that, he wandered off to the kitchen, grabbed a beer from the refrigerator and sat down to watch television.

Maria waited a while before approaching her husband.

"Ethan, can you turn off the television? We need to talk about Ashlee."

"What about her? You talk to her; I'm staying clear of any arguments between you and Ashlee."

"Ethan, we need to talk. I spent an hour this afternoon with her counselor at school. She told me Ashlee's having problems with her studies and with the friends she makes."

"Like I said, you need to talk to her. She doesn't listen to a word I say. We've had that discussion before."

"Maybe that's the problem. When is the last time you spent ten minutes talking to her? All you do is ignore the family, come in late and have a beer. Don't you think it is time to play a real part in her life?"

"Like I said, that's your department. I gave up trying to understand what makes her tick years ago."

The conversation made Maria even more frustrated than she was earlier, after the conversation with Ashlee. She definitely felt depressed that everything was always dumped in her lap.

To get away from the situation, Maria went back downstairs to do the ironing and keep from starting a real argument with Ethan.

Right now, she was angry enough to really tell him off. She knew it wouldn't get her any place even if she tried.

It was about 10:45 pm, when she came back upstairs. The television was off and Ethan had gone to bed after the news. His beer bottle was on the floor next to the chair where he had been sitting. Maria wished she could give it a kick, but realized it might have a drop or two left in it. As a result, she picked it up and decided to read a book until Ashlee came home.

Checking her watch, it was 10:53. Ashlee was cutting it close.

It was about 12:30 am when Ashlee finally opened the door. Maria had finished her book and was waiting, in a rather upset mood, for Ashlee's return. With every fifteen minutes ticking off the clock, her blood pressure rose another ten points.

When Ashlee entered the house, she was accompanied by an older boy, all dressed in black with chains hanging from low cut pants. When he spotted Maria sitting there, he told Ashlee, "I think I'd better go. It was fun. I'll call you." With that, he abruptly turned and left.

Maria noticed he walked with a limp.

"Did you have to wait up for me?" Ashlee belligerently asked with a scowl on her face.

Maria could tell by her talking that she had been drinking. There was also that telltale odor on her breath. "Let's talk about it in the morning," she told Ashlee, knowing full well that anything she might try and say tonight, Ashlee would simply get upset. Things were already too far out of control.

With that, Ashlee turned and stomped up to her room.

Maria sat back down. Dazed, she wondered what to do next. The counselor was right; unless things changed at home,

Ashlee was not going to change. Ethan was no help. Things were just going to get worse. What if the older boys she was chasing got her drunk and she ended up pregnant? With those nightmarish thoughts, Maria eventually dozed off, still in the chair. All night long, all of her different options were racing through her mind, as she slipped in and out of sleep. Unfortunately, none of them stood out as the easy approach.

Saturday morning didn't bring any rays of bright sunshine to help the problems. Maria was up early. She was still troubled with the events from the evening before.

Ethan was up before Ashlee. When he came down for breakfast, Maria insisted that he listen to her before he ate.

"Ethan, Ashlee was out drinking last night. She staggered in about 12:30 am with an older boy that wouldn't make any of my lists of better boyfriends. If you hadn't gone off to bed, you would have seen it too."

"I told you to handle it," he replied.

"It's not that easy. It takes an effort by both of us. You need to be there too," Maria replied, knowing that Ethan didn't care.

With that, Ethan got up and told Maria, "I'm going out. I'll be home later."

"What if we aren't?" Maria responded looking for a reaction.

"Do what you need to do," Ethan answered, and left the house.

Maria's only thoughts were – *thanks for nothing.* Once again, Ethan was not about to get involved. They had had the same conversation off and on for the past couple years. She wondered why they even got married in the first place.

When Ashlee finally woke up from the light coming directly into her window, she came downstairs. She wasn't moving very fast. The effects of the night before were still hanging in the cobwebs of her mind. That was just fine with Maria. She didn't want her going any place. Maria needed to let Ashlee know that things were going to change. Also, Ashlee needed to understand who was the boss. To do that, Maria understood that she needed to be assertive and start making decisions.

"You were out past the time we agreed last night," Maria told Ashlee as she started looking for something to eat.

"You agreed, I didn't," Ashlee said with a definite lack of emotion.

"We need to have a discussion after breakfast."

"Whatever!"

Maria knew in her heart the only possible outcome of her confrontation with Ethan that had a chance of changing anything. With that, she left the room and called her mother. They had discussed it last night, but now, Maria knew it was the only option.

"Mom, is that offer to move in with you for a short time still open?" Maria asked.

"Yes! Your father and I are still willing to give you a place to adjust your lives if you need it."

"Thanks. I'll let you know later today or tomorrow when I'm ready to make the move."

"Do what you need to do. Just remember, you need to do whatever is best for the long term. This might be your last chance to give Ashlee another chance."

With that, Maria thanked her mother and went back in to talk to Ashlee.

"I have a few things to discuss with you. Do me a favor and just listen until I'm done. I need your attention.

"I made a decision last night while you were sleeping. We need to make some changes that will affect both of us. It's not just you.

"As you know, I have had to work two jobs just to pay the bills. Even with that, my parents have had to help us with the unexpected expenses. Unfortunately, I don't see any miracles coming along that might change the way we are living. I need a better sense of stability in my life, just like you.

"I think we both need a change in scenery. You need a chance to get your grades back up and to have someone there to give you the support you need. I need to go back and get my degree so that I can get a better paying job. Both of our lives need adjustments that will affect us for years to come. If we don't do it now, you'll just end up doing nothing in your life just like me."

"What about Dad?" Ashlee broke in. "Doesn't he have a say?"

"He doesn't want to get involved. I need to talk to him about it too," Maria told her. "I talked to your grandparents. They said the two of us could move in with them for a short time while I was looking for a job that could support us and finish my education."

"What if I don't want to move?" Ashlee asserted. "I have my friends."

"Sorry, that's not an option. You'll make new friends just like me. I'm not sure when we will move, but my hope is that we can make it soon, so you don't fall further behind in your classes. I realize that making a change in the middle of the semester will be tough. The new school might be ahead or behind your current school in their curriculum. Hopefully, your new teachers will make some adjustments along with you to make the transition a smooth one."

Maria could see that Ashlee was not happy with the decision. She just sat there with a look of contempt on her face. The surprising part was that she seemed to be accepting what Maria was saying. Perhaps there was more going on than she knew. On the other hand, maybe it was still the hangover from last night. Whatever the reason, Maria decided the quicker they made the move the better.

"I would suggest that you do not mention anything to your friends at school until we get a date figured out. Then we can let people know."

Ashlee just barely shook her head – yes. Then, dragging her feet, she went up to sulk in her room and think about the changes that were coming. Right now, her head was aching from the whole set of events. She looked for some aspirins.

Maria knew she had an even harder discussion coming. Ethan didn't want to be involved. What was he going to say when Maria told him she wanted a separation? Maria was fretting about this discussion even more than talking to Ashlee.

During the day, Ashlee asked a few questions about the move. Maria did her best not to make it look as though they were moving because of the boyfriends Ashlee was making. Even though she could tell that Ashlee was definitely unhappy with the decision, Ashlee was, at least, willing to attempt to talk to her about it. Unfortunately, not moving was not negotiable at this point.

It was close to suppertime when Ethan came back home. He had been hanging out in the bar all day trying to avoid any arguments about Ashlee. Maria caught him as he came in the door.

"Ethan, we need to talk," She told him. She figured she might catch him by surprise.

"What now?"

"Let's go in the other room and talk."

Hesitantly, Ethan followed her into the living room figuring Maria wanted to continue the discussion from this morning.

After getting up the courage, Maria finally told him. "Ethan, things just aren't working the way we hoped when we were first married, and I don't see anything that is going to change it. Every time we talk about our lives and the future, things just stay the same. I think we need to live apart to see if there is anything left in our marriage."

Maria figured that it was not what Ethan was expecting her to say. It probably caught him by surprise. Then again, perhaps not.

"You made up your mind?" he asked.

"Yes. I talked to my parents and they are willing to let Ashlee and me stay for a while to see if we can get our lives back together."

"Then what?" he asked.

"Then, we'll see what the two of us want to do. It will give you time to decide what you want to do the rest of your life, also. I think we both need to assess the future to see where we want our lives to lead us."

Ethan just sat there, silently.

"How do you propose to do this?" Ethan asked.

"I think we can sit down and decide that part tomorrow after we have both had time to think it through. We don't have much, so there isn't much for us to divide up."

"Ashlee OK with this?" he asked.

"So far. I'm sure it is a shock to her. We'll see tomorrow when she has had time to consider what changes will happen."

"Do I still get supper?" Ethan asked.

"Yes, nothing has changed. I'm not mad at you. I just feel we all need to get our lives back. Look at what we have done in the past couple years. Nothing! We are no better off, and in Ashlee's case, she has gone downhill. I think it is time for all of us to take a deep look at where we want to be in ten years, and figure out what it will take to get there."

Supper was rather quiet that evening. Everyone was thinking and no one wanted to open any blind doors.

Sunday wasn't much different. Before working at the restaurant, Maria had a chance to talk to Ethan about splitting things up.

The rent on the duplex was paid-up until the end of the month. That gave Ethan three weeks to decide if he wanted to stay or find a cheaper location. However, if he wanted to move, they needed to let the landlord know next week. They didn't have a lease, so Maria didn't think it would be a problem.

Both of them had old cars that were not worth as much as a set of new tires. The important thing was that they ran. Even the furniture was second hand. Maria would leave the bed and television.

With their next paychecks, after paying the bills they would probably have $800 left in the checking account. It was not very much to show for the number of years they were married. They agreed to split it 50/50. Other than that, it was just a few items scattered around the duplex.

Heading to work at the restaurant, Maria still had a hollow feeling that was wrenching her stomach. Was she doing the right thing? Maria wished she had a close friend that she could talk things over with, in confidence. What she really needed was a sister that lived close.

She decided not to tell her boss until Monday. Maria had had enough discussions at home and she didn't want to have to go through everything, all over again at work. One positive thing, Sundays usually brought good tips from the customers.

When she got home that evening around 7:30, things were quiet. Perhaps too quiet. Ashlee had gone out. Ethan had watched the football games on TV and was patiently waiting for supper. It was almost as though nothing had happened. Perhaps that was what Ethan had hoped for.

"Did Ashlee say anything to you? Maria asked Ethan.

"No! Well, she came down once to get a coke and gave me a look – as if it was all my fault. Then, she just sat in her room until she got a phone call. She said to tell you she would be back early. She seems to be taking this better than I expected her to."

"I think we all knew we needed a change. Hopefully, we can all get through it without a lot of anger. You still okay with it?" Maria asked him.

"I'll survive. Think Ashlee will even miss me?"

"Probably! I'm hoping that after a month or two the two of you can connect on a higher level. Perhaps both of you will miss each other and want to talk again," Maria told Ethan.

"I guess I haven't been much of a father to her in the past few years. You're probably right; maybe a separation for a while will allow the two of us time to get back to thinking again."

Maria was surprised. Where was that basic logic the past couple of years? Ethan had showed very little desire to communicate with Ashlee. In fact, he had gone out of his way not to get into long discussions with her. That was some of the problem.

That evening Ashlee came home about 9 pm and headed straight up to her room to put her earphones in, blocking out the world. Both Maria and Ethan were shocked she was in early.

Monday morning, everyone cleared out early. Perhaps in an effort to eliminate any conversations. Ashlee was off to school, Ethan had a porch-rebuilding job to help with, and Maria had a house-cleaning job before her job at the restaurant. In-between those two jobs, Maria planned to meet with the Job Services people in St. Cloud. She was hoping that they might have suggestions for jobs in the St. Paul area.

When she reached the Workforce Center, she sought out a woman that had helped her a few times in the past, in locating part-time jobs. After informing her that she was going to move to St. Paul with her daughter next week, she asked if there was a local office down there that she could get the same courteous help she had experienced in St. Cloud. The woman just smiled.

"You know, Maria, this is going to be tough on your family. But, you are doing the right thing. Things will work out in the future." She wrote down the name of a friend that worked at the Center in North St. Paul. "Now, when you get there, look him up. I'll let him know you are coming. He'll give you the same assistance I've been giving you. You'll see."

Maria left the office feeling somewhat better about the move. She had a contact, now she just needed a job.

On the way to the restaurant, she stopped by the school and told them that Ashlee would be moving at the end of the week. They told her they would send the records to the new school as soon as they requested them.

It was harder at the restaurant. She had worked there for three years and they had become part of her family. One by one, she informed them that she was leaving at the end of the week. It was an emotional evening. Every time she waited on one of her regular customers, she realized she would probably never see them again after they left.

That evening, Maria told Ashlee that she could let her friends know she was moving.

"I doubt they'd care," she told her. "I only have a couple people that might even know I wasn't there anymore."

"You'd be surprised. People act differently when they haven't seen you in a while. Besides, you will develop a whole new set of friends down there. It won't take long."

Ashlee just gave her a blank stare. She was going along with this change, but it didn't mean that she had to like it.

Saturday morning, Maria's father pulled up in front of the house with a truck he had rented to help them move.

"Where's Ethan, he asked Maria."

"He had a carpenter job. He said goodbye earlier. I think he was glad that he didn't need to be here when we left."

The three of them loaded up the truck with their essentials and left for St. Paul.

***

The next week was kept busy with adjustments. Everyone needed some time to get adjusted to the larger family in the house.

The Schmidt's, John and Helen, had been gracious enough to let Maria and her daughter have as much room as they needed in the house. They didn't mind. They knew it was temporary until Maria got her feet back on the ground. They also realized it might take a year or two. It gave them a chance to become closer to their granddaughter.

Ashlee started back at school – this time in the North St. Paul district. The Schmidt's home was just over the border from St. Paul into North St. Paul.

She felt awkward and strange in her classes. Everyone else knew each other. Even though they tried to make her feel welcome, Ashlee knew it was going to take the rest of the year just to make new friends. On top of that, she had to adjust to where the new school was in their teaching. It was close, but she felt as though she might have missed a few chapters in the books.

Since she didn't have any friends, reluctantly, Ashlee put her nose in the books and tried as hard as she could to catch up to the rest of the class.

Her biggest help was her history teacher. He made her feel as though she was part of the class, and intentionally made sure the questions he asked of her were not the difficult ones linked back to earlier in the semester. When Ashlee figured it out, she realized that she had a teacher that cared. It felt different.

Chapter 6

The Search

The employment offices, located in North St. Paul, Minnesota, were a busy location. People came for assistance in finding a job from the lists of opportunities compiled by the state. For those new to the unemployed roles and without a computer at home, it was a good link to the many temporary and permanent jobs available in the area. For others, it was a required stop for their unemployment check, proving they had gone on interviews, before going over to the Target store nearby to spend their money.

Carl Johnson had been working in the employment assistance office for over 25 years. As such, he had seen all kinds of people with vast circumstances over the years. Usually, he could make an educated guess about an individual within a couple minutes of interviewing a new client to his department. The way they talked, dressed, and even their expressions on their faces, told the story to Carl long before he looked at the forms they had filled out prior to meeting with the job counselors.

Today was just like every other day in the office. He expected to meet with about eight people looking for jobs, check over the new listings that came in over the weekend, and try to assist matching up as many new and previous clients to the jobs on-line that he could, which might make a good fit for them as well as for the perspective employer.

Carl's first appointment for the day was with a man that had just arrived in the country a couple months prior and was looking for a part-time job, while attending school to learn, amongst other things, English. Carl often wondered what it must feel like to be in a new country, not speak the language, and look for a job.

He admired the determination it must take as well as courage to leave his homeland and settle in a new country. What might seem like a difficult job, trying to match up a job for someone with limited language skills, had become Carl's specialty. He kept a running list of other job seekers that spoke foreign languages that had passed through his doors, and where they had found employment. Whenever possible, he would try to see if he could find a good match, so that the new hire might have someone that spoke the same language in the company to help them learn the job and customs of the new country.

Unfortunately, easy matches seemed difficult to find this morning. Nevertheless, Carl reassured the applicant that he would keep an eye open for him and give a call to the family he was temporarily staying with when he found something. The man thanked him and shook his hand as if he had just found a long lost friend.

It was that kind of relationship, which made the job interesting for Carl. He knew the odds were about 75% that either he would be able to find a job for him or teach the person how to use the system to find a job himself. If he was patient, there would be an opening. For the other 25%, they would generally pick up a job directly by means of an acquaintance, who had heard of a job opening.

Carl looked at the clock. There was just enough time for counseling one more applicant before his morning coffee break. He hated to time it wrong and miss the group discussions. This was Carl's opportunity for talking to other counselors, comparing notes of good matches.

His second appointment was a young woman in her mid-thirties that just went through a separation with her husband and was hoping to go back to school and get her degree. This one – Maria Wagner, was a referral from a colleague in St. Cloud. She had given him a brief overview, so he knew what to expect.

After marrying young, she had gotten pregnant. As a result, she was forced to drop out of college during her freshman year. Unfortunately, her child died in childbirth. A year later, she found herself pregnant again with a second child – a daughter.

Many years of an uncomfortable marriage followed, with a husband that had problems holding down a stable job. It led her to her decision; it was time to break it off. With the separation freshly in her past, she realized it was time to make a new start by moving out of the town of St. Cloud, Minnesota, back to the St. Paul area. She found herself moving back home to live with her parents until she could find a stable job.

These were the type of background stories that Carl hated to deal with. Even though he had heard the same story at least 100 times in the past, it still broke his heart to hear it again and have to try to find a good match of a job that would provide the flexibility for her to attempt to finish her schooling. From his years of experience, he knew of a couple employers that might have temporary jobs opening soon. After meeting with Maria, Carl promised that he would call her by the end of the week with an update. For today, that was the best help he was able to give her along with a tour of the facilities available to her at the center. Perhaps a sympathetic ear and a glimpse of hope were what many of his applicants really needed to hear and see. Either way, it was hard for him to tell someone that there was currently very little in the system that was a good match for them at this time.

After watching her leave the office, Carl checked his watch. Five minutes left until the coffee break. Just enough time to file his notes on the previous interviews. He usually tried to get through five people in the morning and then leave the last three applicants for just after lunch. That would give him the last hour and a half of the day to go over the lists of his still active back applicants. Hopefully, later in the afternoon, he could brighten someone's day by giving them a call with the hope of an interview.

At the gathering around the coffee pot this morning, there was a lot of discussion about what everyone had done over the weekend, but very little about job openings. The specialists that tried to contact the larger employers had not found very many openings after the busy weekend. Monday mornings were always a little slow in that area. Usually, Wednesdays and Thursdays were much more promising.

Of the remaining applicants, he was able to find a job interview for only one of them. A man that had been cut during a company rollback and was looking for an industrial job. It was his lucky day. Carl found a company that needed someone for a light duty production line. After a quick call, Carl sent him directly from his office to the employment office of the company.

Ah yes, one happy client today. Somehow, moments like this kept the job from becoming depressing – especially with all the sad stories, he had become used to hearing every day.

By the time he was finished with his eight consultations, Carl spent the next hour trying to make contact with six past clients he had in the last two weeks, trying to determine if they had found jobs or not. So far, he and his clients were batting 50%. One by one, he crossed the lucky ones off his lists.

The last half hour of his busy day was taken up by an office meeting before he could head home and try to forget everyone else's problems.

Maria headed home after the meeting feeling okay. Yes, she didn't find a job, but the person her friend told her to meet with sounded like someone that really cared about the people he met. Perhaps it was his warm smile, or maybe his fatherly gray hair. Either way, she would keep looking for a job. He had suggested a couple of group classes with an advisor. They would help in resume' writing and show her any other state benefits she might qualify for. Maria realized her expenses were going to keep coming in and she needed some cash flow to keep her parents from paying all of her bills.

Later that week, Maria found a cleaning job on a bulletin board at the grocery store that would hopefully allow her to start taking some of her classes at the local college next semester. It wasn't high paying, but it gave her the expense money she needed until she found a better paying job. Fortunately, she didn't have to worry about paying rent. And now, she could start helping out with the food bill.

The immediate adjustments required by the move were starting to settle down. Time would tell if it was a good move long term.

***

By Christmas, Maria was starting to realize the move was indeed a good move. Ashlee's grades at school were improving according to her counselor. Maria asked her to monitor Ashlee for the first couple of months, and let her know if Ashlee needed extra help. Okay, she didn't have straight A's, but several B's and a couple C's were a definite improvement over her St. Cloud grades.

The best thing; Ashlee and her grandparents were developing a close bond. Perhaps that was the thing she needed most – someone close that cared about her. She was even spending time with them instead of just staying in her room. On many evenings, she would watch Ashlee sit down with one or the other grandparent, asking them to review what she wrote for her homework assignment. That was a definite change from the past.

Even Ashlee's attitude towards Maria was improving. She seemed more willing to sit and talk. It was interesting to see the bond that was developing between Ashlee and her grandfather. It was probably the first time in years that Ashlee had felt comfortable with anything close to a father figure.

Ethan had moved out of the house they had rented and was living with a friend in an apartment to save money. He had talked to Maria several times over the past month and seemed okay with the arrangement. However, he was starting to realize life was not the same. Still, he had not worked up any desire to change things. The other thing that had not changed was his reaching out to Ashlee.

Maria figured he was still feeling awkward that Ashlee might blame him for having to move, and as a result, they did not spend time talking to each other.

As January approached, Maria started looking into starting a few classes at the local college. She found out that she could take many of the preliminary classes on-line from home. That would make it easier for her to get back into the studying thing.

One morning, a couple of weeks later, there was a knock on the front door. It was Ethan. He wanted to talk.

Maria was taken by surprise. He hadn't called or anything. Ethan just simply showed up at the door.

Maria's parents went to the kitchen area so that the two could have space to talk. They didn't want to get in the middle of any arguments. They told her to call if she needed anything.

Without any emotion, Ethan told Maria that he had moved in with someone, and he wanted a divorce. They were planning to move to Oregon, and he wanted to cut the ties before they did.

It came as a complete shock.

"What about Ashlee?" Maria asked.

"She'll be okay. She doesn't talk to me anyway."

Apparently, his new girlfriend had pushed him into making the change. He came prepared with a set of papers to sign making it official. It was a simple dissolvent of their marriage. No actions or divisions.

"And then what?" Maria asked.

"I guess we just go our separate ways," he answered. "We've sort of done that anyway."

He was right. There really was no connection other than the fact Ethan was Ashlee's father. Now, he was going to slip out without any support for her as well.

"Are you going to at least say goodbye to Ashlee?"

"I'll let you tell her. Then, before we move, I'll call and say goodbye."

It was the coward's way out and Maria knew it.

She signed the paper and slammed down the pen. I guess that makes it official, she said. They each had a copy and put one copy in an envelope addressed to the court in St. Cloud.

Ethan hardly even said good-bye. He just turned and said, "See ya."

After he left, Maria explained what had happened to her parents. They were not surprised other than the fact that he actually did it. Must have been his girlfriend's pushing, they thought.

Ashlee came home from school that afternoon. After dinner, Maria went to her room and told her all about the visit by Ethan.

"He didn't even say good-bye?" she asked.

"I'm sorry. When it came to good fathers, I guess he never learned what to do. You still have us. Just remember, we do love you."

Maria noticed just a glimmer of a tear in Ashlee's eyes. Ethan had been so far removed from her life that his leaving hadn't even cracked the shell she had built up between them.

A few days later, it was as if Ethan had never appeared at their door. He was out of their lives and was quickly falling out of their memories.

About two weeks later, I noticed that Ashlee got a letter that was postmarked St. Cloud. She never showed it to me or told me what the letter said.

Once again, it appeared that Ethan took the easy way out. My guess was that he didn't want to talk to Ashlee.

I waited to see if he would call her or not.

***

It is amazing how things can juggle your life. Just when it finally felt as though things were starting to settle down for the entire family, one cold day in the middle of February, I received a call from the Workforce Center.

"Maria, this is Carl Johnson at the Workforce Center. I just heard about a job that sounded interesting and thought I should call to see if you were still looking for a promising opportunity. Did I catch you at a good time?"

Maria wondered what Carl could have found. She hadn't talked to him in over a month. How was it that he remembered her from that long ago? Still, she was curious enough to hear what he had to say.

"I have an opportunity for you to manage a Bed and Breakfast in a scenic town about thirty miles from here. They have a staff, but they are looking for a manager to oversee the operation and promote the business. It is a good opportunity for you while giving you the freedom to finish your college work. I think it's a good fit for you and your daughter.

"I remembered that you were looking for an opportunity to get back on your own. The person I talked to said that you would get paid for staying there and the majority of the daily work would be done by the current staff."

The call was totally out in left field and definitely not something I was expecting. Move? We had just gotten adjusted to the last move. What would happen to Ashlee? She was just starting to build a good relationship with her grandparents. What would happen to that? Could Ashlee really handle another move? What about her grades? New school, again? That's a lot to ask for.

All those questions flew through my mind, while Carl was talking. The only thing I could say was, "Thank you. It sounds really good, but I have to think how this will change our lives again. Can I call you tomorrow, in the morning? I need to think about it overnight. Thanks again for thinking of me. Bye."

Now, I had another decision to make. This one might be tougher than the last.

***

Chapter 7

The Offer

Jason Willard Investment Services

I was having one of my update conversations with Edward Gray. We were going over the finances, or should I say lack of finances, at the Bed and Breakfast, along with some of the positive growth seen in his other investments, which Edward had established in the portfolio I managed for him.

"Edward, we are still losing money on that B&B you purchased. Have you come up with the plan you said you were working on? I realize that in the long scheme of things, it is not a lot of money for you to lose, but what are you planning on doing with the property? I really think you need a full-time manager at the B&B to handle the reservations and books. I can keep doing it for the short term, but you really do need to come up with a plan."

"Well, Jason, as a matter of fact I do have an idea. This is probably a good time to talk about it.

"I was talking with an old friend last week and he mentioned that he might have an idea of a good manager for the business. She doesn't have any experience in the business, but from the information about her, and her abilities, I think you could train her in quickly."

"Edward, that's not what I meant by finding a manager. You need someone that is experienced in website development, advertising, and one that is a good promoter."

"Jason, I have a lot of confidence in you. You'll have her up to speed in a very short time."

As we finished our conversation, I just sat back in my chair. Once again, Edward had pulled a rabbit out of a hat and surprised me. There had to be more to the story. I knew him better. I also knew I would find out in short order what it was.

It was time for an extra strong cup of coffee.

***

Maria

The call from Carl Johnson at the Workforce Center was the last thing I was expecting this morning. As I listened to the opportunity he was expressing to me, I saw as many misgivings in the opportunity as pluses.

We had talked for almost a half hour before I hung up.

"That must have been an interesting phone call," my mother inquired. "You want to talk about it?"

I was glad that Ashlee was still at school. It gave me a chance to digest the call while talking to my parents about the opportunity. So far, I did not know what to say. I sat down with my mother and father to see what they thought.

"That was Carl Johnson at the Workforce Center. He told me that one of his friends had talked to the owner of a Bed and Breakfast. They were looking for a live-in manager. Carl suggested that I might be a good candidate. I really don't know how he got that impression.

"Anyway, it pays a starting salary of $32,000 a year and includes a furnished two bedroom apartment that Ashlee and I could live in. I would be keeping the books, making sure it was staffed, while doing the promotion work for the B&B."

"Do you have to do the cooking or cleaning too?" her mother asked.

"No, that's the duties of the staff."

"So, you do the office work and get $15,000 worth of lodging for free, at the same time? Where is it and what about your schooling?" her father asked.

"It is up in Marine on the St Croix. He said I could arrange my schedule, so I could have evenings or specific days off as I needed. If someone quits, I might have to help out until I could hire a replacement."

"That's a nice town. Sounds like you have some serious decisions to make," her father told her. "When do you need to decide by?"

"Dad, I haven't even had an interview yet. Besides, what about Ashlee? Remember how bitter she was when we moved? She is just getting adjusted and is doing so well."

"Maria, I think Ashlee would do very well in Marine," he told her. "Besides, we could visit you whenever you wish or she could come here. Plus, if it didn't work out, you could always move back in. It will finally give you a positive cash flow. Isn't that what you've been trying to find?"

My mind was racing. This was too much, too fast. What was I to do? My biggest concern was Ashlee. I needed to sit down and talk to her when she got back from school. I just didn't know if Ashlee could handle another move this school year.

My mother and I talked all afternoon about the job opening and the emotions I was going through.

Ashlee came home after school and started working on her homework. I waited until after supper to talk to her.

My concept of another move was not met with a warm look on Ashlee's face. Ashlee had just gotten used to the last move.

"What do you mean? We just got here, and now, we have to leave, and I have to go to another school?"

It was going to take some time to get an agreement on this one. I could see the problems and could also understand where Ashlee was coming from. My parents talked to Ashlee for an hour before she finally went upstairs to finish her homework.

"It's going to be hard for her, and us, if you leave," my mother told me. "I think Ashlee understands more than you give her credit for. I think you should, at least, go for the interview. Maybe it's not what you want. You'll never know unless you go look at it."

My father agreed.

I decided to sleep on it. It was a long night – too much churning and thinking.

The next morning, I called Carl Johnson, at the Workforce Center, and Carl arranged an interview for me for the end of the week with a Jason Willard. I figured I could always back out of it if the deal did not feel right for Ashlee or me.

***

Jason Willard

Saturday afternoon, Maria met me at the Meadows Bed and Breakfast. It was on the edge of town, on a secluded gravel road.

At her first glance, she seemed to like the setting nestled back in the woods and it appeared to be a very nice place. It was well maintained and the inside was very clean. One drawback appeared to be the railroad tracks that ran back in the woods behind the Bed and Breakfast.

"Maria, my name is Jason Willard. I'm the accountant for the firm that owns the Bed and Breakfast. Thank you for coming. Let me show you around and then we can sit and talk."

I showed Maria the entire house including the guest quarters, which included a rather large two-bedroom apartment, living quarters and kitchen area on the second level, which had been added above the house when the garage was enlarged. "This would be your apartment if you take the job," he told her.

"Why did they build this large apartment into the house?" she asked.

"I think it was meant to be a mother-in-law's apartment at one time. I'm not the builder. I'm just the accountant."

It was quite spacious. In fact, it was bigger than the duplex unit they had in St. Cloud. So far, Maria was impressed.

"The one drawback to the house is that it is losing money. Your job will be to help advertise the B&B and hopefully bring up the balance sheet."

Maria looked it over. It was in a poor location for a Bed and Breakfast, however, it was what it was. The setting nestled against the woods was diminished slightly by a set of railroad tracks running behind the property. Maria wondered why someone didn't move it to the main street of town, or down by the river. If it was down there, it might have been full every night.

"Does the railroad track bother the customers? Maria asked. "Doesn't it keep them up at night when trains go by?"

"It is not a major track anymore. There is probably one freight train per day that goes by. They usually go by during the daytime, although if they are behind schedule, I guess it is possible for one to go by in the night. I haven't heard any complaints."

"How many people do you have to interview?" she asked.

"Excuse me! I'm not sure you understand. My job is to hire you and train you. It is your decision. There are a couple requirements, but I don't feel that you will have any problems. The job is a three-year job, with an option at that point for you to renegotiate your salary."

Maria didn't know what to say. That was not what she expected. What about her background? What about whether she would make a good manager? He was to hire and train her? Her mouth almost hit the floor, as she digested the words.

"But, you don't know anything about me," she told me.

"Yes, I agree. Nevertheless, someone else does, and apparently, they feel you would make a good manager. From what I see, you are intelligent, polite, and good-looking. With some training, I think you will do quite well."

Now, Maria really did not know what to say. Who recommended her? Carl Johnson? Perhaps her friend back in St. Cloud. No, neither of them knew her that well. Who then?

"How soon do you need an answer?" she asked. "I need to talk it over with my daughter. I've already moved her once this school year. This might be tough on her."

"Take your time. I realize it is a hard choice. Give me a call next week and let me know your decision." As I said it, I handed her my card. "I'll let you look the place over. Perhaps you might want to talk to the staff."

"Please do not discuss any of the financial arrangements with the staff. They might be jealous, realizing they did not get the offer."

With that, I left Maria to look things over and got back into my car.

***

Maria

I stood there, still in shock. The person at the desk knew that someone was being interviewed for the office manager position. I had so many things I would like to ask her. Yet, I didn't know how to approach her without the person showing an interest in the job as well. What special training did I have that the other person at the desk didn't have? I stood there afraid to talk to her, fearing that my lack of experience might show through.

I took the chance to look around a little more before leaving. Then, I decided to drive around town, looking the town over. It had been years since I had been in Marine. It was a small town along the river. Much smaller than St. Cloud and much smaller than I remembered.

I stopped at the General Store to ask the clerk some questions about the town and schools. "What you see is what we have," they told me. "There is a store, bank, a couple of restaurants, coffee shop, post office, and a gas station. Oh, I forgot the church up on the hill." I was surprised to hear that the closest high school was in Stillwater, 14 miles away.

The people in the store seemed friendly. It must have been that small town personality where everyone knew everyone else.

Ashlee! The thought of her kept ringing in my ears. What would she think of it? Could she adjust to a town that everyone would know everything she did?

All the way back home, I kept thinking about Ashlee. Would she adjust to a small town of perhaps one hundred or fewer houses?

On the trip home, I drove by the Stillwater High School. It looked nice. Hopefully, Ashlee would take it as one plus.

Returning to my parents' house, I discussed what I saw with my parents and Ashlee.

"Only a hundred houses?" Ashlee asked.

"Maybe less," I answered. "There is another town only a few miles away about the same size.

"However, the living quarters is really big. We'd have more space than we did in St. Cloud," I told Ashlee.

My father just sat there laughing. He grew up in a small town. He figured Ashlee must be thinking they were moving to Hicksville. He perceived, perhaps, Ashlee was envisioning getting the permanent job of turning off the only streetlight in town at midnight.

My father was a little puzzled when I mentioned the fact that they were offering me the job – not interviewing me.

"Really?" he asked.

"That was my thought," I replied. "Why me?"

After discussing the offer over Saturday night dinner, it was decided that we would all drive to Marine the next morning and get a better look at the community. Perhaps we could find something positive that Ashlee might enjoy.

That evening, I spent most of the time discussing the job opening with my parents. There were a number of good things about the job and just as many concerns.

The next morning, our little group showed up for church in the town. Fortunately, it was not snowing that morning. The bright sun put a warming glow on the small town sitting on a hill. Since there was only one church, a Lutheran Church, we felt it would be a good way to assess the community to see how friendly they were.

So far, so good. The people seemed very friendly. Since most of them knew each other, it was easy to recognized visitors. A number of members made an effort to come up and introduce themselves to our family.

For me, it felt good, and I hoped that Ashlee was paying attention to the fact that we were genuinely welcomed.

We stopped by the Bed & Breakfast. I took them for a quick tour. Bonnie was working that morning and she introduced herself to Ashlee. Ashlee's face was starting to show signs that she was slowly warming to the community.

It didn't take long for us to do a driving tour through the entire town. Perhaps ten minutes. Most of the town was closed except for the General Store and restaurant, so there was very little we could do.

We drove up to Scandia, just up the road from Marine to check it out. Once again, it was a very small town about the size of Marine. What we saw were two communities that were friendly, and once again, all of the people knew each other.

After settling in for a lunch at the Scandia Cafe in Scandia, we headed back home, by way of the Stillwater High School, letting Ashlee check out the outside and the athletic fields.

It had been an interesting day. However, the question still stirring in the pot; do we want to move or not? All afternoon we discussed the options. I kept watching Ashlee's face. So far, she appeared neutral. That was better than the "no way" I had expected.

I decided to wait until the middle of the week to make my decision. I didn't want the job to disappear. However, Ashlee was more important to me than the job. I needed to make sure Ashlee was onboard with the move.

During the week, Ashlee started asking her friends at school in North St. Paul what they thought about Stillwater High. The general consensus was that it was okay to pretty nice, depending on what you were looking for. Some thought their high school was the best; others thought Stillwater had more choices. For Ashlee, nothing stood out that would allow her to insist that her mother leave her in her current school.

By Wednesday, when we were having supper, Ashlee told me that she was okay with the move, if, she could spend a few weekends with her grandparents. My parents, John and Helen, just smiled when they heard Ashlee say she wanted to spend time with them. It was what they hoped for all the time she lived up in St. Cloud.

***

Jason Willard

Thursday, Maria nervously called me to inform me that she wanted the job.

I told her I was glad to hear her decision. She could start March 1st. I told her that she would never regret the decision. Also, I suggested that they could start moving their things into the B&B any time before that date.

Maria sounded excited, but also hesitant at the same time. She told me she would probably move in a day or two before the first of the month.

"Good enough! We can start your training on the first of March. Welcome aboard."

***

Maria

I hung up the phone and breathed a sigh of relief. It had been a hard decision. If it worked out, it might be the best opportunity I had in years. Time would tell.

The last couple of days of the month found Ashlee and me moving some of our things into our new location. Spring was just starting to show its presence. The dirt road was still firm with the winter frost. We didn't need to move very much furniture into the apartment. It was already furnished with beds, chairs and televisions. There was even a computer in the apartment for working on the B&B's reservations and advertisements. It would allow Ashlee to take over my computer for her schoolwork.

All we needed to do was move the small things that we would need to make it our home, and once again, transfer all of Ashlee's school records to her new school.

For me, it seemed strange moving into a new location while the desk staff was working out front, wondering what kind of new boss was moving in. It was definitely a new experience for all of us.

As time went on, I was starting to become nervous about my meeting with Jason Willard once we were moved in. I wished that he had set up another meeting to meet with me before we took over. I just had so many questions. I was still worried about knowing everything that was expected of me.

If I felt uncomfortable, I had a good feeling what Ashlee was going through. Now, she had to change schools and friends for the second time this current school year.

As a result, whenever Ashlee gave me a short answer or sort of snapped at me, I understood. Hopefully, after a week or so, we would start settling into our new environment and things would relax between us.

About then, if things were not unsettled enough, my parents told me that my aunt's health was failing. I hadn't seen her in a few years even though she lived in a retirement home, north of where we used to live in St. Cloud.

My mother encouraged me to take the time and take Ashlee to visit her before something happened to her. She felt it would be good for both of us. We could get away for a day, and think about something other than the move.

Unfortunately, as schedules have it, because of school and everything else going on, the only day we could visit her was the day we were planning on moving into our apartment at the Bed and Breakfast.

I'm not sure if it gave us the break my parents thought we were going to get or not.

***

Chapter 8

Adjusting

The adjustment to our new home and school was indeed a tough one for Ashlee. She felt very "out of it" when she attempted to adapt.

It was five weeks into the new school's semester. Once again, Ashlee found herself playing catch up with her school transition and her class work at Stillwater High.

The first problem she encountered was getting up early for the school bus. We were not at the end of the route, but it sure seemed like it. On top of that, she had to meet the bus out on the blacktop road.

The bus picked her up almost an hour before school started. Everyone else on the bus knew each other, so Ashlee stuck out like a sore thumb when it was her stop to catch the bus.

For the most part, the other students were quite friendly to her. However, each of them had their preferred seats, and she was stuck with whichever seat was open. That meant that she was usually sitting next to one of the boys to and from school that first week. Somehow, the ride home seemed longer than the ride to school. To her, it seemed that the bus aimed at every pothole in the road, which had been created by the melting of the winter ice.

The long ride did allow her to meet some of the students that lived in the Marine area. It wasn't a very formal meeting, it was more like catching a partial conversation here and there.

However, it did give her a hint as to what they were like. Many of them on the bus lived out in the country.

By her second week, one of the girls in her math class asked her if she wanted a ride to and from school. Leslie lived in Marine and her mother had heard through the grapevine that there was a new girl in town. She had suggested that since Leslie had met her in math, it might be nice to offer her a ride since Leslie was lucky enough to get car rides both ways.

It did not take Ashlee very long to accept and thank her for the offer. Ashlee definitely preferred to ride in a mini-van compared to the bus. Plus, she didn't have to arrive at school with muddy shoes. It was going to make her school adjustment a tiny bit easier.

Ashlee also liked the fact that Leslie lived close to her, so she could call her with any math questions. Other than Leslie, Ashlee was having problems making friends. Most of the other students had already migrated into groups of friends with common interests during the year.

Ashlee decided she would make an effort to find one or two people she could talk to in each class. By fall, when class lists were re-scrambled, it would be easier to find some additional new friends.

I spent some of my time with the Inn's staff going over the systems they used for reservations, ordering supplies, and accounting for working hours. Tomorrow, I planned to meet with Jason Willard to find out the parts of the job that I was hired for. Jason had delayed that meeting a few days to let me get a feel for the operation.

The person that was having the hardest time adjusting with the move was my mother. She already missed the opportunity to sit and talk to Ashlee and me. To make up for it, she had invited both of us for dinner on Saturday. It would give her and my father an opportunity to find out what was happening in both Ashlee's and my life.

My mother was still concerned how Ashlee was going to adjust to the new school without losing the momentum she gained the past few months at her school in North St. Paul.

The first two weeks, Ashlee needed to work hard to catch up in her schoolwork. I heard her make a few calls to Leslie and to her grandparents for help. Actually, it was a relief for me to hear the communications. Ashlee was making the effort to find the answers she needed.

***

Jason Willard

When I met with Maria to go over the books and budget for the B&B, I found her very nervous. I definitely think she felt underqualified for the job. However, after showing her the expectations we had for the B&B, I could see in her face a sign of relief. I hadn't dropped any tasks outside of her ability level on her so far.

We talked for a while. She asked me again how I got her name, and how we knew she could handle the job. It was a good question. It was also one that I was not prepared to answer at this time. So, I told her we asked for some names from the Workforce Center and then did some preliminary research on them before picking a candidate.

"Weren't you worried that you might get someone that didn't take the job seriously or might have ripped off the B&B?" she asked.

I told her we had a set of requirements, and she met all of them on the list. She still looked rather puzzled.

"So, you are saying that as long as I do the things on the list you gave me as well as maintain the business, I am free to adjust my time as needed?" she asked me.

"Yes, you are the manager. Keep the staff happy and you will find the job much easier. We will meet off and on for the first couple of months to see how you are doing. If you have any questions, you can simply give me a call. I'll try to help you.

***

Maria

On Saturday, Ashlee and I joined my parents for supper. It felt good to be able to talk to them again.

I told my mother and father that I was still puzzled by the business meeting with Jason Willard. "I kept waiting for some hidden agenda to show up. Somehow, the job didn't seem that difficult that one of the women who had worked there for years couldn't have taken over."

"Perhaps they turned it down," my father replied.

I didn't have an answer. However, it looked like I could still squeeze in the couple classes at the local college I had already enrolled in, and my work at the B&B might even help me if I take a few business classes.

The other item that bothered me was the room reservation rate. I was surprised at how low it was. The good thing was that I probably couldn't affect it too much in that it might cause it to get worse. The unfortunate thing was that it didn't look like it was going to create a profit anytime soon. They really needed some marketing. I was hoping my Introduction to Marketing class might give me some ideas. How long could the B&B exist on a losing path was in the back of my mind. I really didn't want to have to move again anytime soon.

Both of my parents noticed that Ashlee had lost a little of her charisma, or she was much quieter than when we left their house. I hoped that they could talk to her and bring back the Ashlee we were just starting to see before the move. As a result, I let Ashlee deal with most of the questions about Marine and her school in Stillwater. The more she talked about it, the better it would be. So far, Ashlee had not mentioned any real problems with her school, other than having to work hard.

As we were heading home, I asked Ashlee, "You still wish we were living with your grandparents?"

"Yes. I realize you needed to take the job. I'm just glad they are close to us. You think I can spend a weekend with them when I get my school assignments caught up?"

"I'm sure your grandparents would love it," I answered. We talked all the way home about how nice it was to be close to them.

Monday was a beautiful day. Almost all of the snow had melted from the warm sun. Things were starting to turn green. It was a welcoming hint that summer's beauty was just around the corner.

Ashlee was going through a normal day at school when she was surprised by an assignment in her English class. Her teacher informed the class about a group paper assignment that she was going to have due in several weeks. Ashlee's teacher expected the students, who were to work in groups of three, to write a paper about their town. To keep from having to read numerous papers on the same topics, she had thrown in a few twists into the assignment:

1. They could write about the town they live in or any other area within twenty miles of where any one of them lives.
2. The paper had to talk about interesting facts or history.
3. Only five topics could come from the internet, and those

topics could only be 20% of your paper. Which meant, they would need to talk to people about interesting facts. This was done to prevent all the groups from talking about the historical lumber industry.

4. It would be a combined grade for the group on the paper.
5. Each group would have the opportunity to read their paper to the class when they were finished.

Ashlee felt the blood slowly running out of her face. She didn't know very much about the area and definitely didn't know a number of people she could talk to about it.

Most of the students quickly glanced around, making eye contact with those they wanted to work with. There was a sign-up sheet in the front of the class. For those that did not find a group, the teacher would assign the working groups. Ashlee held her breath. She was hoping that she would end up in a good group. She knew her grade depended on it.

At the end of the class, her teacher combined one boy and one girl with her. She didn't know anything about either one, other than she was pleased to hear that they were picked because they lived in the Marine area. The teacher announced that she was going to give them some time tomorrow to get together and decide on their project.

On the way home, Ashlee was talking to Leslie and told her about the assignment. "I'm really worried about this one," she told her. "I don't know anything about our area and I really don't know the other two students."

Leslie listened to her problem. "Well, the good thing is that you don't know any history. It will give you a fresh slate to decide what is interesting and what is just general history. I know your teacher. I had her first semester. She is looking for interesting facts, not just old history. Most of your class probably won't realize that and will list one fact after another."

"Who are you working with?" she asked.

"I'm not sure. I have their names written down," Ashlee told her. Digging through her backpack she found the list. Let's see, there is Oscar Davis III and Dawn Swenson."

"You got stuck with Spider-Boy? Oh, poor you. Too bad your teacher didn't scramble up the class and put you with an "A" student. At least, she gave you two people from the area."

"What do you mean "Spider-Boy?"" Ashlee asked, envisioning all kinds of undesirable thoughts.

"You probably saw him on the bus. He's usually sitting all by himself. Reddish hair, kind of skinny, doesn't say much. He wants everyone to call him Red, but most know him by Spider-Boy."

"That could have been one of two or three on the bus," Ashlee answered. "What do you mean Spider-Boy?"

"I probably shouldn't give you the wrong opinion. I'm not sure if he is autistic or just strange. He likes to write poetry."

"That doesn't sound that strange, what else?"

"Well, this is second hand, but I have heard that he likes to sit in a tunnel just to get away from everyone. I think that's where he writes his poetry."

"Is he a good student?" Ashlee asked.

"I had him in a junior high class. He did okay."

"Alright, I guess I can live with it. What about Dawn Swenson?"

"Well, like you, she just moved into the area about a year ago. Lives down by the river. She does have an advantage, though, she has a relative that lives in town. So, she knew some things about the area before they moved in.

"Let me know what your exact topic is going to be. Perhaps my mother and I can give you some tips."

"Leslie, I would appreciate that. I'm not about to go hide in some tunnel to finish any paper."

When Ashlee got home, she told me all about the paper and what Leslie told her about the group. I sat there and laughed. "I'm sure it won't be as bad as you envision. Why don't you give your grandfather a call? I'm sure he might get a good laugh at your conversation as well."

Later that evening, when Ashlee called her grandparents, her grandfather did indeed get a good laugh out of the story. "You don't have arachnophobia do you?" he asked.

"What's that?"

"Fear of spiders. I'll save a few of them for you."

"Thanks! I'll tell grandmother about your hiding place for chocolate if you do."

"OK! Truce! Keep me informed."

In the short time we lived with her grandparents, Ashlee managed to locate her grandfather's secret stash of candy. He used it to bribe her into talking about her classes. It did not take very long before she realized it was their common secret.

The next day, Ashlee spent her free time in English to get an agreement on what they were going to write about. Dawn felt that stories about the Marine area would be easy to find. She lived just a few miles south of town.

Red told the girls it was fine, he didn't care. Ashlee just stared at him. She kept thinking, *"Is he lazy, doesn't like working with girls, or does he figure he can work on any area?"* She could not determine the answers from his expressions. He was hard to read. She did find out that he lived just west of Marine.

They agreed to meet at the library in Marine later that week and again at the Museum in town on Saturday. The museum was only open from 11:00 to 2:00. Hopefully, they would get some ideas either from what they saw or from talking to the librarian and museum director.

By midweek, I asked Ashlee if she was going to talk to her grandparents about staying at their place over the weekend.

"I wish I could. I think I'm stuck working on that paper for English this weekend. We need to put together a list of topics we can research. I guess I'll have to wait until next week."

I was impressed. Last fall, she would have done anything to get away from studying all weekend. Weekends were for partying. Maybe the move was a good thing for both of us.

I was taking two on-line courses at the local college along with managing the B&B. So far, I had more spare time on my hands than when I was working two part time jobs in St. Cloud. Things were indeed starting to look up. I called my mother and gave her the weekly update. Also, when she asked, I accepted an invitation to Saturday dinner.

Ashlee met with Oscar – Red, and Dawn at the town library Thursday after school. They wanted to get there before any of the other local students did the same thing.

It was a small library with very few books. Hopefully, most of the students would be searching the high school or the Stillwater library. If necessary, the Marine library could request books from any of the county libraries.

Their group's objective: Find something interesting about Marine on the St. Croix that most people in Stillwater didn't know about.

After informing the librarian about their paper, the librarian suggested some books by a local writer – James Taylor Dunn. Most of his books gave a chronology of the history of the area, from the lumber days to the present. She felt it might give them a list of items from which they could start researching. There was one book where the author seemed to give a little more effort to create stories about some of the topics.

The librarian also suggested several local residents whom she felt might have a good knowledge of the history of the town. They picked up a couple of the books along with another book that included a history of Washington County. Hopefully, the books would give them a starting point.

Leaving the library, they agreed to divide up the books they found; reading and taking notes so that they could compare their lists on Saturday at the Museum.

Dawn seemed okay about quickly reviewing the books. Red still seemed quiet and standoffish about getting involved. It bothered Dawn, but Ashlee had hung around with a few boys like him back in St. Cloud, and it didn't seem to faze her as much as it did Dawn. However, it was important that the three of them finished the assignment on time. One way or the other, this assignment was going to get done.

At school on Friday, they compared lists of topics they found in their books. Red told them he hadn't finished his yet. Telling them, "I'll finish them by the time we go to the museum. Besides, it's the stories behind the things at the museum that we are probably going to find the most interesting."

Ashlee could see that Dawn was unhappy. She wanted to see the list right now. Having to wait a day was an imposition. After all, she got her's done on time. It was one of those shortcomings that the other students in her classes picked up on earlier. Dawn appeared to be a person with little patience for others. Perhaps that was why she was assigned to her group. The others in her class probably didn't want someone criticizing their work.

Ashlee had never been to the Marine museum. The others had been there several times and knew what to expect. It was a rather small, very old stone building dating back to the 1800's. Inside, were numerous exhibits of relics from the past. Old lumbering equipment, photos of the lumbering, some fishing stuff, and a few books. As they wandered through the exhibits, Ashlee looked at a document.

"Are you kidding me?" she said. "They made buttons out of that stuff?" She was looking at a chart and examples of the button industry that was popular before the creation of synthetic buttons. It showed how they caught mussels from the river and then stamped out buttons from the shells. The literature said the factory was downtown Stillwater.

Red leaned over. "You going to check your old clothes to see if they smell like fish?"

Ashlee noticed that he had a small twinkle in his eye. It was the first expression Ashlee had seen from him.

"No, but I'll bet you never cut down a tree using one of those huge manual saws." She pointed to a big two-man crosscut saw on the wall that had teeth almost an inch long.

"You'd lose. We've got one of those in the shed. However, we also have a thing called a chainsaw. Not my cup of tea. You'd be surprised to see what is in people's sheds around here. Most people don't even know what they have."

"I know what is in our shed," Dawn quipped. "Did you see the remains of the old jail in the back? It looks like a closet. In fact, my closet is bigger than that."

They looked at the back room. When the museum did some remodeling, they discovered writing on the wall left there from early prisoners. It actually was the town jail at some early point in time. It was definitely not the kind of place that you wanted to spend more than a day. Hopefully, they never put more than one person in the jail.

Just before they were going to leave, Dawn started looking through a book on the counter. It was a collection of newspapers from the Marine Messenger, an old newspaper. The group leafed through several years of the book. It was indeed interesting. It had articles that they had not seen anywhere else.

"I think we need to spend more time reading these," Dawn mentioned. "This might give us the type story we are looking for. I can come back tomorrow for the short time the museum is open, how about either of you?"

"I'm busy," Red answered.

"I'll join you," Ashlee replied.

The museum was closing. The group had just started discovering some interesting things. However, with the stack of old newspapers, they were hoping the papers might disclose something everyone else in her class overlooked.

That evening, Ashlee and I drove to my parents for dinner. It was an enjoyable dinner with good conversation. That was until Ashlee's grandfather asked her how "Spider-Boy" was for writing with. I almost swallowed my food whole. I hadn't heard that title before.

"Who's "Spider-Boy?" I asked.

"It's what the kids call Red. He's the one I met at the museum today along with Dawn."

"I can't wait to hear the history behind this one," I told her. I was trying to decide if I needed to pay more attention to Ashlee's boyfriends once again.

As we were heading back home, I asked Ashlee again about "Spider-Boy." "How did he get that name if he already has a nickname of Red?" I asked.

"Well, I haven't asked him directly," she answered. "Some people say it is because he likes to sit in a tunnel and write during the summertime. Wonder what they would call me? The person that sits up in her room and does homework? Can't think of a good name for it, can you?"

"How about "student who is doing a good job of getting her grades back up?" I'd settle for that," I told her.

"I'm trying," Ashlee replied.

Chapter 9

Digging for Facts

Sunday afternoon found Ashlee and Dawn leafing through the back pages of The Messenger at the museum. The local newspaper was a treasure trove of stories that allowed them to see back into the history of Marine on the St. Croix.

<u>Ashlee</u>

After about fifteen minutes of additional time looking through the book of past newspapers, which we had discovered Saturday, Dawn said, "I think we should write about how the initial investors in the lumber mill developed the town. It's interesting to see how they shaped the politics and early construction of Marine."

"Perhaps! But, remember what our teacher said and what Leslie told me she would be looking for. Our teacher is looking for interesting events that are not well known. Everyone can read about how the team of investors picked this location to build a lumber mill because of the stream they found that could capture waterpower. How are we going to take that to the next step and make it interesting?"

"You don't think it is interesting that the same people developed the store and rooming house? And later, one of them became the Post Master for Marine?"

"Well, if Red was here, I think he'd label it "boring.""

"Well, he isn't, is he. What was his excuse? We need to

get this done and until we agree on what to write, we can't even get started."

"Dawn, he was here yesterday, wasn't he? And, he joined us at the library. Just because we decided to come back today for an hour, you can't expect everyone to instantly change their schedule. Maybe he has something else planned with his family. I didn't get time to finish my book last night because of having dinner with my grandparents. Maybe he had something for today."

"He could have told us if he did," Dawn snapped back. "You sound like you like "Spider-Boy.""

"I just met both of you. I think we should give him a little slack. Just because he is quiet and likes to be by himself, it doesn't make him a bad person or someone that doesn't know what he is doing."

"See, you are already defending him."

"Whatever! Let's finish looking through the pages and start a list of what we have. Then, we can get together later this week to organize the paper. I think we are going to have a problem with too much to write on, versus too little. We'll need to rank the topics by their "wow" factor."

As we were leafing through the pages, I pointed to a picture of the Marine ferry. "I didn't know there was a ferry in town. When did that stop?"

"I saw it in James Taylor Dunn's book. It looked like it stayed in existence until 1954. According to what I saw earlier, it was first started in 1856. That was almost one hundred years of operation."

"Why didn't they just build a bridge?" I asked.

"Who knows. You can put that on your list. It was down by the landing, where they dock the boats."

I wrote it down on my list. How did it operate? What happened to it? How many cars could they put on it? What happened in the winter?

The museum worker was listening to the two of us digging into the town's history. "Did you know that the stone by the door was from the grain mill?" she asked.

We gave her a blank stare. "What grain mill?" I asked.

"I have a few pictures of it over here in my file," she answered. "If you are looking back into the town's past, you need to understand what made it tick after the sawmill died. Also, you might want to look into the history of the sawmill, and see why it closed. I think that's just as interesting as the fact that they had to pay a ransom to get the squatters off the land the log mill's founders had already deeded."

Dawn and I quickly jotted down a note about the tidbits we had just heard. Since I had just moved to the area, it was natural that I had no background on the historic facts of the town. However, Dawn lived in the area for only a little longer and many of the one-line facts we were discovering were new to her, as well.

Were their stories behind each one of them? Where could we find them?

We left the museum with a short list of new topics to look at for their paper. Both of us agreed to have our books we were reading completely finished by Monday. Hopefully, Red would have his close to finished.

***

Maria

Back at the Bed and Breakfast, I was pleased to see Ashlee working so hard on her school assignment. The assignment was forcing her to learn about the community, and hopefully, she might develop an attachment to the area. Besides, she might be able to be helpful by telling customers interesting facts about the town.

For now, I was looking over the books, trying to see which way the budget was trending and see if there were any places we could trim, without hurting the business. As I looked through the data, I remembered a statement from my marketing class: "You have to spend money, to make money. If you cut your way to profitability, you might go too far and cut your way out of business."

Looking at the history of the B&B, I wondered if that was the problem here. For the past five years, everything that could be cut, had been cut. Maybe, they had gone too far.

Jean had just left, so I decided to talk to Bonnie, who was working the desk that evening. Perhaps she had some suggestions.

While Bonnie was talking to a customer that had just arrived to stay a night, the phone rang. I offered to answer it allowing Bonnie to finish the registration.

"Meadows Bed and Breakfast, can I help you?" I politely answered.

"Yes, this is Edward Gray, I would like to book few nights at the Bed and Breakfast. Is this Bonnie or Jean?"

"No, I'm sorry, this is Maria, the manager. Did you want to speak to Bonnie? She's working tonight. Or, is there something I can help you with?"

"Well, I'm sure you can help me. I would like to reserve the corner room with the reading window for a few dates this spring."

"Okay, please give me a second; I need to grab the reservation book. Have you stayed here before? When would you like to reserve the room?"

"Yes, I have stayed before, and I really enjoyed the room. I would like to reserve it for Friday and Saturday night the last weekend in March, and for the same days on the first three weekends in May and June."

I was surprised. She was expecting a reservation for two or three days. "Those days are all open. I can put you down for them. I'll need a credit card number to hold them for you," I told him.

Edward gave her his credit card number. Then, he told her, "Why don't you put a hold on July and September for that room, on those weekends, at the same time. I have some trips I need to take, but it would be good to have those dates reserved ahead of time."

The number of nights made me stop and count the dates. That was twenty-six booked nights. "Alright, I have you down for those days. When you come the first night, perhaps we can meet. I'm curious to see what attributes about the Bed and Breakfast keeps you coming back."

"I'll be looking forward to meeting you," Edward said as they concluded their conversation.

When Bonnie was finished with their customer, I approached her.

"Bonnie, I just had an interesting reservation. Do you know an Edward Gray?"

"Yes! He stays with us every once and a while during the summer and fall seasons. When is he coming?" she asked.

"Well, he made reservations for the Friday and Saturday for the first three weeks of May, June, July, and September plus the last weekend in March. That's twenty-six nights, and he didn't even ask for any discounts for multiple nights. What do you know about him? That's a lot of nights, does he ever cancel? A couple more customers like him and we could turn a profit."

Bonnie told me, "He's been coming here for as long as I've worked here. He's an older man. I think he used to live close to here years ago. Ran a couple businesses in the area, I believe. Anyway, he always wants the same room and rarely have I seen him in the winter. Probably travels somewhere where it is warm.

"That's a lot of nights, even for him. You'll enjoy him."

I was excited. Twenty-six nights was twenty percent of her personal goal for the period. With the reservation, I started thinking about ways to publicize the Bed and Breakfast. Maybe if there was a way of making it profitable for half the year, I might impress my boss, Jason Willard. From what I had seen in the books for the past four years, the Bed and Breakfast had lost money each quarter. If I could increase the bookings, he might be impressed.

I was trying to decide whether or not I should mention my goals to Mr. Willard at our next meeting. Perhaps it would be better to hold it back unless the subject came up. After all, bookings only counted if the person actually shows up.

Ashlee

On the ride to school the next morning, Leslie and I discussed the work our group had done over the weekend looking up facts about Marine.

"So, is Marine more interesting than you expected? Leslie inquired.

"I really didn't know what to expect. I knew a little bit about the lumberjacks, but after looking at the newspapers, it is getting more interesting."

"When do you have to start your writing?" she asked.

"I'm hoping we can start by the end of the week. Dawn wants it "done" by then, or so she implies. If we can have a list of possibilities by mid-week, I think we are doing about as good as we can expect. That will keep us within the five-week deadline to complete it."

Leslie asked me, "Remind me when you get the topics done. I'm curious to see what makes your list. Also, I'll bet you'll find more things you could have written about while you are writing it, than you found ahead of time."

"That's what worries me. How do you narrow it down to just a few good stories? From what you said, it sounds like my teacher is more in tune to a few good stories, rather than a long list of historical facts," I told her.

"Well, if it was my paper, I would start with a minor history of how Marine was founded. Everyone expects that, including your teacher. Then, find some things other people don't know."

"Thanks. I'll show you the list when we complete it. You think Red will come through with his share? Dawn doesn't give him very much hope."

"I've known Red for years. If you give him some space and don't push him, he'll surprise you. Don't let Dawn push you guys out of the way and control everything. That seems to be sort of her standard way of working with people."

I thought about that statement the rest of the way to school. If Leslie was right, I needed to be the middle person between Dawn and Red.

Before I could do anything about the paper, I needed to be concerned about passing my quiz in math. With the busy weekend, I only had a short time to brush up for the quiz. Now, I used every minute available before class to review my notes.

The quiz wasn't that bad. I was surprised to see that I had a higher score than Leslie on the test. It gave me a good feeling. In fact, I had almost all the problems correct. I couldn't wait to tell my grandfather that I had beat my friend on the first quiz.

When I got to English, I caught Red out in the hall. "Missed you yesterday, at the museum."

"Well, I've been to the museum before a few times. I figured that the elbowroom was getting a little tight around those newspapers. Did you find anything?"

"We came up with a few items. I'll show you after class. Dawn wants us to have our lists by Wednesday. Think you can have your list done by then?"

"Perhaps. You think she even wants my list?"

"I do. She has only one vote. There are three of us," Ashlee told him.

He put a small smile on his face. Thanks, I don't enjoy Dawn's pushy attitude. I did spend three hours on the project Sunday."

"Really! Were you reading?"

"No, I was talking to people. Remember, we are to find hidden stories. The two of you were pushing the books to find the history. I was trying to find a few good stories about the facts."

"Did you find something?" I asked.

"Let's talk after school. You can see if they sound interesting or not," he told me.

During English, Dawn asked me, “Did you get your list put together? I’ve got mine.”

“Almost done! I’ll be ready by Wednesday.

I asked her, “On Wednesday are we meeting after school or during lunch? Actually, I have a better idea. How about meeting at the Bed and Breakfast after dinner? It will be quiet and we can spread out what we have, to see how to put the topics together.”

It sounded okay to Dawn. I figured she could catch Red and ask him about it after school. The B&B would give them a good neutral site to discuss the paper, and so far, I knew the B&B didn’t have any reservations for the week.

Red caught me by my locker just before my last class. “Ashlee, I’m stuck staying after school for an hour. How about meeting me at the General Store about 4:00. I’ll buy you an ice cream, if it doesn’t ruin your supper, and we can hike back up the hill while I tell you a few stories.”

It caught me by surprise. “Oh, okay!” I didn’t quite know what to say. Now, I had to hike down the hill just to hike back up. It was a good thing it was a nice sunny day and the temperature was up in the 50’s, it was a long walk. Was this Red’s way of being nice, after I told him not to worry about Dawn? I wondered about it a couple of times during my last class.

On the way home after school, I wondered if it wouldn’t have been easier just to have Leslie’s parents drop me off at the General Store instead of going home first and walking down there after about a half hour.

I figured the exercise might do me some good. Besides, it would give me the opportunity to pick up my almost finished list of topics at home and show it to Red ahead of our meeting with Dawn on Wednesday.

***

Maria

"Would you like me to drop you off at the store," I asked after Ashlee explained that she was meeting Red and was not sure about being back exactly at supper time. "I need some milk, orange juice, and some ice cream."

Ashlee wasn't sure. It was definitely a crimp in her style. "Okay! But, only if we leave 15 minutes early and you're out of there by the time he comes. He's too shy as it is."

I was trying to kill two birds with one stone. I was trying to be nice and give Ashlee a ride down the hill while trying to find out what "Spider-Boy" looked like. After watching some science fiction movies lately, I wasn't sure what to expect.

It wasn't until we were on the way to the General Store that Ashlee told me that the three of them were hoping to meet at the B&B on Wednesday. I told her it was okay.

I took it as a positive. If Ashlee was actually having them meet at our place, she must feel they would be acceptable to her. On the other hand, it was only to work on finishing an assignment, not a date.

When Red got to the General Store, I was already packed up and getting in my car. Until Ashlee told me later, I didn't even know he had passed me at the door.

Ashlee

I was patrolling the counter at the back of the store when Red approached. "The ice cream shop, which is in a separate building in back, is still closed for a few weeks. However, they have some in the cooler up front. What would you like?" Red asked.

I smiled. "I'll take something small. My mother will kill me if I come home for dinner and tell her I'm not hungry." We picked out an ice cream sandwich each and went up to the cashier by the door to pay for it.

"Let's sit outside on the bench and eat it, where the warm setting sun against the building will make it feel like summer," he told me.

The sun did indeed feel like summer where it was baking against the white building.

"You had to stay after school?" I asked.

"They wanted to organize an outing for my art class. The teacher appointed a couple of us to help pick the location where we were going. I told him Hawaii. However, I don't think they have the budget to let all of us fly out for a day."

"What are they doing?" I asked.

"It's a display on perspective. The whole class is planning on meeting one Saturday morning and free-drawing a landscape. When they are finished with the drawings, the drawings will be displayed out in the hall at school. I think we decided on the outlook by the new bridge over the St. Croix River. It has a number of items that will definitely show perspective in our drawings."

"So, the teacher picked you to decide what to paint? Are 'you' any good?" I asked.

"That's an interesting way to ask," he told me. "No, there aren't any Leonardo da Vinci's in the class that I know of. However, it is an attempt by the teacher to give us a chance to put into practice what he has been teaching. Unfortunately, the backup plan, is to draw it from a projected photo, if it is raining."

I told Red, "You'll have to let me know when they display the drawings. I'd like to see yours.

"So, tell me, what interesting stories did you find talking to people?"

Red looked at me and said, "Let's talk as we walk up the hill." We threw away our ice cream wrappers and started hiking up the hill using a very indirect route.

"Let's head down by the old log cabin in the park, first, before we head up the hill. I can tell you about my meeting with Bob."

"Who's Bob?" I asked.

"He's a hermit that lives just out of town. You don't need to know his last name. I met him a few years ago by the railroad tracks. If you ever see a guy in his 50's or 60's, dressed in clothes that look like they needed a wash a year ago, that's probably Bob. I wasn't too sure of him when I first met him."

That sounded a little weird. It had me wondering once again about our group. On the way to the old log cabin, we walked by the site of the old lumber mill.

Red told me, "Bob told me a few stories about the mill and about the log cabin. Now, he's not one for talking, but he remembers all the stories he's heard over the years of living in the area. He has a great memory – names, dates, and places.

"The original site of the lumber mill was on the creek that flowed next to the restaurant on main street, only it was located right on the river. There is a sign in the small park telling people of its history.

"Have you ever been here on the 4th of July?" Red asked.

"No, we just moved here the first of March. I'd never even been to Marine before."

"Well, don't go anywhere on the 3rd or 4th. On the 3rd of July, they have fireworks that they light off from the area near that sign for the lumber mill. Over 10,000 people flock to our little town for the event. Cars are parked almost all the way to the top of the hill on the highway."

"Why the 3rd?" I asked.

"So people can go other places on the 4th. Marine isn't your normal town. Plus, on the 4th we have a parade. That's when you see how un-conservative our little community really is. Everyone thinks that Marine is a very conservative town. What they don't understand, is that the conservative attitude stops with physically changing the town."

As we approached the cabin, Red told me, "Now, according to Bob, the cabin was owned by Mary Smith's great grandparents. You'll get used to name dropping. Around here houses are still known by the person who built them even though there have been five or six owners. In this case, I'm not sure of the name of the owner, you'll probably have to ask Mary Smith.

"Anyway, she's in charge of the Marine Museum. She wasn't there Saturday. The person left in charge told me she was on vacation somewhere warm.

"According to Bob, Mary Smith's great grandparents lived in the cabin for about 11 years. It was up on the hill just a mile west of the railroad tracks on County Road 4. Almost across the railroad tracks and up the hill from your place.

"Well, County 4 didn't exist back then either. It was a wagon rut trail just outside of town.

"Bob told me an interesting tale about her great grandparents. Apparently, the guy was a currier that took packages from Marine to Taylor's Falls and Scandia before they had good, well, let's just say, roads. I heard that his wife fell down their well one day and drowned."

"Down a well?" I asked. "That's terrible."

"You have to remember, they didn't have well drillers back then. They dug a deep hole and hoped to hit water. Most of the time it was runoff water that seeped into the deep hole through the ground."

"Sounds gruesome," I remarked. "So much for pure water."

"That's not the whole of it. One-day Mary's great-grandfather was recruited by the Army to guide them towards Taylors Falls, to talk to some Native Americans since he knew the roads or paths. When they got there, the Army killed some of the Indians. I'm not sure why or what the problem was. But, get this, when he returned home to the log cabin, he found a spear in the yard sticking out of the ground with a foot attached. I'm not sure if they were Dakota or Sioux, but they definitely sent the man a message. He moved out of the cabin right after that."

"Wow, I'd move too. I didn't get that from reading the sign next to the cabin," I told Red.

"Like I said, I heard a few stories. All of them need researching to make sure they are accurate. However, I can't imagine anyone making up a story like that. Apparently, the historical group took the cabin apart and reassembled it here in the park some time ago."

I told him, "Good thing they didn't put the whole story on the sign. It's not what you want to hear when you are having a picnic in the park. What else did Bob tell you?"

"He told me to go and talk to Bert and Louise Hudson. Bert used to be on the Marine town council, on the police force, fire chief, and on the rescue squad. Louise, his wife, was a nurse on the rescue squad."

"I'll bet they could tell a few good stories," I told Red.

"Bob said they could tell us about some Russian investment broker, from the cities. He must have lost a great deal of money from the wrong kind of investors. One day, one of the people from Marine was up at the old waste dump just north of town and saw a black plastic bag. When they opened it, they found the broker's body parts – minus his head. Later, they found his head up by

Taylor's Falls. Kind of makes one wonder how much money he lost."

"You had a rather interesting afternoon with Bob. In a way, I think I'm glad I was at the museum. At least, we didn't find any bodies popping up there. I don't even remember seeing those reports in the papers we looked through."

"They were probably mentioned. You just needed to be looking for the right heading. Didn't you see the reports about the Indians in town?" Red asked.

"Yes, I wrote down a couple reports. I guess, coming from St. Cloud, I didn't give it much thought."

"There are hidden signs all over the valley that were left from the original inhabitants of the area. Most of them are hard to see unless you know where to look. There are even Indian burial grounds just north of here that are visible from the highway," Red informed me.

"So, did Bob tell you any other stories?" I asked as we started hiking up the hill.

"Yes, I don't know where Bob got them, but he said he heard many of them at the bar when he was younger, and from his father.

"He told me to ask Bert Hudson about putting out a fire on the high bridge."

"Where's that?" I asked.

"It's down past Dawn's house. I'll show it to you if you want. It's a railroad bridge that is about 200 feet over the river."

"That's okay, I'm not too keen on heights."

"You don't have to go on the bridge. In fact, they have cameras to watch for people on the bridge. Ever since some girl fell through a missing board on the bridge one night, they have been strict on keeping people off."

"Another "Bob" story?"

"No, I heard that from my father. I go down there a few times every year. Now, that's a place our class should go to draw perspective. Too bad it is way out of town."

Red and I passed the Lutheran Church as we approached the bridge over the creek. The church was one of those classical white churches built years ago, with a steeple that could be seen for miles.

Red showed me the dam on the creek and the falls that came over the dam. "It is really something in the spring. Some people called it "Oceana Falls." A water flume came from above the falls to the grain mill. The water that turned the mill was transported by wooden troughs all the way down to the grain mill."

"I remember seeing pictures in the museum," I told him. "It was winter and there were icicles all over the flume from the leaks. It was a cool picture. Hard to imagine that there was a grain mill in town. There hardly seems like there was room for it below the dam."

"It was just beyond the red walking bridge that crosses the gully," he told me.

As we approached the turn in the road, where County Road 4 parallels the tracks, Red mentioned, "Here's another one for you. The town's cemetery, which looks as though it has been here since day one, used to be on the road just south of town. It was moved up here."

The two of us just stared at the majestic looking cemetery with the old headstones. The stones look as though they had been there for a hundred years.

It was only a few more blocks until we hit the dirt road that led past the Meadows Bed and Breakfast. Red walked me all the way home. As we walked along the dirt road leading to the B&B, we could hear the bell ring in the steeple of the church. It was 6:00 pm.

"So, did you learn anything today?" he asked.

"Yes, and I expect you to present all of that on Wednesday and make Dawn jealous. By the way, I forgot to mention, we are going to meet here at the Bed and Breakfast after dinner to plan out our course of action if it is okay with you."

"Just let me know what time," he told me. "Thanks for listening. It was fun."

Then, he cut through the trees and started walking the mile and a half to his place.

Chapter 10

Slippery Situations

Maria

Ashlee walked into the B&B about 6:15 pm. The sun was already behind the hills and I was wondering what time she was going to get home. Even though it was an early spring, it was still cold at night, and as the sun set, the temperature started dropping off quickly.

I approached Ashlee, "You had a long walk, did you have a good conversation?"

"Mom, you wouldn't believe what Red just told me."

"Well, let's sit down for some food, and you can tell me all about him."

It was an interesting conversation at dinner that evening. Even I had to admit, the stories kept my interest. The only problem, I still wanted to know about Spider-Boy."

"The cabin was only a little over a mile from here," Ashlee told me excitedly. "How'd you like to come home and find a foot impaled on a spear in your yard?"

I had to admit, that was one topic that could have waited until after supper. We talked for almost an hour before Ashlee told me that she needed to call her grandfather – she had passed her math quiz. She even beat Leslie on the test.

When Ashlee was finished talking, she went to her room to finish her homework. I used the time to call my parents.

"Dad, can you believe it's the same girl that was up in St. Cloud and couldn't pass a math test? I can't believe that I have to find out about her test by her wanting to call you and tell you about it. Maybe this move is what she needed."

"Well, I can tell you one thing, she sounded more excited today than she did two weeks ago. Whatever is going on, it seems to be working. Just make sure she doesn't blossom out too far."

"You mean "Spider-Boy?"

"No, I mean a small town with little to do. It's easy to get into trouble when you start to feel your freedom." He was definitely lecturing me.

"Okay, I hear you."

While Ashlee was working on her homework, I started working on my class assignment in website development. Hopefully, there might be tips in the class that would improve the website for the B&B.

Wednesday evening brought Dawn and Red to the Inn for their organization meeting. There were no guests so with the exception of Bonnie who had been working the desk and was about to leave, they had the place to themselves.

When Dawn's mother dropped her off at 6:30, Dawn asked Ashlee, "Why do they call the Bed and Breakfast 'The Meadows'? You are nestled back into the trees."

"I think it is because of the wildlife meadow that is close by. We weren't here when it was named." Ashlee told Dawn as she showed her to the dining room where they could spread out their research on the large oak table.

About ten minutes later Red arrived. "Sorry, I'm late," he told them, "I was trying to get some last minute information."

Dawn gave Ashlee one of those looks – *oh yeah sure*.

About that time, I walked in with a plate of cookies and some soda for them to munch on while they were working. Ashlee thanked me and introduced Dawn and Red to me.

"I've heard all about both of you the past week. Sounds like you have an exciting project. I'll let you have your space to figure it out. Ashlee, if there is anything else you need, just ask," I told them as I headed back to the apartment. Finally, I got my first good glimpse of 'Spider-Boy.' He seemed pretty normal from what I saw.

Ashlee

We spread our papers out on the table. Everyone had finished their lists compiled from the books they reviewed. Dawn definitely wanted to take charge.

Dawn told us, "I put everything on my list on paper and on the computer. I suggest that we look at each of our lists and add the events on the computer arranged by date. Then, we can decide what we want to highlight and it will all be in order."

It was a good starting point and Red and I agreed to start from there. I figured it wouldn't stay that way very long.

Dawn's list started with the historical beginning of what was originally called Marine Mills.

"Well, these are the items I found that I think are important."

Her list included:

1838 David Hone and Louis Judd arrived on steamer Ariel. Land claim made at Marine Mills. Group of 8?

1838 December Jerimiah Russell, Levi Stratton, (Robert McMasters stayed in cabin) erected a cabin jumping Hone claim.

1839 May 13 found claim jumpers Jerimiah Russell, Levi Stratton. Hone and Judd paid $300 to get them to move out.

1839 August first logs cut at Marine Mills

1844 George Judd moves to St Louis to sell the lumber.

1845 Orange Walker became manager of Marine Lumber Company $300/yr. Stayed until mill's end.

1863 Saw Mill burned. Took three years to restart.

1884 Sept 9th Tornado hit town. 1/2 million feet of stacked lumber blown away along with mill's smokestack and damaged every building.
It caused mill owners to file bankruptcy in 1885.

We studied her list. It was good background information and it included a few twists that could make a good start to the paper.

Then, it was my turn.

"My research includes a few things that Dawn had on her extended list as well, plus I picked out a few more," I told them.

It included:

1855 Gaskill Grain Mill built.

1898 Northwest Telephone Exchange formed, running long distance lines from Marine, Scandia, Osceola, Stillwater, and Taylor's Falls.

1898 A 10 coach train brought 400 people to board the towboat Park Bluff, for a trip to the Falls.

1901 Huge excursion by the Soo Line Railroad. 28 coaches filled with 2000 Soo Line conductors brought for a tour of Interstate Park and Falls, then loaded the steamer Columbia and Lora for the trip downriver pausing at Marine.

1904 1st newspaper The Mascot

1954 Ferry officially stops. It carried up to 55 cars per day at one point.

I told them, "I think these events are things that most of the students from Stillwater probably never heard about in the area. In fact, some of the locals probably don't know about them either. I'm still amazed they were able to run big paddleboats all the way to Taylor's Falls. Heck, from what I was told, you can almost walk across the river in places. If we look, I'm sure we could develop the information into a story."

Dawn looked at the list and agreed. Between her findings and these events there appeared to be enough for a good paper.

Then, I suggested that Red might have some rather interesting bits of information he found. We listened as he told us about his research.

"Well, as I mentioned to Ashlee, I picked up a few stories that probably are not listed in many books," Red said.

He proceeded to tell everyone about the old log cabin located in the park in town, and its strange history. "If you look into the history of Native Americans in the area back in the 1830's to 1860's, it is much more significant than you realize. There was definitely no love lost between the Dakota-Sioux and the Chippewa-Ojibwe.

Red's list included:

1855 200 Sioux Indians came through town

1862 During the Sioux Uprising, 47 volunteers from Marine signed up for 17 days to protect the territory. They decided to use their own guns because they knew how to shoot them.

I found out that there is an old Native American trail from the Croixside Development along the river that leads to Big Marine Lake that is still visible in some areas.

Finally, one day all the Ojibwe Indians that were staying near Big Marine Lake up and disappeared. They moved up north.

"Where did you get that information?" Dawn asked. "I live near Croixside. I've never seen or heard about a trail?"

"The information about the Sioux coming through town was in the museum. The other information came from talking to a few local people. You know, Marine has a number of secret stories. Things people know about, but unless you know what to look for, you would never find them in print."

Then, he told her the story about the Russian investment broker's body that was found just north of town.

"That's horrible!" Dawn replied. "I thought Marine was a nice quiet scenic town."

"Well, it is," Red said. "It's just that things happen. Like the train wreck they had by William O'Brien State Park, just up the tracks from here. One night, after a storm, the engine from a freight train went off the tracks and right into a pond. And then, there's the story about the train fire on top the high bridge. You know where that is, don't you?"

"Well, yes. It is south of my place, about half way to Stillwater. What happened?"

"I still need to talk to a fireman. However, according to the story, a freight train car caught on fire one night, and they had to go out on the bridge, 200 feet over the river, to put it out. I think there is a good story in this one.

"Then, there is one other story I'm still working on," Red said. "It appears President Herbert Hoover came to town one day. Some say it was to go fishing. My grandfather had mentioned that he had seen him in Marine. Apparently, he was in the animal tunnel under the tracks when Hoover's train arrived. He said he actually saw him getting off the train.

"I'll have to show you two the tunnel someday. It's up by the cemetery. I like to go there when I need peace and quiet to write."

I thought about that for a minute. By the cemetery, I'll bet there was lots of peace and quiet.

I just smiled. "And, you thought this paper was an easy done deal," I said to Dawn. "I have a feeling that we can turn this into a few good stories that will wow the class, instead of just listing a few events from old history. It may take a little more work to put it together, but it might be worth it. We'll probably be pushing our teacher's page limit. What do you think?"

For once, Dawn was caught short of words. Leslie was right, if we brought in a few current stories, it would definitely be more interesting. As for the page limit, we would have to decide what to cover and what should be edited out. However, where would we find the exact information to document these reports?

Red had a list of people we could talk to who might be able to fill in the stories beyond the headlines.

By the end of the evening, we had revised our proposed list three times. The paper would start with the expected history of the town, along with the fact it was started by someone jumping the claim for the site of the mill.

Next, we would lead with the story of the movements of the Dakota-Sioux and Ojibwe-Chippewa in the area, along with the story of the old cabin. That should start to get the attention of most of the class.

Finally, we could use some of the sensationalism reports of dead bodies, train wrecks, and fires. If the Herbert Hoover thing materialized, we could probably use it as our final topic. If not, we would pick something else from our list to use as the wrap-up story.

It had been an enjoyable meeting with everyone going away feeling that no one was having to pull the entire load.

Dawn sent a text message for her mother to pick her up. When she left, Red hiked back to his house.

"Who picked up Red," my mother asked me as I came back into the apartment.

"He walked," I told her.

"Didn't you ask if he wanted a ride? It's dark out and late. I could have taken him or I'm sure Dawn's mother could have dropped him off."

"He told me he wanted to walk," I replied.

My mother and I sat and talked about the meeting we had. It was interesting and it seemed that all of us were indeed working together. She reminded me that I needed to keep all of them involved in the next parts of the investigation stage. They all needed to buy in that it was their report. Also, she suggested that she could help if they needed some transportation.

The following day at school, Thursday, we talked to our teacher before class. She had set a general guideline as to the size of the paper due, which was probably there to make sure the students did enough work to make it feel worthwhile, and not too long as to keep all the readings for the class from taking the next month.

We didn't give her our proposed outline, deciding that we needed to be able to modify it on the fly if any of the stories proved to be false or uninteresting. However, we told her that what we were working on had both historic and recent stories that we felt the class would enjoy hearing.

After listening to what we were considering, she told us it sounded good. We should go ahead with the paper the way we planned. However, she would probably set a time limit for reading to the class. So, if it gets too long, we might have to edit what we read after handing in the full paper.

That was fine with us.

***

Chapter 11

Updates

Jason Willard

It had only been a couple weeks since I had met with Maria, but I decided it would be best to meet with her a couple times a month the first few months to make sure she was adjusting to the job and there were no problems. The last thing I wanted to have to tell Edward was that after three or four months I had to fire her because she was driving the help nuts or was changing too much at the same time.

It was just a short meeting to keep the atmosphere light and review what was happening at the Inn and in her life. So far, Maria seemed to be adjusting just fine.

"You know, Mr. Willard, I was really leery about taking the job. I was worried that the change in location was going to be too quick for Ashlee, and I would be spending too much time worrying about her along with the Bed and Breakfast. I just wanted to let you know that Ashlee appears to be making the change with flying colors."

Maria went on to explain to me how Ashlee had gotten off to a good start at the new school and was enjoying a project she was working on. She felt it was giving Ashlee an appreciation of the small town atmosphere and at the same time, through her school project, Maria was learning about the area. It was a win for both of them.

Looking over the work Maria had been doing at the Bed and Breakfast, she was pretty much on schedule from our last meeting and we only needed to discuss some minor issues she had discovered with the maintenance of the building.

"Maria, you are doing fine. I was hoping you were adjusting, and so far, I can't find a lot of suggestions to help you out. You seem to have it under control. Get a couple estimates for the work. If they seem in line, you can just get them fixed. That's all part of the normal maintenance of an older building. If something comes back out of the ordinary, then we should probably discuss it. Sometimes the solution is not to fix something. If it is going to be a constant problem, we can look at modifying whatever it is."

We sat and talked for another hour over a cup of coffee. It was nice to hear how the two of them were adjusting to the new environment. In addition, I was enjoying sitting and talking to Maria. For me, it was another plus of my flexible schedule. Time was no longer a major event that controlled my daily life. I told her to let me know what new information Ashlee dug up about our little town. I was curious to see if any of my friends ended up in the story.

The two of us set a meeting date and time for our next meeting. If things continued as they were so far, I was wondering if we needed to meet every two weeks. However, I was enjoying the time talking with her. I hated to change the pre-set schedule.

After Maria left, I called Edward Gray to give him an update on the Bed and Breakfast along with his other investments. He had a couple bonds that were coming due to expire shortly, and I needed to know if he wanted me to find new investment bonds available on the market, or if he had some other wild schemes going in the back of his mind.

***

Maria

When I got back to the Bed and Breakfast, I quickly got started contacting a couple contractors about a problem we discovered over the porch. We noticed that one corner of the ceiling appeared to be hanging down over an inch. The question was; was it a loose board or was this just a sign of larger problems in the roof that was just starting to show.

The first company I called said they could send someone over tomorrow to look it over. I was glad they could look at it that quickly. It would give us a clue if it was a minor or major problem. It would make it easier for getting a second estimate.

Reservations at the B&B were gradually starting to pick up. The sight of green grass rather than white was making people anxious to get out after the long winter. It was nice to see the Inn busy. The smell of food being prepared for the table early in the morning was a welcome odor. We were still looking for our first full booking of the season. However, as I looked at the rate at which the reservations were coming into the Inn, it looked as though it was just a matter of time.

As part of my coursework, I put together an improved website for the Inn. It was fun to work on something for my classes that I could use immediately and still get credit for the work. I decided to continue my classes during the summer with the thought of working towards a degree in business.

While I was fiddling with my course work, I started wondering how Ashlee was doing on her project for school. It was interesting enough that it had caught my curiosity. What other facts about the area remained hidden? I decided to keep a close eye on what they were finding. If it was really interesting, Ashlee might be able to put parts of it into a short booklet that could be left in each room for visitors to learn about the area. Imagine, still in high school and having a book published. That would be something for her to brag about someday when she went to college.

It was an interesting thought. Then, I came down from my dreamland. Well, I guess I needed to get her through high school first.

At dinnertime, we had a chance to talk about her schoolwork. So far, she sounded excited about most of her classes. I think she really liked working as a team on her English assignment. It was something she had not done before.

Ashlee told me how the team had hoped to talk to several people in town during the next week to make sure the stories they had heard about were real.

Ashlee and her crew stayed with their concept. One by one they made appointments to meet with key people around town to check out the stories they had heard.

Towards the end of the week, I was looking forward to meeting Edward Gray. I had been curious about him ever since I took his reservations for several weekends. What kind of man was he? Why did he like to stay in the same room on Friday and Saturday nights? What was so special to him about the Inn?

I had asked Bonnie and Jean about him after he made his reservations. Both of them told me he seemed to be a very nice, older man that read a lot and enjoyed the reading nook in the room.

I decided to keep an eye open for him when he checked in on Friday. Bonnie could let me know if she saw him drive into the parking area. She told me that he usually arrives early in the afternoon.

It was about 2:30 in the afternoon when Bonnie poked her head in my office to tell me that Edward Gray had just pulled up in front of the Inn. I waited until he was checking in before coming out and introducing myself to him.

"Mr. Gray, I'm Maria Wagner the manager of the Meadows Bed and Breakfast. Welcome to the Inn. We spoke a few weeks back when you made your reservations."

"Yes, I believe so. It is nice to meet you.

"Bonnie, is there anything else you need? Well, then, I think I will bring my stuff upstairs.

"Ms. Wagner, nice meeting you. I'm sure we will run into each other before I check out. Right now, I need to put my things away."

With that, the mysterious Edward Gray picked up his bag and headed up to the front bedroom.

"Is he always that short and in a hurry?" I asked Bonnie.

"Yup! After dinner, he usually spends more time talking and is more relaxed. I think he usually eats down at the Brookside this time of year. Later, when it warms up, he likes to have lunch at Quack's Restaurant at the old landing on the river."

"Well, I guess I might try and talk to him later or in the morning. I'm still intrigued as to why he likes the Meadows B&B over other places."

I headed back to the apartment just as curious as I was before meeting our frequent guest. My brief meeting had not allowed me to develop any additional knowledge of his background or why he liked staying at the Inn.

After a short while, I called my mother. She had been asking us about dinner either Saturday or Sunday and in my attempting to get other things accomplished, I had not gotten back to her.

My mother and I talked for almost a half an hour before Ashlee came into the room. I guess it was the excuse we both needed to stop chatting and do other things.

"Ashlee, how was school?"

"Okay! We decided to meet with Mary Smith Saturday. She said she could meet with us in the morning, before the museum opens. It should give us some direction before we meet with others in town."

"Sounds like a plan. By the way, Mr. Gray checked in. Be polite if you see him in the lobby. So far, he seems to be our best customer."

"Alright! Have you met him yet?" she asked. "What's he like?"

"Just briefly. I'm hoping to talk to him tomorrow if I can. I'm still curious about his connection with the Inn. There must be a reason that he likes it as much as he does."

I suggested that Ashlee tell her grandparents about her project on Sunday when we went over there for dinner. I told Ashlee that I felt Sunday would be better than Saturday. I wanted to leave most of the weekend open for both of us.

Ashlee agreed. In addition, I dropped the hint to her that her grandparents were starting to miss talking to her.

Bonnie was right. About 6:30, just a little after sunset, Edward Gray left the Inn for dinner at Brookside. I saw his car driving out the road as we sat down for our own dinner and mentioned it to Ashlee.

"Bonnie said he always goes to the Brookside?" Ashlee asked. "What's the attraction?"

"Not sure. That's another question to put on our list. We'll have to see when he comes back."

About 7:00, I heard our other guest for the night checking in. We had two guests tonight and three for tomorrow night. That meant hot, sticky buns for the morning, Ashlee's favorite. Yes, there were a few perks that came with the Bed and Breakfast. The smell of them coming out of the oven in the morning was just enough to get her out of bed without an alarm clock.

It was about 8:30 pm, while Ashlee and I were discussing parts of her homework, that I heard Edward Gray return from his trip for dinner. He stopped to talk to Bonnie for a few minutes before heading straight upstairs to his room. I decided I would wait until tomorrow before making an attempt to talk to him.

It was about 6:30 am, when I got my first whiff of the rolls in the oven. Jean was working this morning and was preparing the breakfast for the guests. With our bedroom over the kitchen area, the aroma had a way of sneaking up the old walls and into the room. I laid there for about fifteen minutes thinking about the day, before slowly getting up.

Ashlee must have smelled the rolls as well, as she was already in the bathroom. Whatever happened to the theory that high school students couldn't get up in the morning? Here it is Saturday, a good day to sleep in, and she was out in the real world by 7 am. On top of that, she beat me in there. I guess those psychologists just did not understand the amazing power that fresh baked rolls had on teenagers in the morning. I decided to add the rolls to my list of attributes for why people come to the B&B.

Breakfast was served at 8:00 am on Saturdays. Sunday's breakfast was more on the continental style from 7:30 to 9:00. It allowed our guests to travel earlier or go to church if they desired.

Jean had put a couple sticky buns in a separate pan for Ashlee and me. As she was starting to bring out the food for our guests, I slipped into the kitchen to catch her progress as well as steal the pan of rolls along with a couple pieces of fruit for Ashlee and me.

"Everything okay?" I asked Jean as I stole the buns.

"Yes, I just put out the fruit, buns, cheese and sliced meat. The coffee and orange juice is already on the table. The quiche is ready to go out, also."

"Sounds good, and thanks," I told her as I headed back into our apartment.

I figured I would give them about thirty minutes before I came back down and tried to get into a conversation with Edward Gray. The other guest for the night had not been a return customer.

However, I decided that I might use the excuse of obtaining an evaluation of the Inn to get my conversation going.

Ashlee and I enjoyed the rolls and some cereal for breakfast. The rolls had become a Saturday morning treat.

"You know Mom if you made rolls like this when we lived in St. Cloud, you probably wouldn't have had to fight to get me up for school every morning."

I laughed. "Yes, and both of us would have been at least twenty pounds heavier by now if I did. I'll have to go for a mile hike later today just to wear this one off," I told her.

I asked Ashlee if she would clean up the table while I went out to see how our guests were doing. She told me to go ahead and perhaps I could find out more about Edward Gray. Ashlee also reminded me that her group was meeting with Mary Smith later in the morning at the museum. Even though it did not open until 11:00 am, she told them that she had some organization work she was planning on doing in the morning. She could meet with them around 10:00 am.

Before I went out into the dining room, I reminded her that I had someone coming around noon to look at the porch. They wanted to remove a couple pieces of trim to see what they needed to purchase to brace up the ceiling.

As I peeked out from the kitchen area, the guests appeared to be just finishing their breakfast. They were sitting at the table drinking their last cup of coffee.

In preparation for my introduction, I had quickly prepared a short survey that I could give my guests, asking their opinions of the Bed and Breakfast. My timing was perfect. I went out and introduced myself to our guests.

"Good morning," I introduced myself. "My name is Maria Walker. I am the manager of the Meadows Inn. I hope you have enjoyed your night's sleep and breakfast. If you don't mind, I have a request this morning. As part of a marketing course I am taking, I am asking our guests this week to give us your opinions of the Bed and Breakfast. In class, we are working as teams to evaluate the criteria as to why customers like several different businesses and what important things customers are looking for. So, if you don't mind helping me out, I would appreciate your input. Besides, you might have some suggestions we could use to improve your stay. No guarantees! I think Jean told me hot sticky rolls in bed, in the morning, was not on the list."

Mr. Gray and the other couple that was staying in the back bedroom laughed. Then, they willingly agreed to fill out my short form. I asked them to please leave it on the front desk when they were finished, later in the morning.

The couple that was staying in the back room thanked me for the hospitality. They said they really enjoyed staying at the Inn. As they left to head upstairs, Edward Gray and I had a short conversation.

He told me that it was nice that they had a live-in manager for the Inn that guests could interact with. Even though Jean and Bonnie were very pleasant and easy to talk to, it was nice to see who was in charge and that they were interested in the comments of the guests.

I sat down at the table and asked him if they had done any surveys of the customers in the past that he could remember.

"No, I don't believe they have. They had always asked me how my stay was, but I think that was about it. I never thought about sticky rolls in our room before breakfast. I'll have to put that on the list."

I smiled. "How long have you been coming to the Inn?"

"Oh, I'm not sure. It's been a while. I like sitting in the reading window. It gives me a chance to reflect on the past and decide what I need to do next without having my phone ringing constantly and other distractions. When I arrive at the Inn, I simply turn my phone off. People that know me know that I will not answer it until after I leave."

"Aren't you worried someone will really need to talk to you?" I asked.

"No! Life is not that important anymore. Five days a week is enough time for people to ask you questions. God said he gave us a day of rest. I just took it a step farther. If one day is good for us, two might be better. As you get older, you will find it takes a day to start to relax. It makes the second day feel even better."

"What did you do before you retired?" I asked. "I assume you are retired?"

"Yes, I was in the shipping business. Then, I decided to go into investments. I would invest in companies. When the time was right, I would sell my investments for a small profit. Most of the time my timing was right."

"So, why do you come to Marine?" I asked.

"I used to live here. It feels good coming back to the area you spent many years. Kind of allows you to re-live the past."

"How about you? Where did you come from?" he asked.

"I grew up in the Twin Cities and moved to St. Cloud. Finally, I decided I preferred this area for my daughter growing up. I think the change was good for both of us."

"I'm glad to hear that. Family is important. You need to cherish the moments."

Just then, Ashlee came out and whispered to me that she was hiking down to the museum.

"Mr. Gray, this is my daughter Ashlee."

"Nice to meet you," he told her.

"She is working on a school project on some the history of Marine and is meeting some friends at the museum this morning."

"Ashlee, that sounds interesting," he told her. "You will have to let me know if you find something others do not know."

"Thank you, I will," Ashlee told him as she turned to leave.

"Nice daughter. You should be proud."

"Thank you, Mr. Gray," I told him. "I am."

"Edward would be just fine," he told me.

With that, he excused himself and headed up to his room.

About 12:30 pm, a construction worker showed up to evaluate the sag in the porch roof.

It didn't take him very long. He pulled down several pieces of slats that made up the soffit above the porch, and with a stepladder, he evaluated the supports up above.

"Well, you're lucky. From what I see, there isn't any rot from water leaks. Looks to me like someone did some modifications to the porch some time back and when they did, they nailed the supports together at the house wall instead of using a tie-in brace. I should be able to come back on Monday and fix it in a few hours. You were lucky. Most of these calls I get are wood rot. In many of those cases, I have to tear down the affected roof area and rebuild them."

It was nice to hear that it was not going to be a major repair. I was still hoping to stay close to my proposed budget for the spring.

The contractor left the pieces of soffit he tore down on the porch floor because it was in several pieces at this point. As he picked up his ladder, he told me he would return sometime on Monday with new boards and some braces.

As I was walking back inside, I met Edward Gray. He told me he had heard the commotion outside his window and was wondering what the noise was.

"Oh, fortunately, it was not much. We had a board in the porch roof that was sagging. They told me they would have it fixed on Monday."

"Good! I was worried you might have to rip out the wall in my room. Gets drafty at night, you know, with large holes in the walls."

He was joking. I got it. I told him I was considering a slide mounted just outside his window. That way, it would be quicker to get down for breakfast. Part of our improvement program.

"Progress! Good idea. Well, let me know if you need any other suggestions," he told me as he smiled and headed up to his room.

It was unusual. Most of our customers came late in the afternoon and left after breakfast - even on the occasions where they stayed a few days. Mr. Gray preferred to stay in his room most of the time. Only occasionally, did he come down during the day with the exception of heading out for a meal.

It wasn't too much longer that Ashlee headed on back to the Inn with her friend – Spider-Boy. I don't know why, but his nickname just hit a funny bone whenever I thought about it. I had to pinch myself to remind me to call him Red.

"You're back early. Did you find out all the info you wanted to locate?" I asked her.

"Yes, Mrs. Smith confirmed the story that Red had heard and told us all about. A relative of hers did indeed own the old cabin in town. The story about the man guiding the army to talk with the Indians, and then after he returned home, finding a spear with a foot attached to it in his yard was all true."

"Well, looks like you have your story for the paper you are writing. When do you have to get it done?"

"We have three more weeks," Red told her. "That will give us time to finish out the other stories for the paper."

"Want anything to snack on?" I asked them. "There are still a few sticky rolls left over from breakfast."

They snacked on a warmed up roll while discussing what they were going to write. Apparently, Dawn was going to write up a draft of the town history portion of the paper and they were going to tackle the draft of the later day events. So far, they sounded like they had it under control.

After Red left and walked back home, I mentioned to Ashlee that I needed to get out for a walk. The rolls from breakfast were still depositing their sugar on my stomach.

"Can I walk with you?" she asked.

Surprised, I answered, "Sure!"

"I have an idea," Ashlee suggested. "Mrs. Smith told us about the train accident that happened just down the tracks a ways – towards the State Park. I want to see where it was. I can tell you all about it as we walk down the tracks."

"You're really getting into this paper I can see. Sure, we can head down the tracks. Probably less mud that way compared to the dirt road. I'll be glad when summer is here."

The two of us put on a light jacket and hiking boots to trek down the tracks. "How far are we going?" I asked.

"Oh, maybe a mile. It's not supposed to be too far."

I was glad I had put on my hiking boots. Walking on the coarse rock used for the railroad bed was just rough enough that the boots felt better than shoes.

"Okay, Ashlee, tell me the full story about the train wreck."

"Well, according to the story Red heard, and it was confirmed by Mrs. Smith at the museum, one day after a hard rain, a train went off the tracks and ended up nose first in a pond just up ahead.

"The story goes that beavers had blocked up a couple of the creeks in the area that naturally flowed under the tracks by means of a culvert. When there was a big storm, the beaver dam gave way and washed out the culvert under the tracks.

"Later, when a freight train came along in the storm, they did not see that the culvert under the tracks was washed out. The tracks gave way and the freight train derailed. The engine ended up point down into the pond. Fortunately, for the two-man crew, no one was killed. The Marine Fire Department was called out with a reported train derailment between Marine and Copas. In the dark, it took a while to find the wreck even though it was only a mile out of town. From the main highway, in the rain, nothing was easily visible.

"The railroad crew got the cars back on the tracks. However, to get the engine out of the pond, they had to cut the huge diesel engine into pieces to get it out of the mud. I'll bet that cost them a fortune."

"Are you going to build that story into your paper for school?" I asked Ashlee.

"I doubt it. Unless we discover some additional information about it, it will sound like just another train that went off the tracks."

We walked on down the tracks over a mile before coming to the stream and pond where the train was reported to have ended up. Most of our hike along the railroad track had been surrounded by the flat meadow along the west side of William O'Brien State Park on one side and trees and a hill on the other side. We heard a few birds, but other than squirrels, that was all the animals we saw on our walk along the tracks.

The rail bed had been fairly flat to slightly downhill. From this point on, the trains would slowly descend to the old swing bridge crossing the St. Croix River.

Fortunately, during our walk, we had not seen any trains. Thinking back on it, we probably shouldn't have been on the tracks. It was marked "No Trespassing" and the Canadian National (CN) Railroad owned this stretch of tracks.

A little further down the tracks, the Minnesota Transportation Museum ran an excursion train along a short stretch of the same tracks from Osceola, Wisconsin, across the swing bridge over the river, to the edge of the William O'Brien State Park in Minnesota.

It didn't seem like a problem hiking down the tracks. Since we had not encountered any narrow areas where the tracks were restricted while running along a narrow ridge, we weren't too worried about accidentally meeting a freight train. Most of the rail bed had originally been made for two tracks. Some time back, they removed the one set to save money. The new rail bed had been sloped from the one main track.

We figured that we should be able to hear a train coming a long way off. If a freight train was coming up the long hill from the crossing over the river near Osceola, the engines would be working hard, making a lot of noise and not moving very fast. If one approached the downhill from the south, it should have been slowing down anticipating the switch tracks ahead as well as the river crossing. The sound of the steel brakes would sing in the tracks. Crossing the highway at Marine, the train's air horn should give us plenty of notice that a train was approaching, as it blew its warning at the crossing.

As we stood there looking over the spot where the train derailed, you could see the problems they might have had in locating the train.

If the diesel engine and its bright lights were buried into the mud, there were no major roads within eyesight to see it. With no houses close to the spot, reporting the crash and finding it had to come by heading down the tracks.

As we started walking back, Ashlee told me that so far Red had been correct with his stories on the rumors. It seemed that his sources had been extremely accurate on all his stories that they had investigated so far.

Also, she confided in me that Dawn had finally grimaced in her defeat. Instead of leading the tasks, they had appeased her by giving her the assignment of working on the beginning segments of the paper. She even started to admit to Ashlee that Red was doing an equal part to the rest of them in gathering the information.

I knew that that had been a problem from the start and Ashlee was concerned about it.

Ashlee felt that the team dynamics had finally changed. It was indeed a team now with all of them working together.

It was interesting to get away from everything and hear Ashlee tell me in her words how things were changing. And to think, this was coming from my daughter. A year ago, I'm not sure if she would have cared if someone else was working with her or not on a project? It goes to show, people do change if you give them the room.

As I was thinking through the changes I had seen in Ashlee in the past six months, I was suddenly startled by something that flew right by us. It was as if the sky had suddenly turned black in front of our eyes. What was it? It almost hit us.

They came out of the meadow, flying low and fast. Just like an overgrown pheasant. Then, they quickly rose to just above the level of the tracks, gliding right in front of us, perhaps three feet over our heads, as if we were not even there. We could even feel the rush of the wind coming from their wings. Finally, flapping their enormous wings, they rose up in flight and landed in one of the trees, high along the hill, on the side of the tracks.

"What was that?" Ashlee shouted.

Neither of us heard them coming. Both of us jumped back in defense as they almost hit us.

"Stupid birds. Didn't they see us standing on the tracks?" Ashlee said in disbelief.

They had flown less than ten feet in front of us.

In a moment of panic, I was startled and jumped to get away from them. However, I felt my foot catch on something. The next thing I knew, I was laying on the rocks next to the tracks. "Ouch," I shouted to Ashlee.

Looking down, Ashlee saw me flat on my back sprawled on top the railroad ties. "You okay?" she asked.

"No, I think I have hurt my ankle."

I looked down and saw a piece of heavy cable lying next to my foot. In my highly distracted moment, caused by three flying objects, I had somehow stepped into a loop of a cable that was partially buried along the track. In jumping back, I had twisted my left ankle in the loop. And, I was starting to realize, just as the derailed and disabled train was out in the middle of no-where, so was I.

I looked up at Ashlee. "I'm not sure I'm going to be able to walk back. I don't know if my ankle is broken or sprained. Either way, it really hurts. I think it's telling me it is not going anywhere."

Ashlee looked at my foot. Fortunately, I had been wearing my hiking boots. If it was my walking shoes, the cable might have cut into my ankle. My boot was still pointing the right direction. That was one positive sign. Maybe it wasn't broken. Then again, there could be a cracked bone. So far, I had not moved it and I was not about to remove my boot. I probably would not be able to get it back on if it swelled up.

"Think you can stand?" she asked.

"No, I can hardly move it."

"Okay, let's sit here a little while. See if the pain comes down a little bit. We need to think this one out.

"You're too close to the tracks. If a train comes, we don't want to have to move your leg in a hurry. That would really hurt. We need to get you off the tracks."

She was right. I didn't remember hearing any freights go by the B&B today. That was not a good sign either. One might come by later this afternoon. The tracks were not heavily used. However, a train a day was not uncommon.

"Alright! Just let me sit for a minute. What the heck was that creature?"

"I think it was three wild turkeys. I've seen them in some of the fields on the way to and from school. They probably came out of that field. Maybe a fox or coyote chased them out. This is the first time I've ever seen one fly. Are you sure you are okay?"

"I'll be okay as soon as I take up hunting. Let's see if we can drag my foot and ankle over a few yards, to the area next to the tracks. I don't need any more surprises."

It felt like it took hours for me to move ten feet. My ankle and foot were not about to let me put pressure on it. I assumed that I probably broke something. Inch by inch Ashlee helped me up and then slowly move the little bit needed to get off the track area.

"Your head is bleeding," Ashlee told me.

I wiped the back of my head. She was right. There was a small trickle of blood on the back of my head. I must have hit it on one of the railroad ties. Fortunately, it was just a scratch.

I looked at Ashlee. We were, at least, a mile down the tracks from the B&B. It was going to be a long walk to get back. I didn't think I would make it in any time under a month. I'd probably freeze before that.

"I think you're going to need some help to get me back home," I told her.

We looked at the alternatives. We were on the edge of the state park. However, there was nothing near us but a soggy meadow. Ashlee would have to hike across the field area to get to the service road, and then hike to the Welcome Center. Hopefully, someone would be there. It was almost as long as hiking back to Marine. At least hiking back to Marine, she would be on the rail bed and not tracking through swampy fields. Besides, help would have to come from the tracks either way. There were no easy accesses from the park property to the tracks.

It was decided. I would patiently wait by the tracks (as if I had a choice), and Ashlee would hike back and bring the Calvary.

I could already envision in my mind the Marine Fire Department arriving with a fire truck, rescue squad, and I suppose I might even throw in a highway patrol car in the parade of lights coming down the tracks. The guests at the Bed & Breakfast would love the attraction. They would probably line up and stand next to the tracks to watch the event.

Oh, why not throw in one more addition. How about a freight train that had to grind to a stop because of all the trucks on the tracks.

I might even make the paper. Worse yet, it might make Ashlee's paper.

I sat down and watched as Ashlee made the hike back up the tracks. She kept looking back at me to make sure I was all right.

Ashlee hadn't gone two hundred feet down the tracks when the turkeys flew back out of the trees, heading back towards the field. At least this time, they didn't fly over my head.

After a little less than two blocks, the tracks made a slight turn to the right. I was about to lose sight of Ashlee from that point on when I spotted someone on the tracks about 100 feet beyond her.

Ashlee was still looking at me when I started pointing at the person on the tracks. Who was it? Could Ashlee see me?

From my distant perspective, the person's clothes appeared rather sloppy. Was there a bum on the tracks?

Oh my, did Ashlee even see him? How could I get her attention? If only I could get up and start waving. She probably couldn't hear me either. The wind was blowing in the wrong direction.

With me down in the ditch, where the trees and hillside made it dark with the setting sun, she probably couldn't even see me desperately pointing at him.

I was desperate, but there was nothing else I could do.

Chapter 12

Rescue

My anxiety levels were all peaked out. I could no longer feel my ankle and foot throbbing. Who was on the tracks? Did Ashlee see him? Was she in danger?

I watched as she turned around and started walking again. I don't think she ever saw me trying to get her attention.

As she got closer to the person standing on the tracks, she stopped. Then, I watched as the figure slowly approached her.

They stood a few yards apart talking to each other for a couple minutes before I saw Ashlee turn and start to head back towards me. Who was it?

It felt like it took an eternity for Ashlee to get back down the tracks to where I was sitting. Unfortunately, with my anxiety settling down, my foot had gotten my attention once again. It was definitely swelling up inside my boot.

I asked her, "Who was that person you were talking to?" as soon as Ashlee was in hearing range.

"He said his name was Bob. He knows Red. Anyway, he said he saw the two of us walking down the tracks, and when only one of us headed back, he was worried that something had happened to us."

"Oh, thank goodness. I thought for sure you were being stalked by a bum on the railroad tracks," I told Ashlee.

"Probably a good thing you weren't the one walking up the tracks," she told me. "He's not too far from that description. I think he is a hermit. Anyway, he said he would go get Red. I guess we'll just have to wait."

"You think he's dependable?" I asked.

"I think so. Red has mentioned him a couple times in our discussions about the area. How's the foot?"

"Well, let's just say, I hope they don't have to cut off my new boots to get my foot out."

"That swollen? Wish I could do something for you. I guess we're stuck here until someone comes."

"I hope they have a soft riding truck. I'm not sure my leg is going to like bouncing on the rocks all the way back."

We chatted as we waited. Soon, the sun would be setting. I hoped they would come for us before it got dark.

Ashlee asked if the turkeys frightened me when they flew back into the field. She heard them fly by her.

"No, I just wish I had a gun. If I could have stood up, I might have tried to throw a rock at them."

It gave us something to laugh about.

Ashlee

It was almost an hour, and still no one was in sight. I was starting to get worried about "Bob." Maybe I was wrong in my assessment of him. It was getting dark. What would we do if he didn't come back?

Then, I caught the faint sign of a light shining up the tracks. Train? I hoped not, as I pointed up the tracks.

"Someone or something is coming," I told my mother.

We watched. Whatever it was, it wasn't moving very fast. I could just make out the reflections off the shiny tracks. Finally, as it made the corner, we could see what looked like a flashlight on a small rail car coming down the tracks. It definitely wasn't a train or a truck, and there were no flashing lights.

It looked as though there were two people riding on whatever it was. It was definitely on the rails. You could hear the grinding sound ringing on the tracks. Slowly, it was coming closer.

When it was about fifty feet from us, I first recognized Red and then Bob. They were riding on the car. Or, should I say pumping it down the tracks. It took them almost all of the fifty feet to bring the thing to a stop. Apparently the brake did not work, so they had to apply resistance to the pump mechanism.

"Someone call for a cab?" Red called out, as they got close.

My mother took one look at the rig. "You got insurance on that thing?" she asked. I could see her staring at Bob, as she was answering Red.

"Probably not. Plus, I had to steal it from my neighbor. I figured he wouldn't mind. Want a lift?" Red asked.

It took the three of us to move my mother from the ditch to the three-wheeled sidecar. It had two seats – well boards, to sit on. Those lucky two had to push and pull on the lever that made it go. The third wheel was suspended out to the other track to balance it, and someone had fastened a work platform between the three wheels.

"Unless you want to drive, we'll let you sit on the bed," Red told my mother. "You want to sit facing forward or backward?"

My mother laughed as much as she could. "I'd prefer to see where I was going," she answered.

We picked her up and gently set her down on the plywood.

"It's going to get a little crowded on this thing," Red told us. "Ashlee, I suggest you sit next to your mother and help her stay balanced. You can squirm until you are comfortable. I don't think your mother has that luxury and I forgot to mount a rocking chair on the platform."

Once my mother and I were onboard, Red and Bob gave the cart a push. Then they jumped on, propelling it slowly down the tracks.

It rolled very smoothly down the tracks.

Maria

"I appreciated the ride, but I have to ask, what if we see a train? Are the three of you going to jump and leave me here?"

Red laughed. "Well, I see you still have a sense of humor. That's good.

"It's Bob's job to watch for trains coming from behind us. I figure we'll see the light long before it reaches us. A freight coming up from the river probably won't be going over 30 mph. Fortunately, this thing is fairly easy to lift off the tracks – even with you sitting on it. That's the advantage of only three wheels. We only need to lift the side-wheel to pivot the cart.

"Just to make sure we didn't find a visitor coming from the direction of town, when I borrowed your carriage, I also took an impact signal. I put it on the tracks back in town. When a train runs over it, it explodes. It's an old train signal that tells the engineer there is trouble with the tracks up ahead. If it still works, they should hit the emergency brakes."

I was impressed. Ashlee's friend Red had thought this through before they came to my rescue. Riding on the car was much smoother than a four-wheeler or pickup truck driven on the rocky rail bed. Plus, it was level.

Our speed was slow – although it was probably faster than one could walk. Since Ashlee and I were not doing the work, I figured we shouldn't complain.

Ashlee was asking Red all about the car he "borrowed" and how he got it to the tracks.

Apparently Red and Bob hauled it in Red's father's old pickup. Red said they might have left a few new scratches on the truck bed from the wheels. "Since it had not been washed or waxed for a hundred years, I figured no one would notice."

Red's father told him he would wait for them at the crossing in town with his van. He would take us to the Stillwater hospital's emergency room to have my mother's foot looked at, while Red and Bob returned the sidecar to his neighbor's collection. Also, he reminded Red to remove the impact signal from the track. No sense scaring a train engineer accidentally.

As we approached the siding for the Marine station, which had been removed long ago, we paused at the switch track. Instead of throwing the lever to switch the tracks, they simply stopped and lifted the wheel, setting it down the couple inches over on the switch track.

I remember breathing a sigh of relief when we were safely on the sidetrack. Not that I didn't trust everyone, I just didn't need the feel of panic if a train approached. A least for the next couple of blocks, I didn't have to worry about trains.

The siding wasn't very smooth compared to the main track. I guess the track maintenance people didn't feel high-speed trains would be using it. Seeing Red's father in his van with the lights on at the crossing was comforting as well. Now, I had to figure out how to get from the planks to the van.

Red's father was very nice. We had a long discussion as he drove Ashlee and me to the hospital in Stillwater for some x-rays.

Fortunately, it was just a bad sprain. They did cut the fancy laces off my new boot.

It was 2 am by the time we were back at the B&B. I told Red's father how I really appreciated everything they had done. I suggested that once I was back on two feet, they would have to come for dinner so that I could show them the appreciation I really needed to give them.

By 3 am, the pain pills were working and I was out cold in my bed. I didn't feel a thing until morning.

About 9:30 am, I heard a knocking on my door. It was Ashlee.

"How are you feeling?" she asked. "Everyone is asking about you."

"Everyone?" I asked.

"Well, all our guests and staff. Word travels fast at a Bed and Breakfast. They were all asking about you at breakfast. In fact, they insisted that I had to bring you breakfast in bed. They said it was part of the new suggestion process."

I felt embarrassed. However, first things first. I needed Ashlee to help me down the hall to use the bathroom. With all the tape on my ankle, it wasn't as bad as I thought it might be this morning to walk on it.

When I got back to my bedside snack, Ashlee told me the other thing they wanted to tell me. She was to tell me that the railroad police were at the door. They wanted to know why I had disrupted traffic on the railroad all night. April Fools!

I laughed, it was indeed April Fool's day. I guess I knew who felt like the biggest fool on this day.

I didn't move around very much the rest of the morning. I did ask Ashlee to thank everyone that was worried about me and to let them know that the patient will live.

When I called my parents to let them know we couldn't come for dinner, my mother insisted that they would bring the meal to us, just to make sure I was okay.

That evening, at dinner, we got a good laugh at everything that happened on our simple walk down the tracks.

During the day, while I was keeping my face (and foot) out of the public, Ashlee ended up having a conversation with Edward Gray.

Mr. Gray apparently caught Ashlee as she was getting some ice for my leg and after she helped me get comfortable, she went back out and talked to him for almost an hour.

After asking questions about why we were hiking on the railroad tracks so late in the day, the two of them got into a discussion about Ashlee's paper on Marine.

"You know, that train derailment wasn't half as exciting as the fire that almost burned the town down," he told her. "Have you heard about that one? Bert Hudson could tell you all about it if you haven't. He was on the fire department. If it wasn't for the DNR's help in dropping water on the fire, it would have burned all the way from the railroad tracks to the river. That fire was started by a train also."

"How do you know about it?" she asked.

"I used to live in the area."

For the next forty-five minutes, Ashlee and Mr. Edwards discussed some of the proposed topics for her paper.

"I think you have a good topic in that visit by President Hoover. Make sure you check out the old William Edgar residence," he told her. "It has changed hands many times. Plus, there's a great deal more important history in that place than you think.

"Next time I'm here, you will have to show me your finished paper. I have a feeling you'll do a great job."

Ashlee was feeling good. Even though I didn't get time to talk to Mr. Gray, she had some time with him and in between the lines of their conversations, she started to get a better feeling as to what he was like.

Now, I was jealous. That had been my goal for Saturday and Sunday morning before we took that detour.

Monday morning before she left for school, I asked Ashlee to once again thank Red for all the help. She told me she would, and asked if she could use my name in her paper for the wild events of the area. It would make a great story.

"Absolutely not," I replied. "Maybe in twenty or thirty years."

About 9:00 am, Bonnie knocked on my door and told me the porch repairmen were here to fix the porch. I almost forgot about it. I went downstairs and got a bag of ice for my ankle, and found a comfortable chair inside. There, I could observe the work and be handy if they had any problems and needed to talk to me.

By 2:00 pm, they were done. I hobbled out to the porch. It looked great. Now, all that was needed was a couple coats of paint.

As I was watching them pack up their tools, I heard the faint whistle of a freight train up at the crossing in town. A few minutes later, I watched it lumber by on the tracks.

It definitely brought back thoughts and memories of what might have been. I was really happy that I did not have to hike all the way back on the tracks. Ashlee might have heard a few words I had not spoken in a long time.

When Ashlee got back from school, she came looking for me, expecting to find me flat on the bed packed in ice. To her surprise, I was at my computer working on my homework, which had suffered somewhat over the weekend. I had an assignment due this week for my marketing class and I needed to wrap it up.

"Did you thank Red for me?" I asked.

"Yes! He was hoping you were feeling better. I told him to thank his father and Bob. I forgot to ask, what did you think about Bob?"

"You were right. If I was the one going for help, I'm not sure I would have gone near him or not. You were much braver than I would have been," I told her. "You think he sleeps in those clothes? I could still smell them for an hour after we headed to the hospital for x-rays."

"I know what you mean. It helped to have Red tell me about him beforehand. I'm still not sure exactly where he lives."

"Next time you see Red, ask him if there is anything we can get for Bob. He may have an idea of what he might appreciate. Perhaps a new jacket.

"Meanwhile, let's see if we can arrange a dinner for Red and his family perhaps next week if that's okay with you," I suggested to Ashlee.

"I think they earned one," I told my mother.

"Did you mention anything to your friends at school today?"

"No, I figured you got enough notice from our guests yesterday. However, Marine is a small town. I'd give it till – well perhaps three tomorrow afternoon before the rest of the town calls to see if you are okay."

"Thanks! I'll let you answer the phones."

Chapter 13

Giving Thanks

Fortunately, the entire town did not call to see how my ankle was the next couple of days. Yes, I did get a couple comments when I limped up the steps at the General Store using a cane. However, I survived the incident thanks to ice packs, ACE wraps and some help from Ashlee.

By Thursday evening, I was starting to walk with only a slight limp. Ashlee and I decided we would invite Red and his parents over for dinner on Monday night to show our appreciation for all they did. So far, the calendar was open for the Inn that evening and looking at our past history of customers on Mondays, we figured it would be our best opportunity. If we did get some customers, we could close the door to the dining room and put cookies out for them in the gathering room.

In all our rush and the confusion of the evening, I never did catch Red's mother's name, or if she even lived with them. I asked Ashlee to subtly ask Red some questions about his parents at school tomorrow, along with inviting them for dinner on Monday.

Friday, Ashlee met with Red and Dawn, nailing down the list of topics that were to be used for their paper. Now, they had two weeks to finish the paper. They had two options for the final topic just in case they ran into some problems with the story of the President's visit to Marine.

When she got home, Ashlee told me the latest scoop about Red and his family. She had picked up parts of the story from Red at school and the basics from Leslie on the ride to school.

"Well, Mom, here's what I found out today. Red's mother had died several years ago. Apparently, she had cancer. The last year of her life, Red lived with his grandfather, while his father and mother sought cures for her illness at several different clinics. Red was in grade school at the time.

"Red's grandfather lived somewhere along the river. He died a year later, after Red moved back with his father.

"I guess that's why he seems so introverted. Probably separated him from any friends he might have had in the area."

"Yes, I'm sure it affected him greatly," I replied. "It might explain his walking instead of getting a ride from his family. If his father works, Red might be used to doing things on his own.

"So, did you ask Red if he and his father could come for Monday?"

"He said he would ask him and get back to me tonight," Ashlee answered. "I feel sorry for him. All the kids calling him "Spider-Boy." It would be tough enough to lose your mother without kids making fun of you."

"Well, it sounds like you made him a good friend. Sometimes it's all you need – one good friend. How about Dawn. Has she mellowed in her opinion of Red?"

"Sort of! I'm not sure she likes anyone that might be close to her equal in knowledge. For now, we seem to be working fairly good as a group. We'll have to see after our paper is done how Dawn act towards all of us. Miracles do happen you know."

Later that evening Ashlee received a phone call from Red informing her that he and his father could come for supper. His father wanted to know if he could bring some bread.

I told her that would be fine.

I had a feeling that he wanted to contribute something to the dinner. Whether he brought homemade bread or picked it up at a bakery, it did not matter. It was his contribution to the meal.

The Inn was busy over the weekend. Ashlee spent hours working on a section of her paper along with her math homework. I was curious to see how they could blend their voices in the paper to make it sound like one storyteller.

Monday, I spent part of the afternoon cooking. I wanted to prepare a dinner that was fit for my rescuers. My foot was better and I made use of the extra mobility. My menu included a beef roast, green beans, and new potatoes. For dessert, an apple pie would finish off the meal. Fortunately, my mother had picked up several pies at the orchard at the end of the season and still had one in the freezer. I had picked it up from her over the weekend. I did not think anyone would mind if I hadn't fixed one from scratch.

As dinnertime approached, the Inn had the smell of a good restaurant. Too bad there weren't any guests to enjoy the splendid odors. Then again, they would have been upset that it was not prepared for them.

At 6:00 pm, just as the final chime rang on the wall clock, Red and his father Benson came to the door of the Inn. We welcomed them to the Inn, introducing Bonnie to our guests. Then, before showing them to the table, we offered to show Red's father the Inn. Although he had seen the Inn from the outside, he had not been inside before.

Benson was surprised to see how someone had modified the Inn. It was obvious that someone had made modifications to the rooms for modern conveniences. Private bathrooms and whirlpool baths were probably not standard to the house when it was built. Fortunately, the rooms had been big enough that they could be retrofitted easily.

After a brief tour, we settled in for dinner and hopefully some good conversation.

We had a wonderful dinner. After giving thanks to my rescuers, we enjoyed a perfectly prepared meal. The meat was moist and tender.

Red's father, Benson, told me that he was pleased to see that I had recovered from my injury. He had heard bits and pieces of the event and was wondering exactly what had happened.

I told him, "You know, I only know pieces myself. This might be a good time to hear things from all sides. I have a feeling we might get a good laugh at the sequence of events."

As a result, before we had dessert, we tried to put all the missing parts of the story together. I had to admit, now that I was not lying on the ground in pain, it was definitely more interesting.

Ashlee started it out by telling Benson that in doing the research for their paper for school, she and Red had discussed a freight train wreck that had happened years ago down by the State Park.

"You see, a storm had washed out a beaver dam and the resulting water flow washed out the culvert that ran under the tracks. As a train approached, the engine derailed sending it nose first into a pond. It had to be removed by cutting the huge diesel engine up into parts to get it out.

"My mother had suggested that she needed to go for a walk and I suggested that we hike down the tracks to see where it happened."

"I remember hearing about that one years ago," he mentioned. "As I recall, they were lucky and no one was killed in the wreck. It did shut down the tracks for a few days until they repaired the damage. Did you ever find the spot where it happened?"

"Well, Ashlee and I put on our hiking boots and trudged down the tracks looking for the spot. I think we found it. Unfortunately, no one left a sign saying this is it. We must have been a mile and a half down the tracks from here.

"It was a good walk until all of a sudden, out of nowhere, a bunch of wild turkeys came flying right at us. As I ducked, my foot caught an old cable near the ties and before I knew it, I was flat on my back lying on the railroad ties."

"She was really hurting," Ashlee told them, "and I tried to move her off the tracks. I think both of us were worried that the afternoon freight had not come through that day.

"After trying to determine if she broke her foot or not, I managed to help her off the tracks and into the ditch. Then, we realized she was not going to be able to walk back to the B&B."

"I picked a good spot to twist my foot. Not a house or road in sight. I had to convince Ashlee that she needed to hike back to the Inn and call for help.

"It was getting late and it was a long walk. As she was almost out of sight, I saw this person, dressed in sloppy clothes, ahead of her on the tracks. She was so far away, I couldn't warn her or get her attention. I was starting to panic."

"That's a good description of Bob," Red stated.

"Good thing we talked about him a couple times," Ashlee told Red. "How old is he?"

Benson just laughed. "Oh, I suspect Bob is about fifty something. He still looks the same as when I first spotted him over thirty years ago. I'm surprised you talked to him, and even more-so that he approached you."

"So, what did he say to you?" Ashlee asked Red.

"Well, first of all, it took five minutes before I got a word out of him. He must have run all the way from the tracks to our place. He was so winded, I thought he was going to pass out.

"Anyway, he told me that the girl's mother, the one who lived at the B&B, hurt her leg and I needed to get help.

"By the time he got all of that out of his mouth, my father came by wondering what all the hassle was all about. It took another ten minutes to finally get the whole story from him."

"Red figured he could borrow the four-wheeler from our neighbor and go get you while I waited at the crossing in town," Benson added.

Red told us, "Yeah, but the neighbor wasn't home and the keys for the four-wheeler weren't where he normally kept them. He collects all kinds of old railroad stuff in his barn. I remembered that he had this old railroad sidecar in the barn. So, we went back and got the pickup and took the sidecar out of the barn."

"Then, we took it down to the tracks along with the warning device our neighbor had shown me. I knew he had it on the shelf. After we set the charge, we headed down the tracks to find you."

"I sat in the van with the lights flashing just in case a train came from the south and the warning device didn't go off," Benson told us.

"So, you see it was a piece of cake," Red told us. "Well, that was until the neighbor came back home early. We didn't leave a note. He walked into the barn and saw his prize 1919 Sheffield Linesman Cart missing and almost had a kitten.

"You know, they are pretty rare, and this one is in great condition. The carts were made to be adjustable so that they could be used on narrow and regular gauge railroads. A lineman could follow the wires next to the tracks and fix any problems they found. There was an area that a ladder could be placed next to the linemen. I took the ladder off when I borrowed it so there would be room for the two of you on the platform.

"Anyway, he was all set to call the Sheriff, when he spotted my hat. I had accidentally dropped it when we were carrying the cart.

"Then he saw the tire marks outside. The tires were bald in back, just like my father's truck.

"After wondering why I took the ladder off the sidecar, he put two and two together and tried calling our place. Later that evening, when Bob and I brought it back, he was calling our place again. I wasn't sure if he was happy to see us or waiting to lynch us on the spot.

"He was really ticked. He just kept looking at Bob wondering how he fit into everything.

"He also knew that I was one of the few people that knew where the key to the barn was kept. So, I guess he knew where the cart was. He just couldn't figure out why we took it.

"Also, we forgot to relock the door. He wasn't too happy about that one either.

"When we explained everything, he wasn't quite as angry. I told him to leave the key to the four-wheeler in sight next time."

"So, he's okay with your heist?" I asked Red.

"As long as I don't do it again," he answered. "Well, he did ask that I spend a couple days helping him move things in the barn. I guess I earned that one."

"Why didn't you drive the pickup down the tracks?" Ashlee asked.

"Good question," Benson told Ashlee. "Remember, Red told you it had bald tires in back. It would have blown a tire on those rocks before we got down to where you were. On top of that, riding in the bed of that two-ton truck, on that railroad bed, would have bounced you right off the truck. You might have gotten a broken arm trying to catch yourself back there.

"No, Red was right. The cart was the best choice," Benson told us.

"Well, I'm just glad everything worked the way it did," I told them. "I was waiting for the whole fire department to come down the tracks for Ashlee and me. I'm not sure I could have lived this one down. I want to thank all of you for the help."

We laughed at the thought of the rescue squads coming down the rail bed.

As I brought out the ice cream and apple pie for dessert, I asked Red and his father if there was anything I could do for Bob, and for their neighbor for all the help they knowingly or unknowingly contributed.

"Well, our neighbor is pretty quiet and reserved. I think a personal thank you would go a long way with him. As for Bob, we've given him things in the past. Somehow, we never see them again. I'm not sure if he gives them away or what happens," Benson told us. "You see, there are a lot of bums that walk the tracks. I think he gives away things he feels he doesn't need. For years, they used to have a hobo reunion under the tracks at the bridge at the State Park."

"Was he one of them," Ashlee asked.

"No. He just lives like a hermit and does his own thing. He's done it for years out there, no electricity and no phone. He just watches what's going on in the area.

"Fortunately for you, he was watching the tracks that day. You were lucky," Benson told us.

After dessert, our discussions turned to the paper Red and Ashlee were writing.

"So you are going to put a section in the paper about President Hoover coming to Marine? How'd that come up?" Benson asked.

"We saw it at the museum," Ashlee told him. "Also, Red said that his grandfather saw him. Did you know anything about it?"

"Not really. That was Red's grandfather on his mother's side. Even though I've lived here for years, I've spent a lot of time traveling. I guess I'm not a lot of help on the local history. Too bad his grandfather isn't still alive. He seemed to know everything about the area. Red, do you still have his books?"

"Yes, I've been reading some of his notes every evening. There's a lot of information in those that the museum doesn't have."

"Good! I'll have to read your paper when it is done," he told Red. "Have you checked out the William Edgar residence?"

"Not yet. That's on the list," he told him.

"Well, we need to thank you for the dinner and get moving. I've got a meeting in Minneapolis tomorrow morning and I have to put some drafts together before then," Benson told us.

It had been a fun evening. I thanked them once again for the rescue and told them I would be looking forward to seeing them in town.

As they left, Ashlee turned and told me, "Now I think I know the other side of Red's personality. It probably explains why he talks to Bob."

"I think you are right. So what is the William Edgar residence? I think I have heard that name a couple times this week?"

"Red's working on it. He asked me to go over there sometime after school. He said his grandfather had a whole notebook about the place. I'll let you know what we find."

Chapter 14

Information Gathering

Tuesday was one of those days that you wish you didn't have to have.

I was trying to check over the Bed & Breakfast's books before meeting Jason Willard at the end of the week, while at the same time I was trying to finish a project for school. Right in the middle of everything, I got a phone call.

It was the county inspector. He was in the area and wanted to do his yearly inspection of the Bed and Breakfast later this afternoon. What timing. How do they know when we are too busy for routine inspections?

As a result, we instantly dropped everything we were doing and made our own inspection of the B&B prior to the inspector's arrival. The kitchen was our primary concern. Cleaning behind the stove, refrigerator, etc., had to be checked. We also made a quick check of the temperatures of the refrigerator and freezer. The last thing we wanted was a problem with our food service area.

After our two-hour whirlwind, we thought we were set to go. Now, it was just a matter of waiting for the inspector to arrive.

About 3:30 pm, the inspector arrived.

Upon his arrival, he introduced himself to Jean and me. I was glad to see that the inspector was not a new hire. He had been in the business for years and had inspected the Inn for the past ten years.

He told me that he thought it would take about an hour for the inspection. If there were any problems, he would show them to us before leaving.

While I was talking to the inspector, Red and Ashlee went over to check out the old William Edgar residence. I told them to call me when they were done and I would give them a ride back.

Just as I expected, a large part of the inspector's time was spent in the food area. Since this was my first official inspection as manager, I followed the inspector closely watching to see which areas he paid attention to. Cleanliness and maintaining proper food temperatures were critical. He had his checklist, and checked off each item one by one.

Jean had gone through it several times and I was glad that she had inspected many of the places the inspector was looking.

The kitchen passed inspection. I was surprised to hear the inspector ask both of us if we ever allowed customers in the kitchen area. We had a sign on the door informing our customers that they could not enter the kitchen, however, he wanted to drum it in that they were not allowed.

After the kitchen, he inspected the rooms. I figured that he would look for bugs, especially bed bugs. To my surprise, he was concerned with the screens on the windows. He told me that 90% of all bugs come through the windows. As a result, this was one of his critical inspection areas. If he spotted a problem, the customer would have a limited amount of time to replace the window.

Once again, fortunately, we passed.

The only caution he gave us was for the bathtubs in the rooms. The state had come up with an improved suggestion for sanitation of the recirculating system in the tub and he recommended that we change our cleaning materials.

If that was the only problem he could find, I was relieved. I didn't want to have to tell Jason Willard that we had numerous problems at our meeting on Friday.

Finally, he gave me a written copy of the inspection record, told me that he enjoyed meeting me and said he would be back next year.

With that, he was done for the day.

Ashlee

On the way to school Tuesday morning, I mentioned to Leslie that I was curious about the William Edgar house. We were going to mention it in our paper and we keep hearing rumors about it.

Leslie's mother mentioned that she knew the owners. "The house is being sold and if you want to see it, this might be a great time to do it. I can call the owners and see if you can talk to them."

Who was I to pass up an opportunity like that? "Sure! Can you send me a text message to let me know if we could stop over there today or tomorrow?" I asked her.

"Sure!"

Just before second hour, I got a text message from Leslie's mother. "Visit approved for today after school. They will be waiting for you."

Red and I had met with Dawn during lunch at school and went over the progress each of us had made on the report.

Dawn had her part almost done. Since most of it came straight from history reports in books and the museum, it was just a matter of trimming it slightly to keep the size in line with the other parts of the paper. She gave both Red and me a copy to look at and give her some feedback by the end of the week.

Red gave us a hint of his discoveries on the section about President Hoover's visit. He had gone through his grandfather's notebooks and found a number of interesting notes in them regarding the visit. Combining them with the information from the museum, he felt he had a solid story. Dawn and I agreed.

I told him that my friend's mother knew the current owners of the property. She told me they were in the process of selling it. When I told her you wanted to get a look at the property, she told me that she would call them this morning.

"As a result of her phone call, she set up a meeting for us to meet with the owners after school if you are available. We could ask them the questions we might not be able to find other places."

Red looked at me in surprise. "Sure, let's go."

Red wanted to make sure I could go with him to look at the William Edgar property after school. Since he did not know them, he felt awkward just going over there. He told me that many of the aspects of the property needed visualization to get the full understanding.

He was hoping to take some pictures that we could include in the report. My being with him would give him a second eye as to which pictures would show the concept the best.

I told him I could, if he helped me with my last segment. We could talk about that one later this afternoon.

After school, Red and his father picked me up at the Inn and his father dropped us off at the old William Edgar house. I still wondered what Red's father meant when he said the house had a lot of history. Then again, why did the President of the United States come and pay a visit to Marine? This wasn't exactly the hotbed of entertainment and it would have been a long way from civilization back then.

The house did not appear to be anything exceptional. Located almost a mile from the river, up on the west hill just before the railroad tracks, it appeared to be a nice house. It was a white, two-story house with a porch and a white picket fence around the yard. Out back, there appeared to be a garage and a small cabin next to the woods. They had just slightly over eight acres of land. Why would a President come here?

Red's whole concept was to be written around proof that President Hoover made a historic visit to Marine before running for President. He had found some proof from the museum and from his grandfather's notebook. It was an interesting fact, but my question was still why? If he could put the "why" into the paper, it would make the report much more substantial.

Somehow, I kept feeling that Red was holding back something additional that he knew about the subject. What else had he found?

When we knocked at the door, Cynthia Jepsen and Fred Hundt met us. They were pleased to hear that we were writing a paper about Marine and invited us in. It didn't take long to feel comfortable talking to them. Even Red started to relax.

They told us they were selling the house and this was a great time to see it before a new owner moved in.

"I am trying to write a segment on President Hoover's visit," Red told them. "I've found a couple articles at the museum; however, I understand you have some knowledge of the visit."

"Well, if it is proof you are looking for, I can show you his signature on the fireplace," Fred told him.

He took us to the fireside room. There, written very lightly in pencil was indeed Herbert Hoover's signature. "Is that what you are looking for?" he asked. "You realize, he wasn't President at that time."

"Wow! Yes, that is definitely what I was looking for. I had no idea that he had signed the stones. Do you know why he came here?" Red asked. "My grandfather had written in his notebook that he saw Herbert Hoover when he arrived in town."

"Well, we are only one of many owners of the property. The Kavanagh's owned it before us. However, I think it will always be known as the William Edgar house. Do you know anything about William Edgar?" Cynthia asked.

"I don't believe I've ever heard of him," I told her.

"Fred, can you get a copy of the book you had published about Edgar. I think it will provide some of the background they need, to understand William Edgar."

He brought back a small paperback book about Five Essays that William C. Edgar wrote. We looked through it as Cynthia and Fred told us the story of William Edgar.

You are aware that Marine started with a sawmill on the large stream that ran through town. Later, in 1858, they built the Gaskill Grain Mill further up the stream. It lasted for many years.

Many people only think of lumber when they think of the history of the St. Croix Valley. However, there were many areas just over the hills where grains were harvested.

Apparently, William Edgar was at the heart of the grain industry in Minneapolis. He wrote a weekly trade journal that was the hub of the industry – the Northwestern Miller, from the 1880's until 1924. It told about the major industrial players, equipment, and industry news. The journal's information was read in Washington DC., and all over the world. You have to remember, at that point in history, Minneapolis was the center of grain milling for the US, and for all reality, the whole world.

Sometime around the 1920's William Edgar fell in love with the Marine area. At first, he would come out for a weekend. Then, as his love for the property grew, he built his house and moved to Marine with his wife. I think he was planning for his retirement.

"So, what made him come here?" Red asked.

They explained that it was the trout fishing in the small streams. It drew many of the wealthy from Minneapolis to the area. The small stream that flows next to the little cabin in the yard was his favorite spot. He loved to sit in there and write. His Five Essays were a tribute to his love of the area; the streams and getting out of the city. As a joke, he built a miniature grain mill on the stream and claimed in his articles it produced the finest grain in the area. The mill was called the Fish River Roller Mill and had sacks of flour, Fetchit's Pride – the finest baking flour in the state, stacked next to it.

Red commented, "When I was reading my grandfather's notebook, he mentioned a number of trout streams my grandfather liked to fish. I remember seeing a couple pictures at the museum from 1904, with people with a long stringer of fish. Was fishing really that popular back then?"

Cynthia told him, "If you look, you can find articles in the papers from out east talking about spectacular trout fishing in the area. One of those writers wrote from Minneapolis. Plus, there were a couple of other authors that lived in the Marine area that wrote about exploring the north country and about the history of the area. If you check, you might run into names like John Dunn, Calvin Runtstrum. Even F. Scott Fitzgerald and Sinclair Lewis stayed in the area a couple times.

"Apparently, there was a great deal of interest back then about our area. The scenic St. Croix River, and the streams that flowed into it were a magnet for the wealthy people that wanted to escape the heat of the cities in the summer.

"From what we know, Hoover was up here to catch trout. When he didn't have any luck, he stopped to visit an old friend – William Edgar. He found the trout fishing fantastic. He took some back with him to Chicago on his train car."

"Was that parked at the station siding?" Red asked.

"Yes, I believe so," Cynthia answered.

I could see in Red's eyes that he had hit pay dirt. Somehow, he had confirmed the rumors he had heard and started to put the pieces of the puzzle together from what he was now hearing. The question was; what did Red know? It had to be a lot more than what we had just been told. Something had just connected the dots in his memory. I decided to wait and ask later.

We walked out in the yard and Red took some photos of the house, the creek, and the little cabin sitting next to the babbling stream where William Edgar sat and wrote his journals and messages. It was just a small creek. However, back in the 1920's, it contained his precious trout.

We finished taking pictures just before the sun started ducking behind the hillside. Then, we thanked our hosts for the information. They told us to come back if we needed any additional information.

As we left the house, I sent a text message to my mother that we were ready to be picked up and started walking down the road in the direction she would be coming from.

While we were walking, I asked Red if he would do me a favor. I asked if he would help with the perspective of the high bridge article and let me use a couple of his pictures. I wanted to make sure the parts of my report were as accurate as possible.

Red laughed. "Sounds good. I think we need to get together Saturday morning to go over the information we have on our parts of the paper. Then, Dawn will need to make sure her material and ours appear to come together into one article.

As my mother's car approached, I asked Red, "Did you figure out something I don't know from that visit?"

"We can discuss it Saturday. You got your article finished?"

"We'll see on Saturday. Wouldn't want to spill the beans ahead of time." I said with a twinkle in my eye and a quick smile.

Two could play that game.

We took Red back to his house. On the way, we passed the house of his neighbor that had the railroad collection. He pointed it out to us as we passed by. It reminded my mother that she was going to stop over there this week and thank the owner for the unapproved usage of the railroad cart.

As we approached Red's house, I asked him, "Red, I forgot to ask you, how did you get your father to agree to your driving the pickup? You're not 16 yet."

Red laughed. "Long story. The pickup was my mother's. She used it for hauling some horses we used to have, along with hay and other things they needed. When she died, my father put it in the shed. We rarely use it, that's why he hasn't put new tires on it. I'm surprised he puts up-to-date license tabs on it.

"Anyway, we rent out most of our land. My father just doesn't have the time or interest in farming. However, the person that is leasing our land needs help every once and a while.

"I talked my father into letting me apply for a farm license so I could help him move his equipment in and out of our land. My father doesn't let me use the truck for anything else. In fact, I rarely drive. I usually walk.

"I guess your accident qualified for the truck coming out of the shed."

After dropping Red off at his house, we headed back to the Inn.

On the way, I told my mother that Red and I were going to get together on Saturday to rough out our parts of the paper. Then, we would meet with Dawn to blend all the sections together.

Chapter 15

Writing

Maria

I was glad that we took Red back to his house yesterday. It gave me the opportunity to see where Red borrowed the rail car. I decided that I would pick up something today when I went to Stillwater for groceries. Hopefully, I could find something that his neighbor would appreciate. Not knowing anything about the man, I wasn't sure what to pick up.

I picked up a card, some flowers, and a lemon meringue pie. Hopefully, the thought would count.

I dropped them off at his house after dropping our groceries at the Inn. He was a little on the quiet side, but he seem like a nice man, and he thanked me for the thought. I wasn't sure if he was still upset or not. At least at the moment, he was putting on a pleasant face. He told me that he was glad to see that I was walking okay.

On the way home, I got to thinking about the people I had met in the past month in Marine. Many of them had complex personalities and without knowing anything about their backgrounds, several of them were difficult to understand. Bob being the farthest from the norm. I still had to get something for him.

When I arrived back at the Inn, I started working on the financials of the Inn for my meeting with Jason Willard on Friday.

So far, we appeared to be right on target and I wanted to impress him that I was keeping good records.

Friday came quickly. Jason and I had our third update meeting. It went okay, though, it seemed that he was more concerned with how my foot and ankle were, than inspecting the financial records. Somehow, he had heard through the grapevine all about my fiasco.

He told me to call him the next time I had a physical problem. He could have gotten help much quicker. I told him I appreciated the offer. However, he probably could not have provided all the excitement we had experienced in my rescue. Besides, not expecting anything greater than a walk, we had left our phones at the Inn.

Going over the Inn's books, we were ahead of a year ago. That was a good sign. Expenses were limited and future guest reservations were up. Jason was glad to hear the possible roof leak turned out to be a minor support repair. He told me that he liked the changes I had made to the website. I had added some updated photographs of the rooms and showed some pictures of the typical breakfasts.

As our meeting was breaking up, he asked me how Ashlee's paper was coming.

"You know about that too," I asked. "I really need to do some staff training. There must be a serious leak somewhere.

"I think they are hoping to have it done by the end of next week. Right now, I'm trying real hard to stay out of the extreme episodes. Jason, there's still time for you to do something to qualify, and I'm sure they would love to add it to their report."

Jason laughed. "I suppose I could get one of those large rubber ducks and sit on it in the pond, down in the park. Think that would get a laugh?"

"Almost as much as twisting my ankle," I told him.

We agreed to meet the end of the next month. Things were going so well that he didn't think we would need to meet before then unless an emergency came up.

Ashlee was back from school and was holed up in her room by the time I had a chance to pay her some attention.

Entering her bedroom, I asked, "How's it going?"

"I'm working on my article for the high bridge train fire. I've got all my notes. Now I'm just trying to invent some dialog that would make it sound a little more exciting."

"Want me to take a look at it?" I asked.

"Maybe after dinner. I'll let you find the stupid mistakes before Red looks at it tomorrow and laughs. I have a feeling he is a much better writer than I am. If he can write poetry, he is probably better with grammar than I am. I'm really not looking forward to meeting with Dawn next week to blend it into one paper. Think she will want to take control again?"

"I think the two of you were smart giving her the historical background of the town. You are going to have to work with her to blend in the old log cabin article with the origins of the mills and territory. Are you finishing that part or Red?"

"Red wanted me to clean up his draft of it. He told me that he wanted to spend more time on the Hoover visit. It's taking a lot more effort to get the research right."

"Well, here's a suggestion. If you set up the history of the cabin to refer to Dawn's writings, I think you'll be able to work together easier.

"Let me know when you would like to have me look it over."

I left Ashlee alone to work through her thoughts. Actually, I was dying to see the final paper. So far, it sounded exciting to me. I just hoped their teacher appreciated the work that the group had done in putting it together.

Ashlee

I was starting to get nervous about our paper. It needed to look as though we worked together as a team. I wasn't sure what our teacher would say when we told her we divided it into three section, each one of us working separately to draft our section.

Also, I really did feel like I wanted my mother's opinion before Red looked at it. If she told me it was good, I could breathe easier.

We still had the time to get it right. If we edited the paper next week, it wasn't due until the Monday the following week. Hopefully, we would not have to spend the next weekend as well on re-writes.

I finished the history of the old log cabin article, listing Mary Smith as a contributor to the story. Now, I could attempt to put the finishing parts on all the notes that went into the story about the bridge fire.

Before I started, I looked at the photo of the bridge Red had given me at school. Whoa, you wouldn't catch me out on that bridge. Two hundred feet over the river. And at night! No way!

After thinking about it for fifteen minutes, I decided to write the fire article from the eyes of the firemen. It would make it sound more exciting.

It was a quiet evening when the call came into the New Richmond Fire Department. There was a report of a fire on the railroad high bridge. A boxcar was on fire. It put the fear in the hearts of the firemen as they assembled to head to the bridge.

From there, I wrote about how on arriving at the bridge, they saw a train car on fire out on the bridge. It had been detached from the rest of the train and the engine was stopped over on the Minnesota side of the bridge. No one was out on the bridge.

Apparently, the car had a hot box on the axle, and the resulting heat caused the grease and wood to catch fire.

Looking over the scene, it was obvious that they did not have any hoses long enough to reach out on the half-mile long bridge to put the fire out. They tried approaching it from below. Too high. The water pressure in the hoses could not reach the top of the bridge.

Finally, in desperation, they called the Marine Fire Department for assistance. The car could burn itself out. However, if it got too hot, the extreme heat might damage the bridge. That would be a serious problem. This was a working bridge. Steel girder replacement might take the tracks out of use for months.

When the Marine Fire Department arrived, the fire had spread to the top of the boxcar. Once again, it was too far out to reach with hoses. Pulling water from the river in buckets would have been a futile effort as well.

As they walked out to the burning car, the firemen could smell the sickening smell of their rubber boots melting as they touched the hot rails. "Get off the rails," the fire chief told his men. The fire needed to be put out quickly before the wood ties caught fire and the entire structure had permanent damage.

Finally, a decision was made. The Marine Fire Department would work from the top of the bridge and the New Richmond Department would work from the river's edge.

A rope was lowered from the bridge and a fire hose from the New Richmond pumper was pulled up. The pumper could draw water from the river. Then, with a great deal of strength and concern with the weight of the water in the hose and the pressure that would be exerted by the nozzle, they sprayed the car until the fire was out. It worked. No one lost their balance and fell off the bridge.

The bridge was saved.

My draft was done. Just in time for dinner.

I was glad. I needed the break.

After dinner, it was back to the writing.

Okay, that was the rough draft. Now I needed to go back and put some emotion and action statements into the article:

As the firemen approached the bridge, a full moon rising over the hills silhouetted the huge bridge over the river. Even with the moonlight, the half-mile long bridge looked like it went on forever. The tracks were aglow with the reflections from the fire as if a train's light was shining down the tracks. When they approached the bridge, they stopped short, looking at the danger of being high over the river. Cautiously, they wandered out to assess the situation. As the firemen walked out on the tracks, they could smell rubber burning from the soles of their fire boots. Don't touch the hot rails, they shouted to each other. They knew the rails were so hot that they wouldn't feel the heat melting their boots until it was too late to keep the molten rubber from severely burning their feet.

"Good start!" I told myself. "That put a little life into the article." Now, I went through the rest of the dangling notes on my page that I had drafted from Bert Hudson, putting in the action phrases wherever I could, without changing the actual story.

When I was finished, it sounded like a story told by the firemen, just what I was hoping for.

Now, it was ready for its first test. I asked my mother to look it over and see what she thought.

"Ashlee, I'm impressed. I think you did a very good job on both of these articles. What made you use two different styles of writing?" she asked.

"Well, the first article is more historical, a tell it like it is story. First person wouldn't work. The second article needed the dramatics. That's why I put it in the firemen's voice. Did it work okay for you?" I asked.

"Yes. Hopefully, your other writers will agree also. I'm sure most of the class's papers will be written in one voice only."

"Well, Red is coming over tomorrow around 10:00 am if that's okay. Also, is it okay if he has some lunch with us?"

"Absolutely. I'll try to stay out of the way," she told me.

As my mother left to do some work, I breathed a sigh of relief. Finished. Just in time. I wondered how Red was doing with his article. My guess was that it was not going to be one or two pages.

Chapter 16

War Preparations

Ashlee

The next morning, Red showed up at the Inn right on time. His father had given him a ride instead of having him walk. As Red walked in the door, I noticed that he had an old notebook along with a laptop.

We went off to the kitchen table in our apartment to compare writings. I didn't want to bother any guests of the B&B.

My mother greeted Red as he came into the apartment. "Good morning Red. I hear you are here to tell us an interesting story."

"Well, when we are done, I hope we'll all say we like it," he told us.

My mother went off to work in the Inn, leaving the area for us to spread out our papers.

"So, did you finish?" I asked him

"Like I said, you show me what you have, and I'll show you my writing."

I laughed. "OK, just don't laugh too loud."

I gave him the two articles for him to read. It didn't take very long. When he was finished reading, he told me, "You wrote the second one in the voice of a fireman. Did you talk to Dawn about that? Good idea. I like it."

I took a deep breath and thanked him. I had been nervous about what he might think of the article.

"Any changes you think I should make to the draft?" I asked.

"Just leave it as it is," he told me. I don't see anything you need to change. I think you did a good job."

Now, I was beaming inside with pleasure. I had a hard time keeping from showing my emotions. He actually told me I did a good job. I'll bet Dawn won't say that. I wondered what she would say about using the voice of the firemen.

"Okay, your turn. Show me the story you have been working on. You better have some good information that you kept hidden from me."

Red laid down the notebook along with pulling up his article on his laptop.

"Sorry, I didn't print it out. I figured it would be easier this way, just in case we needed to move some of the paragraphs around. There is so much information, I wasn't sure which part I should tell first. I might need help editing it before our teacher sees how long it is."

Red told me the story behind his research before I started to read his article.

"Well, I started with two separate articles, and by the time I was done with my research, it sort of blended into one story.

"It is interesting that only a few people in the area know about President Herbert Hoover visiting Marine on the St. Croix. The book by William Edgar – Five Essays, dropped the hint it was to see his old friend and go fishing. I think there was a lot more to the story. I hope everyone will be impressed when they hear our report.

"The story really has to begin with William Edgar. He is just as important to the story as Hoover. So, I jumped to his story first.

"William Edgar was the editor and president of a weekly journal called the Northwestern Miller in Minneapolis. He became the editor of the trade journal in 1886. With Minneapolis being the center of world trade in grains, this magazine was the who's who in the industry. He didn't move to Marine until 1920.

"So, the question everyone will want to ask, why was he important?

"In 1891, he organized shipments of American flour to Russian peasants. Under his supervision, the collection, shipment, and distribution of the flour made sure the relief shipments made it to the peasants that needed the relief.

"He received an award from the Russian Emperor for his efforts.

"In 1914, he was called upon once again to direct American relief efforts to Belgians. The Germans had invaded and their crops were ruined.

"We tend to forget that Minneapolis was indeed the center of US milling during those years and we supplied much of the world flour and grains during times of poor harvests and war.

"As World War I was breaking out, Edgar assisted a man in Washington DC. named Herbert Hoover, who was the Food Administrator for the United States. Their task was to improve the US's organization, regulations, and methods of directing the milling industry during wartime. It was imperative that the United States be able to assist Europe and provide timely shipments of aid.

"For all William Edgar's assistance to Europe and especially Brussels, he was awarded a bronze medallion in recognition of his relief work from the Belgian government.

"However, it was his contacts with Herbert Hoover that were becoming cemented into a firm friendship at the time.

"Edgar continued publishing his trade journal until he retired in 1924. He became a very well-known man in Europe as well as in Minneapolis. In fact, there is a museum named after him in Brussels."

"So, is that the same William Edgar that owned the white house on the hill that Hoover is said to have visited?" I asked Red. "How come there isn't a sign about him in front of the house?"

"I don't know. Maybe he kept things quiet once he moved here. Anyway, let's get back to the story.

"Did you know that President Hoover was only elected to public office once in his whole life?

"His story is almost as interesting as William Edgar, and it seems that people around here know almost as much about his early days as William Edgar's.

"I did some research on him including checking on him at his presidential library in Iowa to make sure our facts are correct.

"Here's another little-known fact. In 1914, when the war broke out in Europe that led to World War I, many Americans were stranded over there. Hoover's wife – Lou, organized a relief organization to supply clothing, lodging, and food. You see, it wasn't just Herbert that was involved in the war effort. Both of them provided important leadership in helping with the war effort.

"With all his efforts, Herbert Hoover was appointed by President Woodrow Wilson to become U.S. Food Administrator on May 5, 1917.

"Both political parties wanted him to run for President in 1920. However, Hoover declined.

"He was later appointed Secretary of Commerce on March 5, 1921, under President Warren Harding's administration. It was a title he continued to hold under the two-term President Calvin Coolidge administration as well, until Hoover resigned the office on August 21, 1928."

"Okay, both men were important, but what does that have to do with the town of Marine?" I asked.

"Patience, without the background, the importance of his visit here gets overlooked," Red told me.

"Now, where did I leave off? Oh, yes, I remember.

"Since both of these people were not full-time politicians, they were involved in many activities.

"Herbert Hoover was involved in the Izaac Walton League when it was formed in 1922. He served as an unofficial president for some time. The League was involved in maintaining rivers and streams for fishing.

"On the other side, William Edgar's wife, Marjorine, was highly involved in the Girl Scouts. She played a leadership role in establishing the Girl Scouts in Minnesota and attended national conventions with other leaders from Minnesota.

"Coincidentally, during the 1920's, Lou Hoover was also involved in the Girl Scout Council in Washington DC. as well as advancing women's athletics. She served two terms as the Girl Scouts of America president, once in the 1920's and once in the 1930's. It was during her second term that the concept of selling Girl Scout cookies was approved.

"With the men becoming friends earlier with their war efforts and bringing food to war-torn Europe, the women renewed that friendship over their work on the behalf of the Girl Scouts. In fact, I found a letter written by the Girl Scouts mentioned both Herbert Hoover's and William Edgar's wifes, thanking them for their efforts.

"These two families had become entwined in many circles over the twenty or so years of working together."

"Alright, I understand there was a connection, but how does that lead to a link between them and why do you think Hoover was in Marine?" I asked again.

"You really don't like waiting for the answers. You should have written this section. It took me two weeks just to figure out when the event happened.

"It all starts with the presidential race of 1919. The run for the presidency in 1920 found both parties looking for candidates. Both wanted Herbert Hoover to run for them. Hoover declined, and was once again reappointed Secretary of Commerce by the newly elected Republican President – Calvin Coolidge. With Coolidge winning reelection, it gave Hoover a total of eight years to consider running for president.

"Politics is a strange mixture of promises, shoe polishing, and greasing the skids. It's amazing that anything positive actually happens from our political leaders.

"A glimpse of the two years before Herbert Hoover was elected president will convince you of that fact."

Chapter 17

The Sport of Presidents

Red continued his story about the research he had done on Herbert Hoover.

"Over the years, Presidents had a way of escaping from Washington DC. during the summer months. I guess I can't blame them. Before air-conditioning, it was probably rather hot and sticky on the east coast, not including the hot air of politics. Even Congress shut down over the summer.

"President Coolidge had been trying to encourage Herbert Hoover to run for the Republican Party in the 1928 election. The two had met and discussed it several times.

"For Hoover, it was untested ground. He had never run for any office. He had no background in the politics it would take to be elected, not to mention the fundraising he would need to do. It was one thing to raise support from the political leaders. It was a totally different thing to raise support of the industrial leaders of the country. Without both, he would probably fail.

"I looked through several books and called the State Historical Society to find out when Hoover was in Marine. Even after calling Hoover's Presidential Library in Iowa, I could find no evidence of a visit to Marine by Hoover. I was starting to think we had picked a topic that was beyond our capability to resolve. Why weren't there any records? Then I started checking his speaking engagements looking for something in Minneapolis or St. Paul. That's where I found the clue. There were three meetings around that time. Two were in the winter months.

"From what I was able to find in the files of the Historical Society and from Hoover's Presidential Library, Herbert Hoover made a speaking stop in Minneapolis and St. Paul on or about July 20th, 1926. It was a low-key effort to drum up support for a possible run at the presidency. With his long record of Secretary of Commerce, he knew many of the leaders of the milling industry in Minneapolis. He was hoping their connections with other industrial leaders would lead to their endorsement of him for President in 1929, if he ran.

"President Coolidge had been telling people all along that he would not run again and tried to convince Hoover to throw his hat in the ring. President Coolidge's biggest fear was that the 1928 nominating convention would draft him into running for a third term as president. As a result, he sent representatives to the convention to make sure they did not draft him for another term.

"The meetings appeared to be a success. His old friends encouraged him to run for office.

"However, in an effort of putting the icing on the cake, he decided to call on another of his old friends – William Edgar, to ask him for his advice and to sound him out as a possible cheerleader for his cause.

"He took a day off after his meetings to go fishing. I'm not sure exactly where, but my guess is that it was with some of the prominent people in the area. Many of the rich people in Minneapolis had summer cabins in the Marine area. These people were always bragging about the excellent trout fishing in the area and if they could convince a prominent politician to visit their cabin, it would give them bragging rights with their friends for at least a year or two.

"At the same time he accepted their invitation, he left word with his old friend William Edgar that he would like to stop in Marine to see him on the way back to St. Paul.

"This is where things are a little sketchy.

"If you read William Edgar's book, Hoover stopped to go fishing and have dinner with him after not catching anything all day. He went on to talk about how Hoover enjoyed the fishing so much that it didn't matter if his flies or catch ended up in the branches of the trees lining the stream or not. He wanted to fish until he was forced to leave to catch his train.

"I think William Edgar had a deep sense of humor when he wasn't writing for the milling industry trade journal.

"An example of this might be the flour mill located on Edgar's property. According to his book, it produced the finest flour in the area for baking.

"Well, the stream had little if any milling power and was only a few inches deep. In reality, what he had bragged about in his essays was a miniature flourmill placed on the stream for his personal enjoyment of making fun of it to his high power milling friends in Minneapolis. It was from this mill, which he called the Fish River Roller Mill, that he had sacks of flour stacked up labeled Fetchit's Pride.

"So, the question is, did Herbert Hoover stop to go fishing in William Edgar's stream?

"One thing for certain, Hoover was definitely in Marine. There is a picture of his railcar on the siding in town, at the museum. However, that's almost all the proof I found about his visit at the museum.

"There is a signature on William Edgar's fireplace rocks by Herbert Hoover that looks authentic. But, no one in town seems to have taken pictures.

"Then, I talked to Bob."

"Don't tell me he was there in 1926," I interjected.

"No, he's not that old. However, he did tell me that he had heard that my grandfather had played a part in the stop. Remember me mentioning that my grandfather was in the cattle tunnel, under the rails, when Hoover came to town? I always wondered how he knew to be there. Was it pure luck?

"I'm sure the stop was not announced ahead of time. There would have been a whole town full of people there to see him, perhaps as many as twenty-five people.

"According to Bob, it was my grandfather's job to make sure Hoover caught some fish. He spent two days catching fish from some of the better trout streams in the area, and "enhanced" the stocking of the stream at Edgar's property. It was legal back then. If you read Edgar's book, he even tells how the ice on his stream took out the trout one year.

"That shallow stream may, or may not, have had a few natural trout in it. I'm not sure how much water was flowing naturally back then. It may have been twice the flow it has now due to changes in the topography caused by housing in the area. However, just to make sure, and make his old friend happy when he stopped for a visit, Edgar made certain there were enough hungry trout in the stream to keep Hoover busy for a couple hours.

"That's how my grandfather knew about Hoover's visit and why he was sitting under the tracks waiting to get a look at the man."

"And you can prove that?" I asked Red.

"Most of it. I spent an evening looking through my grandfather's old notebook. Once I knew what to look for, there was indeed a reference to moving trout to William Edgar's stream. I think Bob got another one right."

"If Bob's that smart and knows all these things, why is he a hermit?" I asked.

"That's another long story. Perhaps, someday, we can discuss it.

"Anyway, I think Hoover's reason for the visit was to ask William Edgar to help him with the industrialists of Minneapolis in his proposed election bid. I'm not even sure it had been announced to the public yet that he was considering running. Somewhere between William Edgar's book and Herbert Hoover's need to talk to Edgar, lies the truth.

"With Hoover's reputation for liking to fish, the conversation might have started out in the house, or even at the edge of the stream. If William Edgar put his favorite fishing pole in Hoover's hands as he said in his book, the conversation may have happened right there on the edge of the brook for the next two hours.

"That's probably the best guess of what might have happened.

"Hoover was such a fishing addict. I saw an article printed by the National Park Service.

It read, *"When Herbert Hoover was honorary president of the Izaak Walton League, he declared in an intriguing article that it should be the inalienable right of every American to catch a nice string of fish at least once each year. He touched upon the ennobling and uplifting effect this would have upon the American's soul and indicated that as a panacea for unrest, discontent, and so on, there was nothing in the world like goin' fishin'. He advocated the expenditure of sufficient funds to see that all good fish waters of the country be adequately stocked with the right kind of fish. Then, at least, the fish would be there to be caught, and the man who could not catch his share would have nobody but himself to blame."*

"Rumor has it Hoover left the area in great spirits, having gotten what he wanted both in advice and with enough trout to fry up for breakfast.

"Except for a couple of the town's people that saw an empty train car at the siding, the station master and my grandfather watching from the tunnel, no one probably paid attention to the events at the William Edgar house. I'm not sure if his train car was picked up by a private locomotive or added to a scheduled passenger train. There is no record of the stop.

"History is made in strange places."

"And you think that somehow fishing in the stream played a part?" I asked.

"Well, let me tell you another story that probably won't make our report.

"When I was digging into everything I could find trying to trace down the year Herbert Hoover visited Marine, I ran across another story that had a surprising similarity.

"I wondered if somehow Hoover had played a part in it.

"In 1927, President Coolidge located his summer residence in the Black Hills of South Dakota. The report I read stated that the Governor of South Dakota devised a plot to entertain the President, while he spent three weeks in the Black Hills, and perhaps gather some positive press about South Dakota.

"Somehow, 2,000 trout were moved from the state hatcheries at Spearfish and driven eighty miles south to the area where the Coolidges were staying at their Presidential retreat. To make sure the fishing stayed great in the local stream, they released some fish every fourth day to keep the President happy. President Coolidge found that he couldn't help but catch fish.

"Well, not only did President Coolidge learn how to catch trout on the trip but in his enjoyment of the summer days, he extended his visit from three weeks to the full three months.

"There had been another rumor floating around our area that President Coolidge was going to travel from the Black Hills and visit a cabin on the St. Croix River later that summer. However, it appears he might have canceled his visit after deciding to extend his stay in the Black Hills.

"President Coolidge was already enjoying the thoughts of private life even before he was out of office. The Black Hills had provided the final nail to any thoughts of his running for a third term.

"The following summer, President Coolidge decided to spend the hot months of 1928 at a small remote cabin up in northern Wisconsin. His summer retreat for 1928, was at Cedar Island on the Brule River. It was in the same area that has been enjoyed by several presidents as a summer retreat over the years starting with President Grant. The later Presidents preferred staying in elaborate retreat cabins.

"Once again, during the summer break from Washington, the Secretary of Commerce Herbert Hoover took his train car up to the Presidential retreat area in Wisconsin to discuss the upcoming Republican Convention, asking his mentor for suggestions as well as determining the timing for Hoover to resign the Secretary's title before the convention.

"They spent the day, as a photo event, fishing trout in the Brule.

"Hoover had hoped to stop in Marine on the St. Croix once again to visit his old friend William Edgar on the return trip. However, an illness in the family required him to travel directly to Iowa.

"In order to avoid the high bridge over the St. Croix River, Hoover traveled to Duluth before heading down the tracks to St. Paul and then further south. The security team that was traveling with him at that point did not want him using the high bridge.

"I kind of questioned that, until I found another report on the bridge from World War II. Apparently, the government was so concerned about shipments over the bridge that they actually had guards on each side of the bridge to protect it. They were worried about someone damaging the bridge."

"So, not only did Marine have some very important guests that made history, it is quite probable that the outcome of the 1928 elections was in some way influenced by Hoover's stop in Marine in 1926.

"The sad part of history is that as soon as Hoover became President, as fate would have it, the Great Depression started with the collapse of Wall Street. All the positive history that had followed Hoover for the past couple decades would be erased by the events of 1929 and the early 1930's.

"His friend and long term advisor William Edgar died in 1932.

"Now, President Hoover would have to bring into play many of his own abilities to lead the relief efforts here in the United States."

"Wow, that's quite a tale," I told Red. "Maybe you should consider including the whole thing in the report. I think it finishes off the entire story."

We spent the next two hours splicing together our stories, polishing it off with a few glittering words, and reviewing it two more times for typos and other errors.

Now, we needed to meet with Dawn to get her agreement and seam her portions to the beginning of the story.

I called Dawn and we set up a meeting for after church on Sunday, where we could look at Dawn's section and get everyone's opinion before we made our final edit of the paper. Barring a serious re-write, we should be able to have it done by Wednesday or Thursday.

<u>Maria</u>

Ashlee was excited that Red liked her writings. Looking into her eyes, I wasn't sure if it was the fact that one of her peers had approved of her writings or if she was starting to fall for a boy.

I made the offer to Ashlee that we could take Red home instead of his walking since he had his papers and laptop.

Before leaving, he copied over to Ashlee's computer the draft of their paper. Both of them agreed that they might make slight changes to their sections before meeting with Dawn tomorrow. If they did, they would copy each other with any changes before then.

On the way back home, I asked Ashlee how Red's section turned out.

"I think it sounded great. You won't believe this, but Bob helped him fill in some of his information."

"Bob! He's like a ghost that pops up here and there with a miracle crystal ball to know when to be there and have an answer or solution. I think you should have written the whole paper around Bob. Who is he? Where did he come from? How does he know so much about the area?" I told Ashlee.

"You might be right. I still wonder what might have happened if I sprained my ankle and you ran into him on the tracks. That might have been a chapter all by itself."

We both laughed at the thought.

When we arrived at the Inn, I asked Ashlee if I could look at the draft. I was curious to see what they had found about President Hoover's visit to Marine.

When I was done reading it, I told her that I thought it was very good. When they added Dawn's section to the paper, it should get an 'A' from their teacher.

"Mom, don't forget, we still need to get this past Dawn. She may want us to change things."

I told her, "Don't worry. I think she's going to be blown out of her chair when she reads both of your sections. She may worry that her section is not as exciting as the rest of the paper."

I wished I could be a fly on the wall when they got together tomorrow to put the sections together. They were meeting at Dawn's house. I had offered to take Ashlee and Red down there. Dawn's mother had offered to drive them back when they were done.

Ashlee

On Sunday, my mother gave Red and me a ride down to Dawn's house, about four to five miles south of town and just off the river.

Neither of us had been to her house. It was a nice single story house nestled in the woods about a block from the river, in a small development of houses.

Her mother greeted us at the door when we arrived. Dawn was ready for us and had a number of papers spread out on the dining room table along with her laptop computer. She almost looked disappointed as we walked in. All we had with us was a flash drive with our parts of the paper on it.

We decided that it made sense to have Dawn explain and show us her sections of the report before we showed her ours. It was the way it was going to be put together in the final report and if things did not fit, we would spot it quickly and could make any adjustments on the fly if necessary.

Dawn's section was the history of Marine and the surrounding area. We knew the only conflict might be the old log cabin. As a result, we listened to see how my piece would fit into her discussion. It needed to sound like the same author wrote it.

As most of the class and our teacher would expect, Dawn started with the history of the founding of Marine; the claim for Marine Mills and the claim jumpers that ransomed their claim for $300.

After that, she talked about the timber industry and how vital the St. Croix River had been to the industry. A discussion about cutting and floating logs down river along with having to brand each of the logs followed.

The lumbering section ended with the history of the mill's problems including a couple years of low water levels and the tornado that almost leveled the town in 1884, that bankrupted the mill the following year.

She had a short discussion about the presence of the Ojibwe-Chippewa and Dakota-Sioux tribes' presence in the area. It described the ease of hunting in the hills along the river as well as raising crops on the flat areas from the Croixside area to the Big Marine Lake area.

Dawn concluded it with the large Ojibwe gathering in the Big Marine Lake area and the killing of two hundred deer, only to have all of the tribe permanently disappear a few days later and head north.

The final section about the history of the town included the building of the Gaskill Grain Mill, the history of the local church, and the history of the town hall that presently contains the library and an auditorium upstairs. She concluded it with the long history of the Marine ferry.

Dawn figured that the majority of the class would not know about any of the items mentioned except for the lumber mill and the church. She had intentionally left out the riverboat parts figuring that other papers about Stillwater would have discussions about them.

It sounded good. It was a good history lesson about the area and most of the class should learn something reading it. Dawn was pleased that we didn't want to change anything she had written.

When we looked at her writing style and what she found about the native tribes in the area, Red and I concluded that my section about the old cabin could either be inserted into her discussion of the movement of the tribes or would work as a stand-alone discussion about current buildings.

Red and I explained and showed Dawn the sections we had put together in one file on the flash drive.

After reading it over, she agreed that they appeared to fit in very well with her section. If we put caption headings indicating History, followed by Interesting Events, it would bring the entire paper together and give an explanation to the class, as well as our teacher, how the paper was composed.

We all felt relieved that we didn't need to sit down and do any major editing to any of the sections. It would have made for awkward situations of "I think" versus "but we think" discussions. None of us really wanted to spend the entire week arguing about changes.

The only thing left to do was to list all of our references and then have one person do a final edit to make sure the language sounded like one author. So far, we only saw a couple spots where the sentences sounded like they needed a little polishing.

To my surprise, Red volunteered to give the final edit a run, and equally surprising, Dawn agreed. I was so shocked, I was not going to disagree with giving him the final reins.

In just over two hours, we were finished. Well, all of us except for Red. He'd have a couple hours of checking the final wording. Dawn's mother offered to take us home.

Before we left, I asked Red if we could see the high bridge from the Croixside landing. Unfortunately, he told me it was too far down the river to see it. There was, at least, one bend in the river between us.

I had to go by the photograph Red had given me.

When I got back to the Inn, I told my mother that she would have to wait until Tuesday or Wednesday to see our paper. Dawn had wisely let our poet do the final edit of the text. We both figured Red was probably a better writer than we were.

On the way to school on Monday, I told Leslie that we finished our paper. She was glad to hear it and was curious about what we found for the topics we used.

We discussed it all the way to school.

To my surprise, when we walked into our English class, Red handed Dawn and me a disc with our finished report on it. He had worked on it after getting home from Dawn's, and told us that he thought it looked really good.

As a group, we decided not to turn it into our teacher until we had both looked at Red's final edit. Tomorrow or Wednesday would be soon enough.

Chapter 18

Relief

Ashlee

Our paper passed the final review of our writing group. Breathing a sigh of relief, on Wednesday, we turned it into our teacher. It was done and on time. Now we just had to sit back and see if she liked it.

When I got home, my mother asked if she could read the final version. She spent that evening reading it instead of watching her favorite television drama.

When she was finished, she told me, "Ashlee, you and your group did a really good job on this paper. I think you should print out a couple copies and put a copy in the fireside room of the Inn as well as in the guest rooms. I think our guest would love to read some of the history of the area."

I gave her a big smile. It would be fun to have a few guests read and comment on our paper.

After talking to Dawn and Red, I printed out a few copies along with inserting the photographs at the end of the paper. All three of our names were on the cover of the report. It will be interesting to see if anyone even notices.

Maria

Things had quieted down at the Inn. Friday was May 1st. That meant the town was preparing for a May Day festival in the park. It was one of those Scandinavian events that were carried on in several of the local towns. Many of the early settlers of the area came from Sweden or Norway. For them, May Day marked the returning of the sun, especially in locations above the Arctic Circle where the sun had been behind the globe all winter.

In the park, next to the log cabin, festive musicians danced around a May Pole marking their heritages, as few people actually knew the real history of the cabin nearby or the fact that a grain mill had once stood near the site.

Just before dinnertime, Edward Gray checked into the Inn. I managed to spot him as he was checking in.

"Ms. Wagner, how's the ankle?" he asked me.

"Just Maria please," I told him. "Thank you for remembering. It's just fine. Only my pride was left with a little dent from the incident.

"It is good to have you back. Are you heading back out for dinner?" I asked him.

"You pay attention," he told me. "Yes, I guess I'll check out the Brookside. Any word when the restaurant at the landing – Quacks, will open for summer?"

"No, I haven't heard yet. I'll have to check that one out myself when it opens up. Have a good dinner," I told him and I headed back to my apartment.

The next morning, at breakfast, Bonnie had five people to serve. Edward Gray asked Bonnie if Ashlee was here. He was hoping to talk to her.

"Well, it's a weekend. My guess is that she's exactly where most teenagers start out the weekend – lost in her pillow. I usually see her moving around by 9:00 am. Would you like me to leave her a message?" Bonnie asked.

"Yes, could you tell her that I would like to talk to her about the paper she wrote. I read it last night. It was a fun thing to have in the room."

"I'll tell Maria to let her know," Bonnie told him.

When Bonnie popped her head into the apartment, she told me about her conversation with Edward Gray.

"Oh, Ashlee is going to be pleased to hear that she got a comment already. I'll let her know."

I was wondering what customers might think about the paper. I was hoping that someone might write in their review that they enjoyed the paper about the local history.

When Ashlee got up for breakfast, I told her that she had an admirer of her writing already. Mr. Gray had read it last night and wanted to talk to her about it. She looked pleased.

Ashlee put on some better clothes and started to go to meet with Edward Gray.

Ashlee

I heard a loud ruckus out in the lobby of the Inn. In a couple moments, my mother came back into my room and shouted, "There's a bear in the bird feeder."

We ran back out to the fireside room of the Inn. Sure enough, the couple guests we had were enjoying the sight of a large black bear feasting on our bird feeder. Not just one, but all three of our feeders. It went from one feeder to the next as soon as it was empty.

Everyone was laughing. I heard one of the guests ask Bonnie, which room the bear was staying in.

It stayed outside the window for almost twenty minutes. We had three bird feeders hung from tall wrought iron shepherd's hooks. The bear would simply lay against the hook and it would bend all the way to the ground. Easy picking for the bear. It didn't even have to work to get the feed out of the feeders. Once on the ground, the feed just spilled out. With its huge paws with claws that looked like bent over nails, it could have smashed them to toothpicks in seconds.

Finally, when a train blew its whistle up at the crossing, the bear snorted and slowly lumbered back into the woods.

"Must have just come out of hibernation," one of the guests told me as we headed back to the apartment. "It was pretty small and its coat was shabby like it just came out of a cave."

I was surprised. It looked huge to me. How big did they get by the end of the feeding season? It was big enough to keep me from wandering into the woods for a few days. How do you chase away a bear? It was a problem I had never worried about in the past. I'd have to call my grandparents and see what they thought of the situation.

I was curious to see what Mr. Gray had thought about my paper. We had briefly mentioned it the last time he stayed here and he told me that he would like to see it when it was done.

I went up to his room and knocked on the door.

When he came to the door, he asked if I had seen the bear. He had watched it from his side window. He also told me he had read my paper.

"You did a great job," he told me. "Please come in and have a seat at the reading window. I have a couple questions about it I would like to ask you."

Cautiously, I went in his room, leaving the door open. My mother had given me instructions as to what to do if anyone asks you in their room. Leaving the door open, and making sure someone else knows where you are, were two of her instructions.

On the desk of the reading nook sat my paper.

"You know, I've lived in the area for a long time. I remember hearing a couple of the stories you wrote about, but you and your classmates did a good job researching the other stories. Where did you come up with the information on Herbert Hoover? I didn't know anything about that one.

"Oh, I heard rumors that Hoover had left his signature on the fireplace at the Edgar home, but I always thought it was more a joke than reality," he told me.

"People up here like to brag about important people they know, and somehow they tend to forget the names of anyone they are not happy to know. But, your group actually dotted the I's and crossed the T's on this rumor. So, how did you find the connections?"

I was surprised. He was genuinely interested and wanted to know how we did it.

"Well, I can't take very much credit on that story. I was working on the train stories. A friend of mine did most of the research on Hoover.

"A lot of our information came from talking to some of the town's people. They gave us the start to the rumors and in the case of Hoover, we saw a photo of his train car at the Marine siding in the museum. That gave us the starting point to trace down the story."

"Well, I enjoyed that story as well as the story on the train fire. I know Bert Hudson. I'm sure he was excited to tell you the story of the fire.

"I'm curious, how did you pick these stories from all the other stories about the area? Don't get me wrong, you did a great job. I was just wondering how you determined what made your paper?"

I told Mr. Gray about the assignment at school and how we were told that it had to be about where we lived. Since our small group lived in a four-mile circle of the town, we tried to keep our stories within five miles of each of our houses.

A friend, who I ride to school with every day, told me our teacher liked to hear exciting stories about the area most people had never heard. So, we started with the normal history of the area and then picked a couple stories we figured the teacher and class would enjoy.

“Well, you did a good job of selecting your stories.

“Did you ever hear the story of “Boozer?” he asked.

I was wondering which town drunk he was talking about. “No, his name never came up. Why?” I asked.

“Well, this summer if you and your mother go down to Quack’s restaurant at the old ferry landing, look and see if you can see the sign on the side of the building. It says, “Boozer slept here.” It has an interesting story to it as well. You see, Boozer was the town’s dog.”

“A dog? I thought you were going to say it was the town drunk. How did the dog get so popular?”

“Well, you’re the writing detective, if you are curious, look it up.

“Oh, you might want to tell your mother that in the springtime, you might want to hang the feeders high up from a tree. Until the berries come out, the bears are looking for anything they can get their paws on. Next time she might lose the feeders.”

That was not the conversation I was expecting. We did a lot of research. Now, I was expected to check into the town’s dog? I thanked him for reading my paper and sharing his thoughts. As I did, I left his room as puzzled about our frequent guest as my mother was.

When I got back to the apartment, I told my mother all about our conversation, including his suggestion about the bear.

“He liked my paper and said he knew about several of the things we mentioned. Then, he asked me if I knew “Boozer.””

“Who’s Boozer?” my mother asked.

“He told me it was the town’s dog and if I was curious, there was a good story behind it. Apparently, there is a sign at Quack’s restaurant saying “Boozer slept here.””

“Well, maybe you should go and find Bob and ask him. He seems to know everything that ever happened in Marine.”

I knew my mother was getting a dig in on me. Bob was still this mysterious person that popped up all the time in our conversations and we still had no idea of who he actually was, except for helping us when my mother fell on the railroad tracks.

I figured I should call Red. He might know the story.

Red laughed when I told him about the bear. I didn't even get a chance to ask him about Boozer.

"Didn't someone tell you there was bear in the area?" he asked. "You are lucky any of the feeders are still in one piece. You better take them down or they will go missing by morning. Bears keep coming back if there is something they like to eat.

"If you like, I can come over and help you put them on a rope from one of your trees. Then, all you have to worry about is the squirrels. Your guests will love them too."

"The squirrels already know where the feeder is," I told him. "If you could help, I'm sure my mother would appreciate it. I'm not sure if we have any rope though."

"I'll bring something," he told me.

Just after lunch, Red arrived. He had ridden an old bike. Around the handlebars were a coil of rope and a couple coils of wire that looked as though it was meant for fencing.

My mother joined the two of us as we tried to figure out which tree branch had the best chance of holding the feeder without the bear reaching it or climbing up to it.

After selecting three good branches coming from the oak trees, my mother left the two of us to our bidding.

It didn't take us very long. Red used the rope and a stick to throw a line over the limb. Then, he used it to pull the wire over the limb. Using a loop at the end, he was able to snug off the wire to the limb and tie the feeder to the other end about eight feet off the ground.

He told me it needed to be that high to keep the bears out of it. In the winter, we could put a short section of rope on the wire and lower it down to where we could fill the feeder easier since the bears would be in hibernation. Until then, we needed to use our ladder to fill the feeders.

By 3:00 pm, we were finished. The bear would have to look elsewhere for food.

Edward Gray

After the morning's excitement, I was starting to relax in the reading window watching a few squirrels jumping from tree to tree. I really missed the relaxation of sitting in the window and watching nature go by when I was away from here.

As I was starting to doze off, I heard a clatter outside. I wondered if the bear had returned. To my enjoyment, I watched as Ashlee and her friend attempted to bear-proof the bird feeders. I remembered doing exactly the same thing years ago.

I remember my family watching me. My wife – Kathleen, was worried sick that I would fall off my long extension ladder when I tried to attach a rope to a tree limb. It was a long way up.

At the same time, my kids were worried that I would chase away all the wildlife. They liked seeing the bears and especially the squirrels. As I recall, they even had names for a couple of them. One squirrel had gray ears. I think they named it Moses. The other one was a red squirrel. They named it Rosy.

After the commotion settled down outside my window, I sat back in the chair in the reading nook and dozed off.

Ashlee

My mother thanked Red for his quick assistance in keeping the Bears out of the feeder and out of the Inn. The last thing she wanted to see was a bear that was sticking its head in the door looking for food.

I asked Red about Boozer. "Who was he and why was he the town's dog?"

"Where did you hear about Boozer?" Red asked.

"Our guest, Mr. Gray read our paper. He liked it. He also told me to look up the story about Boozer. Do you know anything about it?" I asked.

I was almost expecting him to say, "Well no, but let me talk to Bob." If he did, I think I would have hit him. However, in this case, his answer was better. He knew some of the background stories about the town's dog.

Chapter 19

More Stories

Ashlee

Red told me that his father had joked about Boozer and told him that if he didn't shape up, he would be just like him. I wasn't sure what the likeness would be between his son and a dog, but my curiosity was up and I wanted to listen to Red's story.

"You see, Boozer was called the town's dog because no one could remember who exactly the dog belonged to. He would attach himself to one family, and then a few months later move on to another house to stay.

"It wasn't as though someone was trying to lure him away from someone else, Boozer just figured it was high time to move on to another location. He would sit there on someone's doorstep until they finally fed him."

"Sounds like the cat we used to have," I told Red. "He'd disappear for weeks only to show up on the doorstep looking for food.

"Well, after a while, the whole town knew who Boozer was. He had his rounds. He would go sit in the sun on the porch of the General Store, or he would sit in the cool shade of the bank building. He knew where people would stop and pet him when they walked by. Everyone knew his name.

"This went on for quite some time. No one could remember when Boozer first showed up in town. After a while, it became the town joke. If Boozer wasn't at the store, the restaurant or at the bank, where was he?

"If you are interested, we can go down to the library after school on Tuesday. It is only open around the noon hour on Monday, so Tuesday would be better. From what I heard, there were a number of articles in the paper about Boozer. He became a sort of celebrity in the area. The newspaper articles are probably more accurate than my memory. I wasn't exactly listening for details when I heard the story.

"Okay, you have my curiosity up. Let's meet on Tuesday.

After thanking him for all the help with the bird feeders, Red picked up the rope and leftover wire and placed them on his bike. Then, he headed back down the gravel road from the Inn.

<u>Maria</u>

Late that afternoon, when a couple was checking in for the weekend, I saw Mr. Gray in the fireside room. He was checking out some of the books we had on our bookshelf.

"Looking for a good book to read?" I asked him.

"Just wondering if you had any other books about the area or the river at the Inn," he told me. "I thought the paper Ashlee wrote was a great idea. Just wondering if you had anything else for the customers to see in Marine."

It was a good idea. I decided I would look to see if I could find some books at the bookstore the next time I was in Stillwater.

"Are you enjoying your stay?" I asked him.

"Yes! I'm afraid I spent most of the afternoon lost in thought after watching your feeder project. Reminded me of the old days when I had to move my feeders.

"How about you? Are you enjoying managing the Inn? You seem to be doing a good job from what I can see."

"Well, thank you. Yes, it was what my family needed. I think it was good for Ashlee as well as for me. Both of us are adjusting to the slower pace and we are enjoying the time Ashlee has spent learning about the area.

"Ashlee said you used to live in the area. How long ago was that?" I asked him.

"I moved away about twenty years ago. Somehow, I just enjoy coming back. Something about the area I guess.

"I better get going. Time for my stomach to find some nutrients. We'll talk again sometime."

With that, he left to head out for dinner. It seemed that every time I had a chance to find out something about Edward Gray, he had a way of leaving me a small tidbit and exiting the conversation. Ashlee seemed to be able to get more information out of him than I could.

Bonnie was finished checking in our new guests. I walked over and talked to her about our bear event. I was wondering if the sight of a bear was a positive thing or negative event for our guests.

"No, I think they enjoyed seeing the bear. I doubt that many of our guests plan on walks down the railroad tracks, so seeing one in the wild was probably something special."

I caught the dig – a walk down the tracks. I was glad to hear it didn't frighten anyone. Either way, I suggested to Bonnie that we use caution out in the yard for the next couple of weeks just in case it comes back. "You might want to warn customers that the bears are coming out of hibernation."

That evening, I tried to decide if I wanted to include wildlife on our web page. For some, it might be a draw to the Inn. The thought of a chance to see bears, deer, etc. in the wild might draw in customers.

On the other hand, I didn't want to scare anyone away. I was still trying to increase our reservation rate. That reminded me; I still needed to set a date with Jason Willard for our next review.

I was starting to feel more comfortable with our reviews. At first, I was scared silly that he would find something wrong. Now, it was more like a friendly meeting just to make sure nothing had changed.

I was thinking, we have been here for two full months. Hard to believe that in that short of time with us being at the Inn, it could start to feel like our home.

With all the events that had happened during the two months, it felt like we had been living here a much longer time.

Sunday morning, I was feeling a little frustrated that I still did not know anything about our most frequent guest. I didn't want to bug him at breakfast. However, from his past stays, he seemed to check out about 11:00 am. I decided to be in the lobby area about that time.

He was still on his clockwork schedule. At 10:55 am, Edward Gray came down the steps to check out.

"Did you have a good stay, Mr. Gray?" I asked him.

"Well, I was looking for that bear hug this morning. Little disappointed that I did not get one. But, other than that, yes, it was very nice."

"Where are you off to this week?" I boldly asked.

"I have a meeting in Iowa. Someone is interested in purchasing some land I own down there," he stated as he paid up his bill with Jean. Then, he picked up his bag and headed for the door.

"We'll be looking forward to seeing you next weekend," I told him.

"Thanks! Oh, please let Ashlee know I enjoyed talking to her."

With that, he was out the door.

Ugh! Just one more morsel of information slipping out of his hat. This is becoming a real challenge. I wondered if I would know anything more about him by the end of the summer.

Ashlee

Red came up to me in class on Monday with a big grin on his face. I was wondering if he had found out the grade on our paper before the rest of us.

"Did you see the pictures hanging in the hall by the office?" he asked.

"No. Is it your art class's project?"

"Yes! The teacher put my drawing first. There was a gold ribbon attached to it."

"Wow, I'll have to look at it at lunch time," I told him.

Today was the day all the papers were due in our English class. As our teacher was collecting the papers that had not been turned in the previous week, she turned and told the class, "Tomorrow, I would like to start having each group read their papers to the class. I have read a few of them over the weekend and I was very impressed."

When she went through the order that she wanted them read, ours came up second tomorrow. I was hoping to hear a couple others before we had to read ours. Of course, the benefit of going early was that there was no pressure to compete with all the others we heard. They would have to compete with us.

At the end of class, our teacher passed out the papers that she had read. When I saw our's, I turned and smiled at Red. We got an 'A'. There was a note on the top of the paper – "Very well done." When I looked over, Dawn had a big smile on her face as well.

At the end of class, we got together and decided that each one of us should read the section we wrote in class tomorrow. That way, if anyone had any questions, the one that wrote the section could answer them. We were all wondering how the readings of the papers would be taken by our class. One thing for certain, there was bound to be someone that had to ask a few dumb questions about the paper.

On the way to lunch, I passed by the office area and looked at the drawings Red's class had done on perspective. They were very good. Much better than I could have done.

I saw Red's drawing. Wow! He was good. Now I understood why his teacher had him on the committee to decide where the class would go to do the drawing.

When I spotted him later in the day in the hall, I went up to him and whispered in his ear. "I saw your drawing. I think you're really good."

He looked puzzled as if he didn't know how to react. Then, he simply smiled at me and said, "Thank you."

That night, Red called and told me that he would pick me up when we went to the library in town tomorrow. I told him my mother could pick us up, but he insisted on picking me up.

I reminded him to look like a presidential aid tomorrow. I got a laugh out of that suggestion.

The reading of our paper went perfectly the next day. From the look in the eyes of the other groups, you could see that they were both surprised at what we came up with, and at the same time worried how they were going to compete.

The first group that went before us had mostly historical facts about Stillwater. They spent considerable time talking about the riverboats that came to Stillwater. We made a good guess leaving that out of our paper.

The class asked one or two questions about it. However, on an interest level, I would have said it was a 6 on a scale of 10 with the class.

When we got our chance, you could see by looking at everyone's faces that they thought it was going to be another historical review. However, the moment we shifted gears and got into the interesting events, everyone's ears picked up. The story about the foot attached to the spear caught everyone by surprise.

When we got to the story about a fire out on the high bridge, I could tell just by looking which students had been there and which ones had not. It made them think about going out on the bridge at night to put out a hot fire.

Finally, when Red told them about Hoover's visit to Marine, I think they realized that they had met their match. An investigative report? How were they going to match that? Even our teacher was impressed with the work that went into it.

Fortunately, the bell rang only a couple minutes after we finished our paper. It looked like half of the class had their hands up with questions on our paper.

On the way out of class, they were still asking us questions about the stories. I guess we earned our 'A' on this one.

All the way home, I told Leslie about the paper and how the reading went. Even her mother was interested in it. She kept asking me questions about how we found all the information. When I told her that Red even contacted the Hoover Presidential Library, she told me, "I'll bet no one else in your class did half that much research for their paper." She was probably right.

I was all excited when I got home. I didn't tell my mother about the grade yesterday. I wanted to wait until we read it to the class to tell her. Now, I had to tell her quickly before Red picked me up to go to the library.

She was excited to hear the news and congratulated me on all the hard work, including getting my group to work together on the project. For her, that was a real accomplishment.

As we were talking, I saw Red drive up in the parking area to pick me up. He was driving the old red pickup truck.

Chapter 20

Boozer

<u>Ashlee</u>

When I saw Red driving the old red pickup, I told my mother I had to go, and I ran out the door to meet him.

"Hey, I thought you weren't allowed to drive the truck unless you were on the farm or doing farm work," I told him. "How'd you talk your father into letting you drive it?"

"Well, when I got back from helping you with your minor bear problem, my father surprised me and told me he had an appointment on Monday to convert my farm license into a full driver's license."

"And you passed?"

"It was easier than I thought to convert it."

"So, when did you turn sixteen?" I asked.

"Saturday. It was just another day so I didn't tell anyone."

"Saturday! Now I am ticked. You came over to help with the bird feeders and didn't even tell me it was your birthday? I'm not sure I can trust you to drive into town if you couldn't even tell me it was your birthday."

"Well, we can walk if you prefer," he told me.

With a look of disgust, I climbed into the truck. It was a lot cleaner than I remembered it the last time I saw it. As we were leaving, I could see my mother looking out the window. I'm sure she had the same questions I had about Red driving.

I didn't realize she had heard the whole conversation through the open window. In my excitement, I guess I was a little loud.

The old pickup was still in good shape. Red's father had put new tires on the truck before allowing him to drive it. In fact, he had surprised Red after getting his license by giving him the keys. The icing on the cake, he even had it waxed. His father told him it was all his, on one condition. If they needed it for hauling something, he needed to be willing to help.

Red had quickly agreed.

Maria

I had a feeling in my gut the second Ashlee saw Red drive into the parking area that my peaceful spring had just jumped a track.

Things had been moving far too well with the move; improved grades, improved moods with grandparents and with me. It had been a totally different girl.

And now, a boyfriend with wheels. I took a deep breath as they drove out the road.

Bonnie was working today. She came up behind me and said, "Don't worry. It's going to take her a month to realize she has a crush on him. Besides, if she has to pick a boy, at least, she found one that you can trust."

I thought about it for a minute. She was right. I was hoping I had the full summer before she woke up to the boys in the area. But, as things had it, at least, I liked "Spider-Boy."

I couldn't wait to hear my father's thoughts on the subject.

Ashlee

I was still ticked off with Red that he hadn't told me it was his birthday. At the very least, I would have gotten a card for him.

It only took five minutes to get to the library. I kept telling myself to cool it. I didn't want to ruin his day. After all, he was probably showing off his truck, to me, for the first time.

When we got to the library, the librarian helped us find a number of articles that were published about Boozer.

I was surprised how many there were. You would have thought it was a town founder that had died. There were articles in the local and Twin City newspapers. Every columnist seemed to want to get in as part of the act.

"So, tell me again, why was this dog so popular?" I ask Red.

"According to Don Boxmeyer, who wrote for the Pioneer Press, Boozer was a research survivor from the University of Minnesota's Medical Institute where he and other dogs, were used for training veterinary technicians. The students practiced giving shots and other procedures on the animals. When they were done using the dogs, they were orphaned out. Chris Olin, an Institute student, and Marine resident, brought one of those dogs home in the spring of 1982.

"However, I think the story has roots that travel much deeper into Marine's history."

As we looked into the articles in the various papers written about his death, there was indeed an underlining trend that seemed to follow. During the 1970's and 1980's, the residents of Marine were an interesting bunch. They had fundraisers for almost anything you could imagine. Now most of these fundraisers didn't run high profits. Instead, they became excuses for gatherings and parties. It became the thing to do in order to have a public party.

There was the save the river, save the tree, save the island, and no doubt, save Boozer.

Boozer was a mixed breed dog. He was mostly Bassett with some Dachshund and perhaps a touch of German Shepherd. It really didn't matter.

The dog was given to one family to keep. However, it didn't take long for old Boozer to decide he wanted to live with another family. It didn't take long for the family to realize that Boozer wanted to be at the other house and before long, the dog's dish was moved next door. I guess that was the start of things.

They tried to tie him up to keep him in the yard. He yelped until someone let him in the house. It was winter, so they tried a kennel. Somehow he got out. Soon, people were realizing it was easier to let him roam than try to keep him tied up.

Reading one article on the dog, they said they tracked him one day. The dog's day started at 5:00 am. with Dan Froiland. He fed him wieners heated in the microwave. Dan said the dog was fussy. It had to be the right kind of wieners.

From there it was off to the Voyageur Café for a piece of ham or off to the Village Scoop for some ice cream.

Boozer didn't raid trash cans or garbage. He was fussy about his food and he knew his sources. I'm not sure if the town trained the dog, or if the dog trained the town. On a sunny day, he might want to lie in the street and take a nap.

At sports day at the local grade school, Boozer was there to be with the children.

By 11:00 pm, his day was over and he would show up at whichever home he was staying with that month.

And so it went, with only a few exceptions.

According to the articles, one person Boozer did not make friends with was the area animal control officer. Many times he was picked up only to have a Marine resident show up to bail him out.

Claudia Moffitt and Jackie Miller came up with the idea of a fundraiser to pay for Boozer's trips to the pound. They were going to sell T-shirts to pay for his fines. Somehow, this fundraiser got out of control. It raised so much money that they actually opened a bank account in Boozer's name. Later that year, Boozer had his own float in the Sesquicentennial parade.

"Remember, when I told you that Marine was a little different when it came to 4th of July parades?" Red told me. "This is not your typical conservative community."

Apparently, KMSP television in the Twin Cities got wind of it and soon there were stories on the national network show Good Morning America. It was even picked up by a London newspaper. Things appeared to snowball out of hand.

Finally, when Boozer was diagnosed with cancer, he was treated with chemotherapy. However, at the same time, they found an inoperable tumor on his artery. It was time for Boozer's day of roaming the town to come to an end.

"That's unbelievable," I told Red. "All that for a wayward dog. Why don't they put the same effort into helping some of the people in town?

"You think they would put that kind of effort into getting your friend Bob a new coat?"

Red just shrugged his shoulders. "That's Marine. Like I said, they do some weird things here. Besides, I doubt that Bob would like the attention that Boozer got."

We headed back out of the library after our short research project.

"I'm just glad we didn't use the Boozer story for our paper. I think the class would have laughed us out of the classroom. A bank account set up just for getting a dog out of jail???" I told Red.

"Don't forget they used some of the money for his vet bills too."

On the way back up the hill to the Inn, we were passing the church when Red asked me if I would like to join him for church on Sunday. It was the church's day, which they set aside, for inviting a friend to church, and he was wondering if I would join him.

I thought about it for a minute before saying, "Sure, I'll join you."

Except for the Sunday our whole family attended the church when we were looking at moving to Marine, I hadn't been to church since early Sunday School days.

I could remember my mother taking me to church when I was in kindergarten. Then, as she found herself working at the restaurant on Sunday's, she would often drop me off at Sunday School, only to have my father pick me up when it was over. He never did come to church. Then again, he never did much with us as a family.

"Oh, if your mother would like to join us, I'm sure she would be welcome," he told me.

"Okay, I'll ask her. Got room for her in the back of the truck?" I asked.

Red laughed. "Well, in that case, we might have to meet you there. I think there is still a restriction as to the number of passengers I can carry with my license for the next year. Although, it doesn't say how many people I can put in the back of the truck."

"I'll talk to her this evening. Perhaps she can find an old motorcycle helmet she could donate to your cause for the back of your truck."

Red dropped me off at the Inn and headed back for dinner at his place. I thanked him for taking me to the library.

When I got back, both Bonnie and my mother were waiting for me.

"So, he got a new truck and took you out as his first date using the truck to the town library? Last of the big spenders?" Bonnie joked.

I just turned red in the face. She knew she had me on this one. Even my mother cracked a smile when she said it.

At dinner, I told my mother about the fact it had been Red's birthday last Saturday and how he didn't tell anyone.

"Well, from what I've noticed, I think he is rather shy and doesn't like a lot of attention. Is that your take also?" she asked.

"Yeah, I guess so. I'm waiting to see if the kids in my class will stop calling him Spider-Boy after hearing our report and seeing his drawing at school."

"You didn't tell me about that one. What drawing did he do?"

"His art class had an assignment to do a drawing showing perspective. They all went to the outlook in Stillwater and drew the new bridge. You should see it. It's real good. He even got a gold ribbon for it."

"So, Red has another talent. Besides writing poetry in a tunnel, researching historic people, and saving damsels on the railway, he knows how to draw. Any other surprises?" she asked.

"Well, he asked me if I would like to go to church with him this Sunday. They have a "bring a friend day." I told him I could, if it's okay with you. Also, he offered to take you if you were willing to sit in the bed of the pickup."

I was waiting to see her expression. Her eyebrows raised when I said I was going to church with him. When I mentioned picking her up in the truck bed, it broke the silence.

"He said he would do what?" my mother asked.

"I told him you could probably find an old motorcycle helmet to wear back there. Besides, it's only a mile or so. You couldn't fall out, could you?"

With a sharp clank, she dropped her fork.

After a minute of silence, I told her that Red suggested the two of us could meet him there if you would like to come along.

She just shook her head.

“I’ll take back what I said about this shy kid. I think you have been quite the influence on him. Are you sure you want me tagging along?” she asked.

“I’m okay with it,” I told her.

“Okay, maybe we can fill one of their pews on Sunday.”

“Oh, one more favor. Since he was working over here on his birthday, you think you could take me to the store this week to find him a birthday card and gift?”

“We’ll work it out,” she told me.

Chapter 21

Bear Hugs

Maria

Ashlee was on the phone after dinner letting Red know that we would be joining him on Sunday. I wasn't sure if he really wanted me there or not. Probably not!

Anyway, it was a nice offer on his part. I looked at it as a chance to be with Ashlee at church. We had sort of let that one slide over the years.

I had just one week left in my current classes at the college. You guessed it; I had a paper due and finals. I was glad I was only taking two courses. I had the papers done, and only one of the classes actually had a test at the end. For this one, I needed to drive in and actually take the test in person on Thursday. I think they did it just to make sure they had some personal contact with their adult classes.

Jason Willard had suggested meeting later this week. I put him off until next week. I told him I was booked solid this week. I could hear the pause on the other end of the line. "No, the Inn's not booked solid, just me. It's the last week of classes so I'm struggling to do the work at the Inn, pass my classes and keep an eye on Ashlee."

"You're having problems with Ashlee?" he asked.

"No, I'm just a little concerned that a boy has found her. I guess I'm just the standard mother that wants her little girl to stay her little girl."

"Now, that I understand. You want to put her in the closet and not let her out until she is twenty-six."

"I didn't know you were a family consultant as well as an accountant," I told him. "Maybe you do have another job waiting for you when you retire."

Jason laughed. "No thanks. I'll pass on that opportunity. Just keep good notes. You might be able to sell your experiences to someone else that runs the same course with a daughter."

I thanked him for the advice and told him I'd see him next week.

We were doing spring cleaning this week. Time to refresh things, including changing the colors in the Inn. A different hanging here and a different table cover there made a difference. Even the bedspreads were changed. Gone were the spring colors and out came the cooler summer colors.

It didn't take long for customers to notice and make comments.

Speaking of comments, ever since we put Ashlee's paper in the rooms last week, almost every one of the guests commented on it. As a result, I planned to pick up a couple books about the St. Croix area tomorrow when I picked up Ashlee at school and took her shopping after my test. I had the option of taking the test in the afternoon or evening. I chose afternoon.

I was looking at the reservation sheet. We were running about fifteen percent above the past two years so far. That was good. Perhaps my job was safe for a couple more months. I was still looking for that big weekend when we could actually turn customers away. I figured that was the real turning point.

Looking at the records from last year, only one weekend did they come close to that scenario. They had one opening on that weekend.

So far, we were still ahead on the budget as well. I figured Jason Willard's meeting would be a short one next week when I showed him our results.

Thursday afternoon, I went in to take my final. As it turned out, I didn't need to panic about it. The instructor made it an essay exam – one question. Well, two. The first question, was related to the main topic of my marketing class. It was an opinion as to why a long-established store failed in Minneapolis. That one was fairly easy as we had discussed it in some of his on-line lectures. The second question caught me by surprise. What grade do you expect to get?

I didn't know how to answer it. I assumed the instructor was looking to see any comments about how hard the coursework had been. At the same time, even if it had been extremely easy, our grade should be based on how well we learned the concepts.

I wrote a short paragraph and ended it with an 'A'. I had a feeling that the instructor would expect most of his adult students to answer the question that way.

It turned out that I had time to kill before picking up Ashlee at school for her shopping trip.

When she came out, we drove to the Maplewood Mall to see if she could find a present for Red.

On the way there, she told me that Red had asked her the other day if she wanted to ride to and from school with him instead of Leslie.

I hesitantly waited to hear her answer.

"I told him that this week was really busy. I didn't tell him you were picking me up to go shopping. But, I told him that I would talk to you about rides. Do you think it would be okay to ride with him since we only have a couple weeks left of school?"

I was really pleased that she had asked me before saying yes. If we were still up in St. Cloud, I doubt it would have even been a thought on her part.

"I think that sounds reasonable. I assume he checked with his father also. Just make sure he is a good driver and keeps his eyes on the road. What about next year? Leslie's parents have been good dependable transportation for you."

"I will. Actually, he is a slower driver than you are," she told me. Then, she changed her statement and made it sound a little less direct to my driving.

"Besides, Leslie's mother said she might have a different job next year. I'm not sure if we would still get a ride or not."

"You might want to be careful how you tell them. No sense burning bridges."

Ashlee told me she would wait until next week before making the transportation change.

While we were in the car, Ashlee told me about some of the other papers that were read in her English class. So far, she thought that her group's was the best. Almost every other one stuck to stories about the history of the town; founders, industry, and how the town developed. Some of them had relatives that were actually there at the founding of the town. Others looked for stories from "old timers" who were often swamped by more than one group looking for information. Overall, she said she learned a great deal about the area and the abilities of some of her classmates to work together.

Ashlee told me that her teacher told her she liked theirs the best. I'm sure Ashlee was proud.

When we got to the mall, we walked through some areas looking for ideas. As I did, I remembered that I had not purchased anything for Bob. What do you get for a hermit? That was a real problem and probably why I had let it go this long.

It would help if I knew where he lived, or actually been to his house. All I knew about him and all Ashlee knew about him were the clothes we saw him dressed in. That left everything up for grabs or perhaps he needed nothing. One thing for certain, he definitely saved my bacon that day out on the railroad tracks.

As Ashlee walked through the stores, we both kept our eyes open for something for Red that would instantly stand out.

I told Ashlee that she should look for something in the $15 price range. Since they didn't know each other that well, anything over that amount might give the wrong impression. I think she understood what I was getting to.

It took her a little while. First she stopped in a card shop and picked up an "Oops, I missed it" card. It was cute and looked like it would work for Red.

Then, as she was walking through a stationary store, she spotted a leather notebook that she thought Red might enjoy.

I kept thinking about his writing in the tunnel with the spiders. "Need a can of bug repellant I asked," and immediately wished I hadn't said it.

She gave me a look that could kill a horse.

"Mom, I thought you, of all people, would say better things."

"I'm sorry. That's just one of those things that I can't quite get out of my head. I'll try to be better."

Ashlee purchased a light-tan leather notebook to go along with the card she had picked out previously. She also picked out a pen to go with it.

Then, I asked her for help with Bob. Both of us were struggling with him.

Gift cards – no, no way of knowing if he could get to a store or not. What then?

Once again I was stymied. How can you buy something for someone you don't know, you don't know where they live, and you don't know how they live?

I decided I needed Red's help. I would ask for his help selecting something appropriate on Sunday. Besides, I needed his help to get it to him. I had no idea where he lived.

We got back to the Inn just before 6 pm. As we were unloading the car, I heard the church bell ringing.

I know I had heard it ringing at 6 pm before from the Inn, but I was surprised at how loud it sounded since it was about a mile away. Perhaps it was the fact that we were outside and not inside with all the windows closed for winter.

Later that evening, I checked my computer. When I went into the college system, I saw I got A's in both classes. It definitely made my day.

Ashlee didn't waste very much time in taking care of the gifts she had bought for Red. By the time I had the dishes done after dinner, she had her present wrapped. I figured she didn't want to be caught with it unwrapped.

Friday, just before dinner, Edward Gray checked in. I was sure we could set the Inn's clock by him. Was he always that prompt in everything he did?

As he was checking in, I walked up to him and told him that I heard a rumor that Quack's restaurant was opening up June 1st. He turned and gave me a smile.

"Well, I might have to check it out when they open. If not, I can always go back to my usual eating spot," he told me.

When he was done checking in, he headed off to his room.

About forty-five minutes later, he came back down. He stopped at the desk and told Bonnie to tell me he liked the sign. Then, he headed out the door.

Bonnie caught me a few minutes later and asked me about the message.

I told her I had left a stuffed bear with a note on his pillow. It read, "Bear hugs accepted."

Bonnie started laughing. She knew it was a reference to our bear visit last weekend.

We had two other couples join us that night. Both of them checked in just after dinner. That made five people for breakfast. I had Bonnie leave a note for Jean in the morning giving her the number of guests.

About 7:45 pm, Edward Gray came back from dinner. I was out in the dining room helping Bonnie set up for the morning when he stopped in to let me know that dinner was excellent. He decided to try something different. He went over to Scandia tonight, and ate at Meister's Bar and Grill.

He really wanted to thank me for the delightful note in his room. He was planning on making sure the bear did not go looking for the honey jar set out for the morning breakfast.

I told Ashlee about his comments. She smiled. She knew I had picked up the bear when we were shopping and was wondering what I was up to.

Unfortunately, the next morning was uneventful. No bears for the guests to watch and be entertained. In fact, we had not seen any sign of the bear since Red tied the feeders out of reach.

I wondered if the bear had returned later that night and found its treat out of reach. It was probably at some other feeder in town enjoying its snacks. Either that or some camper at the William O'Brien State Park might have an uninvited visitor looking for food.

I didn't get a chance to talk to Mr. Gray all day Saturday. I was wondering if he had seen the books I left in the fireside room and one in his room about the valley. However, he simply stayed in his room working or reading.

It had been a nice sunny day. Most of our guests were out enjoying the weather taking walks or a drive along the river.

Later that evening, Bonnie popped her head in my door.

"We did it," she exclaimed. "Even though we had one room check out this morning, we had two sets of walk in's. We have a full house tonight."

I was ecstatic. "Really! That's great," I told her. We had finally hit our target – a full house on a weekend. It was our first time we had all four rooms rented at one time. That made seven guests for breakfast. I left a note for Jean.

Sunday morning, I checked with Jean and made sure everything was on time for breakfast with our full house. Then, Ashlee and I left for church.

Red and his father met us in the entryway to the church, where we said our greetings. Then, we found a pew that could fit all four of us together.

It was a nice small church. You could see the early Scandinavian design of the church with a round ceiling and walls tied across from each other with metal rods. My guess, it was probably built before 1900. I hadn't checked the cornerstone to see how old it was.

When the service began, the pastor greeted all the visitors. I had a feeling with this small congregation he knew exactly which ones we were.

It was a nice warm feeling church. It gave off a friendly feeling from the time you walked in, hearing the bell ringing outside the church.

I was surprised to hear both Red and Ashlee singing the hymns. I hadn't heard Ashlee do very much singing. Yes, she had music classes in school, but at home, it was primarily junk music off the computer. She actually had a good voice.

Red wasn't too shabby either. He was doing his best to keep Ashlee on the right pages of the hymnal. Red's father didn't look like he did a lot of singing. He participated in the liturgy, but left the singing to the others.

For me, it was almost like old home week. I was raised with many of these songs and it had been a long time since I sang them. The liturgy had changed slightly, but it didn't take long for me to remember the words.

The pastor caught me by surprise when he announced that on visitor Sunday, visitors were not expected to put an offering in the plate. He said we were their guests. I thought it was a nice touch.

After the service, they had coffee and cookies in the gathering room outside the sanctuary. I could see it was a favorite of most of the kids that had attended the service or had been in Sunday School.

While we were talking to a few people I had met in town along with a few people Ashlee knew from school, the pastor came up and greeted both of us. After finding out where we lived, he invited us to come back again. We were always welcome.

The pastor asked if we could put a few greeting cards at the Bed and Breakfast with the churches name and phone number on it. I told him we would be pleased to put them out.

Shortly after the service, Red's father – Benson, asked us if we would like to join them for brunch at the Scandia Cafe. Looking at Ashlee, I told him we would be glad to join him.

He suggested that Ashlee could ride with Red and he could ride with me to the restaurant. He had something he wanted to discuss on the way there. Whatever it was, I knew it had to be a short discussion. It would only take ten minutes to get there.

On the way to the restaurant, Benson told me that he wanted to thank me for the accident I had on the railroad tracks. It was not that he was happy I had my accident, but he told me that he realized that evening how families act and react together. Ever since his wife died, he hadn't really taken the time to be with Red like he should have. After my little fiasco, he realized he had been wasting many of the years he needed to be in Red's life.

"I suppose you heard the story of Red's truck?" he asked.

"Parts of it. He drove it over on Monday to take Ashlee to the town library. He seemed pretty proud of it."

"Well, it was his mother's. Red helped her pick it out. That's why it was red. When she died, I put it in the barn. I just couldn't drive it unless we needed it as a truck.

"When you hurt your leg, I told Red he could use it. You should have seen the expression in his eyes. You would have thought I gave him a million dollars. When I got back that night, he had it parked back in the barn where we keep it.

"I started thinking. Why did I keep the truck? I could have sold it a few years ago for a good price and bought another truck when I needed one.

"So, with Red's birthday coming up, I took it to town, put some safe tires on it and had it waxed to bring back the faded red color hidden under years of dust.

"You should have seen his face when I told him to get it out of the barn. It was just like when he borrowed it for your ankle mishap.

"So, I just wanted to thank you for providing me the opportunity to reconnect with Red like you connect with Ashlee. I guess I needed my bell rung to wake up."

I didn't know exactly what to say. I guess I had somewhat the same experience moving from St. Cloud. Fortunately, we were arriving at the restaurant.

I told him, "I am glad you remade the connections. Red seems like a nice boy. He needs a strong father at this point in his life for guidance."

We had a good meal. Everyone seemed to enjoy it. As we finished, we thanked Benson and Red for the invitation and for taking us out for the meal. It made a great morning.

Before we left, I told Red I was having a problem trying to figure out something I could get for Bob as a thank you for his help. I asked him if he could come up with something to let me or Ashlee know. He told us he would think about it.

On the way back to the Inn, Ashlee asked me what Red's father wanted to talk about.

I told her, "I think he just wanted to give the two of you an excuse to be able to spend some time together."

Ashlee gave me a big smile. "Thanks!"

Chapter 22

Drawings

<u>Maria</u>

When we got back to the Inn, it was a little later than I had expected. It was just after noon.

It had been a nice day. The sun was starting to warm the earth to the point you could enjoy a sunny day without a jacket. It was hard to imagine that in another month, it would be the summer solstice, and the days would start to get shorter just as summer was starting to show its warm presence. Nature has a strange way of allowing us to adjust to the seasons.

The good thing was that our phone reservations were up. People wanted to get out and walk the trails over at the William O'Brien State Park as well as enjoy the river valley. Looking at the calendar, almost every day from now through September had at least one room reserved.

I realized that I needed to talk to both Bonnie and Jean about taking days off. It was unrealistic to think that one of the two sisters needed to be at the Inn every day this summer. I had been pleased that they had not left me with an open day since I took over. However, in valuing their service, they needed to be able to take a few days off if they wanted them. I decided to talk to them Monday or Tuesday.

Our spring changeover to summer colors and pictures was completed last week. Now, I looked at the list I had put together of "other" areas that needed attention. The lawn company had the grass green and looking good. The leaves left over from winter that always blew onto the grass just after it was raked, had blown back out of the yard and down by the railroad track.

With our summer lawn furniture out on the deck and in the yard, we looked good. The only task left on the list was cleaning the attic and the basement. We needed to straighten out the winter decorations we hastily put away and make some room for a crew to spray for the summer creatures that love to creep into houses out in the countryside. The pro's would spray the inside and outside of the Inn.

I set Thursday and Friday afternoon for a quick cleanup of the basement and attic on our daily task list. We could do the basement one day, leaving the attic for the next.

Looking at my schedule, that left Wednesday for meeting with Jason Willard. I gave him a quick call and confirmed a time we were both available.

Meeting with Bonnie and Jean to discuss vacation ability, I was surprised at how the two of them offered to cover for the other one if they wanted a vacation. I was expecting more of a problem with both of them wanting two weeks off at the same time to go travel somewhere. You would think that sisters might want to travel together sometimes.

I realized I was the emergency backup for the pair, however, I felt it would be good to have a third person trained to come in a day or two a week. I could see from the expression on their faces at my meeting that both Bonnie and Jean had figured it would cut into their hours if I hired a third person. I needed to figure out a solution to the problem before one of them got sick or found a better job someday.

So far, the best solution to adding a part time person appeared to be increasing our customer reservations. If we could keep the reservations up by twenty percent, it would give me additional dollars to bring in a part-time person.

When I met with Jason Willard the next day at my office in the Inn, we discussed the issue. In fact, it was the only issue we needed to discuss. He liked the fact that the room rate had increased, and felt the Inn was in fine shape.

When I told him my concern about staffing, he smiled and told me, that's what we hired you for. You need to plan for things so that you don't end up in chaos. When I showed him my suggestion for adding a third person on a very part-time basis once the reservation rate hit my magic point, he just nodded his head.

"Sounds like a good plan. Let me know when you decide to do it. There may be a few local people that would love to fill in a day here and a day there," Jason told me. "I think you have things in good hands. Unless there is a problem that you need my help, I don't think we need to meet until fall. The way you are going, you'll probably be asking for a parking ramp by that time."

I smiled and laughed. Obviously, Jason felt I was doing the job they hired me for. To me, it was job security. I guess that was what Bonnie and Jean were worried about as well. I needed to put that on my list as something to work on to affirm their importance at the Inn.

As we were finishing our conversation in my office, we noticed Red and Ashlee drove into the parking lot.

"Looks like Ashlee has a friend," Jason told me.

"Yes, he just got the truck in his name and convinced Ashlee to ride with him to and from school. So far, he seems like a nice boy and they appear to be taking things slow."

"Well, keep an eye on her. You only have one daughter."

With that, Jason greeted Ashlee as she came in the front door, and then left the Inn to handle his other customers.

"Looks like you got a ride from Red. Have you switched taxis, or is it just for the day?" I asked Ashlee.

"Leslie told me this morning that she had a doctor's appointment after school. So, I asked Red if I could have a ride home instead of taking the bus. It was nice, we talked all the way here.

"If it's okay with you, can I shift over to riding with Red on Friday?"

"As long as you thank Leslie's parents and let them know your plans," I told her. I was glad she was still keeping me in the loop. In this case, I thought she would enjoy getting a ride to and from school from a boy more than a girl friend's mother.

She headed off to her room to work on homework.

Thursday and Friday, I had both Jean and Bonnie working since we were doing some cleaning during the day.

On Friday afternoon, Jean and Bonnie were cleaning out some of the storage cabinets up in the attic when they discovered something tucked away in the corner.

It was a small booklet with pictures drawn in it. Someone had used it to draw on and then somehow it had been tucked into a corner and forgotten. There were no names on the drawings.

They brought it down and showed me what they had found.

"Any idea who may have made the drawings?" I asked.

Neither of them had any ideas.

We didn't see any names or initials in the booklet.

The drawings looked as though they were made by some young children, perhaps six to eight years old. They had very good drawing skills. Most of the objects in the drawings were drawn to proper scale. After looking it through, I decided to place it on the mantle in the fireside room for guests to look through. If I knew the artist, we would have gladly called them and told them what we found.

At the end of the day, that was our only rare find. Other than a couple spiders, there was very little to get excited about. It gave us a good opportunity to get the Inn sprayed and make sure we didn't have any non-paying guests staying at the Inn.

I was glad we did not have the exterminators come today. It had been raining all morning and when it cleared, it was cloudy with little wind. We had three rooms reserved for this evening including Mr. Gray. I really didn't want any lingering smell of the spray to deter customers from coming back. Fortunately, I had scheduled the spraying for Tuesday, which is normally one of our slowest days.

I didn't see very much of Edward Gray this weekend. He checked in at the same time another couple was checking in. When they were finished, he headed out for dinner. I'm not sure what time he returned. I was assisting someone with reservations.

Saturday was a busy day at the Inn. We needed to turn over two rooms for the guests coming in that evening. So, while Jean was cleaning up the rooms, I volunteered to help with the front desk.

In the middle of things, Ashlee went off somewhere with Red just before lunch. She told me she would be back in time for dinner. With all the hassle of people checking out, I never did catch where they were going.

When she returned, she showed me a sling backpack she picked up for me to give to Bob. Wow! It shocked me that she had solved my problem. I never did figure out what to get him. Apparently, she and Red had discussed it on the way home from school yesterday, and they went to some wholesale place to pick one up. Now, all I had to do was figure out how to get it to him. I figured I needed to pick up a card to go along with it.

I asked if Ashlee and Red wanted to go to church in the morning. If they did, I could get a card this evening and discuss it with Red tomorrow as to how to deliver it to Bob.

Bonnie came in late in the afternoon and finished the day. I let her check in the evening guests before running out to get a card in Stillwater. On the way back, I couldn't believe that I had procrastinated this long in getting a gift for Bob. I needed to become more focused on what was going on, and set priorities.

The smell of rolls in the oven woke me up early in the morning. Ashlee and I had a taste of the rolls before heading off to church. Two weeks in a row for us set a record. I hadn't done that since moving to St. Cloud. That was years ago.

After church, Red and I discussed getting the backpack to Bob. He told me that I had a choice. He could take it to Bob for me and give it to him, or, I could wait for a day or perhaps weeks for Bob to come to us. The answer was easy, I thanked Red and gave him the backpack to take to Bob along with my card.

It took us a little while before we got back to the Inn. Edward Gray had just checked out. Before leaving, Jean told me that he had spent time after breakfast looking at the coloring book we had discovered up in the attic, before heading up to his room. We had placed it on the mantle in the fireside room.

Then, she told me, "He came down later in the morning looking for you. When I told him that you and Ashlee had gone to church, and didn't say if you were coming straight back, he headed back to his room.

"Then, as he was checking out, he handed me an envelope to give to you. He didn't say what it was about."

She handed me the envelope.

I waited until I was in my office to open it up. I was curious as to what it was about. Opening the envelope, I read the note inside.

Dear Ms. Wagner,

I wanted to write you a note to tell you how I have appreciated what you have done with the Bed and Breakfast since you took over the helm.

I think you have done a very good job in making it clean and comfortable for your guests.

Also, I have enjoyed your personal touches. Where I was really expecting a bearskin rug in my room after seeing your visitor to the Inn, the bear on the pillow was a nice touch.

I especially enjoyed seeing a copy of Ashlee's paper in each room. It gives the Inn a home-like touch.

Finally, when I was looking at the books you purchased about the area in the fireside room, I came upon the coloring book you placed on the mantle. It finished off the home away from home touch – just what it took. Please do not throw the drawing book, I enjoyed looking at all the pictures and will enjoy it again the next time I return.

One more request. If you have time, I would like to take both you and Ashlee to Quack's restaurant next time I am here. They have a great meal on Friday nights and since you have never been there, I would love to take both of you, my treat, to dinner. Just let me know when I check in next time if you are available.

Sincerely,
Edward Gray

The note took me by surprise. While I was working hard trying to get to know him, he turns and asks to take Ashlee and me to dinner. I thought about it a couple minutes.

Interesting, he wasn't just flirting with a single woman, he invited Ashlee as well.

Later in the day, I showed it to Ashlee.

"So, did you say we were going or not?" she asked.

"The next time he will be at the Inn will be the first weekend of June. I guess I'll just have to see how busy our schedule is by then. Quacks should be open. I think you need reservations for Friday night.

"Remind me, let's talk about it next weekend and see how your plans look," I told Ashlee. "Maybe we will take him up on his offer."

Chapter 23

The Encounter

It took a couple days, but when Red brought Ashlee home from school on Tuesday, he told me that he had brought the backpack to Bob last night. He said to say thanks.

"That's about as good as it gets with Bob," Red told me. "He's not one for a long thank-you or a lot of emotion."

The backpack Ashlee and Red had purchased was one with a design in bright orange over black. I figured I could watch the railroad tracks to see if I could spot him walking with it over his shoulder during the summer. I still wondered where exactly he lived.

Ashlee and Red went for a walk towards the State Park before Red needed to head home for dinner.

<u>Ashlee</u>

While we were walking on the dirt road, I asked Red if he would do me a favor. I asked him if he would go with me to the high bridge over the river and help me take a few pictures. I wanted to see it for myself if all the parts of my report had been as accurate as possible.

"I told you it was," he told me.

"I know. It's just that I'd like to see it in person sometime. You know how that is. Everyone seems to have seen it, but me. Even Leslie told me she had seen it."

"So you want me to take you? I thought you were scared of heights?"

"I am. That's why I was hoping you would take me. That way I don't have to go too close to the bridge. I was hoping we could go just the two of us. Since school is almost over, we shouldn't have any homework to worry about.

"Besides," I told him, "after the episode with my mother on the railroad tracks, I think we need to do this without telling her. She might be a little paranoid, after her rescue, if she hears that I want to go near the high bridge."

"How about Saturday. That way we don't have to worry about it getting dark and a bear jumping out at you."

That was the last thing I needed to hear. I was nervous enough without having to hear stories about bears. We decided on 11:00 am on Saturday. I would pack some sandwiches and we could find a place with a view for lunch.

When we got back to the B&B, I asked my mother, "What smells?"

"Did you forget we were spraying for pests today? You should have been here a couple hours ago. We've had the windows open ever since. I can't smell it anymore. I take it you can. I'll light a couple candles to try and take the odor out for the one guest we have tonight. Fortunately, they said they would be arriving a little late. I can't remember where they said they were driving from."

By the time our guests arrived, the smell was almost gone. I was glad, my room had smelled just as bad. I had the windows open and three candles lit to try to get the odor out. Then I realized, they had sprayed just outside my windows as well. Closing the windows helped.

I didn't tell my mother what Red and I had planned for Saturday.

School was starting to ease up for homework. I think the teachers knew that the last week or two, with really nice weather outside, was not a good time for homework. It just wasn't going to get done. On top of that, they probably didn't want to correct the papers.

Yearbooks had arrived, and I had reluctantly purchased one. Everyone else was going to have half the world sign theirs the last couple of weeks. I figured I'd be lucky to have ten or fifteen sign mine.

We weren't supposed to pass them around until the last week, but since the seniors were already passing theirs around, the rest of the students did the same thing.

To my surprise, I'll bet sixty people signed my book. I didn't think that many people in our school knew me. Even my teachers wrote something.

Most of the students in my English class wrote something in my book and many of them commented on how good our paper was. I was impressed. When I read comment after comment, I knew we did a good job on our report.

Then, there were a couple comments by a few of the shy boys in my classes. I hadn't even talked to them all spring. Somehow, they had the courage to say something nice in writing when they hadn't had the nerve to talk to me face to face. I wondered what they would be like come fall. It seemed like many of the students were maturing right before my eyes. I wondered if I appeared that way to them.

The note I cherished the most was from Red. He wrote in my book that I was the best thing that happened to him this year. He thanked me for our friendship.

Then there was one note from a kid that I always thought was a little weird in math class. *"The multiplicity of life is matched only by the logarithmic nature of same. Your close classmate, Arlo."*

Close classmate? When I read it a few hours later, it took me ten minutes just to figure out who he was.

At the end of the week, I showed my mother my yearbook. When she saw Red's comment, she just smiled at me.

"See, you can make a difference," she told me.

I told her that Red and I were going for a walk along the river tomorrow and that I was going to bring sandwiches for lunch.

"Don't fall in," she told me. "The river is too cold for swimming this time of the year."

I laughed. I didn't tell her that several of my friends had an end of year beer party on Crunch Berry Island, just out from the old mill site on the river, last night.

They were talking about the fact that they swam the short distance to the island. Burr! I wondered about the swim. I figured they didn't have their swimming suits with. Who would want to stay on the island in wet clothes? Even with the beer they were drinking, it would have been cold. I would have thought that one of their parents would have had a boat they could have used.

Then again, if the police broke up the party, they probably didn't want a boat that someone could confiscate. A quick dash through the water was quicker in case they needed a fast exit. If they had to, they could even make the dash to the Wisconsin side of the river. Most of the way there, the river was less than four feet deep from that location.

I got to thinking, if I was still in St. Cloud, my friends and I would have been at a party like that every weekend. Now, it didn't even appeal to me. Times had changed.

As my mother and I were talking, one of the guests came in and told Jean that there was a suspicious looking person in the woods just behind our Inn.

My mother heard them and tried to look out the back window to see what they were talking about.

After looking through a couple windows, my mother spotted him. It was a grubby looking man in a coat even though it was 65 degrees outside. It took her a second, then she realized it was Bob. He was just standing there about twenty feet back into the trees.

Looking at him, she could understand why a customer would be concerned. He looked just like he did the first time I saw him on the railroad tracks.

My mother walked over to Jean and our customer. "It's okay, I know him. I think he wants to talk to me," she told them.

With that, she went out the door and around the back to the woods that lined the railroad tracks. It was where Bob stood there waiting.

I was surprised that my mother did not ask me to go with her. I knew she must have been real nervous meeting him in the woods.

I watched as she approached Bob and stopped about ten feet from him. The two of them appeared to be talking. Or at least, my mother was talking. Then, after a few minutes, I saw Bob turn and head back into the woods. When he did, I noticed the orange backpack on his back.

It took a few minutes before my mother got back into the Inn. Jean looked at her, wondering what it was all about.

"That was Bob," she told her. "He was the one that went for help when I sprained my ankle. We bought him a backpack as a thank you for his help. He wanted to thank me, but he was too nervous to come to the door."

When she came back in the apartment, she turned to me, "I'm glad he didn't come to the door. I'm not sure what Jean might have done.

"That was one of the strangest conversations I have had in a long time. He wanted to thank us, but he really didn't know how. I just told him it was me that needed to thank him."

Looking at my mother's face, I could tell how stressed she was in meeting Bob. Fortunately, it was over. She had her chance to tell him in person that she appreciated his efforts.

I called Red later that evening. I told him about our encounter with the stranger hiding in the woods. He laughed. "That's Bob," he told me.

Chapter 24

The Picnic

Ashlee

The next morning, Red picked me up for our walk to the high bridge. As I instructed him, we didn't mention to my mother exactly where we were going.

I threw a backpack with our lunch in his truck along with my camera. Then, we headed south of town.

"It seems like everyone in our English class had seen the bridge," I told Red. "How did you find it?"

"Well, remember I told you my grandfather used to live on the river. He used to take me out in his boat and we would pass under the bridge. It's just as impressive from the water as it is from shore.

"When I heard some of the guys at school talking about walking to it, I asked them how to get there from the road. That's how I found it. There was a small trail that led from the road all the way to the river. It was really neat. Lots of woods, gullies, and then the railroad bed shows up on a hill, just before you see the bridge.

"You'll see. Unfortunately, the National Park Service almost ruined the trail through the woods. Last time I was there, they cut the forest with a brush cutter, eliminating all the trees less than eight inches in diameter, and a few that were greater than that. There was so much debris on the ground, I couldn't even find the trail. It was a good thing I knew which way to go. Even the signs were gone. The start of the old trail was really nice. You could walk fifty feet into the woods and leave all traces of the road behind. Now, we have to walk a few hundred feet just to lose sight of the road."

"So is it worth the walk?" I asked.

"I think so. Some things even the Park Service can't damage."

After parking in a spot that held only a couple cars, along the road, Red and I hiked back into a forest that looked like it had been hit by loggers.

I was glad Red knew the way. From the start of the trail, I would have had no guess as to which way the trail led.

We were probably two blocks into the woods before we started to pick up signs of the old trail. I was expecting it to lead east to the river. Instead, the trail that was about eight feet wide led off north and south.

"Which way?" I asked.

"We'll head north towards the train tracks."

From the direction we came on the road, which had been from the south, I had no idea where the tracks were.

After another couple hundred yards, the woods changed. Gone was the flat forest covered with branches and bark. Oh, the cutters had hit some of this area too, but it became hilly. Their machinery had stopped at the edges of the ravine that laid ahead of us. Beyond the ravine, I could just make out the slope of a steep hill leading up to the railroad tracks.

"Wow, that's way up there," I told Red.

"Actually, we have dropped that far on the trail. We started out higher than the tracks back at the car."

It was looking more and more like a beautiful wooded trail. As the trail ran east paralleling the tracks high above us, we passed some large cedar trees and a few large white pine trees.

"You see that pine?" Red asked.

"The forest used to be full of them and oak trees. North of Taylor's Falls, it was mainly pine. That's what brought the lumberjacks here in the first place. That huge white pine is probably almost eighty feet tall. My guess is that it is a second growth tree. You can tell by the large diameter of the trunk. When Marine was founded, they harvested trees that stood two hundred feet tall. You think that they made a noise when the lumberjacks fell them to the forest floor? I'm just glad they left a few of these second growth trees since then."

It was indeed impressive to see the huge white pine tree. There were a few of these in Marine, but standing up here on the hill, it really stood out.

Just before the path took a drop heading to the river, there was a spot where you caught your first glance of the river bridge.

Looking at it from a distance, I remembered Leslie saying that she had walked out on it. No Way! Even from here my fear of heights was starting to become active. How could anyone even consider it?

There was the remains of an old road that led down a steep hill to where a cabin was located on the river. My guess was that was why the trail was as wide as it was. We had been traveling on an old dirt road created there in the forest eighty to one hundred years ago.

"This is the easy way," Red told me. "Before they tried mulching the forest, there used to be the remains of an old trolley system the original cabin owner must have used to move things up the steep hill in the winter. Even after all these years, the metal eyelets are probably still in the hillside. I was told they were made of Swedish Bell Steel. It doesn't rust. That's why they still exist.

"If you go up to Taylor's Falls, you can see the same eyelets in the rocks by the landing. They used them to tie up the riverboats."

"If they don't rust, why don't we use that metal now?" I asked.

"Sorry, you'll have to ask a metal expert. I wondered the same thing. My guess is that it might have something to do with cost.

"I'm not sure if the old trolley cart exists anymore. Someone may have taken it. It's too bad they couldn't have left everything the way it was."

We headed down the road closer to the river. About forty feet above the river it turned north towards the bridge.

As we followed the path, we came to a flat area that was protected on the hillside by a tall wall made of rocks cemented in place.

"This is probably where the old cabin was located," Red told me. "Their barn was probably up on the hill, just above where I pointed out that the trolley trail came out."

I looked at the view of the river. "Wow, I think I know why they built a cabin here. That's quite a view."

From this spot, you were protected by the hills from the setting sun. It would have made it cool in the evenings. The rising sun over the river valley would have warmed the area in the early mornings.

A creek flowed down between the homestead and the railroad bridge. And then, there was the bridge!!!!

"Oh, my!" I told Red. "It is even more impressive than your photograph."

I took out my camera to take a few pictures.

"Not yet," he told me. "Wait until we get down by the river. Then you will get the pictures you wanted."

We crossed the creek and followed the path to the river, which was only a short distance. From there, I had an unrestricted view of the bridge, the river, and the river valley.

"You want to take pictures first or have lunch first?" Red asked.

Looking at the blue sky and how the light was hitting the bridge, there was no option. “Let me take a couple pictures. Then, we can sit and eat as we talk.”

I spent the next fifteen minutes taking picture after picture.

Red suggested a place where I could really get a good shot. The reflections of the bridge in the water really made for a fantastic view. I could see his artist’s eye coming out in his selection of how to frame the picture.

Sitting on a log near the river, I took the sandwiches out of my backpack along with a couple drink boxes. “I hope this is okay?”

"It will be fine," he told me, "I'm just enjoying the company."

We sat there looking at the bridge. Now, in all fairness, this was not your everyday bridge you would see going across a river. This thing was massive, and at the same time delicate looking.

"How did they build this bridge?" I asked. "Surely, they didn't float it up the river and lift it in place?"

"Probably not. Although some of the material may have come up the river. The cement footings were probably poured from down here.

"You have to remember, this wasn't computer designed like modern bridges. Someone built it like an old erector set – one piece of steel at a time, bolted or riveted in place.

"I saw an old picture of them building the bridge. They started at both ends and met in the middle. You say you are scared of heights? They brought a crane out on a train from each end putting the next pieces of steel in front of them as they built it.

"Think it swayed in the wind when it wasn't attached to the other side? I don't understand how they could have driven the crane out on the incomplete bridge," he told me.

"What happened if it didn't meet in the middle?" I asked.

"I guess someone would have gotten fired. I don't see a jog in the bridge do you?"

As we were watching, a work crew drove out on the bridge.

Looking at them, I told Red, "It looks like a toy truck up there."

"So if the bridge looked huge before, how does it look with something that you recognize the size on it? That's called perspective. Now, that would make another good picture for you."

He was right. With the truck up there looking like a miniature toy, it gave the size of the bridge an entirely different look.

We were enjoying sitting on the log, enjoying our sandwiches and just talking. It was a great location for a picnic. Even on a Saturday, it was quiet down here.

"We picked the wrong time of day to do this," Red told me. "It's a full moon today. We should have come here later in the day and we could have watched the full moon rising over the hills. Now, that would have been impressive. Think of the pictures you could have shot.

"Do you know there is going to be a blue moon tonight?"

"What do you mean?" I asked.

"You never heard of a blue moon? Well, I guess I need to teach you everything on this walk.

"First of all, it's not blue. That's just the name. I looked it up in the Farmer's Almanac once. Maybe on a super cold January day up north, it might look blue. Who knows, maybe that was where the Native Americans were when they made up the names.

"You do know that the time between full moons is not a month, right?"

"Yeah, I guess so. They said it was 29 days in science class."

"Okay. Let's start from there. The Native Americans had names for all the full moons. There was the harvest moon, the snow moon, the wolf moon, the flower moon, the corn moon, the hunter's moon and a few others that I can't recall off the top of my head."

"I've heard of the harvest moon. That's the full moon closest to the harvest season that looks red from all the dust," I told him.

"That's close. Actually, there are other moons that correspond to harvests. Like the corn moon. It takes place in September when the corn is ready to harvest."

"I thought that was the harvest moon," I told him.

"The harvest moon can happen in September or October. It occurs at the equinox – you know equal day and night. It signals the time for corn, pumpkins, squash, and wild rice to be harvested."

"So, what's the difference between the harvest moon and the corn moon?"

"Let me go back a little."

"The Native Americans named the twelve full moons. But with 29 days per moon cycle, that means we get almost 13 full moons in a year. It doesn't come out to an even number.

"The harvest moon is the name given to the closest full moon to the equinox. Therefore, that moon may have two names.

"Then again, we have the blue moon. It started out as the 3rd full moon in a 3 month period with 4 full moons. It was a little complicated and most people didn't understand it. They changed it to the second full moon in any given month. That people could remember.

"So, if there were two full moons in September, the first one would have been the corn moon. The second would have been the harvest moon or the blue moon. The full moon in October would come late in the month and would be called its regular name – the hunter's moon. Understand?"

"I guess so. So, why do we say once in a blue moon?" I asked.

"Because it only happens once in a very long time. The moon's cycle and the calendar have to match up. It happens in a different month each time.

"One more odd event. With only 28 days in most Februarys, every once in a while there is no full moons in that month. Save that fact in the back of your head for some trivia contest when you need it."

"Okay, how about this; the next time we have a blue moon, you have to take me to a location where we can watch it come up over the horizon. I want to see if it is blue."

"Deal. But, only if I can pick the spot. How about on some cliff where we can get a good unobstructed view?"

"You'd be sitting there alone," I told him.

Chapter 25

Scenery

I was really enjoying sitting on the log next to the river with Red. We could have stayed there until the moon rose over the hills. I'm not sure I would have complained.

"Well, are you ready for a hike?" Red asked as he finished his food."

"I thought this was the hike. We heading back already?"

"No, I want to show you the view."

I looked at him. This wasn't the view? Where were we going now? Oh no! Not up on the bridge?

I told Red, "I'm not going up on the bridge. No way!"

"Good. I wouldn't go there either. It's not safe. We're going to go up above the bridge. I want you to see the view that Bert Hudson and his firefighters would have seen when they reported to the train fire."

"I'm not climbing any cliffs," I told him.

"No cliffs. Just a big hill to go up."

He pointed to the hill next to where we had been sitting. From where we sat, I could not see the top of the hill. There were too many trees blocking my vision. The trail led under the bridge to the opposite side of the tall railroad bridge. Before we hiked the trail, I took a few pictures from the riverbank directly up at the bridge.

Wow! Two hundred feet up and you could see right through the railroad ties on the bridge. What a picture. As we stood there, you could hear the bridge creaking.

"What's that?" I asked.

"That's the sun expanding the metal on the bridge. Sounds eerie doesn't it. And they say a bridge is not a living thing. This one grows and contracts every day."

I just kept looking at the bridge. A bridge that moves with the sun? What does it do with the wind? How old was it?

I think we said it was completed in 1911 in our report. What keeps it up? Its five arches loomed like an old Roman bridge. Was it really built to last this long?

I saw a rope hanging from one of the arches. No Way! Someone must have tied it there to swing from the bridge. It was supposed to be 184 feet from the bottom of the arch to the water. No wonder I had heard stories about the bridge. Many of them did not turn out very good.

We should have been mountain goats. Climb a hill. It could have been a mountain. Unlike mountains that use switchbacks to make climbing easy, this one was straight up. And up, and up.

When we finally reached the top, I was glad we had finished lunch on the bottom. I didn't want to carry anything up that hill.

I stopped to catch my breath. Ugh! I thought I was in good shape. I almost didn't make the climb.

Red was ahead of me by about fifteen feet. He was motioning me to come over to where he was standing. Looking back, I was worried that he had found an overhang to get a good view of the river. Even looking down the path we came up made me dizzy.

He was standing next to a steel pipe, driven into the ground.

"I always wondered what this pipe was for," he said. "Did they use it for surveying the bridge or was it used to run a cable that would prevent it from swaying as they built it?"

I had most of my breath back. When I looked out to see what he was talking about, I saw we were on a hill probably thirty feet higher than the bridge. The crest was back from the cliff so I was only slightly nervous.

"Oh my gosh! What a view," I told him. I took out my camera.

You could see all the way across the bridge from one side to the other. At the same time, you could see probably a mile up and down the river.

"Now you know what it is like to be an eagle flying over the river valley. Only they aren't stuck here on the hill. Want to sit and catch your breath?"

We sat there for quite a while.

"Who owns this property?" I asked.

"The National Park Service. So far they haven't gotten their cutters up here. Over the years, they have been systematically taking over the valley from north of Stillwater to Taylor's Falls. Anything close to the hills, they pick up on a forced long term contract. They buy out the land with an option for the original owner to live there. Once they die or want to give up the land and not pay taxes, it goes over to the Park Service.

"That's what happened to my grandfather's property. When he died, they simply took it over. The cabin he lived in was moved out. He had a great setting just back from the river with about forty acres of the hillside on his property."

"I'll bet you wish you could have it back."

"Yes. But it will never happen. They want to protect the valley and keep it for future generations. It sounds good. However, I'm not sure it works for our generation. Take that forest we walked through. If they keep their hands off of it, it will take at least twenty years before it looks the same as it was before they "improved" it.

"Even the fishing area I used to fish with my grandfather is almost impossible to get to. They closed the river to boats from the south. To get there from the north, the river is too shallow and the bottom is lined with huge rocks. Last time I tried fishing the Apple River outlet, the person I was with lost two propellers on the rocks getting there and back. That makes fishing from anything but a canoe or kayak impossible. With the current, it is hard to paddle any distance back upstream."

Red pointed to the split in the river way upstream where he used to fish with his grandfather.

"I used to watch eagles, otters and turtles up there when we were on the river. I'll bet most of the kids in the area never even get a chance to get out there anymore."

I saw his point. When we were having our lunch at the base of the bridge, I saw signs that stated that no river travel was allowed upstream from the bridge.

"They were trying to prevent zebra mussels from getting upstream. With the high current in the area, boaters would not have gotten very far. The strange thing, the National Park Service allowed boaters to come down to that point and then go up as far as they could. Did the magic shadow in the water, caused by the bridge, really stop the mussels from getting upstream?" he asked.

Red didn't think so. He said that the waterfowl could carry them up river, especially the herons and egrets. They could stick to weeds or sticks and be carried right past the bridge.

I could tell he didn't like the way the National Park Service was protecting the valley. He was probably right. They needed someone local to manage the area that knew the history of the river and what areas to respect. It didn't work to bring in someone from some other part of the nation that only stayed for a few years. Typical government in action.

I wondered how long it would take for them to take over the river front along the Marine area.

My attention slipped back to the bridge. The work crew we saw earlier had disappeared long ago. Now, the long empty stretch of tracks seemed to go on forever from hillside to hillside.

We discussed Bert Hudson's tale of the burning train. It was hard to imagine showing up at night and seeing a train parked on the Minnesota side of the tracks having left a car on fire out on the bridge.

We looked at the situation. If the car was closer to Wisconsin than Minnesota on the bridge, they had to walk a long distance at night without lights. I remembered that you could see up through the ties from down below the bridge.

Looking at the tracks, there was only room for one train and there was a small walkway next to the track. I could see why they couldn't drive the truck out on the bridge to put out the fire.

The river was split under the bridge. The mainstream was under the Minnesota end of the bridge. Under the other end, there was a smaller cut. That must have been where the New Richmond Fire Department parked a truck and got the water from.

I looked. From that point, it was still 200-feet up to the top of the bridge. No way, I would have stood there and raised a hose up on a rope to the bridge. They should have given all of them a medal for putting out the fire. How did they keep from losing someone over the edge of the narrow bridge?

Red and I just sat there talking about the event. Somehow, it seemed incredible that they pulled it off and put out the fire. If the heat of the fire got to the railroad ties, the whole bridge could have caught fire. That would have definitely made the national news.

We wondered if they would have let them rebuild the bridge if it collapsed.

Then we got to thinking about Red's report on President Hoover. I remembered him saying that his guards did not want his train to cross the high bridge.

Were they afraid of the height or worried that someone could easily sabotage his train on the bridge? All it would take would have been a few missing spikes.

It was a chilling discussion.

I told Red, "You know, right after we read our report in class, one of the girls came up to me and told me a story about her cousin and the bridge. I looked it up. Apparently, it really happened." I gave Red a description of what she told me at school.

"Apparently, her cousin lives about a mile from the Wisconsin end of the bridge. She told me that several times the two of them would hike to the bridge and walk out on the walkway of the bridge.

"She told me it was scary as the bridge actually moves with the wind.

"They never went very far. There are cameras set up to detect people on the bridge. When they spot someone, they call the railroad police or the county sheriff's department.

"Well, one day her cousin and her friend went down there and her friend talked her into crossing the bridge with her. She said it was only a half a mile. They could do it in less than ten minutes. No one would ever know.

"After a short discussion, they agreed to go out there. It was mid-afternoon on a cloudy day. No one would be looking for two people crossing the bridge, they thought. Besides, think of the stories they could tell everyone at school the next day."

"How old were they?" Red asked.

"Old enough to know better. I think they were high school students.

"Anyway, according to our classmate, they walked out on the Wisconsin end of the tracks. Apparently, they looked but did not see the cameras aimed at the tracks. They thought they were in the clear.

"Walking out on the bridge, there was a steel grate on the side of the tracks for maintenance along with a railing just on one side of the bridge."

As Red and I looked at the bridge from our angle, we could see the narrow grate she was talking about. It was very close to the tracks.

"The two girls went out over the Wisconsin channel and apparently were enjoying the view from there. They were looking for bald eagles, but only saw one flying high over the hills. Along with seeing the eagle, there were a couple turkey vultures flying over the valley.

"Obviously, they weren't like me. They must not have been scared silly of heights.

"As they stopped and enjoyed the view, they blew their estimates as to how long it would take to cross the bridge.

"They were almost to the center when they heard it. It started as a ringing sound on the tracks. As it got louder, they saw a set of three lights coming from behind them. It was a train, and the engine was coasting downhill towards the bridge. To their shock, it was only a half a mile from the bridge. And, it was heading their way.

"Panic set in. It was too close to run back towards the oncoming train to get off the bridge. Even if they ran as fast as they could, it would be a race to the edge of the bridge. Since the train was heading towards them, they might not make it. They knew the train was moving faster than they could run. How much faster was the question? Train speeds are hard to judge at a distance.

"The only other option they had was to run the other way. It was slightly longer, but it would take the train longer to get there as well. Hopefully, the engineer would see them and slow down. If they did, the girls might make it to safety.

"Their dark clothing made them blend in with the dark tracks and railroad ties. So far, at that distance, they were just a dark spot on the bridge to the train crew.

"From what I picked up on news reports of the incident and the Sherriff's Department, the train was pulling about 100 loaded cars. It was slowing down to the safe crossing speed of 30 mph on the bridge.

"The train crew had no idea that two people were on the bridge ahead of them until they were a couple hundred feet from the bridge.

"There was one more item that the two girls had no idea of. Due to the weight of a fully loaded freight train, the crew was not allowed to apply the brakes on the bridge. Even if they could, it would have taken them a distance longer than the bridge just to bring the freight train to a stop.

"As solid as the bridge looks, it is not built to withstand the braking force of several million pounds of train straining to come to a stop. Not even the wheels or tracks could take the stress of a quick stop even if they were not on a bridge. At that speed, it would probably take over a mile to come to a full stop.

"Before reaching the bridge, the train sounded its air-horn. For the girls, it was time to run for their life.

"Shortly thereafter, the two-man crew spotted the girls running on the bridge. Their flailing arms caught their attention. Unfortunately, it was too late to do anything. All they could do was to lay on the air horn.

"The screaming could probably be heard coming from the bridge. Both girls were running as fast as they could. The bridge looked like it stretched all the way from Wisconsin to the Dakotas as they desperately tried to reach the other side. Neither girl had ever run over a half mile before, and never at full speed.

"As they looked over their shoulders, they couldn't believe what they saw. Or should I say what they didn't hear. They didn't hear any screeching of brakes coming from the train. Couldn't they see them? Why weren't they trying to stop?

"The bridge was shaking like there had been an earthquake. It made running in a straight line on a narrow surface harder.

"After looking back at the train, the one girl's foot slipped off the walkway as she ran. Fortunately, she landed squarely on a railroad tie and didn't tumble to the tracks. She stumbled for a second, regained her stride and kept going.

"The other girl shouted to her – Don't look back.

"The fact the girls didn't understand, was that not only could the engineer not apply the brakes on the train, fifty of the cars were still on the gradual slope downhill to the bridge.

"Even on neutral power, the train was not slowing down.

"The numbers were not in their favor. The train was still traveling at 30 mph. The girls could run at about 12 mph if they were on a good road. On the metal mesh next to the tracks, it was much slower.

"How long could they keep up the pace? Panic was setting in. They were not breathing evenly as they tried to run.

"By the time they hit the two-thirds mark of the length of the bridge, it was obvious to both the train crew and the girls – they were not going to make it to the end of the bridge in time.

"So far, one girl was thirty feet ahead of the other one. The slip off the walkway had slowed the one down for a stride or two. It was our classmate's cousin that was behind. She was not a runner and was running out of gas.

"There were two options; jump into the river or cling to the railing of the bridge with all the strength they could muster. It was 200 feet to the water. Even if they held onto the railing, they might be swept from the bridge from the wind of the passing train. That was if there was indeed room between the railing and the train for a person. This was a maintenance walkway. It was not designed as a pedestrian sidewalk.

"The crew on the train were already thinking the worse. The girls could stumble and get run over by the train, or get swept off the bridge to their death in the river. It was only a question of which would happen.

"Even if they clung to the railing, if there was a branch that was picked up by any of the cars during their long travel, it could easily knock them off the bridge.

"The train was only two hundred feet behind them on the track. Now the bridge was shaking from the weight of the approaching train and the two big diesel locomotives in the lead. Even the tracks appeared to be moving up and down.

"The girls were screaming. They had run out of energy from the distance they had run, and the chances of stumbling onto the rails were increasing.

"Finally, our classmate's cousin decided to give up. She shouted to her friend to cling to the railing. Stopping, she hung on for all she could.

"Looking down, she could see the ripples in the water two hundred feet below her. Perhaps the turkey vultures knew more than the girls did when they circled the bridge.

"Her friend could barely hear her over the noise of the train. Looking back, she saw her friend clinging as tightly as possible to the railing. The train was almost up to her friend now. She realized she was not going to make the hillside either. It was now or never. The girl stopped and grabbed the top metal railing as hard as her fingers could grab it.

"As the train rolled by, the girls could see the look on the faces of the train's crew. They were that close. Everyone on the bridge that day wondered if the one-hundred car train would clear the girls and if they had the strength left in their bodies to hang on that long.

"The crew on the train strained to look back, out the window of the engine. Did they hold on or did they lose the battle and end up in the river? If the fall didn't knock them out when they hit the water, they'd probably drown fighting the current.

"In the old days, a crew member riding in the caboose could have let them know the girls fate. With no caboose anymore, all they could do was hope.

"Why didn't the girls observe the sign that said "No Trespassing on Railroad Property?"

"As the train rolled by, the girls kept an eye on each other. They were hoping it wasn't the last time they saw each other alive.

"There were no other options. They kept telling each other to hang on tight as the cars kept rolling by inches from them on the track. It felt like it took an hour before the train finally passed by.

"Once the engine was off the bridge a safe distance, they applied the dynamic brakes on the engine to slow the train. It made a loud crashing metal sound as the couplings of the cars felt the sudden backward pressure of the engines. Combining that noise with the shifting bridge from the weight of the cars, for a second, it sounded as if the whole bridge was coming apart.

"The engineer could not apply the air brakes on the cars until the entire train was off the bridge. It was all or nothing with the air-brakes. You couldn't apply the brakes to only part of the train as it left the bridge.

"After they brought the train to a stop, when they checked the train, there was no evidence that there was anything sticking out from a car that hit the girls. The question still in their minds; did they make it, or did they end up in the river?

"The crew had close calls before, but this one was the closest they had ever had to killing two people.

"According to our classmate, both girls made it off the bridge. As soon as the train passed by, they quickly got off the bridge and ran into the woods. They were worried the police had been called about trespassers on the bridge.

It was terrifying. "She told me that both of them thought they were going to die. The wind from the train passing inches from them felt like a hurricane attempting to push them off the bridge. The top railing they held onto was the only thing that saved their lives.

"They stayed in the woods for over an hour trying to get their nerves back, and keep their knees from shaking. When they got their composure back, the one girl called her brother and talked him into picking both of them up on the Minnesota side of the bridge.

"Neither of them were about to cross that bridge ever again.

"They told our classmate that the train was so close to them that their hair and clothes smelled of diesel smoke the rest of the day. Even a shower, once they got home, didn't get the odor out of their noses.

"She wasn't sure if their parents found out about it or not. From what I looked up, both the Sheriff's Department and the television crews had reports on the story, and they did not list any names. They got lucky."

Red told me, "Good thing we didn't know about that story when we wrote our paper. The fire was one thing. Out running a train, is another. I'm glad we didn't tell her story.

"Since we are telling stories, I found a couple about the bridge as well when we were doing our research," he told me.

"The story I read said that the bridge is haunted.

"It claimed that when they were building the bridge, someone fell to their death from the bridge. The story claimed that every once and a while, the person can be seen at night carrying a blueish-green lantern on the bridge. It is supposed to be the railroad worker that died.

"Legend has it, if you see the light, you might die in the next few days.

"There was another story of a family that lived near the bridge in a small cabin. The man went nuts. He killed his family and burned down their cabin. That person is supposed to haunt the bridge as well.

"There were a few more stories online about the bridge too. Maybe that's why the National Park Service gave up on the cabin that used to be down at the base of the bridge where we had a picnic. Maybe they heard it was haunted as well.

"From what I heard, the Park Service wanted to have it really bad to use as their headquarters. They finally gave up and took a cabin on the Wisconsin side.

Speaking of haunted, "You know, I don't remember eating the second side of my sandwich. You don't suppose…"

"I gave him a jab to the ribs. "Enough! It's time to head back before my mother comes looking for us. She's probably checking 'Find My Phone' as we speak. I'm not sure even Bob could save us from here."

We hiked back down from the hill, under the bridge and back up through the woods to Red's truck.

It had been a great day. One that both of us would remember for a long time.

Chapter 26

Reservations

Maria

I was waiting for Ashlee to come home. She didn't say exactly where they were going, but she did pack sandwiches for a picnic lunch. That was something I was not used to her doing with a boy before.

My parents had asked us to come for supper on Sunday and I told them I needed to check with Ashlee before I made any commitments. When I accidentally mentioned she was out with a boy, I caught all kinds of questions.

What I found out in the conversation was that Ashlee had told my mother almost as much as I knew about him. She was using her as a sounding board.

When Ashlee and Red pulled up in the parking lot, I spotted them out the window. As they came in, I was surprised when both of them took off their shoes, just before coming into the garage entrance to the apartment.

Looking at them carrying their shoes, I had to ask, "Looks like you found a picnic area that wasn't paved. Did you have fun?"

Red looked over at Ashlee as if to say – I'll let you answer the question.

"Yes, we had a great time," Ashlee answered. "We went down by the river and found a comfortable log to have lunch and watch the geese swim by. I wasn't sure if we stepped in some debris or if it was just some mud.

"I thought you might prefer that we washed off our shoes before we tracked some of that in the apartment."

"Good idea," I answered. "Otherwise, I can tell you who might be cleaning the floor later tonight."

Obviously, I wasn't going to get a lot out of the conversation this afternoon. I watched as they went to the laundry room to wash off the soles of their hiking boots.

When they came back, they put their shoes out in the garage area to dry.

Red didn't stay very long. He told Ashlee that he had told his father he would be home by 4:30 to 5:00 pm. I watched as they went back out through the garage area.

When Ashlee came back inside, she still had the look on her face like she had enjoyed the day. I figured I'd hear about it when she was ready to tell me.

"Ashlee, your grandparents called. They would like to have us for dinner tomorrow. I told them I would check with you. Is that okay with your tight schedule?"

"She looked at me. Then she laughed, and said, "I'll check with my secretary. I think I can squeeze you in."

"Well, I know it is a tight schedule. You think you might be ready for dinner in about an hour? I have it in the oven."

I thought she might tell me all about her afternoon at dinner. I was wrong. Still, I decided to wait until she wanted to tell me about it.

<u>Ashlee</u>

After dinner, I called Red and thanked him once again for the fun afternoon. I wanted to tell him that I was watching the Full

Strawberry Moon out the window. I thought he might be impressed that I looked it up on my phone.

"Did you tell your mother that you were up by the high bridge and were looking for a man carrying a lantern?"

"No, she still thinks you are a good guy. I didn't want to change that thought this quickly. Besides, I decided to let you tell her. I wanted to see how fast you could run."

We talked on the phone for over a half an hour.

I told him that I thought we were going to church in the morning, and asked if he was going, also. He said he would meet me there.

The next morning, my mother and I went to the church service. We sat next to Red and his father.

Maria

At dinner that evening at my parent's house, I almost choked on a piece of ham, when my father asked Ashlee, "So I hear you have a new boyfriend. Want to tell us about him?"

"He's just a friend," she answered.

"That's not what your grandmother told me," he replied.

I laughed. The expression on everyone's face at the table was priceless.

My mother looked like she could strangle my father with her cloth napkins. Ashlee looked like she just swallowed a red pepper. Her face was slowly turning red.

I just sat there waiting for her next answer.

It took Ashlee a few minutes to worm her way out of the situation. She explained that it was a friend from school that had worked on her English paper with her, and he was giving her rides to school.

The look on my father's face told me he was not buying it.

The look on Ashlee's face told him that he had caught her by surprise. Gracefully, he dropped the subject until after dinner.

For some reason, the conversation seemed a little more reserved right up until dessert.

There was an hour-long television show on this evening that my parents liked to watch. My mother suggested that we have dessert in the family room while the show was on.

I helped my mother clear the table while my father and Ashlee went in to turn on the television. While we were clearing the dishes, I picked up on bits and pieces of their conversation.

Somehow, my father knew about the picnic they had yesterday and was asking Ashlee about it. Reluctantly, after getting him to agree not to tell me about it, Ashlee was letting my father know some of the things they did on their picnic, including where they went.

I was starting to get jealous. Here I was patiently waiting for her to spill the beans to me about her day, and the only one that finds out was my father. Give me a break.

When we were going to bring out the cake my mother had made, I heard the words bridge and great view. New clues. Where had they gone? My thoughts turned to the new bridge in Stillwater, perhaps the old lift bridge over the river. Then again, did they go up to Taylor's Falls and take the hiking path under the bridge? So where was the mud and geese? Too much current at Taylor's Falls for the geese.

I figured I had to wait for my next clue. That, or I would have to ask my mother tomorrow morning. She would definitely find out from my father.

I never did figure it out that evening. As promised my father kept his mouth shut. Whether he got the whole story or not, I was not sure.

The next morning after Ashlee when to school, my phone rang. It was my mother.

"Okay, give me the story. I know she promised dad, but Ashlee hasn't said a word to me. Where did Red and Ashlee go for their picnic?

After a few minutes, my mother told me that they had a picnic at a place called the high bridge. She thought it was the high bridge in St. Paul, but my father corrected her and told her it was a railroad bridge over the St. Croix River.

Instantly, it brought back thoughts I didn't want to think about.

"I thought I told her she had to stay away from railroad tracks," I told my mother.

"Relax. It's not what you think. They hiked through some woods and took pictures of the bridge from down by the river. I'll let Ashlee tell you about it. I don't want her to think we told you everything."

When I was done talking with my mother, I was more puzzled than I was before. Why hadn't Ashlee told me about their picnic?

It was Tuesday at dinner before Ashlee finally told me about her picnic with Red. She figured she might as well tell me since she knew my parents would tell me eventually.

As we were eating, she told me all about going to see the bridge that they had written about in their paper. She wanted to see for herself what it was like, and what the firemen had to go through to put out the fire on the tracks.

"You didn't go out on the tracks, did you?" I asked in a rather impolite sounding voice.

"Are you kidding. Remember, you are talking to your child that does not like when you drive over a high bridge. No, I just wanted to see it."

She told me all about sitting at the base of the bridge and taking pictures. Then, how they hiked up the steep trail to an advantage point above the bridge to get the real view. When she was done, she showed me the photos on her camera she had shot.

"Why didn't you tell me all this before?" I asked.

"After your ankle mishap, I figured you might be worried if I told you we were going to hike to the high bridge. You okay with it?" she inquired.

"I will be tomorrow," I told her. "That's one scary bridge. Just don't ever let me find out you tried to walk out on it."

"That's one promise you can put in stone," she told me.

Ashlee

On the way to school the next morning, I told Red that he better keep his distance from my mother for the next day or two. He laughed when I informed him that I had told her about visiting the high bridge.

"So, she's mad at me?"

"No, just upset that we were anywhere close to train tracks. I told her there was no way I would ever go out on the bridge. By the way, I didn't tell her the stories about the bridge. I was worried I would be grounded for the summer."

"So, you want me to tell her…"

I suggested to him that he keep his mouth shut. He promised he would.

I started thinking. In a few days, school would be out. I was enjoying riding with Red to school. I liked talking to him. Now, I started wondering what would happen once school was out. Would he even call me?

Maria

The rest of the week was quiet. I was anticipating the arrival of Mr. Gray on Friday. Perhaps this time, I could finally find some information about him.

Friday afternoon, Edward Gray checked in a little earlier than his regular time.

When he arrived at the desk, he asked Bonnie if I was in, and if I had left any notes for him.

Bonnie knew that I was waiting for him to check in, so she came and got me.

"No note?" he commented. "Are we still on for dinner?"

"I think we are," I mentioned. "I asked them to hold a table for us."

"And so did I," Mr. Gray told me. "I called and they said you had reserved the table. Is Ashlee going to be able to join us?"

"Yes, she is looking forward to it."

"Fantastic! About 5:30 pm okay for the two of you?"

He went up to his room to unpack and freshen up. While he was up there, I went to talk to Ashlee.

I mentioned to her that we were still on for dinner at Quacks. Since the seating was outside on their deck overlooking the river, she might want to dress for a cool breeze as the sun might drop behind the hills while we were there.

As I was waiting for 5:30 pm, I got to thinking, *"What was I thinking about when I agreed to go to dinner with Mr. Gray? I didn't know him. In fact, the only thing I knew was that he made reservations for a large number of nights. Why did he want to take me out to dinner? Better yet, he invited Ashlee, also.*

"He was too old to expect a date. He was twice my age and then some. At least, I hoped that wasn't what he had in mind.

"This was not something I would have normally done with any of our guests. In fact, I would have said no if someone else asked Ashlee and me. I definitely would not have approved Bonnie or Jean going to dinner with one of our customers without really knowing them."

The more I thought about it, the more uncomfortable I was feeling about it. I asked Bonnie to call me about 6:30 pm. If I was still uncomfortable with the situation, I could use the excuse that we needed to get back as soon as we finished our meal. Bonnie said she understood.

At 5:30 pm, Ashlee and I met Edward Gray at the front desk.

"Thank you for joining me this evening. It is always more fun to have someone to talk to when you are eating outdoors. I heard that you have never eaten at Quacks. I hope you will enjoy it."

We headed out in his car. It didn't take long, it was less than ten minutes away. When we arrived, they had a table all set for us.

"Ed, welcome back. I haven't seen you since last summer," the waitress told him.

"Thank you. I invited the new manager of the Meadows Bed and Breakfast and her lovely daughter to join me this evening. I figured you could use some good referrals at the restaurant."

"In that case, I hope you all enjoy the meal," she told us as she seated another customer addressing them by name also.

"As you can see, the locals know when to come here to eat. Friday nights are their specialty night," Edward Gray told us.

We had a great view from our table. Then again, every table had the same view. The restaurant was only a few yards from the boat dock and the river. Looking out, you could see a quarter mile down the river in both directions.

As we were looking over the long line of pontoon boats that lined the dock along the shoreline, Ashlee asked, “Is this where the ferry went across the river?”

He smiled when he gave her his answer, “Yes, for a very long time it ran from the ramp on the other side of the river to the ramp next to the boat dock on this side. Did you see pictures of it when you did your paper?”

“Yes. It looked like it would only hold a couple cars. I’m surprised they didn’t replace it with a bridge.”

“Well, the people of Marine didn’t want one back then. That’s why it was never built. Did you know that they claimed to find the remains of the old ferry? They say it is buried in the sandy river bottom at the end of the boat dock.

“It’s fun to watch people putting their boats in the river on the other side. Every once in a while, I watch someone that doesn’t realize how quickly a river can go from very shallow to a quick drop.

“Last summer I watched someone back their boat in, only to have the trailer drop into the slightly deeper water. By the time they reacted, in only a couple feet, the river was up to the driver’s door when the car came to a stop. I wondered if, in their panic, they didn’t have their foot slip off the brake. The water was even with the top of the trunk in the back when they finally stopped. Good thing they had front wheel drive. I always wondered how much water they got in their trunk.

“You never know what you will see on the river,” he told us. “Sometimes it is very entertaining.”

I was paying attention to the fact that Edward Gray seemed to know a lot more about the area than I had taken him for. On top of that, he knew several people from the area. Had he met all of them at Quacks or the Brookside restaurants?

The waitress came back to take our order. It was rib night. So, we all had the ribs along with something to drink.

"You seem to know a great deal about the area. Did you say you used to live around here?" I asked him.

"Yes, I moved here from the east coast when I was in my twenties. We built a house on a strip of land that came all the way down to the river. The house was built on a small ridge near the trees, so we had the wonderful view, and most people didn't even know a house was back there."

"Where about was that?" I asked.

"Oh, I suppose it was five or ten miles downriver from here. Hard to give you an exact number. Too many zigs and zags in the river."

"So you moved out? Where did you go?" I asked.

"Well, the Park Service was rumored to be granting land rights to the valley. I sold my property. The developers moved the house and divided up the land for houses before they weren't allowed to sell land overlooking the river.

"My business was expanding and I stayed in Minneapolis, while I traveled all over the US. Somehow, now I keep coming back to the area. It brings back good memories."

About that time, our food started arriving.

"Ashlee, we haven't heard very much from you. I read your paper. It was very good. Are you enjoying Marine?"

Edward Gray was acting as a host and polished gentleman. He knew how to divert the discussion from himself, and to make others at the table feel good. He knew that Ashlee would enjoy the praise for her paper.

Most of the rest of the time we were eating, he kept the discussion on how we were adjusting to the area and how the Bed and Breakfast had never had better hands running it.

As we were finishing our dinner and the sun was starting to set behind the valley hills to the west, Mr. Gray picked up the check for the three of us, over the effort on my part to pay for our meals.

"Absolutely, not," he commented. "I invited you. Besides, I enjoyed the splendid company this evening. It was just nice to get to meet the two of you and to get to know you."

Funny. That was the reason I considered accepting his invitation to dinner in the first place. I wanted to get to know him. I had the feeling though that through our dinner that Mr. Gray had been peering into our lives wondering what made us tick.

As we were about to leave, Edward Gray saw someone else he knew and went over to say hi before we left.

So, how was it that he knew so many people and yet I had very little connection between him and Marine, other than the fact that he used to own a house in the area years ago? My curiosity was still getting to me.

On the ride back to the Inn, I finally asked him.

"Tell me, you seem to know a lot of people in the area, or at least, they know you, what am I missing. What's your connection to the area? There has to be more to it than the fact you moved away from here years ago?"

He shrugged his shoulders. "It's been such a splendid evening, why spoil the atmosphere. Let's leave that discussion for another day. I'd rather leave this day as this day and not talk about the past."

Well, that just got my mind thinking more and more. He's hiding something. Obviously, he is a control freak. He only wants you to know, what he wants you to know.

I thought about it for a few minutes.

"Okay! Today was your treat. We'll play under your rules. However, tomorrow is another day. I can duck your questions just as good as you can duck mine."

"Sounds like a deal. Ashlee, you can keep us in line. By the way, I forgot to ask, how's that new boyfriend of yours? I heard he was giving you rides to school."

Smooth. He did it again. He changed the subject and diverted the attention. He must have been a master of that technique when he was running his businesses.

It caught Ashlee by surprise. I'm not even sure she had a response ready for him before we got back to the Inn.

When we got back to the Inn, we thanked him for the dinner and went our own ways.

"How'd he know about Red?" Ashlee asked.

"He saw him when he fixed our bird feeders I suppose."

"Okay, but how did he know that Red gave me rides?"

"Good question. You might want to ask Bonnie and Jean. If they didn't say anything, he has a spy in town."

It did not take Ashlee very long to check with Bonnie. In a few minutes, she was out at the desk, grilling Bonnie.

When she came back into the apartment, Ashlee told me that Bonnie told her that she had not said a word to anyone.

Ashlee told me that she would check with Jean tomorrow morning. Someone must have told him.

Chapter 27

Detective Work

The next morning, it didn't take Ashlee very long to corner Jean.

Breakfast was over, and she was cleaning up the dishes when Ashlee caught her in the kitchen.

"Jean, I have a question for you. Did you mention to Mr. Gray that Red was taking me to school?"

"No. He didn't ask anything about you this morning."

Ashlee was puzzled. She really didn't mean this morning with her question. However, she asked Jean not to say anything to Mr. Gray.

It didn't take Ashlee very long to realize that Jean wasn't here last night when Mr. Gray checked in, and she had not been getting rides from Red when he was here last time.

She popped back into the apartment. "It wasn't Jean. If it wasn't Bonnie, where's he getting his information from?"

Now, we had two people that were interested in the mysterious Edward Gray. I didn't want to pry into his personal life and lose a customer, but somehow we needed to discretely figure out more about him.

I didn't see Edward Gray again until just before he left for dinner. He had spent the entire day up in his room. I was hoping he wasn't trying to avoid us.

As he came down the stairs to go out for dinner, he saw me at the desk.

"I hope you don't mind, I borrowed the drawing book from your mantle this morning. I was enjoying the drawing style that was used on the pages. It is always interesting to see how children express themselves in drawings. The way they draw something can tell you a lot about their thought process."

He put the drawings back on the mantle exactly where it had been placed. Then, he thanked me again for joining him last night and headed out for dinner.

I didn't ask him where he was going to eat.

While he was out, I put some chocolates on his pillow with a note: Pleasant dreams!

The next morning at breakfast, Edward Gray handed Jean a note to give to me when she saw me.

I didn't see it until lunch time when Jean handed it to me. Edward Gray had already checked out.

The note read, "Thank you for the chocolates. It was a "sweet" treat – Edward."

Ashlee was done with school by Wednesday. On Thursday, I took her to lunch at Quacks. I was hoping the same waitress was working and we could find out something about Edward Gray's history.

We were lucky, she was working today.

After ordering a sandwich for lunch, we asked her how she knew Edward Gray.

"Oh, you mean the man that was with you at dinner last Friday? He's been a customer for the past several years. He eats here about once a month when we are open in the summer.

"I usually make the effort to talk to him. He usually comes alone and sits at one of the small tables on the side deck. I can't remember him sitting with anyone else except for the two of you.

"I don't work every day, so it is possible I missed him eating with someone else."

I told Ashlee – that's another dead end, although we found out that he ate alone most of the time. We'll have to check in town. Someone must know him.

Unfortunately, the people Edward Gray talked to at Quacks were not people I knew, so we couldn't simply stop at their place to get some answers. That's the disadvantage of not being from the area. I still didn't know very many people from Marine.

As we were leaving the restaurant, we saw a sign we had missed when dining with Edward Gray. "Boozer slept here."

Actually, Ashlee saw it first and pointed to the sign. "Remind me to tell you the story about Boozer when we get back," she told me.

Another puzzle. Things were getting interesting around here.

Ashlee suggested that I should stop at the museum on Saturday afternoon when it was open. The person that worked there knew a lot about the area. She might even know Edward Gray. It was a good suggestion. The other place we thought about was the town garage. With one gas station/repair garage, they might have done business with him when he lived in the area.

We stopped at the garage on the way back to the Inn. I had a feeling that the older workers knew who Edward Gray was. However, they didn't offer us any words of wisdom. They simply told us that they really didn't know him.

I took Ashlee's advice and stopped at the museum Saturday afternoon during the couple of hours it was open. When no one else was there, I introduced myself and asked the person working if she had any memory of an Edward Gray that used to live in the area years ago.

To my surprise, she did.

"Yes, I remember Edward Gray. Well, actually I don't remember him, I remember his name being used a lot when the developers bought his property and split it off for houses. As I recall, there was quite a problem with the planning commission, with the splitting of the property. It took a year just to agree on the minimum lot size. People around here just don't like developments. Just try and put up a new store on Judd Street. You might get tarred and feathered before you get your permit."

I looked around the museum before thanking her for her help.

Ashlee had been right when she was researching her paper, people in a small town tend to know something about everyone else. It's just hard to get them to tell you exactly what you are trying to find.

I realized that the best source might be someone at the church that had lived in the area for years.

The next morning, Ashlee and I attended church. After the service, I asked a few people, indirectly, if they knew any members that had lived in the area south of town for the past forty years. It took a few people, but finally, someone came up with a couple names.

When they wrote them down for me, I was caught by surprise. One of them was Red's father Benson. Red and his father had just left a few minutes earlier. Red and Ashlee sat together at church. It was too bad I didn't tell Red and his father what I was going to do.

Later that afternoon, I called Red's father Benson. I wanted to see what he remembered of Edward Gray.

"Yes, I remember an Edward Gray. He had owned the property that was developed against the desires of the whole town council. I haven't heard his name in a very long time."

"What can you tell me about him," I asked.

"That's a long time ago. From what I remember, something happened to his family. His wife and children died. I can't remember how it happened. I remember my wife's father talking about it. I think he knew him. Anyway, sometime after that, he sold his house and moved away. That's the last I heard of him. Of course, they referred to his property as the Gray property for years."

Finally, I had another lead as to who he was. It was not what I was looking for. In fact, it took me by complete surprise.

I thanked Benson for the information. I didn't tell him why I was asking about Edward Gray, and he didn't ask.

***

The weeks seemed to go by quickly once summer broke. By the first weekend of July, we were booked solid for the first half of the week. It was the first time we had consecutive days of a full house.

I was trying to figure out what we had done right to get the bookings when Ashlee and Red walked in.

"Ashlee, I might need a little help this week. We are booked up from Friday night until Wednesday night."

"Everyone is coming for the fireworks on the 3rd and parade on the 4th," Red mentioned.

He was right. That had to be the reason. I had heard that it was a big thing in Marine. I just hadn't placed it as the reason we were booked up.

"Red asked me to go to the fireworks on the 3rd," Ashlee told me. "And we are going to the parade on the 4th."

I told her that it was okay. I just wanted her to know that we might have to help fill in with breakfast on those days if things got too busy.

By Friday evening, the place was hopping. As usual, most of the guests came within an hour and a half of each other. It would usually start around 4:30 pm, and by 6:00 pm we were all checked in. Of course, there were the exceptions.

Once in a while, someone would not be able to get here until almost 9:00 pm. They were usually the travelers.

Edward Gray usually checked in around 4:00. Today, for some reason he was late. It was almost 5:15 pm when he drove into the lot.

Once again, it was Bonnie that had pulled the Friday check-in shift. "You're late Mr. Gray. I was almost ready to give away your room," she told him as he came in.

"You're not that brave," he told her. "You'd lose all those compliments I keep telling management about you."

"Did you leave one this year? I must have missed it."

The two of them knew how to call each other's bluff. It's what comes from being a repeat customer. If any of the other guests were checking in at the time, they would have probably wondered if that's the way we treat all our customers.

"Sorry, I had a doctor's appointment this afternoon. They just don't know how to run an office. Just because someone is bleeding, they shouldn't get in to see the doctor before someone with an appointment. Don't you agree?"

Bonnie laughed. "Remind me not to walk in front of your car at an intersection. You'd probably argue that my foot got in the way of your tire." She finished checking him in and gave him his room key.

"Want me to carry your bag up to your room so you can make dinner on time?" Bonnie said with a smirk.

"I think I can handle it okay. Perhaps next week. I'm getting weaker from all the harassment coming from this Inn each week."

She smiled at him as he headed up to his room. It didn't take long and he was back down, heading for dinner. Bonnie told herself, *"I don't know why he doesn't just head to dinner first and then check in. He knows we will keep his room. It would be a lot easier for him."*

By 8:30 pm, everyone was checked into the Inn, and up in their rooms. Sometimes, I wondered if we were running an old people's home. After 8:30, it was rare to see any of the guests until morning.

On this evening, Edward Gray quietly came downstairs about 9:00 pm and borrowed the drawing book from the mantle. He kept it in his room until morning, when he came down for breakfast.

With the extra hassle of a full house, I spent a little more time than normal talking with our guests this weekend. That was with the exception of Edward Gray. Everyone had questions about the area and we tried to help them as much as we could.

Edward Gray seemed quieter than normal and just stayed in his room most of his stay.

Mr. Gray slipped out of the Inn on Sunday before Ashlee and I got back from church. I had hoped to ask him, at least, one question just to see if I could get an answer from him or if he would simply change the subject. I was hoping that I had not been too rude in my comments to him about his past.

Chapter 28

Fireworks

Ashlee

I was looking forward to the 3rd of July. Red had told me all about the fireworks that were shot off in town.

Even though he had told me all about the celebration, I was not ready for what I saw on the day before the 4th of July. Red told me he would pick me up about 6:30 pm to go watch the fireworks that started at 10:00 pm.

"It doesn't take that long to drive into town," I told him.

"No, we won't be able to get a parking place in town. We may have to hike down the hill."

I was puzzled. No parking over three hours before the fireworks?

When Red picked me up, I found out what he meant. Parking was already limited. We parked by the church and walked down the hill. Already, there was a large number of people in the town square.

"Where did they come from?" I asked.

Red laughed. Just wait another hour.

Apparently, everyone for miles away came for the fireworks. By 9:00 pm, they looked like ants covering the whole town. Some people had claimed their viewing place at 4:00 pm. Others, that had arrived around 9:00 pm, planned on standing. Room for a blanket on the ground or a chair would be hard to find.

Red told me that they estimated that over 10,000 people came just to watch the fireworks. No wonder the Inn was booked for days.

He asked me if I wanted some ice cream while we waited. What I didn't understand was the fact that the line that stretched over a block was for the ice cream. I had never seen so many people standing in line for a cone. It took almost an hour to get our cool treats.

People were barbecuing brats in front of the General Store. Even the garage had people making food in front of it. It was like an old fashion bazaar capped off with fireworks.

By the time the fireworks started, we were standing shoulder to shoulder with everyone in town. Actually, there was something magic about it. As the fireworks were shot up from the site of the old lumber mill, the crowd would "ooh and ah" with each burst of a shell.

With the river and steep hills on each side, the burst of the fireworks shells echoed back and forth across the valley. It was as if opposing armies were on each side of the river firing canons at each other.

Now, I understood why so many people came to watch the fireworks. It wasn't just the fireworks. It was the whole small town effect, and being part of the mass of people enjoying the show.

After the show was over, it took forever just to cross the highway and hike up the hill to get to Red's truck. People were still trying to get out of town an hour later. As far as one could see, in each direction, there was a sea of red taillights heading out of town.

When Red brought me back to the Inn, he told me he would pick me up in time for the town parade tomorrow. Then, he gave me a kiss goodnight.

As I entered the Inn, my mother was manning the desk.

"You missed it," I told her.

For the next fifteen minutes, I told her about the whole event. "You will have to go with me next year," I told her.

"And what will Red say about that?" she jested.

"Probably, one scoop or two?"

As the guests returned from the fireworks, everyone mentioned how great of a time they had.

My mother quickly realized that she needed to add the event to the website along with the customer comments. It was another reason to visit the Inn.

In the morning, after helping Bonnie with breakfast, Red picked me up to go to the parade. After last night, I wasn't sure what to expect. One thing, I was sure that 10,000 people would not come to Marine just for a town parade.

We drove down to the nearly deserted town after last night's fireworks. After finding a parking place on a side street, we walked down and stood in front of the nearly empty fire department building. The fleet was out ready to lead the parade.

It looked as though there were almost 150 people standing on Judd Street waiting for the start of the parade. That was a lot considering we were expecting about fifty local adults and kids in the parade. You could see many of the little kids with their decorated bikes down in the park by the old log cabin. They were excited to be in the parade.

It was a small parade. There was a kiddie section of the parade. With all these kids riding their bikes, it limited the top speed of the parade to about one mile per hour.

In order to keep the parade to about forty-five minutes, the length had to be restricted to two or three blocks. It only ran from the old log cabin to the gazebo in town. If it were any longer, they would have had to use both sides of the street for the parade with groups going in different directions on the street to stay in town.

I hadn't thought about the organization until the start of the parade. It was led down the street by a police car and one of the big fire trucks. Right behind them were the flag bearers.

Obviously, this was one of the first compromises of the parade. The local veterans group wanted to ride their Harley's in the parade with flags flying from their bikes. Trying to ride a heavy Harley at one mile per hour or less is a challenge. Especially, if you are older. They are heavy and tend to tip over.

So, the first compromise for the parade was that they found some bikers that had older bikes with sidecars. Now, the older vets could ride in the sidecar in their dress uniforms, the flag could be flown on the back, and the bike would be stable at one mile per hour.

There was also a group of five veterans that walked the parade route carrying the flag.

Right behind them were about thirty kids with their decorated bikes. They were the stars of the show. Everyone applauded their favorite decorations and shouted at the kids they knew.

From this traditional start of a parade, things changed. Now, the local flavor started to show through. Red pointed out to me who was on the next float. I might have missed it if he hadn't pointed it out.

Riding on a modified garden tractor was the pastor of the Lutheran Church. He was dressed in farm clothes, a straw hat and was pulling a hay wagon.

On the back of the tractor was a wooden hoist made to look like a tow truck with a big hook. On the sides of the wagon were a sign, "Bring Me Your Broken in Spirit."

You had to think about it for a minute. He was following the little kids on bikes, and riding on the wagon were several of the parents of some of the smaller kids.

I finally got the joke.

Right behind the pastor was a real tow truck from the Marine Garage. It had a sign on it as well. "Sent by God – just in case he doesn't keep running or he runs out of gas."

Everyone was laughing and pointing at the sign.

There was a couple floats promoting the local businesses, before the final float in the parade. It was the one the crowd was waiting for.

Everyone that had been to the parade in the past few years knew the final float would be the political statement of the parade. Once again, it didn't disappoint them.

It took me a while to understand what they were saying. Once Red leaned over and explained it to me, it became obvious.

The sign on the float said, "Marine In The St. Croix." As a response to decisions made over the past couple years about the schools and now the threat that Marine would have to upgrade their sanitation system, the group was promoting the secession of Marine from Minnesota.

On top of the float sat the mayor of Marine dressed in a construction outfit complete with a hard hat. She was sitting at the driver's wheel of a backhoe on the float.

In front of the backhoe was the proposed new map of Marine.

It showed a two hundred foot deep, fifty-foot wide trench dug around the west side of Marine, connecting to the river on the north and south ends of town. According to the map, Marine was going to be an island in the river. That way it would be immune to the whims of both Minnesota and Wisconsin politics.

On each side of the float, were three people walking and standing guard of the float. They were carrying long-handled shovels.

You probably had to be a local to understand the underlying principles of the statement.

On top of that, they were handing out pieces of paper. When I got one, I looked at what they proclaimed. In bold print was "Marine In the St. Croix." "Free us from outside interference."

As part of the joke, they had a coupon printed on the bottom of the sheet. It told people that the coupon was good for One Phooey. Additional Phooeys could be purchased at the local merchants listed. They included the Brookside Bar and Grill, the General Store, the ice cream shop – the Village Scoop, and the Marine Garage.

They recommended that the Phooeys be sent to any county or state elected official as a bribe to leave Marine alone. The more they could send the better.

Finally, they declared that a Phooey was issued by the sovereign Island of Marine and it is guaranteed to be worth less than the value of the paper it is printed on. However, it is officially good for fifty cents off any purchase at the merchants listed on the coupon.

They even had some kids handing out Phooeys on the street.

To connect Marine to either state, the ferry would be brought back into service. That way they could control who was allowed to come on the island and keep the politicians out.

"Wow! These people are really serious about politicians," I told Red.

"Well, don't forget who's riding the backhoe. She's the mayor. I think the group was upset that they lost a few decisions the last couple years and didn't feel they had any input to the discussions."

"What happened?" I asked.

"You probably heard about the school issue. Then, the State Highway Department wanted to put a roundabout on the intersection of county 4 and highway 95 here in town.

"The parade committee met at the Brookside. After a few drinks, they came up with this year's float design. Sometimes, I think they have way too many drinks.

"Finally, there was the concession stand on the river. For the committee, it was the final straw. It was to be located just downstream from Crunch Berry Island. Somehow, it had the approval of the city, only I never did see who signed the approval letter.

"They were going to have hot chocolate, coffee, and a few other drinks out at a shack on the sandbar in the middle of the river. It's only a few inches deep out there. Once you clear the underlining limestone rock structure, the river drops off to four or five feet deep right after the sandbar. Boaters could pull up to the sandbar and walk over to the stand.

"Then, when it warms up, canoers could stop there as they paddled down the river. They would have Kool-Aid, candy bars, and a few other items available. It was a sure thing.

"The biggest problem was sales tax. Both Minnesota and Wisconsin wanted to get in on the money. There was a big argument as to which side of the river the sandbar was located. I guess someone finally pointed out that sandbars on a river tend to migrate.

"Finally, they put it up to a general vote. Like many things here in Marine, there were supporters for both sides.

To settle the issue, they even had rallies just like they had for Boozer. In fact, some of the local residents were seen at both of the rallies; for the stand and against. It really didn't matter, they just liked to attend the rally.

Don't forget, Boozer got to ride on a float in one of our parades after those rallies for him. We take things seriously.

"The highly anticipated vote finally came in. It lost by only one vote. Once again, it was the National Park Service's vote. They will probably get some Phooeys sent their way this summer.

"Well, that's the way Marine is run during celebration week. Nothing is sacred and everything is available for making fun of.

"Hey, I'll bet you could nominate your mother for next year's parade committee. They are always looking for new business sponsors.

"I can see it now. Your mother riding on a float, sitting in her nightgown in a brass bed on the float.

"Just for good measure, she could get a few kids to dress up like squirrels to pull it down the street. It would be great advertising.

"I can even see the sign – "I Go Nuts Over The Meadows Bed and Breakfast."

It was time to head out of town before we went nuts. I suggested to Red that he might not want to mention that concept to my mother. He obviously needed to spend more time in the railroad tunnel using all that creativity writing poetry.

As I suggested that to him, he told me, "Oh, I forgot. Your mother asked my father about Edward Gray. I asked Bob about him the other day. After a short talk, Bob told me he knew who he was."

Bob! How did I know that name was going to end up in the discussion before we had an answer?

"You better pull over," I told him. "I need to see your eyes when you tell me another story today. I'm not sure when to believe you and when not."

He pulled off the road into the town cemetery.

"This should be a good quiet place to talk," he told me. The irony of the location did not go unnoticed.

Chapter 29

Revelations

<u>Ashlee</u>

After all the stories I had heard all day, I wasn't sure I was ready for another Bob story or not.

Red told me what he had found out from Bob.

"Bob told me that he actually knew Edward Gray. When he was younger, he would do odd jobs for him at his house. Bob's father would arrange for the jobs since Bob was too shy to talk to anyone.

"He did things like raking the leaves around the house, stacking up firewood, and putting up the storm windows.

"Bob told me that Edward Gray seemed like a very nice man. Usually, he would see him working in his study. He would always wave to Bob whenever he came over to do the work. Bob would see him sitting in the window – just like the one you have at the Bed and Breakfast.

"Bob said he used to have fun pushing his two kids on the rope swing in the yard. That's the type of thing Bob would have been good at. He was good with very young kids.

"He told me that he remembers that one winter day his father told him that Edward Gray's wife and two kids were killed on the dirt road leading to their house. It was real icy and apparently his wife lost control of their car. When they went around a curve, the car skidded sideways and slipped off an embankment into some trees. That was before airbags in cars.

"The force of the car hitting an old oak tree that was rotted on the bottom, caused it to come down and crush the car. Everyone inside was killed instantly.

"Mr. Gray took the accident very hard. Bob said he never saw him again after that day. His work for him stopped.

"About six months later, he heard that he had sold the house and moved from the area."

"Wow! I guess that explains a little more about him. I wonder why he keeps coming back," I told Red.

"He must have had some good memories of the area as well as the tragic ones," Red told me.

While we were sitting there, Red pointed to a gravestone in the cemetery. "If you look, you will see the names of his wife and his two children on the gravestone," Red said. "Bob showed them to me the other day."

"And you didn't tell me?"

"Like I said, I was planning on telling you today when we were together."

I sat and looked at the stone. It was only a half a mile from the Bed and Breakfast. Was this finally the reason Edward Gray stayed at the Inn?

Before I let Red drive out of the cemetery, I told him, "Speaking of promises, you promised a while ago that you would tell me all about Bob. Something tells me there is more to his story, as well, that you haven't told me."

Red looked me in the eye. He could tell that I was not going to take no for an answer. I had that determined look on my face.

"Okay, but let's save that one for tomorrow. It will give us an excuse for getting together three days in a row. Besides, I need to talk to Bob. If it is alright with him, maybe I can show you where he lives."

With a line like that, how could I refuse. He took me back to the Inn.

For some reason, when we went inside, he didn't suggest to my mother that she should join the parade committee for next year as a sponsor. I thought it was a rather wise decision on his part.

We stayed and told my mother all about the parade. When we got to the part about the proposal to dig a mote around Marine, she broke out laughing.

"How can such a conservative town act so liberal?" she asked.

Then we told her about the pastor from the church.

That night Red talked to Bob about taking me to his place. Apparently, Bob was not very happy about it. He didn't like visitors. Somehow, Red managed to convince him that it was okay just this one time.

The next morning, Red called me to let me know that he had talked to Bob. He would pick me up about three in the afternoon and we could go to where Bob lived.

I told my mother. She was shocked. "I can't wait to hear this story," she told me. "Make sure you stay behind Red when you go in."

"Mom, I'm not worried about Bob."

"That's not what I meant. Bob might be nervous about you. Make sure you give him some space and let Red take the lead."

It was a good thought. I really had not thought about how a real hermit lived. I guess I was about to find out.

My mother spotted Red's truck pull in about 2:30 pm. He was early. I rushed to get ready while my mother met him at the door.

"So, another secret comes out of the bag," she told him after greeting him and bringing him back into the apartment.

"I figured I needed to talk to Ashlee a little bit before we went to see Bob. There's a few things I hadn't told her yesterday."

My mother was really curious now. Should she stay and listen in, or give us our privacy?

She waited for me to come downstairs. Then, she went into her office, with the door open. She figured it was fair game if we talked loud enough for her to hear the story.

Red sat and told me the parts of Bob's story that he had kept from me in the past.

"I wasn't sure how you would take this in the past, so I guess I decided I just wouldn't tell you. Even my father didn't think it was a good idea to talk to you about it."

Now, my curiosity was up. Red's father didn't want him to tell me? What was it that they were hiding?

Red went on to attempt to explain who Bob was. "You know how strange Bob acts around people. Well, the reason I didn't say anything, was that I wasn't sure how you would react.

"Bob is sort of related to me. His grandfather and my grandfather were brothers. That's why I know so much about him. My father always claimed he was from the weird side of the family.

"You see, his father was almost as strange as Bob. Bob's father got married, and when Bob was born, his mother died. About five years later, his father was found hanging from a tree. Depression had gotten to him.

"So you see, Bob started out in the world on the wrong feet. I think there were some other underlining psychological problems in that family that might have been there as well. They could have been hereditary for all we knew.

"He stayed with my grandfather until he was thirteen. Then when my grandfather died, the National Park Service got my grandfather's land along the river. Bob just disappeared for about six months.

"Finally, one day he showed up at our doorstep. He looked as though he had been sleeping in the woods all summer.

"My mother wanted him to move in with us. I'm not sure my father was in favor of it. He was worried about what Bob's influence might be on me. Finally, it was Bob who simply wanted a good meal and to get out of the cold rain for a few days, and then leave.

"We had just purchased our farm a year earlier. There was an old shack on the far side of the farm that we didn't know what to do with. My father wanted to burn it down. It was too small for the horse equipment of my mother's, and not much good for anything else. My mother told Bob he could stay in it until he decided what he wanted to do. At least that way, he was out of the rain.

"The shack was on the edge of the woods, about a block from the railroad tracks. I guess Bob decided he liked it there. It had an old well outside, and a wood burning stove inside.

"My mother and I would bring him food once a week. Sometimes, he was there. Usually, not. I think he used to hang out with a few of the bums on the tracks. I remember one time he told me about the hobo reunion at the car tunnel by the State Park. He said there were about 30 men there.

"My father was traveling a lot for his job. I'm not sure if he knew if Bob was at the shack most of the time or not. I know he didn't have much to do with him.

"When my mother died, we didn't see much of Bob. I would take a few things from the shelves once a week and leave them in his cabin. If they were gone the next week, I knew he must have been there.

"Eventually, I would wait until he came back, figuring I was gone. After a while, he would sit and talk to me. It was kind of a strange relationship. Sometimes we would sit for a half an hour without anyone saying a word. It was the way Bob was.

"What surprised me, was the way he could continue a conversation we had the week before. It was as if we never stopped talking. Later I realized that his memory was just that good. He never forgot anything.

"One day, I loaned him some old notebooks I found in the barn. They were my grandfather's notebooks. Bob read everyone by the time I stopped back two days later.

"In the past few months, my father has started to take an interest in Bob. He fixed up his cabin and managed to get electricity to it. He put a solar cell on the roof, and connected to a battery. It's not great, but it runs a light at night. I'm not sure how he accomplished that one since no one in the county knows Bob lives back there.

"So, that's the story. Do you still want to go see him? We have to walk almost the entire length of our farm to get to the cabin hidden back in the woods?"

I sat there amazed. It was amazing that Red was able to keep this a secret. It was more amazing that his family had kept it from the community. What a strange way to live.

"I told Red to give me a second; I wanted to change into my hiking boots if we had to walk the back 40."

Chapter 30

"Bob"

<u>Maria</u>

I sat in the office listening in to the story. No wonder Bob's name always appeared in mysterious situations. I really wanted to run out there and ask Red a bunch of questions. Then, I thought better of it. I didn't want to appear as though I had been evesdropping in on their conversation.

The next time he came over, I figured he was fair game to answer some questions.

Ashlee told me that she might not be back for dinner. She and Red might go into the shopping mall after their encounter with Bob.

<u>Ashlee</u>

I was absolutely blown out of the water listening to Red's story about Bob. Now, I understood some of the strangeness I saw in Red when I first started to get to know him. And, I thought I had a strange family background.

We hopped into his truck and headed to his father's farm. When we got there, no one was home. His father was visiting a customer in Minneapolis. He left a note on the table for Red.

It was indeed a walk to the back corner of their property. The field had not been turned for a couple years, and it was work walking through all the weeds and ruts.

We were almost to the woods, and I had not seen any sign of a cabin back there.

"My mother had gotten a good deal on the extra 40 acres of woods just before Bob showed up. She picked it up for the back taxes at an auction. That's why it has a cabin on it. It was probably an old hunting shack," Red told me. "It didn't have any access since it was cut off by the other farms. Plus, the land is kind of swampy. I guess that's why she got it so cheap."

We followed a small trail that led around a corner. There it was, Bob's cabin. No wonder no one knew he lived back there. We were thirty feet from the cabin before we saw it.

Bob was sitting by the door of the cabin. We stopped, and I waited, as Red talked to him making sure he was okay having a visitor.

Finally, Red motioned for me to follow him. We were almost to the cabin before Bob acknowledged me – "Hi."

As we stood outside Bob's cabin, you could feel the tension slowly decreasing as Red and Bob slowly exchanged greetings. It was really strange. Then again, this was the first time I had encountered a hermit at his home.

After about fifteen minutes, Red asked Bob, if we could go inside. He shrugged and pointed to the door.

The inside of the cabin surprised me. I expected a mess. To my surprise, it was extremely clean. Obviously, Bob had a place for everything he owned. Everything had to be in its place. It was another hint of his possible psychological issues. I wondered if he was autistic. When he was young, they probably never checked him for any psychological disorders.

Bob showed me his backpack. It was on the hook by the door. He was very happy that we had given it to him.

He had several books on a shelf. Red told me that he brings them to him once a week. Bob can read a book a day. I'm not sure he ever sleeps.

After we were there for a short time, we thanked him for letting us see his home and left.

It had been quite an experience for me. One that I'm sure I will not forget anytime soon. I wasn't sure I could live that way. For Bob, he could not live any other way.

The whole way back to Red's house, we talked about the way Bob lived all by himself. Red told me about some of his early encounters with Bob. "It took a long time before Bob would talk to him. Even now, it's like you have to thaw the ice before he warms up to you.

"Bob gets a disability check every month. Red told me the receipt comes to their house. They have it automatically deposited in an account at the Marine Bank. Someday, if he ever gets really sick, it will be there to help him out. For now, he has no need for the money."

When we finally reached Red's house, his father was just driving in the driveway.

"Well, did you meet Bob?" he asked.

"Yes, Red showed me the way. I guess I understand why he acts so strange. That's a tough way to live."

"For Bob, it's the only way. Please keep his location a secret. I'm not sure the county would appreciate knowing he lives out in the woods in an unregistered cabin."

I told Red's father I understood.

We hopped in Red's truck and drove to the mall. Somehow, walking through racks of clothes didn't feel the same after visiting Bob.

Red and I stopped at a Subway for a sandwich. The whole time I was eating my food, I kept thinking about Bob. I'll bet he never had a fresh store bought sandwich.

When I got back to the Inn, I thanked Red for sharing Bob's story with me. It did not make me feel any less about Red. In fact, I admired the fact that he was still watching over his recluse relative.

That evening, my mother and I sat up for several hours talking about Bob. She was glad to see that Bob still had the backpack and that he pointed it out to me. Looking at his place, the backpack was probably the best thing we could have given him. I told her that I was glad Red had suggested it.

Both of us wondered if either of us could even exist in the conditions that Bob lived. The Bed and Breakfast was rather plush compared to his living conditions.

At least, I didn't have to put a log in the stove for heat.

It had been an interesting week with all kinds of revelations. I told my mother that I saw and learned more about Marine in the past week than I learned the whole time we had lived here.

I was wondering what my mother was going to say to Edward Gray at the end of the week. Was she going to ask him about his family? I doubted that she would mention to him that she knew their graves were in the cemetery.

The Inn was finally back to normal occupancy after the busy week. That meant I could finally sleep late in the morning and not have to help either Bonnie or Jean with breakfast due to the full house. After the past couple days, I was really looking forward to the extra sleep.

Friday morning, wouldn't you know it, I was wide awake at 7:00 am. It wasn't fair. Why did it always work that way. I got up early and had an extra roll from the kitchen.

Maria

I heard Ashlee get up early. I was wondering if she was sick so I got up to see what was going on. When she told me she couldn't sleep, I just laughed.

"Just wait until you get a little older. Sleeping late just doesn't happen."

I could see that she was trying to figure out what to do with her day. She had spent so much time with Red that a day without him had left her stranded with nothing to do.

I suggested to her that she could make contact with a couple of her school friends. Keeping in touch would be a great start for the next school year. She told me she would think about it.

When I saw Jean cleaning up in the kitchen, she told me that Bonnie had left a message at the desk last night that Edward Gray had called and canceled his reservation for the weekend.

He told her that he was still hoping to make it next week. Apparently, he wasn't feeling good and decided he had better stay home and not out with other people.

I was disappointed. I was glad he was not canceling because of something we had said. However, at the same time, I was looking forward to talking to him.

On Sunday, we met Red and his father at church. Red and Ashlee sat together.

After the service, I watched as Ashlee went up to shake the pastor's hand.

"I don't see any dirt under those fingernails," she told him.

He looked puzzled for a minute. Then, he realized what her comment meant. "Yes, it took a little while to get the straw out of my hair also. Did you enjoy the parade?"

"I did. I guess I can call you if my car breaks down. Got that tractor gassed up?"

"Just give me a call," he told her.

Ashlee seemed to be enjoying the pastor. I was glad. It was good to see her rekindle an enjoyment for going to church. It had been too long. Of course, Red being there helped.

Chapter 31

The Find

We finally had a rainy week. The good weather had moved in a couple of weeks ago and we really needed some rain. It made everything look fresher.

The rain gave Ashlee the excuse to call Leslie and Dawn. She was calling to see how their summer was going. After talking to both of them, Ashlee realized that her summer had been the most exciting of the group. On top of that, she hadn't even mentioned her meeting with Bob.

It appeared that both of the girls were waiting for school to start just to get out of the house. For Ashlee, that had not been a problem, thanks to her friend Red.

They also talked about going to Lumberjack Days in Stillwater later in the week. There were a couple bands performing and all three of them hoped to go hear them.

Ashlee decided to ask Red if he wanted to go. It would give them another excuse to be together.

To kill some time one afternoon, Ashlee went down to the library when I had a couple errands to run in town.

She wanted to look into the newspaper archives of the county to see if there were any write-ups on the sale of Edward Gray's property. If there was a lot of discussion about the development, she thought there might have been some mention in the paper as to why he moved from the area.

From the town's library, Ashlee was able to pull down newspaper articles on the county's system and sort them by descriptions. It didn't take long to find an article on the development of Edward Gray's land along the river. It gave her a date to work around looking for other articles.

She was there about twenty minutes looking at article after article, arguing about protecting the scenic shoreline, when she spotted it.

The one article showed them moving the original homestead off the land before the bulldozers leveled the forest. It said, "Moving to a different home."

She did a double take when she saw it. It was a house with a reading window on the upper floor just like the Bed and Breakfast. Bob was right once again. Bob had said that Edward Gray would wave to him from his office desk in the window just like the Inn.

"How in the world could Bob always get things right?" she wondered.

As she looked at the article, something kept bringing her back to the photo. There was something odd about it. With the exception of the apartment at the Bed and Breakfast, the house was almost identical. She wondered how many homes were built that way back then. Surely, builders worked off patterns. There must have been a design back then that many large houses copied.

For the fun of it, she asked the librarian if she could make a copy to bring home and show her mother.

About ten minutes later, I picked Ashlee up from the library when I was done at the bank and General Store. I needed to pick up some groceries and make a deposit for the Inn at the bank.

When she climbed into the car, I asked her, "Did you find anything?"

"Yes, I found the date the property was sold and numerous articles about how the development was the start of ruining the scenic valley. I guess people didn't agree back then either. I wonder if they had rally parties back then supporting their views?"

"I wouldn't put it past them," I answered.

"Oh, you've got to see this. I found a picture of Edward Gray's house where Bob used to do yard work. Bob told us Edward Gray used to sit in his office window and wave to him when he came over to rake. He said it was just like the Bed and Breakfast's reading window.

"Guess what, it is exactly like the Inn's reading window."

I glanced over at the photo. Sure enough, it looked just like it. "Let me look at that again when we get back, will you," I asked.

As we pulled up to the Bed and Breakfast, instead of pulling into the driveway, I parked in front of the Inn.

"Now, Ashlee, let me see that photograph," I asked.

When we looked at the photograph and the Inn, they were identical except for the apartment, which we had always felt was obviously an addition at some point in time.

"You don't suppose?" Ashlee asked.

"I think we need another check at the town's record department. It is either a coincidence or someone moved the house up here."

The next day, we checked with the town clerk. Since we had a date from the newspaper article, she was able to find it quickly.

"Yes, here it is. There is a permit to move a house from the south of town to the property where your Bed and Breakfast is located. As I recall, it was only about ten years ago that they put the addition on the property to allow for office space."

That was it. Not only did it resemble Edward Gray's home along the river, it was Edward Gray's old home. Now it made sense that he always wanted the reading room. That was his old office.

"Wait until I tell Red about this one," Ashlee told me.

"Hold on there. We need to protect his privacy. I'm not sure if we should let Red know we found Edward Gray's secret or not. He's still our best customer. I don't want to lose him just as we are starting to build our reservation rate."

Ashlee nodded that I was right.

After we put the car in the garage, Ashlee and I talked about our find all the way until suppertime.

"Can we, at least, tell grandpa and grandma about our find?" Ashlee asked.

I told her I would let her know after dinner. I needed to think this one through.

I knew that it would drive Ashlee nuts to have all this knowledge and not be able to share it with someone. So after dinner, I told her she could call her grandparents and tell them about all the things she had discovered in the past couple weeks. There was one condition – they were to agree not to tell anyone.

She spent the next hour on the phone telling them all about the parade, her visit to Bob's cabin, and all the information she found at the town library. She could hardly wait to tell someone.

My parents commented to me later about how excited Ashlee was in finding out the history of our mystery guest. It was fun to talk to her and hear the excitement in her voice. They asked again, "And, who is this Bob?"

I explained to them that Bob was the stranger that went for help when I hurt my ankle on the railroad tracks.

I made sure they knew that the information Ashlee told them wasn't to leave the family.

Now, I was really looking forward to the weekend. One thing for sure, I was planning to be somewhere near the front desk when Edward Gray checked in.

Chapter 32

Explanations

Friday morning I checked the registry. Edward Gray was still expected later today. We had two other guest reservations for the night as well.

Ashlee and Red had made plans to head to Stillwater this evening for the Lumberjack Days. The main concert that they wanted to hear was scheduled for tomorrow night. However, knowing kids, they were worried they might miss something if they didn't go today as well.

I was busy talking to Ashlee about being crowd wise and missed Edward Gray pulling into the parking lot. In fact, I didn't realize he was here until I walked out with Ashlee and Red, as they headed out to Red's truck. Then, I spotted Mr. Gray's car in the lot.

When I came back in, I asked Bonnie if Edward Gray had checked in. I thought it was his car outside; however, it could have been someone else with the same make and color of car that had checked in.

"Yes. I just checked him in. He looked a little gray in his face and told me that he didn't think he was going to go for supper tonight. He had picked up a sandwich at a fast-food place on the way to Marine.

"I told him there was coffee down here if he wanted some. He told me he might stop down later this evening if he wanted something warm. Right now he just wanted to unpack and relax."

So, he missed last weekend because he was not feeling very good, and Bonnie said he was still a little pale in the face. I was hoping that he was doing okay. I hadn't heard of any summer flu, but if you caught a bad cold, they could still hold on for a couple weeks.

I went back in to call and talk to my mother. She was still a buzz about Ashlee's desire to dig out facts. We talked for quite a while.

Later that evening, when Bonnie was getting ready to leave, I went out to the check-in desk to look at the names of our guests. I always tried to look at the names, and see where they were from. Guests seem to appreciate it if you know something about them when you run into them while they are here.

Bonnie told me she would see me tomorrow, and left for the day.

While I was straightening out the front desk, I noticed that the drawing book was missing from the fireplace. I figured someone had grabbed it to look at it. I left a note for Jean in the morning to check for the book when she cleaned out the rooms of people that were checking out.

It was amazing how people grab a book or a magazine to read, and then leave it in their room. I wondered who picks up after them at home?

I heard Ashlee come in later that evening. To be honest, I had slipped off to sleep and had no idea what time it was.

The next morning, at breakfast, I asked her how the concert was.

"Oh, the concert is tonight. We just hung out with a few of our school friends and listened to the band that was scheduled to play. They weren't the best. Hopefully, the group that is playing tonight is supposed to be really good. We'll head back tonight and see."

I was hoping that the two of them were staying out of trouble. Sometimes teenagers can become carried away when they are in a group. I told her to watch what her crowd was doing. If it looked questionable, just walk away. She said she would.

As Jean was cleaning up the breakfast dishes from our guests, I asked her how Edward Gray was doing. "Bonnie said he looked a little pale last night when he checked in."

"Now that you mention it, he was rather quiet this morning. In fact, he had his coffee and a roll and then headed back upstairs to his room. That's not like him. He usually likes to talk to the other guests."

It still sounded like he wasn't feeling good. If he came down later in the day, I thought I would ask him if he was feeling okay. Perhaps some tea would be helpful. I could make some for him.

I didn't want to bother him while he was in his room. We did our best not to interfere with our guest's quiet time when they were in their rooms.

When Bonnie came in later in the afternoon, I told her that Jean thought that Edward Gray still looked a little pale. I wasn't sure if he was feeling ill or not. I asked Bonnie to let me know if he came down. If he needed some tea and crackers, we could make some up for him.

As we were talking, Red drove up to pick up Ashlee.

I told him to please be careful in the crowd. I was still concerned about them being in a large crowd at their age. He promised that he would.

The two of them took off for another evening of partying. I only wished I had a better feeling about letting the two of them loose in a crowd.

Then again, if they were twenty-five, I would probably still have the same feelings. I suppose every mother has the same feelings when their children are growing up and finding their independence.

I noticed Edward Gray coming down the steps when I was talking to a couple that had just checked in. Politely, I shortened our conversation so that I could talk to Mr. Gray.

I walked up to him and asked, "You don't look like you have your normal hop to your step. If you don't mind me asking, are you feeling okay?"

"Thanks for asking. My doctor changed some of my medications and so far, it has food tasting like cardboard. I hope Jean didn't think that I didn't like her cooking this morning."

"No, I'm sure she didn't feel that way. She did mention that you looked a little pale and didn't seem like your cheery self. If you need anything, tea or crackers, please let me know. I'll be glad to make some for you or if you want some toast, we have a few jams we can put on it that might improve the taste."

"You are kind. I think I'll just head down and get some soup tonight. Hopefully, I'll be better by morning. My old body is probably taking its time adjusting to the new medication."

He thanked me again for my offer and headed out for some soup. Somehow, he just didn't look like his normal self.

Mr. Gray did not stay out very long. After a short time, he returned and went directly up to his room without speaking to anyone.

I'm not sure if I was nervous or just a typical parent, but I stayed up until Ashlee and Red returned from the concert. I wanted to make sure that one of their friends had not gotten some beer for them.

When they came in, I was glad to see they were okay and I did not detect any smell of alcohol on their breath.

I told them I was tired and headed off to bed.

The next morning, Ashlee told me all about her evening while we were having some toast for breakfast. They had seen a few of their friends and then left them to go and listen to the concert. She told me the music was very good.

She also told me that traffic leaving Stillwater was almost as bad as leaving Marine after the fireworks. It took them forever to hike to where they left the car and then get out of town. That was why it was so late when we got home.

Ashlee was surprised I was still up when they got back. I told her that I was concerned about her. Even though Red seemed like a very dependable boy, I was worried about the crowds and traffic. "I just wanted to make sure you got home alright."

I was hoping she would realize that I was just a concerned parent and not snooping on the two of them.

We hurried up to get cleaned up for church. We were running a little late after talking about the concert.

When we got to church, Red's father mentioned to me that the kids seemed to have had fun at the concert last night. I didn't tell him that I had stayed up until they came back. I didn't want to leave the impression that I was one of those that checked up on the exact time her kids came home. At the same time, it was probably exactly what I had just done.

When the service was over, as we were leaving the sanctuary, I heard the pastor joke with Ashlee, "Good morning Ashlee. I checked for straw in my hair this morning just for you."

It caught her by surprise. She didn't think the pastor would remember her name. Apparently, he was one of those people that could remember names easily.

"Well, we're still waiting for you to come over and cut the grass," she responded. "I assume that's your second job."

"Only if you have some flower beds that need cutting," he responded.

I watched as Red just laughed. He knew from experience that the pastor had met his match.

When we got back to the Inn, almost all of our guests had checked out, including Edward Gray.

Jean was starting to strip the beds when we arrived. I asked her if the drawing book had reappeared. “No, but I’ll keep an eye open for it,” she told me.

As I went back downstairs, the last customer was just coming down to check out. They told me they really enjoyed the stay and were hoping to come back again in the fall. It was nice to hear that from customers.

I suggested that they bring their friends next time. They thought it was a good idea. It would make a fun couples weekend.

I was just about to check on Ashlee when Jean came down the steps.

“I found it.”

She was holding up the drawing book. I figured it would turn up in one of the rooms. I just hoped it didn’t end up in someone’s suitcase.

“It was in Edward Gray’s room. He left it on the table in the reading window.”

Jean put it back on the mantle where it had been.

“How did Mr. Gray look this morning,” I asked.

“Oh, I guess about the same. He was really quiet. He just doesn’t look good.”

I wondered about that. We wouldn’t see him for another two weeks until his next reservation. I hoped he would be feeling better by then.

After lunch, I went outside to check the flowers. They were starting to look a little malnourished. After sprinkling some flower fertilizer on them and giving them some water, I came back in the front door to ask Jean a question before she left.

As I approached the desk, I stopped dead in my tracks and thought: The book. The drawing book. We found it when we were clearing some space in the attic for the bug people. If the Inn had indeed been Edward Gray's home, had the drawing book belonged to his children? Was that the reason he had it in his room the last two stays? Was he looking at the drawings made by his children?

Now I really felt bad. I hadn't put two and two together very well at all. I ran back and caught Ashlee.

"Well, Ms. Private Eye. You missed a clue," I told her. "Remember how you placed the Inn at Edward Gray's old property? You missed the drawing book."

"Oh my goodness. You think it was his kids?" she asked.

"Right on," I told her.

That really had to be the reason he showed so much interest in the book. In my attempt to stay out of his business, I missed the fact that the book belonged to him. If he was coming back next weekend, I would have wrapped it in paper and put it on his pillow. Now, I wondered if I shouldn't send it to him.

If I sent it, he would know that I knew his secret. I asked Ashlee what I should do.

"He didn't look very good this weekend. If you sent it to him, it might cheer him up," Ashlee suggested. "If it wasn't his kids, he'll probably bring it back in a couple weeks."

I agreed. I copied his address from the registry and took the book in back, to wrap up for shipping.

Before I taped it shut, I put a note inside the book.

Dear Mr. Gray,

Ashlee did some research lately and saw a picture of the Bed and Breakfast being moved. I wasn't sure you wanted us to know, so I did not say anything to you.

However, my guess is that the drawing book we found hidden upstairs last month might have been yours. I didn't want to take a chance that it might get lost, so I am sending it to you for safe keeping.

I hope it brings back good memories.

Sincerely,

Maria and Ashlee Wagner

The next morning I took it to the Post Office and mailed it to Edward Gray. They told me that officially, book rate would take seven to ten days. However, the carrier told me it would probably get to him in two days.

As I left the Post Office, I felt better about sending him the book.

Chapter 33

Losses

The next week was a very quiet week. No outdoor concerts, no fireworks, not even a parade.

As the weekend came and went, I was wondering if I would get a note from Edward Gray that he received the package in the mail. However, so far there was nothing in our Post Office box.

Ashlee and a group of friends were planning on renting canoes and going down the St. Croix River. It sounded like a fun outing on a hot July day.

It was hard to believe that July was almost gone. It seemed like only yesterday Ashlee and I moved into the Inn. Now, St. Cloud was only a distant memory.

Even the thought of finishing off my third set of college courses by the end of next month didn't seem real. At this rate, I might even get my degree before our contract with the Inn ran out for a lack of customers and profit.

Wednesday, Bonnie popped her head in the door to tell me that Edward Gray's associate had called. He canceled his reservation for the next weekend, which was the first weekend in August. Apparently, he is still not feeling very good.

"Did he mention the drawing book?" I asked.

"No, it wasn't Edward Gray on the phone. Just someone that said he was his associate. Hopefully, he got it. You still haven't heard from him?"

"No. But, if he is sick, that might be the reason."

The next day, I decided to try to call him to see how he was doing and to see if he received the book. When I did, I got his message machine, so I left a short message.

He never did call me back.

We didn't see any sign of Edward Gray the rest of August. I was hoping it was not due to the fact that we had uncovered his secret about the house. On the other hand, was it something I said?

I tried calling him, but each time I got his answering machine.

I remembered that when I spoke to Edward Gray the first time on the telephone, and he gave me his reservations, he told me to put a hold on July, August, and September. We had simply converted them to reservations the end of June.

Perhaps we were premature. He might have had a trip planned and that was why he did not answer his messages. We still put a hold on his room for September hoping we would hear from him.

The end of August, Ashlee was busy getting her things ready for school. She had a list a mile long. Most of them started with a new fall wardrobe. Girls just could not be seen in the same clothes they wore last year. Well, some of them probably didn't fit her this year. The best thing was I inherited some great sweatshirts. It helped to be the same size.

She had already worked it out with Red to get a ride to school. Another no brainer. If he didn't offer her a ride, she would have probably been sitting in his truck when he came out of his house. As Ashlee said it, "One thing good about an old truck. There is only room for two. They didn't put a back seat in the old ones."

It had been interesting watching her the past month. Every Saturday morning, she would go with Red to pick up groceries and bring them to Bob's cabin. Last week, she told me, Bob was even there to talk to them when they arrived.

I noticed that a couple of our books were missing from our bookshelf. The next week, they were back, and a couple other books were missing. I had a feeling I knew where they were going.

Labor Day weekend filled us up once again. Still not a sign of Edward Gray. We held his room until the last minute before accepting a late reservation.

I recruited Ashlee to help with breakfast each day, as I knew the girls would be tired changing linen and doing the wash for quick turnarounds.

To help with her expenses, I even agreed to pay Ashlee for any hours she helped at the Inn. Actually, I was hoping it would give Bonnie and Jean some breaks. They had worked continuously for almost six months. I was afraid they were getting burned out.

When I asked, both Bonnie and Jean told me they were fine. If they needed a day off, they would let me know.

School started the day after Labor Day. For me, it seemed extra quiet at the Inn. Our reservations had slipped down from our summer rate. We were back to a couple reservations per day during the week and three or four on the weekends.

With Ashlee at school, I had time to start a new set of courses. It was also time to meet with Jason Willard.

Jason had told me not to worry the last time we met. We didn't need to meet every few weeks. In fact, we hadn't met for almost three months. Now, it was time for a review of the summer. We had set a meeting for Thursday at his office almost three months ago to the date.

I had prepared a set of charts and graphs showing expenses per month, reservations, rooms reserved for the future, and one showing when we received reservations.

I was hoping to show the trends experienced by the Bed and Breakfast. The graph showing when the reservations were made, gave us the hint that it was important to have someone near the phone on certain days of the month. Since we ran a tight ship, we didn't want to miss any reservations.

Ashlee came back from her first day back at school all excited. Her goal last year was to meet and get to know two or three classmates in each class. This year, she wanted to know most of her classmates before winter. That left the other half of her junior year class to meet come spring.

When she walked into the room, she told me that most of the students that were in her classes last year were in her classes this year. Because of scheduling, it had just worked out that way. Band and orchestra students were on an opposite schedule. I think she was relieved that she didn't have to start all over learning names.

Of course, it didn't hurt that Red was in her last hour class – math. I wondered what she might have done it he wasn't in one of her classes. Something tells me a counselor might have had a long discussion about changing classes if he wasn't. He was also in her advanced English class. Her last year's teacher had suggested that both she and Red move up to the advanced class this year. It was something she was proud of.

I was glad to see that things were working out the way they were for her. It had been a tough transition over the past year. Ashlee had made the hard adjustments and was almost up the level the better students had reached.

The next morning when Ashlee was at school, I received a call from Jason Willard.

He called to cancel our meeting on Thursday.

I was a little disappointed. I was eager to show him the charts I had prepared for him on the Inn.

Then he dropped the news on me…

Jason Willard had called to tell me that he needed to postpone our meeting for a couple weeks because of the death of one of his clients. He needed to prepare a financial statement and put his affairs in proper order.

To my shock, it was Edward Gray.

I didn't know what to say. I had no idea.

"What happened?" I asked.

"He had been fighting a form of brain cancer for almost a year," he told me. "Instead of doing the radiation and chemo stuff, he decided just to enjoy what time he had left.

"His funeral is Saturday, so we will have to delay our meeting until I get things completed."

I asked him where the funeral was going to be held.

He told me, "His service will be held at Christ Lutheran Church here in Marine at 11:00 am."

When I hung up the phone, I was in shock. I had no idea he was that sick. He was a man of many secrets. I guess he had the last one on us.

I talked to both Bonnie and Jean and told them the news I had just heard. Both were saddened by the news.

When Ashlee came home from school, I broke the news to her also. It was almost as though we had lost a member of our family. Later that evening, she called and told Red.

Chapter 34

Respects

The funeral at the Lutheran Church in Marine was attended by just a limited number of people. There were a few of his close friends, along with Jason Willard – his financial advisor, all of us from the Bed and Breakfast, Red, his father, and Bob.

Benson had taken Bob out for some new clothes and had him cleaned up for the service. He figured that Bob would want to be there. He felt there were some ties between them.

It was a short service. Bob sat by himself in the back row of the only partially filled church. The pastor did a good job talking to Edward Gray's friends that had gathered. Then, the procession led the short distance to the cemetery, where he was finally laid to rest next to the rest of his family.

I had arranged for my parents to come and watch the Bed and Breakfast while we were at the funeral. Jean had completed the breakfast and had pre-checked out the rooms that were leaving. All they needed to do was be there to answer any phone calls that might have come in while we were away.

When we got back, they stayed and had lunch with us.

The morning's funeral had sort of taken the wind out of Ashlee and me, and I'm not too sure we were the best of hosts. I still wished that I had talked to Mr. Gray when I had the chance. He might not have wanted us to know his secrets, but it would have made me feel better.

After my parents left, Ashlee and I took a ride up to Taylor's Falls. We figured a little hiking in the hills might get us away from the Inn and give us some exercise at the same time.

It was a nice day. The temperatures hadn't fallen too far and it was light jacket weather.

As we hiked the pathway above the river, I noticed that Ashlee didn't like to get anywhere near the cliffs.

"Still don't like heights?" I asked.

"You got it. You want to head back?"

We cut our walk short. I knew that Ashlee was trying to be good to me in agreeing to hike the path. Nevertheless, it was not worth making her nervous.

Still, it was what we needed. It gave us a chance to be together and get out of the Inn for the afternoon.

A week followed without Jason Willard rescheduling our meeting. I figured he would call when his schedule slowed down. I didn't know how many other clients he had. I was surprised when he told me that Edward Gray was one of his clients. He didn't say very much about it at his funeral.

Towards the end of the following week, Jason called to reschedule out meeting. He wanted to meet on Tuesday evening at 7:00 pm, the following week at the Inn. I told him that would be fine. We could meet in our apartment since we had, at least, one guest that night.

He suggested it would be nice if Ashlee could be there, also. He wanted to talk to her about the paper she wrote. He had heard a number of positive comments about it.

It was a good weekend for us. On Saturday night, we were booked solid. If we could keep this up until Christmas, we might even be profitable for the six-month period.

On Tuesday, I updated my charts and had everything all set for Jason Willard's meeting. Ashlee was interested in being there also. She wanted to see what our meetings were like.

At 7:00 pm, sharp, Jason Willard walked into the Bed and Breakfast. Just like Edward Gray, you could set your watch by him.

When I looked, I noticed that he had another person with him. I wasn't expecting anyone else. I was wondering if Jason was planning on finally retiring and was going to introduce me to someone that was going to take over his job.

"Maria, I would like to introduce you to Patrick Dean. Patrick, this is Maria Wagner and her daughter Ashlee."

"Pleased to meet both of you," he said.

"I asked Patrick to join us. He helps me with my paperwork."

After Patrick had a few minutes to look around, I showed the two of them into our apartment.

"Jason, I put together a few charts for you to look at. I think you are going to be pleased with the number of bookings we had the past three months. We are actually ahead of the number we were hoping to achieve."

"He looked at the charts. You've done a good job. I'm impressed. Did your marketing class help you in putting together the presentation?"

"Yes. It felt good to take a class you can actually use right after you take it."

He showed the charts to Patrick.

Jason told me, "Actually, we needed to talk to you about the Bed and Breakfast. There are some ownership issues and we wanted to talk to you about it."

I looked at Ashlee. This was not what I was expecting. If things were going to change, I was wondering why they wanted

Ashlee here for the meeting. Did someone sell the Inn? Now I wondered, were we about to find out that we needed to find a new home?

Ashlee sat there with a blank stare on her face as well. She didn't know what to expect.

"Let me bring you up to date with a few items you probably did not know. I got the feeling from Edward that the two of you figured out Edward used to own the building many years ago. You probably figured out that his wife and children died in an automobile accident prior to his selling the property.

"A few years ago, when the house was modified to be a Bed and Breakfast, Edward started coming back on weekends when he was in town. I'm sure you saw that pattern as well.

"What you probably didn't know, was that about a year ago, the previous owner wanted to sell the property. He was tired of losing money. To prevent the property from changing to something other than a Bed and Breakfast, Edward asked me to purchase the property under a corporation he had me set up for him. To be quite honest, Edward was a shrewd businessman. He picked it up for far less than it was worth.

"It was right after that, that he found out he had brain cancer.

Jason told us, "I questioned Edward when he had me buy the property. I asked why he wanted to purchase a property that was not going to turn a profit in years. It wasn't his style. He wouldn't give me an answer. He just told me to get it done.

"When he asked me to manage the property, I told him I was retired. I didn't do that, not even for him. He told me to just monitor it and keep the staff. He had an idea and he would let me know when he had it worked out.

"I did that for several months before he called me one day, telling me to hire you. I never did find out where he got your name.

So, when you came for an interview, I was under instructions to hire you.

"I'm glad you accepted.

"He had a plan, he just wouldn't tell anyone.

"He asked me to monitor the Bed and Breakfast for a minimum of one year. If it was losing money, he wanted me to cover it. So, as you can see, I did what he asked."

I was waiting for the other shoe to fall. All along, I wondered if there was something I was missing. Now, as it appeared, the secret owner had died, and my employment and home were about to change.

"A few weeks ago, I met with Edward. His health was heading downhill quickly and he wanted me to get his financial things in order before he died.

"I asked Patrick to help me. He took care of the legal papers.

"Edward told me that he used to come to the Bed and Breakfast in order to remember his family and feel a closeness to them. It was as if they were talking to him as he sat in the window with the sun coming in.

"Apparently, all that changed in the past couple months. He found himself watching the two of you. For him, it was as if you were his family, all grown up. He especially enjoyed the paper you wrote, Ashlee. He said he read it over several times.

"Every once and a while after we met, he would call and ask me how the two of you were doing. He wasn't that interested in whether or not the Bed and Breakfast was making money. He was interested to hear if you were making the adjustment, and how Ashlee was doing at school. I felt as though I was giving him a report each time.

"Last March, he had me write out a contract. It was a contract for you to manage the Inn for the next three years. It had some options in it for you each year. I was to present it to you after Labor Day Weekend. Unfortunately, with his death, the contract expired before you could see it and sign it."

I gave a look to Ashlee. This didn't sound good.

Chapter 35

The Agreement

I was really wishing that Jason Willard had not invited Ashlee to the meeting. Did he hope that I would not react badly if Ashlee was there?

Jason proceeded to tell the story.

"Edward had me prepare a contract that would have allowed you to be a partial owner of the Bed and Breakfast after the first year. Each of the following years, if you were still managing the Inn, you would have gained additional shares."

I just closed my eyes. Was it that close?

"The first weekend he missed his reservation with you, he was meeting with Patrick and me. He realized his days were numbered and he needed to change his objectives.

"Apparently, the dinner he had with the two of you sealed the deal.

"Edward asked us to write up a new contract for you. He was worried about the financial stability of the Inn, especially if you lost your salary and were forced to live on just the income of the Inn. It took a few hours and different solutions to figure out what he was requesting us to do.

"Maria, Edward asked us to transfer the title of the Bed and Breakfast to you. Since there is no mortgage payment on the property, the income has to cover your current expenses – taxes, wages, insurance, supplies, and maintenance. That's where we spent the most time. He wanted projections for this year and the next. He wanted to know if you could make it.

"I told him he picked a very capable manager. If you could make it through the year, you should be profitable.

"So, here's the straight deal. You can take it or leave it.

"The property gets transferred from the corporation to a corporation in your name for the price of one dollar.

"Bonnie and Jean already have a contract with me. I set it up last fall. They were to stay on until January 1st. If they did, they would receive a $25,000 bonus each. That's probably why they are so loyal. After that point, it is up to the manager if she wants to keep them or fire them. So far, both have told me that they are leaning towards staying on. Their salaries are set aside under Edward's agreement and are covered until that date.

"Edward also asked me to set up a contingency fund of $50,000 to cover incidentals. Call it your emergency fund. If after two years, you have found you do not need it, it goes into a fund for Ashlee to go to college.

"I think that's about it. Oh, I forgot, he asked me to give you a package."

Jason reached into his briefcase and took out an envelope. Both Ashlee and I recognized it immediately. It was the envelope we used to mail Edward Gray the drawing book.

"So, as you can see, the decision is yours," he told me.

"What if I shut down the Inn?" I asked.

"Then the house is yours to decide what you want to do with it. It is your property."

I looked at Ashlee. This time, I was not dumb enough to ask if I could think about it for a while. Besides, Ashlee would have me committed.

"Two questions. Will you be around to ask questions when I need answers?

"Edward is still paying me to help monitor the Inn until at least January 1st. What's the other question?" he asked.

"Where do I sign?"

Chapter 36

Notes

When I had signed the contract for the property with the pen Patrick handed me, I gave Jason a hug. "Thanks! I don't know what to say."

"I know Edward would be happy you chose the right option," he told me.

"One more question if you don't mind. Why did he do this?" I asked Jason.

Jason told us, that Edward had told him in April that he had been looking for a family to take the place of his family. "The house was built to please his wife. Between his wife and his children, they were his world. When they died, he felt as though his world died with them.

"It was when they were going to sell the property last year, and he started feeling sick, that he realized he couldn't take everything with him. He decided that he wanted to make someone else's life whole.

"It's funny how each one of us hold on to the images of what things were like in our lives for a short period of time. Even though the valley and people change, we hold on to the hope that somehow everything can remain the same. I think from his frame of mind, he hoped to be able to keep that memory, of a period of time that was important to him, alive through you and your family.

"After talking to some of his friends, your names came up. He didn't tell me who recommended you, but you were one of only a few people he considered. He actually did a lot of background checking on your family. Talking to his friends, about whether or not you could make a go of it, he decided to take the chance. I'm not sure he ever did consider the other choices he received. From what I've seen, he chose wisely. Edward always was a good judge of character.

"In fact, he was the best person I've ever worked for. I tried to retire several times. He just wouldn't let me."

They picked up all of their papers.

"We'll take care of filing all the papers for you," Jason told me. "Call me in a day or two and I'll let you know if it was a dream or not."

With that, they left. Ashlee and I just stood there in shock. It was not what either of us expected. Slowly, the realization sunk in. We were standing in our own house. It was not just an apartment anymore.

About an hour later, Ashlee asked me if we should put the drawing book back on the mantle.

When I opened the package, we found a note inside.

Dear Maria and Ashlee,

I guess you made the last discovery. When I opened the package, I didn't have any words left. My family's drawing book gave me the strength to hang on the past month.

Thank you for sending it to me. I kept it by my side.

All the times I stayed at the Inn, I would dream about the good times I had with my wife and family. It was as if they were there in the room with me. Sometimes, I think it was the only thing that kept me together the last five years.

I hope the two of you have the same memories together. Remember, life is short. You need to keep those relationships alive as long as you can.

Ashlee, keep writing. You do a great job of digging for the facts. I think there is a career there for you.

Your friend,
Edward Gray

I waited until Sunday night to tell my parents. I wasn't sure I could tell them without breaking out in tears before then. I know Ashlee was dying to tell them.

I'm not sure if she told Red the next morning on the way to school or not. It wouldn't have surprised me.

I only hoped that Edward Gray's generosity and wisdom would carry over to Ashlee. In a very short way, he gave her the image of a true father, along with showing her his love for his family.

Author's Note:

I hope you enjoyed "Meadow House."

This book started with an interest in photographing several types of classical style houses. It was fun comparing designs found in several locations and in different states. Sometimes, it seemed that the builders were copying a single picture of a house found in a magazine. Similar designs carried from one house to the other.

It wasn't long before my images branched out to the concept of a person sitting in a classically curved reading nook, staring out the window. It was the most prominent feature of many of these houses.

As the imagination grew, so did the story.

Even though this is a fiction novel, I tried to weave in as many actual stories from the area as I could. You will have to look closely at them to figure out which were real and which were developed simply to enhance the effect of one of the other stories. You might be surprised to see how many were created from historical facts.

I would like to give credit to the people of Marine on the St. Croix for allowing me to intrude on their time, to listen to their stories and give me the important clues as to where to find others. In fact, there were so many stories of the area that I could only pick a few that would fit the theme of the novel.

You might have a hard time making reservations at the Meadow House. Unlike the other locations mentioned in Marine, it was developed just to carry the story. The design of the house was a composite of the many images I found that made it look as if it was actually built in the setting described in the book. Even the setting of the house was created from discussions with past town leaders as to where they would have allowed a house to be moved into the community at that time.

The other primary characters in the story are fiction as well. Any similarities to actual residents are purely coincidental, although many might say they were there.

As a reader, I hope you found the story as interesting as it was to research and write.

David G. Fabio

Acknowledgements:

I would like to give special thanks to the following people and organizations. Without their help and direction, many of the facts in this novel would have never been known.

Cynthia Jepsen and Fredt Hundt – Marine residents

Bert and Louise Hudson – Marine residents

Mary Smith – Marine Museum Director

Hoover Presidential Library

Minnesota Historical Society

Kathleen Luhrsen and Bob Lindell for their suggestions and help.

About the Author

David Fabio is the author of two youth adventure novels – The Hidden Passage and The Second Summer.
He has also written a historical fiction novel for youth centered on life on the Mississippi River – Tales from a River's Bend.

Now, his seven other mystery novels – Search and Seizure, Secret of the Apostle Islands, Bayfield's Secret Notebook, Water Pressure, The Spot on the Wall, The Missing Jewels and Meadow House challenge the reader's imagination.

He is an educator, photographer, and an outdoor enthusiast. His love for nature and learning about the outdoors is evident in many of his writings.

Suggested other mysteries by the author:

Search and Seizure – a suspense mystery about scientific research, espionage, and murder.

When a researcher is killed and another shanghaied, attempts to uncover the killer and solve the mystery by FBI Agent Lawson leads to unexpected places.

Secret of the Apostle Islands – the mystery of a lost sailboat, last seen in the Apostle Islands.

When a woman's husband goes missing, the story leads to adventure, romance, and intrigue in solving the case.

Bayfield's Secret Notebook – a historical fiction.

A long time hidden notebook is discovered that tells about its writer's involvement in the Confederacy's attempt to return gold to England at the end of the war.

The story leads from Kentucky to the Mississippi River, leading to Stillwater, Minnesota and eventually Bayfield, Wisconsin.

Water Pressure – when the state wants to pump water from Lake Superior to supply the major cities, because the rivers are contaminated, the mystery starts.

An international water conference leads to a murder mystery. It is up to Martin Berman and Tracy Saunders to follow up the leads given to their television stations along with the help of FBI Agent Mark Lawson.

This book involves mystery, romance and murder. Locations include: Minneapolis, St. Paul, Grand Marais, Duluth, Williston, and other towns.

The Spot on the Wall – an action fiction.

When two old friends team up to work for a corporation that designs surveillance equipment, imaginations in technology go to work.

This book involves competition, imagination, high technology, mystery, kidnapping, and the FBI.
Located in Minnesota.

The Lost Jewels – an action fiction.

The a long lost relative's mysterious letter turns up talking about imminent danger and jewels, leading to a quest to solve the old mystery.

Locations include: Davenport Iowa, Kansas City Missouri, Alliance, North Platte and Kearney Nebraska

CPSIA information can be obtained
at www.ICGtesting.com
Printed in the USA
LVOW10s1541311016
511023LV00001B/56/P